THROWN BY
LOVE

This book is dedicated to Mikayla who has been my strongest supporter. You have encouraged me to keep following my dreams no matter what. Thank you for helping me get this book published. You are the best cheerleader a writer could have or want.

I also dedicate this book to my husband Mike. Twenty-nine years have flown by and I can't imagine having shared those years with anyone else but you. You are the man who has "checked those boxes" from Diana Nelson's list and who has taught me what true love actually means.

BOOTS AND BULLS
THROWN BY
LOVE

BOOK 1

C. KELLY

Jeanne –
I hope you enjoy the book!!

~Christina Kelly

Boots and Bulls: Thrown by Love-Book 1
Copyright © 2021 by C. Kelly.

ISBN: 9781952976247
LCCN: 2021920638

Cover and Interior Design by Ann Aubitz
Published by Kirk House Publishers

Kirk House Publishers
1250 E 115th Street
Burnsville, MN 55337
612-781-2815
Kirkhousepublishers.com

TABLE OF CONTENTS

CHAPTER 1

"I don't see any way for us to keep the ranch afloat." Joel quietly shared his greatest fear with his siblings.

"Is it really that bad?" Zach asked.

"Dad gambled on there being oil in that northern field. No oil means we don't have the cash to pay our bills."

"So, what do we do now?" Maria asked.

"I'm not sure. We have to find a way to infuse cash back into the operation. Without it, we won't be able to make the mortgage payments through the end of the year."

Both of his siblings sat at the kitchen table with him and thought about what Joel had just relayed to them. After their parents had died, the three of them had taken over running the ranch that had been in their family for five generations. This was their home and their livelihood; it was also the only way of life any of them had known. All three of them loved the ranch and were devoted to it. Joel hated having to tell them about the financial crisis that was upon them. He felt like he was letting them down. *Hell,* he felt like he was letting down every generation that had lived on the ranch previously as well.

Joel watched Zach open his mouth, but he didn't say anything.

"Just spit it out, Zach. What do you want to say?" Joel said wearily.

"I have an idea. It's a really crazy idea. I mean really, truly crazy."

"What is it?" Maria pushed.

"Remember Drake Lewis? We used to hang out at the rodeos together."

"What about him?" Joel interjected, frowning.

"He wants to do a reality show on learning to be a bull rider."

"Okay, I'll bite. What does that have to do with our ranch?"

"He needs a place to film—a real working ranch that also has bulls to ride," Zach answered.

"You have got to be joking! Have you lost your mind?" Joel bellowed.

"Joel, will you please just listen? I promise, if you still don't like it after you hear the details, you can shoot the idea down. But will you at least let me tell you about the concept?"

Joel let out a huge sigh, looked at Zach, nodded, and then waited for him to continue.

"Drake Lewis is now associated with the PRCA, the Professional Rodeo Cowboys Association. They want to expand the exposure of the rodeo circuit. Not only are they looking to get people interested in attending rodeos, but they also aim to educate folks about a rancher's life. We all know that what we do on this ranch is a lot more than just roping and riding, a lot more than what is portrayed in the movies or on television. The show's producers have been tossing around the idea of a reality show where one contestant gets to learn how to ride a bull while also learning the ins and outs of being a ranch hand. They haven't determined yet how the contestant will be selected, but the idea is that he would live and work on an actual operating ranch and learn firsthand how to be a rancher, which would include learning how to ride a bull. The final show would be at the PRCA Championship in Las Vegas, where the new cowpoke would get to ride a bull in the ring."

"And get himself killed?" Joel cried.

"No. I told you this is a different kind of show. Everyone would know going in that he wouldn't be riding one of the contestant bulls but one that was retired. So a tamer ride, hopefully." Zach shrugged his shoulders.

"*Hopefully* being the operative word," Joel replied. "You know as well as I do that even some of those retired bulls can be dangerous."

"Yeah, there will be a certain amount of risk, but that's part of the show—the education on the risks that ranchers face every day."

"So how exactly does this reality show help the ranch?"

"They would pay the ranch to use it as the site for the show."

"Are you kidding?" Joel's voice was getting louder with each response.

"Joel—"

"Zach," Joel interrupted, "how would we be able to run the ranch with camera crews all over the place?"

"Joel, listen to me. There wouldn't be cameras all over. We could limit where they go. Additionally, the contestant would only be here for one, maybe two months. We could really do something great. We could show people what it really means to be a rancher. There wouldn't be any fake drama. All of the drama would be what naturally happens around here. It's a great way to get some exposure for our own operation as well."

"I think it's a great idea," Maria said. This was the first comment she had made since Zach started talking about the show. "Joel, if we're really at risk of losing this ranch, the ranch that has been in our family for *five generations,* I might add, then I say we need to look at all of our options. So tell me, are we really going to lose this ranch without at least fighting for it?" This time she looked pointedly in Joel's eyes without blinking. Maria was their younger sister, the baby. But at the moment, Joel could see only steel in her eyes. It was the same steel that had always been in his mother's eyes whenever she needed to be tough. He had never said it aloud, but he had always believed that his mom was probably one of the toughest people he had ever known. Maria was channeling Mom. There was no way he could argue with her on this. She was right.

"Okay. We'll fight for the ranch with whatever we can."

Maria wasn't going to just let it go at that.

"Even if that means we bring this reality show on the ranch?" she pushed.

"Even if that means the cameras will be here filming everything we do."

"Joel, it really won't be that bad. Let me start the conversation with Drake."

Joel sighed, "Okay. Talk to Drake. But, Zach, if we agree to host this show, are we committing the ranch to being the site of this show for years to come?"

"Actually, Drake and I talked about that. He said he doesn't want the show to be more than just the one season. Drake's afraid that after the first season, it would lose its value. He's afraid that to keep up interest, the show would have to start creating the drama you're concerned about. He doesn't want to have anything to do with that kind of project. So, this really is just a one-time gig."

"Alright, we'll look into what it would take for the Double Spur to host this show and whether the money we'd receive from having the program filmed here would be enough to get us through.

CHAPTER 2

"Carrie, can you take me to the cowboy bar?"

"Which one?"

"You know—that one that has the bull thingy."

"Rusty's?"

"Yes, yes, yes!! That's the one!" Cassie said as she clapped her hands.

"Cassie, why in the world would you want to go there?"

"I want to ride that bull thingy."

"Cassie, honey, you can't ride that mechanical bull."

"Why not?"

"They won't let someone who's in a wheelchair get on the mechanical bull, sweetie."

"But why not?"

Carrie looked at her sister and sighed. She had always told Cassie that she could do whatever she wanted. How could she tell her that because of her disability, the bar would never let her ride the bull? Maybe she could try a different approach than the flat-out hurtful truth. Carrie reached for another reason.

"So—most of the people who ride that bull are guys, right?"

"Yeah . . ."

"So, if you were to get out of a wheelchair and ride the bull longer than those guys, they would feel bad. You wouldn't want that would you?"

Cassie immediately looked contrite. "I wouldn't want to make anyone feel bad."

"Good. I knew you would understand."

"Can we go anyway?"

"Why?"

"I like watching people trying to ride the bull. It's fun!" Cassie was once again smiling from ear to ear. Carrie knew that she would agree to go. She would do almost anything to put a smile on her sister's face.

Cassie was eight years younger than Carrie. Their mom had developed toxoplasmosis during her pregnancy, which had resulted in significant physical and mental disabilities for Cassie. She had been confined to a wheelchair for her entire life. Her comprehension and reasoning skills were diminished, and she had a compromised immune system. As a result, Cassie had spent much of her life in and out of hospitals. Even with all of the difficult things she had endured, Cassie's spirit was insuppressible. It was one of the many things about her sister that Carrie loved. Carrie nodded and agreed to take her sister to the bar.

"Can Becky come, too?" Cassie asked.

"Want me to call and invite her?"

"Yes!" Cassie cheered.

As Carrie watched Cassie smile, she remembered the vow she had made years earlier. She would do whatever she could to bring joy into Cassie's life. If taking her to this bar brought her joy, there was no question about going. Bringing her own best friend, Becky, along would ensure that both she and Cassie would have fun. Becky was gutsy and fun, and Cassie loved hanging out with her. Carrie loved how much Becky could make her sister laugh. She often accompanied the sisters on different outings. For Carrie, that meant that she always had an extra set of hands in case Cassie had problems while they were out. She picked up her phone and called her friend.

"Hey, Becky."

"Hi. How are you?"

"Great. Cassie wants me to take her to Rusty's."

"The cowboy bar? Why?"

"She wants to watch someone ride the bull."

"Are you kidding?" Becky chuckled. "Sounds awesome. I'm in."

"We'll pick you up at seven o'clock."

"I'll be ready. I can't believe she likes to watch the mechanical bull. Your sister is always surprising me."

"I know, right? I think she wants to go because she's been watching some of those old western cowboy movies."

"Did you let her watch *Urban Cowboy*?"

"What? Of course not, other westerns—you know, with *real* cowboys."

"So now she's fascinated with all things cowboy."

"Yep, that about sums it all up."

"Should I bring my six-shooter?"

"Very funny." Carrie laughed. "See you soon."

As Carrie hung up the phone, she was once again smiling at her sister, who was smiling back. Carrie found herself reaffirming her promise to keep that smile on Cassie's face. It was a mere five hours later when Carrie found herself regretting making that vow.

Carrie pushed Cassie's wheelchair into Rusty's while Becky held open the doors. The bar was decorated with a western theme. There were wagon wheels and wooden barrels scattered throughout the entire bar as well as bull heads mounted on the walls. The scarred wooden tables looked as if they had been used in an actual bar during the gold-rush days. Carrie thought the cacti and tumbleweed, along with the occasional animal skull added just the right element to the ambiance to make the customers feel as if they had just stepped off the dusty wagon train and come in for a refreshing cold drink. Of course, there was a limit to the western feel. The bar had your typical neon signs advertising different beers and whiskeys, not to mention the large ring with the mechanical bull sitting in the center. As they walked in, the three were temporarily distracted watching a guy who was hanging on for dear life as the bull moved and shifted. Carrie couldn't believe that her sister had actually wanted to ride the thing. Carrie shook her head and thought, *If bringing Cassie here brings her joy, I'm willing to bring her as often as she wants to come.*

Becky found an open table that was near the bull thingy so that Cassie could watch the riders as much as she wanted. The trio watched several men attempt to ride the bull. Each man was thrown to the mat after riding for only a few moments. Carrie watched them and was glad she wasn't having to pick Cassie up off those mats. The thought of her sister being thrown from the mechanical bull made her shudder. As their drinks arrived, Cassie turned to Carrie and said, "*You* need to ride the bull."

"Me? I can't do that."

"Will you fall off?"

"Probably!"

"Then you won't make the other people feel bad," Cassie said, reminding her of the reason Carrie had given her sister for why she couldn't ride herself. That lame excuse was coming back to bite Carrie in the butt.

"True, but *I* will probably feel bad when I fall. You don't want me to get hurt, do you?"

"But Carrie, you told me the blue mats are cushions that make it so the people don't get hurt."

"Yeah, but Cassie . . ."

"I want to see my big sister ride! I want to cheer for you!"

Carrie blew out a large breath of air. She had made her vow, and she wasn't backing away from it at the first sign of adversity. She nodded.

"I have to go check to see if they're taking any more riders tonight."

Carrie got up and approached the counter near the mechanical bull ring.

"Is this where you sign up to ride that thing?"

"Yep." The guy behind the counter smirked. "You don't look like our usual type of rider, though."

"I'm not. My sister has talked me into doing this for her. She's the one over there waving at us." Carrie pointed over to Cassie, who was sitting at the table waving wildly at her.

"She seems kind of excited for you to ride." He grinned.

"She is."

"Okay, so here's the liability waiver form. Everyone who wants to ride has to sign the form. As soon as you sign the form, we'll get you on the bull."

"Isn't there a waiting list?"

"Nope. We've run through all of the riders that have signed up so far tonight."

"Could you create one?"

"One what?"

"A waiting list?"

The guy laughed and said, "No way! Look at how excited your sister is. We wouldn't want to disappoint her now, would we?"

"Did she pay you to arrange this?"

"Nope." He just smiled and waved back to Cassie.

"So who calls for the ambulance?"

"Relax. You'll do fine."

"Yeah, right." Carrie rolled her eyes as she reached for the form.

She signed the form and handed it back to him. She walked into the ring and stepped on the mats that surrounded the bull. She grabbed ahold of the fake bull's saddle horn.

"Okay, so are you going to climb onto the bull?"

"How?"

"Not much of a cowboy, are you?"

"No."

"Put your foot in the stirrup and swing your other leg over."

"I was just kidding. I have seen at least one western." This time it was Carrie's turn to smirk.

"Once you're on, I'll start the bull. It starts out pretty slow and tame. The longer you manage to stay on, the more it starts to twist and turn."

"The ride is only eight seconds, right?"

"Darlin', this is not the PBA, the Professional Bull Rider's Association. This ride lasts as long as you do."

"Ugh."

"Come on. It'll be fun."

"For you, maybe."

"Trust me, someone in this bar is going to get a thrill when you get on that bull."

They both turned to Cassie and waved. Yep. This was all for her.

Carrie climbed up onto the bull and grabbed the hard plastic imitation of a saddle horn.

"Don't forget to throw your hand up in the air like a real bull rider."

"Not funny. I'm just hoping not to break my neck."

"Ready?"

"Yes."

The bull did indeed start slowly, and as Carrie was getting used to the feel of the bull's movements, it began to change and shift. Just when she thought she was figuring the whole thing out, the bull would move in a different direction, and she would feel her body jerk one way and then the next. *How in the world did real bull riders do this?* She knew that what she was doing was in no way even close to the real thing, but this was really hard. The ride got to the point where she was doing everything in her power to stay on the bull, but finally, the bull won, and she was tossed to the mats below. She took a moment to take stock and make sure that she was unharmed. When she was sure nothing was broken and that she would be able to get up without falling over, she slowly stood up. The guy who had been running the controls met her before she got out of the ring.

"Are you okay?"

"Yeah, thanks."

"You actually did great. You stayed on longer than a lot of people."

"That was sheer fright at the possibility of how much it was going to hurt when I fell off."

"And? Did it hurt?"

"No, I think I'm okay."

"Good to hear. Just let me know if you want to ride again. Your liability waiver is good all night." He winked.

"Aren't you Mr. Funny Pants? Do you do stand-up comedy on the weekends?"

"Nope, they only let me run the bull."

"Run the bull and shovel the bull out after?"

He threw his head back and laughed. "Yep, that about sums up my job here."

"Well, thanks for taking it easy on me."

"Truly, I didn't. You really did good and a lot better than most. Before you leave, I need to give you this flyer."

"What is it?"

"The company that makes this bull is a sponsor of a reality TV show they want to make about becoming a cowboy. I'm supposed to hand these out to everyone who gets on."

"Oh, okay, thanks."

She headed back to where Cassie and Becky sat and dropped the flyer on the table.

"What's that?"

"Nothing. Just some flyer they have to give everyone who gets on that thing."

Carrie reached for her glass of soda. She could really use a nice alcoholic beverage right about now, but she never drank in front of her sister. While Cassie was legal, she was not allowed to drink. The alcohol never mixed well with all of the medications she needed to take on a daily basis. If Carrie didn't drink, then Cassie never felt like she was missing out. Becky never drank around Cassie either. It was just one more of the reasons why Becky was her best friend.

As Carrie was bringing her glass of soda up to her lips, Becky reached over and grabbed the flyer.

"Holy crap!"

"What's the matter?"

"Did you read this?"

"No. I took it and then dropped it here on the table. Why, what's up?"

"This is a contest to get a role in a reality show. The show is about learning to become a real cowboy. The person who gets selected for the contest gets to spend two months on a working ranch and learn all about ranch life. After a couple of months, they get to go to Las Vegas with their family and participate in the rodeo championship in Las Vegas. How cool would that be?"

Carrie merely shrugged her shoulders.

"There's also a prize if the contestant makes it the whole two months and to the Las Vegas rodeo."

"What's the prize?"

"A million dollars."

"What?!"

"That's what it says. Living on a ranch and pretending to be a cowboy—sounds like an easy way to make a million dollars."

"Not sure living on a ranch and learning to be a cowboy would be easy."

"You're right, of course. I just thought it was a huge sum of money for doing something other people do every day. Not to mention you'd only have to be there for two months."

"You should do it, Carrie!" Cassie squealed.

"What?"

"You should do it. You did so good riding that bull thingy—I know you could do it."

"Thanks for the vote of confidence, sis, but I don't think I'm the right kind of contestant. I'm pretty sure they want men to do this."

"Oh, oh well."

Dodged that bullet, Carrie thought.

♦ ♦ ♦

The next morning, Carrie received a call from her mom.

"Good morning, sweetie. How are you feeling?"

"Fine, Mom. Why?"

"Cassie told me you fell off of that bull thingy last night."

"Did she also happen to mention that she manipulated me into getting on top of that bull thingy in the first place?"

"I did get that impression; although to be fair to your sister, I don't think she manipulated you—I think she merely encouraged you." Both Carrie and her mom laughed.

"Yeah, that's probably more accurate."

"Seriously, are you okay? You didn't get hurt?"

"I'm fine, Mom. How's Cassie this morning?"

"Good. We go back to the doctor on Monday to find out the results of the latest round of tests."

"Okay. Well, let me know what you find out."

"Will do. I love you."

"Love you, too, Mom."

Monday evening, Carrie's mom called her back to talk about the doctor's appointment.

"So, what did you find out?"

"They said that all of Cassie's tests results came back indicating that Cassie would be a strong candidate for the spinal treatment in Texas."

"That's great!"

"Yeah," her mom quietly responded.

"Mom? What is it? What's the matter?"

"The treatment is still in the experimental stage."

"In other words, it's really expensive and not covered by insurance."

"Yes." The word came across the phone as more of a breath than an actual answer.

"How much?"

"Between the medications, the physical therapy machines, and the doctor costs, somewhere around three-quarters of a million to a million dollars."

"What?!"

"I know."

"How could anyone afford to do this?"

"I don't know how other people do it, but there isn't any way for us to come up with that kind of money. The hardware store has some value, so if we sold it, we could use that."

"Mom, that isn't a realistic solution. The store is your sole source of income. Cashing it out for a lump sum payout to sink into an experimental therapy for Cassie that may or may not work is not a viable long-term option."

Her mom let out another deep sigh. "I know. It's just so hard to realize that there's a treatment out there that may be able to help her live a better, more normal life, and we aren't going to pursue it. Do you know how much your dad and I feel like a failure? If we were better parents, we'd find a way to make this happen."

"Mom, not having the money doesn't mean that you're a failure. It only means we don't have the money. Let me do some digging. Maybe there's some kind of grant or something out there that would help us cover the costs."

"A grant? Do you really think there could be a grant for something like this? I know grant writing is your job, but you think there might actually be funding out there for us?"

"I'm not sure, but with my contacts, if there's a grant out there, I should be able to find it."

"Thanks, Carrie."

"I'll let you know what I find out."

Carrie sat down at the table and began researching any treatment grants she could find. She looked for not only grants to cover the treatment costs but also for grants that would fund the transportation to Texas and the lodging there while Cassie recovered. After a couple of hours, she had a list of grants that were potential options, but they were all longshots.

◆ ◆ ◆

Carrie spent the next two weeks running down the list of grants. At the beginning, she had been optimistic, or maybe just dreaming, that she would be able to save the day with a grant that would help pay for this treatment for Cassie. So far, none of them were panning out. She was down to her last option. She had put together an application and was hoping to hear soon that this might be the one. She checked her mail and saw a letter from the foundation. She stared at the envelope, afraid to open up one more rejection letter. Before she tore open the envelope, Carrie called Becky.

"Hey, Carrie, how's it going?"

"I'm sitting here in my living room staring at an envelope that could change my sister's life—or just be one more huge disappointment for her and the rest of my family."

"I'm on my way over."

"You don't have to come over. I can open an envelope by myself."

"Don't touch that envelope until I get there," Becky directed. "I'm leaving now."

There was a knock on the door a short while later. Carrie got up and answered the door. Becky hugged her tight, and the two women walked back into the apartment.

"Go ahead and open it. I'm here for you."

Carrie opened the envelope and began to read. Becky watched the emotions cross over her friend's face, first joy and then utter heartbreak.

"What does it say?"

"They would be willing to cover some of the treatment; however, there are a lot of conditions, including moving Cassie down to Texas to work with the foundation's medical team. Even with them covering costs, it still leaves a half a million dollars to come out of my parent's pockets—a sum of money they just don't have."

"Oh, Carrie, I'm so sorry." Becky hugged her friend and sat with her as she cried out her frustration and disappointment. After a while, Becky turned to Carrie and asked, "Did you eat dinner?"

"No," Carrie answered in a soft voice.

"Let me make you something to eat."

Carrie nodded. She wasn't hungry but knew she needed to eat something. Becky prepared a light supper of soup and sandwiches. As it was just about ready, she turned to Carrie's kitchen table and went to clear some space so they could eat. As she was making room, she saw a colorful brochure sitting on the table.

"What's this?"

"Huh?"

"This flyer." Becky started reading it and realized it was the flyer from Rusty's about the cowboy reality show.

Carrie walked over to see what Becky had in her hands.

"It's that flyer from Rusty's."

Carrie grabbed it and turned it over. "It's just what I was using to take notes on as I started researching grants. Might as well throw it out now, as none of them panned out." Just as Carrie turned to throw the flyer away, Becky snatched it out of her hands.

"This thing pays a million dollars."

"Yeah, so?"

"Why not try and get on the show?"

"They're looking for guys who want to learn how to become a cowboy. How could I get on the show?"

"Nowhere on this flyer does it say you have to be a guy."

"What's your point?"

"My point *is*: this is a million dollars, and it could be a way for Cassie to get this treatment."

"Becky, are you crazy?"

"Maybe," she smiled back at her friend, "but that's why we're best friends. Let's eat dinner, and we can look into this show a little more."

An hour after they ate, Becky was winning the argument that Carrie apply to be on the show.

"It's only an application. What's the worst that can happen?"

"They post my video on some website, and I'm humiliated on an international scale?"

"So, who cares?"

"I do?" Carrie questioned.

"I'll continue to be your best friend, and your family will continue to love you. Nothing else matters. I'm getting my phone so we can record your video submission."

"I don't want Cassie to be a part of this show. It's one thing for me to make a fool of myself, but quite another for the show to exploit her for ratings and money."

"Agreed. But you need a catch."

"A catch?"

"Yeah, something that makes you sympathetic to the audience. The show is going to want you to be relatable to all of those *regular* folks watching."

"So, do you have any ideas?"

"What if we use the store?"

"Dad's hardware store?"

"Yeah. You can say that you've worked in the store since you were a little girl and would use the proceeds to buy your parents out of the store to keep it in your family."

"But that's not really true."

"Would you like your parents to be able to retire?"

"Of course. Someday—when Dad decides he's ready to get out of the business. So?"

"So, when he wants to get out, would you want the store transferring to someone else outside of the family?"

"No, I'd like to buy it."

"So, what's the problem?"

"That reason isn't the *actual* reason I'd be doing the show."

"But it is a reason. Not a lie, just not the whole story. This is television. They never want the whole story anyway."

"Okay, fine. But I don't want to come off whiney."

"No, definitely not. Whiney would not work for a reality show about cowboys. Pretty sure they don't whine. You need to be you. That means spunky, not whiney."

CHAPTER 3

When Carrie's phone rang three weeks later, she didn't recognize the number.

"Hello?"

"Hello. Is this Carrie Nelson?"

"Yes," she answered hesitantly.

"Hi, Carrie, my name is Drake Lewis. I'm the producer and director of *Bull's Life*, the reality show about becoming a bull rider and rancher."

"What can I do for you, Mr. Lewis?"

"Drake, please."

"Drake, then. What can I do for you?"

"I'd love for you to come to Texas for an in-person interview."

"Interview for what?"

"To be the participant on the show."

"What?! You can't be serious."

"Why not? You did submit this application, right?"

"Well, yes. But aren't you looking for a guy?"

Drake laughed. "To be honest, that's exactly what I *thought* we were looking for until I saw your submission. I actually think you're perfect. However, there are a few other people who want to meet with you to determine if they think you're as good a fit as what I think you are."

"What kind of people?"

"My assistant director, the president of the PRCA, and a doctor."

"A doctor?"

"Yes. You'll need to have a complete physical to make sure you're up to the challenge. You can choose your own doctor or you can use the one we use for our rodeo circuits. It's entirely up to you."

"If I pass your medical exam and agree to go on your show, are my medical records going to become public?"

"Great question; the answer is no. We're not doing that kind of show. We aren't interested in public humiliation, just true reality TV on what a couple of months in the life of a new cowboy would be like. I'll be honest; I'm not saying there won't ever be moments when you do or say something that's embarrassing, but I promise, we don't intend for you to be the butt of anyone's jokes."

"Okay, so when do you want this interview?"

"I'm hoping you can come out at the end of next week. I'd really like to finalize our choice by then and hopefully begin shooting the show a couple weeks after that. Will that work for you?"

"Ummm, sure, I guess so. Can I ask something?"

"Of course. What do you want to know?"

"How many other people are coming for interviews?" There was complete silence on the other end of the line. "Drake, are you still there?"

"Umm, yeah. I'm still here."

"How many?"

"None," he quietly admitted.

"What?" Carrie asked confused.

"I'll be honest—you're the person I want for the show. If for some reason, you can't do it, then I'm back to the drawing board. There was no one else as perfect for this part as you. At least, that's my opinion."

"So do I buy my own plane ticket?"

Drake laughed again. "No. Let me turn you over to my assistant who will make all of the travel and hotel arrangements for you. Okay?"

"Okay."

"And Carrie?"

"Yes?"

"I can't wait to meet you. I think this show is going to be just what the PRCA needs—and maybe what you need as well."

♦ ♦ ♦

The next morning, Carrie spoke with her parents about the show.

"Can you really take two months off from your job?" her mom asked.

"I just finished up the grant applications I had been working on for the university, and I should be able to complete the application for the pet-rescue shelter before I leave for the interview. I can let the school district know that I'll be out of town for a couple of months, but their applications aren't due for another four months, so I should be able to complete these once I finish with the show—assuming that they even decide they want me for the show. Dad, my concern is that I won't be around to help you at the store."

"Don't worry about me or the store. We'll manage," he replied.

"Carrie, I'm also worried that you could get hurt," her mom said.

"I'm not gonna lie, Mom, doing this show will come with a certain amount of risk. I'm willing to take that risk if it means that Cassie can have this procedure."

"I don't like it. I don't like thinking about you putting yourself at risk just to get the money for Cassie."

"I don't like it either, but how can I turn down this opportunity? This is our chance to get the money we need for her."

"You'll be careful?" her dad asked.

"Yes. I won't take any unnecessary risks. I promise."

♦ ♦ ♦

The time seemed to fly by, and all too soon, and it was Wednesday night of the following week and Becky was dropping Carrie off at the airport.

"I can't believe you're going for an interview."

"I can't either."

"Even more, I can't believe you're on the short list for the cowboy in training."

"Short list? I don't think you can call it a short list if my name is the only one on it."

"True, but I'm still amazed, and, frankly, I'm so excited I'm having trouble sitting still."

"Well, you need to be excited for both of us because right now, I'm nervous enough for both of us."

"Relax. You'll do fine. Just be yourself and they'll love you."

"I'm going to miss you."

Carrie had spoken to Drake's assistant a half-dozen times about logistics. If the other folks interviewing Carrie agreed that she was indeed the most ideal candidate, then she would stay in Texas. If everything went according to plan, she would be getting to the ranch within a week's time. She would then stay for the next two months, possibly longer, filming the show and learning about ranch life.

"No, you won't. We'll talk as often as you can. You're going to be so busy that a couple of months will fly by."

"I hope so."

CHAPTER 4

Carrie and Drake stepped out of the large white SUV and onto the dry, dusty ground of the Roulston Double Spur Ranch. The air was dry and hot. It was nothing like Minnesota, where she had grown up. She wasn't expecting it to be so hot, but she should have. This was Texas, after all. She immediately began looking at everything surrounding her. There was a beautiful brick two-story house off to the right. It was a house that had been built to last for generations, and it had been built with love. She didn't know how she knew that, but she was sure that her assessment was right. There was a picture-perfect white porch with a white wooden swing. All around the porch and the house were flower beds. There were no weeds to be found in any of the flower beds. The gardens were clearly someone's pride and joy. The flower beds contained many different varieties of flowers, most of which Carrie couldn't iden-tify. In addition, the colors of the different flowers blended together per-fectly and were a sight to behold. She took in a deep breath and coughed. She hadn't expected the pungent odor of cow, manure, and hay. This, too, shouldn't have come as a surprise, but it did. Just as she was trying to get a feel for the buildings on the ranch, a tall, handsome man walked out of the house with a smile spread across his face.

"Hey there, Drake, welcome to the Double Spur."

"Nice to see you again, Zach. The place is even more beautiful than I remember."

"Thanks. We're all pretty proud of what we have here."

"You should be," Drake said. He turned to Carrie and said, "Carrie, I would like you to meet Zach Roulston. He's one of the owners of this spread. Zach, meet Carrie Nelson."

"Nice to meet you, Ms. Nelson."

"Carrie, please. I don't stand on much formality. I hope that's okay."

"Perfect for this ranch. We don't tend to stand on much formality around here, either. You'll fit right in." Zach reached out his hand. Carrie, in turn, reached out and shook his hand.

"It's nice to meet you," she responded.

"Let me start showing you around. We can get you settled and talk about what, if anything, you may need."

"Sounds great, Zach. Lead the way," Drake replied.

Zach walked over toward the barns. Drake, Carrie, and a few of the other crew members followed along. Drake and the crew asked questions as they went. Carrie was just trying to take it all in. The ranch was definitely well-maintained, but it was not spotless. Carrie wondered how it would look for the viewing audience. Zach caught the concerned look on her face.

"Why the frown?" he asked.

"Your ranch is beautiful and well-maintained. I don't know anything about ranches, but even I can tell that much."

"So . . . why the frown?"

"Just wondering how it will come across on the television. How will an audience who knows nothing about ranching really understand what an incredibly beautiful and successful ranch this is?"

Zach smiled and looked to Drake.

"Don't worry, Carrie, we'll make sure to do this place justice. I'm not interested in having the Double Spur come across as anything other than incredible."

Carrie smiled, nodded, and kept looking around.

Zach quickly walked them over to the ranch bunkhouse.

As they got there, he turned to Drake and said, "Whenever your guy gets here, he can leave his stuff on the open bunk. The top one in the corner is available for him."

"Guy?" Drake asked.

"Yeah, the one who's going to learn how to be a cowboy?" Zach chuckled. "Remember the show about making a cowboy?"

"Ahh, Zach—" Drake started.

"Actually, the guy is me," Carrie interrupted.

"What?"

"I'm the cowboy in training."

"But you're a woman."

"Yep—been one my whole life." Drake laughed. Carrie's wit was one of the things in her video that made her so appealing for this role. He knew that she would come across to the audience as fun, funny, and utterly charming. She was the girl next door that everyone would like. Her desire to make sure the ranch was shown in its best light possible, put her in a league of her own as far as Drake was concerned. One of a kind—and definitely the best choice to do this show.

"I, ah . . . I just wasn't expecting a woman."

"To be perfectly honest, I wasn't expecting to get selected either. Ask Drake if he's lost his mind. He won't answer the question whenever I ask him."

Zach chuckled. This woman was quick with the comebacks. He loved it. She would certainly fit in well around here.

"Is this the only place for me to sleep?"

"Ahh, yeah. We weren't, ah—"

"Expecting a woman, I know. Can we check with the other hands on how they feel about sharing space with me? If they're not comfortable, Drake, you'll need to find another solution."

"If they don't feel comfortable, then we'll have you stay in the trailer. It's not ideal, but it'll work."

"I'll wait until they voice their opinions before I drop my stuff off. I don't want them to feel as if their votes don't count."

Zach was impressed that her first thought was for the men with whom she would be sharing living quarters and with whom she would be working alongside. She was not only funny but considerate and insightful as well.

"Okay, sounds like a plan. When will the hands be back so we can talk to them?"

"I'll get 'em right now. You've come late enough in the day for most of them to have finished up their daily chores. Whatever they're doing now can wait until tomorrow. It's almost dinner time."

Zach left to round up the hands as Carrie and Drake looked around the bunkhouse. It was somewhat clean but definitely lived in. There were clothes on beds, and not all of the bunks were made. It wasn't dirty, but it seemed comfortable. Carrie would feel right at home.

The men began to straggle in. Carrie noticed that they stopped at a building adjacent to the bunkhouse. She wondered if it was some sort of washhouse.

Zach walked in with a bunch of men and told Carrie and Drake that everyone was there.

Drake went to introduce Carrie and was immediately cut off by her.

"Hi guys. My name is Carrie Nelson. I assume that you've all been told about the reality show that's going to be filmed on this ranch about turning a greenhorn into a bull-riding cowpoke."

Both Zach and Drake's eyebrows climbed up their foreheads. She *had* been doing her research. Carrie waited and watched. After the men nodded their heads, she continued.

"Well, the thing is, *I'm* the greenhorn. I was selected as the cowboy in training, and I'm here to learn from all of you. The reason we wanted to talk with you is that I'm supposed to stay on-site with the other hands. I guess that's supposed to be better television or something," Carrie said behind her hand as if she was telling show secrets. Some of the men chuckled. She continued, "But as you may have noticed, I'm a woman, and I want to know if you're still okay with sharing your space with me. Just to be clear, I won't run around and clean up after you. You're grown men and don't need a mother."

"Maybe we do, sweetheart." The guys all laughed, and Carrie smiled and chuckled.

"Well," Carrie said, "you're going to have to find her somewhere else. It ain't gonna be me, boys. I promise to keep my mess to an area near this bunk, and I won't complain if you snore. I don't mind sharing the space, but, truly, this decision is up to you. I can sleep out in the trailer with the film crew, but I suspect I'll be missing out on some of the experience if I do. Whatever you decide is fine, and you have my full support. Drake and I are now going to leave so you can discuss the issue together. I only need to know what the final decision is so I know where to drop my gear. I don't want to know how anyone voted. I don't want that to impact our being able to work together. Let us know if you have any questions. Okay?"

"Where will you shower, Ms. Nelson?"

"Please call me Carrie, and I can use the shower you all do whenever you're not using it. I don't mind using it at odd hours so as not to interfere with your schedules."

The men merely nodded. No one said anything else, and Carrie and Drake stepped out of the bunkhouse.

Drake turned to Carrie. "You really are amazing, you know that? In a matter of a few minutes, you introduced yourself, made sure each man in there knew you were not a threat, and gave them your respect by leaving the living situation up to them. I look forward to the next couple of months. I knew you would be perfect for this show."

"Thanks. I really hope it turns out just how you envisioned it."

They walked over to the nearest enclosure and watched the bull inside eating hay. The animal was massive. Carrie had never seen a bull up this close. Just watching the beast gave her goosebumps. She had seen a cow once before, and, of course, she had been to a zoo and seen wild animals, but this creature was different. You could sense the power in it, and she was in awe.

After about twenty minutes or so, one of the hands stepped out of the bunkhouse. He was the oldest man of the group. He had deep wrinkles in his tanned face that made it hard to tell exactly how old he was. He carried himself with an air of confidence that said he knew what he was about. He walked with bowed legs and with a purpose.

"Ms. Nelson?"

"Carrie, please."

"Ma'am, I was raised to respect women, and that means calling you Ms. Nelson or ma'am. What's your preference?"

"Not ma'am, that's for sure. You'll make me feel like I'm a hundred years old."

"Ms. Nelson it is."

"And you are?"

"Bull."

"What?"

"It's my nickname—Bull."

"But shouldn't a proper lady address you as Mr.—?"

"Nope. Around here, if you have a nickname, that's the only name you get called."

"Okay, Bull, how 'bout giving me a nickname?"

"Excuse me, ma'am?"

"If I have a nickname, you can quit calling me ma'am or Ms. Nelson."

"You *want* a nickname?" Bull frowned. "You do realize that the nicknames aren't always very nice and that sometimes a person gets one to remind him how stupid he was."

Carrie laughed. "I understand. I'm willing to take my chances." She winked at the old cowhand.

"Hmmm. We'll have to give that one some thought."

"So, was there a decision on the bunkhouse?"

"Yes, ma'am." Carrie lifted her eyebrows at the ma'am address, but Bull only shrugged his shoulders.

"So what's the verdict?"

"You can stay in the bunkhouse."

Carrie let out the breath she hadn't even realized she had been holding.

"Thanks. I really appreciate your hospitality."

"No problem. But if you expect to live in the bunkhouse, you'll be put on chore rotation."

"Obviously. Chores are a part of living there, right?"

"Yep. Glad you understand that. It was what clinched the deal for you."

"Got it. Someone was willing to let me stay if it meant less cleaning for him."

"Yep, that's about it." Bull chuckled.

"Thanks, Bull."

"Now if you'll excuse me, I have to clean up before dinner."

Carrie nodded and turned back to watch the bull in the enclosure behind her.

After a few more minutes, she turned to Drake and said, "I guess I'd better get my stuff."

"Are you sure you're okay with living in that big open room in the bunkhouse?" Drake asked. "I'm ashamed to admit that I didn't think about it being a big open room. The last time I stayed here, I stayed up at the house. I just pictured you staying there. I'm sorry."

"It's fine. I'll be experiencing a lot of firsts over the course of the next couple of months. This will just get added to the list. I do think the show will be better and more realistic if I stay in the bunkhouse. Hopefully, I can get the skinny on how to be a great cowboy."

Zach walked up to them at that moment. "Bull fill you in on the bunkhouse decision?"

"Yep, he said I'm in if I do my fair share of the chores."

"Just a fair warning, you'll need to stand up for yourself. Most of those guys are used to thinking about women in housekeeping roles. They'll try to take advantage of the fact that you're a woman and try to get you to do their individual chores as well as the chores of the bunkhouse."

"Good to know."

Zach looked over his shoulder. "Looks like Joel's done with the books for the day. Why don't we go over, and I can introduce you."

"Okay, just let me grab my stuff from the SUV first."

Carrie left Zach and Drake to their conversation and proceeded to walk over to the SUV and grab her suitcase and duffle bag. She hadn't brought a lot and knew the show would get her anything she forgot. Carrying both the suitcase and the duffle bag, she headed directly toward the house and the man who was standing on the front porch. He was tall and tanned. She couldn't see much of his facial features because his cowboy hat put most of his face in its shadow.

◆ ◆ ◆

Joel stood on the front porch and surveyed the land. He sure prayed that this reality television show paid off. He hated the idea of cameras being all over the place and someone filming their every move. He was also concerned about this greenhorn getting hurt. He knew the guy would have had to sign a waiver before he stepped foot on the ranch, but that didn't mean Joel's concerns for his safety were alleviated.

As he was looking out over the land, he noticed a woman holding a suitcase and a duffle bag and heading straight toward him. *Where was she going?* She walked confidently toward the house with her brunette hair bouncing with every step she took. She was a little thing; she couldn't have stood more than five feet, four inches. While she was short, Joel didn't miss her subtle curves. He noticed her hips gently swaying as she glided toward the front porch. His first thought was that this woman was going to be a complete and total distraction to every one of his hands. How was anyone going to get any work done with this beauty wandering around? As she drew near, he saw her pixie face. He noticed big brown eyes that would make it impossible for any man on this ranch to stay focused on his job. She was going to be trouble. Right now, however, he needed to redirect her. She didn't belong in the house. The ranch hands would see her soon enough, but he was going to delay that encounter as long as he could. She walked right up to the front porch.

"Hi, I'm Carrie." Sunshine and cheerfulness beamed out of her face. Oh, she was definitely going to be a problem.

"You're going the wrong way," he stated flatly.

"Huh?"

"Only family and guests stay in the house. As you are clearly with the television show, you aren't either of those. I don't know where you thought you were going, but it isn't in the house."

"I, ah—" Carrie was taken aback by this man's confrontational manner. Everyone else she had met was so nice. Even the gruff old cow-hand, Bull, was nicer.

"Sorry if I ruined your plans, but we had an agreement with your producer. The house is off-limits." Joel noticed shutters come down over her eyes, and he saw all of the joy drain out of her face. He started to regret his approach.

Carrie lifted her chin, drew her shoulders back, and nodded once. She tried to tell herself not to take the man's growl personally, but she was not winning that battle. It was impossible not to take his comments personally, she acknowledged, when he was aiming them directly *at* her and *only* her. After all, she was the only person around.

"No problem. I'll just be on my way," she replied stoically.

As Carrie turned away from the house, she heard Zach coming up behind her. He called out to the man on the porch. "Hey, Joel, did you meet Carrie?"

Carrie kept walking toward the bunkhouse.

"Who?" the man on the front porch asked.

"Carrie."

As she neared Zach and Drake, she said, "Never mind. He doesn't really want an introduction. He just made sure to let me know I wasn't welcome in the house." Carrie kept walking past the two men and headed in the direction of the bunkhouse.

"What the hell, Joel?" Zach called out.

"Excuse me?" Joel responded.

"What the hell did you say to her?" This came from Drake. "I have never seen that look on her face. What the bloody hell did you do?" he snarled.

"I just explained that the television crew was not allowed in the house."

"Nice manners," Zach growled back. "Mom would kick your butt if she were still alive. You could have at least introduced yourself to her before you made sure she knew she wasn't welcome."

"Sorry. I guess I was a little harsh."

"A little harsh?" Drake snapped.

Joel waived the comment away. "I'll apologize to her later. She really shouldn't be so sensitive if she's going to be working on a film crew for a reality television show. Now where's the guy who's going to be on the show. We agreed I would get to meet him and make sure he understands the importance of safety here on the ranch."

"*The guy,*" he said, waving toward Carrie, "is the woman who just tried to introduce herself to you, and you just ran her off. Nice introduction." Drake pointedly responded.

"What do you mean the guy is a woman?"

"That woman, the one you just made sure knew she wasn't welcome, is Carrie Nelson. *She's* the contestant. I was going to explain everything when we came to introduce her."

"Well, hell. How could you have picked a woman to do this show?"

"At the moment, I really don't feel any need to explain anything to you, *Mister Roulston.*" Drake turned away from Joel and toward Zach. "I'm going to go check on Carrie and make sure she gets settled."

"Where's she staying?" Joel questioned.

"The bunkhouse."

"What? She can't stay in the bunkhouse," Joel asserted.

"Why not?"

"The guys will never go for it."

"On that, you're wrong. *They* at least let her introduce herself and tell them that they could decide whether she could stay in the bunkhouse or not. The decision was unanimous to let her stay. *Including Bull,*" Zach informed him.

"Bull agreed to let her stay in the bunkhouse?" Joel felt his head spinning.

Zach looked up at Joel and stared him in the eyes. "Yes, Bull agreed." Zach was sounding exactly like their father. His voice was tough and unyielding. Yep, definitely sounding like Dad. Joel took a deep breath and started down the steps.

"I'll go and apologize now."

"I hope she takes a bite out of your hide." It was the final thing Zach said as he brushed past Joel and headed into the house. Clearly, the woman had found a friend in both his brother and the producer. Joel supposed that would bode well for her and the show as a whole. Each man sounded more like her champion than a rancher or a producer.

If she takes a bite out of me, it's no less than what I deserve, thought Joel.

◆ ◆ ◆

Carrie had walked straight to the bunkhouse. Drake found her standing next to her bunk bed.

"Are you okay?" Drake quietly asked.

"I'm fine." Her voice sounded brittle. It sounded as though it could break, as though *she* could break at any moment. Drake was afraid that Carrie was about ready to fall apart.

"Carrie, you can talk to me. I don't know exactly what Joel said, but I'm guessing it was rude and cruel."

Carrie took a deep breath and turned to Drake.

"It's fine."

"No, it's not." Drake immediately responded.

Carrie turned back to the bed and began unpacking her things. Drake wasn't sure if it would be better to leave her alone or try and talk to her. Drake decided to give her some space. He left her to her thoughts.

"I'll be back to check on you in a little while," he said as he turned and left the room.

◆ ◆ ◆

In the meantime, Joel walked over to the bunkhouse and saw Bull eyeing him as he approached. Bull moved in front of the door.

"You here to apologize?" the old cowhand asked.

"You too, Bull?"

"That little lady didn't deserve the manure you just slung at her."

"Yes, I'm here to apologize." Joel sighed.

Bull nodded his head and moved out of Joel's way.

Joel walked into the main room and looked around. He didn't see Carrie anywhere. He figured she must be back in the sleeping quarters. He shook his head. He still couldn't believe that all of the ranch hands had agreed to let her stay with them. He knocked on the door frame. There was no answer. He poked his head around the corner. There was no one in the room. He stepped further into the room, and that was when he heard the water running in the bathroom. He walked over to the door and knocked.

"Yes?"

"Carrie?"

"Yes?"

"It's, umm, Joel. I came to apologize."

"No need."

He sighed. He had really messed this up.

"Please, may I have a moment of your time?" he called over the running water.

◆ ◆ ◆

Carrie looked at herself in the mirror. She had started crying when she had entered the bathroom. Once she had known she was completely alone, she had taken a minute to just let the frustration and hurt wash through her. The rancher's comments up at the house had transported her back to her seventh grade. Growing up with a disabled sister had left Carrie open to a lot of ridicule. She didn't mind the name-calling, but when the bullies started targeting Cassie's sweet nature, Carrie had had enough. She still remembered the day when she discovered that a couple of neighborhood tormentors had tied Cassie into her wheelchair and then tied a rope dangling off the back of the chair. They were making Cassie pull them on their skateboards, all the while laughing at her. Carrie had immediately untied the tow rope while she tried to explain to her sister that these boys didn't really want to be her friends.

"But Carrie," she had said, "they said it would be fun."

"Are you having fun pulling them?"

"Not yet. They said it would be more fun if we kept doing it for a while."

How long had they planned on making her pull them up and down the street, Carrie had wondered. As she had untied the rope, the boys began mocking her.

"You gonna save your sister from her new friends?"

"You must be as dumb as she is."

Carrie hadn't responded to any of the mean comments. She just finished getting all of the rope confining Cassie to the chair untied and off of her. As soon as Cassie was free, Carrie had grabbed the handles of the wheelchair and started pushing her sister home. The next day had been terrible for Cassie. She had exerted herself so much trying to pull the bullies that she couldn't get out of bed. It took over three days for her to recover from the incident.

The next few days had also been terrible for Carrie. Not only was she worried about her sister, but the bullies had decided that Carrie should be punished for taking away their fun. Every time she had gone to her locker after that, something had happened. The first time, it was a water balloon that completely soaked her before her first class of the day. Next, it was a shaken can of soda sprayed at her. The antics continued until they pulled their final prank, which was a dozen raw eggs that had been smashed into the vent of her locker. Everything in her locker had been ruined, including the school's textbooks. The school administration had finally stepped in and put a stop to it by expelling the boys. To this day, Carrie could still remember the feeling of opening up her locker and having egg drip down on top of her head from the upper shelf.

Carrie shook off the morose thoughts. *You made it through those bullies in junior high, you can make it through this one as well.* She moved to the bathroom sink and splashed cold water on her face. She couldn't afford to let any of these men think that she was an emotional wreck. She was allowed to be spunky but weak would not be accepted. There was a drastic difference between the two, and remembering that difference would be critical to her success on this ranch. As she looked at her face, she felt better about the mottled skin. It had mostly disappeared with the cold water.

"Just give me a minute, please."

She took a deep breath and gave herself a pep talk. *You can do this. It doesn't matter if he likes you or not.* As far as Drake had described the show, she would have very little to do with this man anyway. He spent most of his time doing paperwork in the office and managing the business side of things. He wouldn't be around. *Just think of him as one of those bullies you had to fend off from school.* He may have opened up the old wounds, but she wouldn't let him know it. If she had learned one thing about bullies, it was that if they smelled blood, they always came back for more. She couldn't let him know how much his harsh comments had upset her. When she was reasonably certain she had her armor in place, she opened the door.

"Hi. I'm Joel Roulston." He held out his open hand and waited for her to respond.

"Carrie Nelson." She reached out her hand and shook his. She tried to remove her hand as quickly as possible. He held hers for a moment longer, causing her to look up.

"I'm sorry. I was incredibly rude. Please accept my apology."

She tugged on her hand a little, and he held on while continuing to look into her eyes.

"Sure, of course." She gently tugged her hand again.

Joel watched Carrie for a moment longer. She had said she accepted his apology, but he wasn't convinced that she had actually forgiven him. He regretfully let her hand slide out of his grasp.

"So can we start over?"

"Mr. Roulston, it isn't necessary."

"Joel. Please, call me Joel."

"I've learned today that names are very important here in Texas and that not using a title is disrespectful. I don't want to make that mistake again."

"We're pretty casual around here."

"I'll make sure to keep that in mind."

"We'll be eating up at the house in about ten minutes."

"O—Okay."

"You're welcome to join us."

"I, ah—" Carrie swallowed. "Thank you, but I have a meeting with Drake about the start of production." Carrie had created the excuse on the fly. She just hoped that Joel Roulston wouldn't run into Drake.

"Are you ready to grab some dinner and talk over the filming for tomorrow?" Drake popped his head in the bedroom. Carrie sighed in relief. So far, Drake had shown he had impeccable timing. "If you'll excuse us, Mr. Roulston? We really do have some work to do."

"Of course. It was nice meeting you, Ms. Nelson." Joel turned and walked out of the bedroom. He continued through the living room and out the door. Bull was still standing on the porch.

"Did you apologize?"

"Yeah."

"Did she accept it?"

"Don't know. She said she did, but—"

"But you didn't see any signs of forgiveness, did you?"

"No," Joel sighed and shook his head, "I didn't."

"So now what are you gonna do?"

"My job—which is to keep this ranch up and running."

"And what are you going to do about Ms. Nelson?" Bull nodded his head in the direction of the bunkhouse.

"Not really sure, Bull, not really sure." Joel merely shook his head once again.

Bull dropped his head and looked to the ground. "You need to make things right with her," he quietly stated.

"I know," Joel acknowledged.

Bull let that thought sit and didn't comment any further. The two men stood on the front porch and looked out over the ranch, each with their own thoughts of the woman unpacking in the bunkhouse.

"Alright, let's head up to the house and eat. The rest of the men are probably starving," Joel said, breaking the silence. Bull and Joel stepped off the porch and headed back up to the house. A few steps off of the porch, Joel turned and looked back over his shoulder. He swore he'd fix the damage he'd done.

♦ ♦ ♦

Inside the bedroom, Drake took Carrie by the shoulders and sat her down on a nearby chair. He knelt down in front of her and clasped her hands.

"Carrie? Are you alright?"

"I'm fine, Drake, no problem."

"Cut the crap, or the stiff upper lip, the tough girl persona, or whatever this is." His arm flited around in front of her, gesturing to her person. "I'm genuinely concerned about you. I would never have brought you down here to be abused: physically, mentally, or emotionally. It's my responsibility to ensure the safety and well-being of everyone associated with the production of this show. That starts with you. So please be honest with me and tell me how you're *really* doing."

Carrie looked up into the eyes of the producer and saw genuine compassion. She hoped she wasn't wrong in trusting him, but she really could use a friend. He had already proven to her that he had her back, and she was willing to continue to trust him.

"I'll be honest, I wasn't expecting the tongue-lashing I received up at the house from Mr. Roulston, but I survived. They're only words, after all. I would like to know how much I'll have to be exposed to him, though. If we can limit that contact, I'd appreciate it. I understand if that isn't an option. But if it's not an option, could you give me a warning when I'll have to deal with him? I would just like to be more prepared."

"You will, of course, have contact with him, but I'll do what I can to limit your interactions. I'll also try to give you a warning when you'll need to be around him."

"Thanks, Drake. I appreciate that more than you can possibly know."

"You're welcome. Now, let's head over to the trailer and dig up something for us to eat for dinner. I, for one, am starving."

Carrie smiled a small smile that was not the big, bright, bold, beautiful smile she wore when she seemed truly happy. Drake missed the joy she had radiated earlier in this room when she was talking with the ranch hands. He hoped that with a little time, she could get some of that back. Without her exuberance, the next two months would be disappointing and quite possibly dreadful. The show would also be impacted, and that would be truly awful for everyone involved.

CHAPTER 5

After Carrie and Drake had found something to eat, they discussed more specifics about Drake's thoughts on the show and how Carrie would be exposed to the ranch. Carrie had been adamant that she learn all aspects of being a ranch hand. She didn't want it to appear that the show was treating her differently because she was a woman. When they were done, Carrie asked if she could have a little time to make a phone call home.

"Of course," Drake responded.

"I'd like to check in with my family."

"I'll let you have the trailer, and I'll go touch base with the camera crew."

"Thanks, Drake."

After he had left the trailer, Carrie called her family.

"Hi, Mom."

"Carrie! I was hoping we would hear from you today!"

"Warren!" Carrie's mom called out to her father, "Carrie's on the phone."

"Carrie!" She heard her sister give a shrill shriek and knew that she was just as excited to talk to Cassie as her parents. She needed the reminder as to why she was doing all of this. Not that Cassie would ever know.

"Hey, kiddo," her father said as her mother put the call on video call mode.

"Hi, Dad. How are things at home?" she asked.

"Same old same old. Nothing new here. We all want to hear about you. How's the ranch?"

"Are the people nice?" her mother wanted to know.

"Have you got to see any cows?" Cassie asked. "Where are you sleeping? Is it hot?"

Her sister asked a few more questions, her excitement obvious with each word.

"Hey, Cassie, why don't we let Carrie get a chance to answer our questions? Okay?" her mother suggested.

"Okay." Cassie smiled and turned her face back to the phone.

"Yes, it's hot here. I was surprised how hot and dry it actually is. And yes, Cassie, I have seen some cows. In fact, I watched a real live bull for a while."

"What was he doing?"

"Nothing much," Carrie answered. "Just chewing his food."

"So how are things going for you?" her mother, Diana, asked.

"Fine. There's going to be a lot of things happening as we begin shooting tomorrow, so I'm not sure how often I'll be able to call home. They really intend to train me to become a ranch hand in just two months."

"We understand. Call when you can."

"So, where are you staying?"

"Um, ah, well . . . I'm in the bunkhouse."

Her dad was the first one to understand the sleeping arrangements. "What does that mean exactly?" he asked carefully.

"Well, I'm in the same building as the rest of the ranch hands."

"In the same room?" her mother questioned.

"Um, well, yeah, it's a big open room with a lot of bunk beds. So it's sort of like a big sleepover party."

"A sleepover party? That sounds so fun! Can I come and visit you and have a sleepover party, too?" Cassie asked.

"Probably not, Cassie. They don't have any extra beds in the bunkhouse for another person."

◆ ◆ ◆

She got back to the bunkhouse well after dark that night. Drake and his production crew had discussed the general plan for the two months and, more specifically, for the next few days. There were so many details about creating the show that Carrie's head was spinning. Drake had walked her back and let her know he would return the next morning at seven o'clock. She nodded and walked into the ranch hands' residence.

The front room was dark and empty. Carrie didn't want to wake anyone. She grabbed her phone out of her pocket. She was concerned that the flashlight on her phone would be too bright, but she thought she could use the screen glow to give her enough light to see as she made her way across the room. She walked quietly back into the bunkroom.

"You can turn on a light if you need it," came a voice in the dark. It startled Carrie. As she sucked in a breath and stopped moving, Carrie realized the voice had come from one of the men.

"I'm alright," she whispered.

There was no further comment. Carrie walked over to her suitcase, grabbed her t-shirt and shorts, and walked into the bathroom. She changed quickly and headed back into the bedroom. As she climbed up into the top bunk, she remembered she had not brushed her teeth or washed her face. She let out a sigh and continued to climb under the covers. One night would not matter, she assured herself. She closed her eyes and tried to relax. She noticed that her hands were clammy and her heart was beating hard in her chest. She was so nervous. Just thinking about tomorrow's filming was nerve-racking enough, but when she thought about sleeping in this room with all of these men she had not really met, she started to wonder if she had lost her mind. *What am I doing? What if I really shouldn't trust these men?* She realized that her breathing was growing shallow and her heart was racing. *Stop it. Don't invite trouble. Keep your wits about you, and don't start seeing trouble where there isn't any. Bull would never hurt you. He wouldn't let any of these men hurt you either.* With that thought, she was able to start slowing her heart rate down and get her breathing back under control. *I have to get my mind off of everything here. Think about Cassie, think about what she will be doing tomorrow.* Carrie began to think of Cassie's daily routines and what she might have scheduled for tomorrow. Then she started to think about the treatment that might actually be possible because of her own involvement with this show. Carrie started imaging all of the possibilities and how Cassie's life could be improved.

The next morning, Carrie's cell phone began to buzz. She had set an alarm for six thirty. She had not gotten a chance to speak with the men in the bunkhouse about when they would be in the one and only bathroom in the building. She was hoping she had set her alarm early enough to get to the bathroom without interrupting their routine. She opened her eyes and tried to let her eyes adjust to the darkness of the room. She couldn't believe how quiet it was. She sat up and listened harder. She didn't hear anything. Could these men really be this quiet when they slept? As soon as her eyes had adjusted enough, she climbed down the ladder and moved to the bathroom. There was toothpaste on the counter that had not been there last night. She stuck her head back out the door. With the light from the bathroom, she could see that the bunkroom was empty. They were all gone. *How could they all have gotten up and used the bathroom without her hearing a thing?* She turned back toward the bathroom and finished her morning routine. As soon as she was dressed, she walked out the front door and headed down the porch steps. Drake was walking toward her.

"Good morning. How'd you sleep?"

"Apparently, soundly. I didn't hear anyone this morning when they got up and got ready for the day."

Drake chuckled. "You didn't hear *any* of them?"

"Nothing. I thought I woke up before them."

"What time was your alarm set for?"

"Six thirty."

"Darlin', they would have been out of the bunkhouse by six."

"Ugh, I'm never going to adjust to their schedule."

"We'll worry about that when the time comes. Let's go to the trailer. I'm sure you haven't had breakfast."

Carrie nodded and followed Drake to the production trailer. As soon as they both had some breakfast, they headed toward the largest barn.

"Bull said to meet him here. He was planning to give you a tour. We'll film a part of it, and as soon as I think we have enough, I'll let the two of you continue to go over all of the things you need to know."

Drake and Carrie walked into the barn. Carrie walked down the center aisle toward the old cowhand. Carrie was amazed at the size of the stalls in the barn. They were twice as big as she thought they'd be. She'd have to remember to ask Bull about the size. As she neared the old man, she heard one of the other ranch hands call out to her, "Good morning, Sleeping Beauty."

"Sleeping Beauty?" Carrie questioned.

"No one sleeps that soundly unless they're Sleeping Beauty. You didn't even stir when we were all gettin' up and gettin' ready." Carrie blushed. She still couldn't believe she hadn't heard a thing this morning.

"There's no way I'm going to allow you to call me Sleeping Beauty. I am *not* a princess."

Bull turned to her and answered, "You did say I could pick a nickname."

"Bull, come on. It at least has to be something that fits me!" she argued.

"Guess I'll wait to see if it's gonna stick." Bull winked.

He turned and started walking toward the end of the barn. After he had taken a step or two, he turned around and said, "Comin'?"

Carrie jumped and quickly followed him. He started showing Carrie around the barn.

"I noticed that these stalls are huge. I wasn't expecting the animals to be given so much individual space."

"This is the maternity barn. We bring the cows in here when they're ready to deliver. Once they deliver and we know they're healthy and recovered, we send them back out to the grazing fields."

"I have so much to learn about how this ranch operates."

"Don't think you need to know how it operates, just how to be a ranch hand and bull rider, right?"

She smiled. "Yeah, I guess that's true enough."

"Let's head over to the next barn." He stepped out of the back door and walked into the next large structure.

"So, have you ever ridden on a bull before?" Bull asked as they entered the next building.

"Does a mechanical one count?"

"No."

"Then I guess the answer is no."

"Are you telling me the only bull you've ridden is a mechanical one and they think you can ride one in Las Vegas at the professional rodeo?"

"Yep, that's the plan."

"Are you *crazy*?"

"Quite possibly, yes." Carrie laughed out loud at Bull's expression.

"We'll see how much you're still laughing with seventeen hundred pounds of bull underneath you."

Carrie swallowed. "How much?"

"Sixteen to seventeen hundred pounds is the average weight of a rodeo bull."

"Is it too late to change my mind?"

"Probably," Bull responded with a smile on his face. "Okay, Beauty, if not a bull, how about a horse? What's your experience riding horses?"

"Do the horses on the carousel count?"

"No, ma'am."

"Then none."

"You're as green as they come. How in the world did you get this gig?"

"No idea."

"Plans are going to have to change, Beauty."

"Bull, quit calling me that silly name."

"I told you I need to see if it sticks."

Carrie shook her head and let it go. "So, what's going to change?" she asked Bull.

"To start, we need to get you on a horse. Tomorrow, you're going to go riding. You can go out and check fences."

"Bull, not only don't I know how to ride a horse, but I don't know how to check a fence. What in the world am I going to do out there?"

"Give me a moment—I have an idea. I'm gonna go speak with Maria."

"Maria?"

"Zach and Joel's sister. I'll be right back." Bull walked away.

Carrie turned around and started walking around the barn. In just a matter of a few moments, Bull walked back into the barn with a beautiful woman. She had long legs and gorgeous thick brown hair. The two walked down the aisle and right up to where Carrie stood.

"Hi, I'm Maria." The brunette held out her hand. Carrie moved to grasp it.

"Carrie Nelson."

"I'm Zach's sister."

"Doesn't that mean your Joel's sister, too?" Carrie asked.

"After the way he treated you yesterday, I'm not sure I'm going to admit to that yet."

With that, Carrie was immediately put at ease. She knew they were going to be friends. Additionally, there was something about Maria that reminded her of Becky.

"Bull tells me you've never ridden a horse, and in a couple of months, you have to ride a bull in the ring in Vegas."

"Yep."

"I'm going to teach you to ride a horse. One of these other guys, however, is going to have to teach you how to ride a bull. I'm not crazy enough to try that one." Maria chuckled.

"So, you can teach me how to ride a horse?"

"Ain't no one better on this ranch to teach you how to ride a horse," Bull answered.

Maria continued, "Come on, let's go meet Misty."

"Misty?"

"Your ride. She's a sweet old mare who's easy to ride and a wonderful teacher. I wouldn't trust you on any other horse to learn how to ride. Come on, she's in the other barn."

Maria gestured for Carrie to walk down a side aisle and out the door. She headed toward yet another large building. When Carrie walked into this third barn, she noticed that this one housed only horses.

"This is our equestrian barn. In other words, it's mine."

"Yours?"

"I'm responsible for all the horse flesh on this ranch."

"She's the horse woman, all right. There's no one better working with the horses on this ranch than Maria."

"Thanks, Bull." Maria smiled at the old cowhand. "So, Carrie, are you ready to be introduced to Misty?"

"Sure. I'm in your obviously very capable hands."

As the two women walked through the third barn, Carrie looked around at all of the horses and at the paraphernalia hanging in the barn. Maria walked right up to one of the stalls and stopped. Inside this stall was a beautiful chestnut mare. Maria held out her hand and the mare nuzzled her palm.

"Carrie, I'd like you to meet Misty. Misty, this is Carrie. She needs to learn how to ride. Do you think you can teach her?" The horse whinnied. Maria reached into her pocket and pulled out a square white cube.

"Hold out your hand, Carrie, palm side up, and make sure to keep it flat."

Carrie did as instructed, and Maria placed the cube in her hand. "Keep your hand flat and steady. Misty will take the sugar cube with her lips right from your hand."

Carrie didn't move. The horse's head leaned down, and Carrie felt soft lips tickle her palm as the horse took the sugar. Carrie was in awe. She had never had such an experience with any kind of animal. She had never even fed a goat at the zoo.

Maria spent the rest of the day helping Carrie learn not only how to ride Misty but how to interact with the mare. Carrie brushed the horse and learned how to caress her on her nose and neck, just as the horse enjoyed. By the end of the day, Carrie felt comfortable and at ease on and around Misty. She would not have believed that was possible in one short day.

"Get some rest," Maria said. "Riding to check fences is a very long day."

"Are you coming with me?"

"Yes."

"I'm sorry," Carrie quietly stated.

"Sorry?"

"Yes, I'm sure there are a ton of things you need to or should be doing other than babysitting me."

"First of all," Maria countered, "I don't consider spending time with a friend to be babysitting. Furthermore, any chance I get to ride, I take it. Training new stock or checking fences doesn't matter. Either way, I'm on a horse, which is where I want to be more than anywhere else."

Carrie smiled. Maria was an amazing, down-to-earth gal. She was strong, confident, and self-assured. If a friendship with her was the only thing that came out of this experience, it would still be an amazing one and worth everything she would endure.

"As I said, get some sleep. See you bright and early tomorrow."

"What time does that mean, exactly?" Carrie inquired.

Maria chuckled. "Don't want to be called Sleeping Beauty?"

"I wouldn't mind it so much if I *was* a princess or even beautiful. But as I'm neither, it just seems to be as if I'm wearing someone else's clothes—uncomfortable and kind of irritating."

"So be out here at seven. That will give us plenty of time to make sure we have everything we need."

"Hey, Dusty," Maria called to one of the hands.

"Yeah, Ree?"

"Tomorrow morning, Carrie needs Misty saddled and ready to go. She's riding fences with me. Can you make sure to take care of that for us?"

"You got it."

"But, Maria, I don't understand. You showed me how to do that. I know I can do it myself."

"I know you *can* do it, but I would rather you focus on your riding and just becoming better friends with Misty. Riding all day will be a lot harder than I think you realize. Not having to saddle Misty will be a little break, even though it will be a break before we even get started." Maria looked Carrie in the eye and asked, "Are you okay with that?"

"I'm okay following whatever advice you have to give me. I *so* appreciate all of your efforts and time today."

"It was my pleasure. I don't get any girl time around this place, and I feel like you're the sister I never had. I'm looking forward to hanging out with you tomorrow."

"Me, too."

With that said, Maria turned and headed toward the small office in the equestrian barn. Carrie turned and walked to the production trailers. She had been so focused on all that Maria had been teaching her that she had completely forgotten about the filming.

"Drake, are you around?"

"Right here. What do you need, Carrie?"

"I wanted to apologize."

"For what?"

"I got so wrapped up in what Maria was showing me that I completely forgot about the show."

"So?"

"Did you need me to do anything else?"

"After the filming of the tour and getting quite a bit of your working with Maria and Misty, I think we have enough for today."

"You filmed my time with Misty?"

"Yeah."

"When?"

"When you were learning how to brush her down, when you were learning how to mount her, and when you were trying to saddle her."

"Are you serious?"

"Yeah, why? What's up?" Drake frowned.

"I never even saw the cameras."

"Good. That's when the footage is the most real and natural. Remember, that's what we're striving for anyway."

"So, we're good?"

"Yeah. Do you want to eat dinner?"

"Sounds great. Can I eat here?"

Drake looked to the house, and for a moment, Carrie thought he was going to say something. He sighed, then looked at her and nodded. "Sure. Let's see what's available for tonight."

CHAPTER 6

The next morning, Carrie made sure to have her alarm set. She was awake by six o'clock. She heard the other ranch hands quietly moving about in the front room. She tossed the covers back and began to climb down from the top bunk. Just as her feet touched the floor, the door to the bathroom opened. She grabbed her clothes and hurriedly scooted into the room. She quickly showered and brushed her teeth. As soon as she finished, she walked out of the room.

"Sleeping Beauty woke up early today."

"Don't know about Sleeping Beauty, but I have work to do," Carrie replied. She was not going to take that nickname lying down. Carrie stepped out of the bunkhouse and walked to the trailer.

"Drake?"

"Right behind ya, darlin'." Carrie turned and noticed that Drake was moving toward her. He must have been in the barns already this morning.

"Maria wanted to meet in the barn in a few minutes, but I just wanted to check in with you this morning."

"Let's grab some breakfast to go, and we can talk about the day as we walk to the barns."

"Sounds great. I'm starving," Carrie said.

They grabbed some fruit and a cereal bar and headed into the equestrian barn.

"Good morning, Carrie," Maria said.

"Morning, Maria. How are you?"

"Great. How are *you*?"

"Actually, I'm pretty excited about getting to ride Misty."

Maria's smile was brilliant. "That's what I like to hear. She's all ready for you, too. Dusty made sure she was ready to go."

"Terrific."

They walked out the back door of the barn. Carrie noticed four horses tied up waiting for their riders.

"Who else is joining us?"

"That would be me and Dusty," a deep baritone voice answered.

Carrie turned and saw Joel approaching them. All of the color drained from her face. *She was going to have to go riding with Joel? How was she going to get through the day?* She had been looking forward to the experience, and now she was dreading the ride. *How was he going to treat her today?* While he had apologized for his initial comments, Carrie didn't trust him not to do or say more things to undermine her every move.

Seeing the distress on Carrie's face, Maria grabbed her arm, "Carrie?"

Once she felt the pressure of Maria's hand gripping her arm, she was able to get out of her own head.

"It'll be fine," Maria whispered. "I promise."

Carrie saw the honesty in her eyes and heard the sincerity in her voice. She may not have trusted Joel, but she trusted Maria implicitly. Carrie took a deep breath, nodded, and moved over to where Misty stood. She walked up to the horse's nose and gently stroked it as Maria had shown her just the day before.

Carrie quietly whispered to the horse. "Okay, Misty, I need you to take care of me today. We need to show Mr. Roulston over there that I can do this. Are you ready?"

The horse whinnied and nodded her head as if she understood what Carrie had just said. Carrie knew that it was impossible for the horse to have understood what she had said, but she felt relieved to have a moment where she felt in tune with this wonderful gentle creature.

Carrie placed her foot in the stirrup and jumped up into the saddle. She took the reins and turned Misty just as Maria had taught her. The horse responded beautifully.

"I'm ready whenever you are, Mr. Roulston."

"You know, you really should call me Joel."

Joel had watched all of the blood drain from Carrie's face when he had announced his presence. She was clearly afraid of him. He needed to do what he could to turn that around. He was incredibly sorry for his comments to her on her first day, and he wanted her to relax and enjoy her time on their ranch. That wouldn't happen as long as she was afraid of what he would say or do next. Hopefully, this ride would help.

Carrie had no response for him. She just couldn't pretend to be on friendly terms with him. She was still waiting for the next shoe to drop. Carrie looked to Maria and waited for direction.

"Joel, what are you doing here?" Maria pointedly asked. She was clearly irritated with him.

"Maria, I'm here because I wanted to check on the cows in the west pasture. Dusty said you were checking the fences around the west pasture. If you want to head over to check fences on the east pasture, you can do that."

"Joel, you know dang well I just checked those fences."

"Ree, I need to check on 1072 and a few of the other cows who are ready to drop their calves. 1072 could calve any day now. Do I need to wait an hour to check on her, just to let you get a head start?"

That sounded ridiculous even to Carrie. She said as much.

"That would be silly," Carrie asserted. "Are we ready to go?"

Maria harrumphed one last time and turned her horse to the west. She turned to Carrie and said, "Why don't you move up and ride next to me."

"Carrie," Joel smoothly interrupted, "listen to what Maria tells you. She's an expert horsewoman, and there is truly no rider on this ranch, or the entire county, who could teach you how to ride better than her. As long as you follow her directions, you'll do just fine."

Carrie swallowed hard. It was the last thing she had expected to come out of his mouth. She nodded her acknowledgment and waited for Maria to give her directions.

"Let's head out. We'll take it slow this morning. Ready?"

Carrie nodded. She gently squeezed her legs together and clicked her tongue. Misty responded to the command just as Maria had said she would. *So far, so good.* Maybe she really could do this, even with Joel Roulston watching her every move.

Joel watched Carrie take control of the reins. He was impressed. She looked relaxed in the saddle, which he didn't think would be possible given the fact that this was her first experience riding. Another reason he wanted to go along this morning was to make sure that Carrie was comfortable in the saddle—he needed to assure himself that she would be okay riding their horse stock.

Even though he was concerned about Carrie's ability to ride, he hadn't lied when he told his sister he needed to check on the cows in the west pasture. He *was* concerned about 1072. She was a high-quality cow and had produced great stock for them. She was actually one of his favorites. However, she had a tendency to drop her calves out in the fields. He always preferred to have the cows calve in the maternity barn. It was easier to make sure the birth went smoothly. Furthermore, if there were complications, they had the equipment nearby. Additionally, if the calves were born in the barn, the ranch would not lose a calf to predators that sometimes claimed the small or weak animals in the herd while out in the fields.

If he was completely honest with himself, he would admit that he could have taken the four-wheeler out to check on the cows, but he wanted to ride with Carrie. He wanted to make sure she did okay on this first ride. He told himself it was because she was on his property and he was responsible for her, but the truth was that he wanted to make sure she didn't get hurt. He was concerned about her, not as a guest or as his responsibility, but just because there was something about this woman. He wasn't sure what that meant, but he wasn't going to analyze it. She was only here for a couple of months. She would be gone after that.

As the group rode out, Maria coached Carrie. Maria was surprised at how well Carrie was doing. She was a natural and handled Misty like she had been riding for years. At one point, Maria turned and looked back at Joel. He was completely focused on Carrie. Maria smiled to herself and thought, *well, well, this is an interesting development.* Maria knew Joel could have taken the four-wheeler out to check the cows, but she figured he needed to assure himself that Carrie was comfortable on the horse. Now, she wondered if his desire to join them was based on something a little more personal.

Joel turned his head and smiled at Maria. He nodded his head and tipped his hat to her. He always did that when he wanted to praise her for something she had done. It was one of their non-verbal exchanges. She understood he was complimenting her on what she had managed to teach Carrie in such a short period of time. Maria only hoped he would also recognize Carrie's efforts and her natural ability.

"I think it's about time to stop for lunch," he called out after they had been riding for a couple of hours.

"Isn't it early for lunch?" Carrie asked.

"Around here, we eat when the opportunity presents itself," Joel answered.

"Let's stop up by Hawk's Tree. The horses can rest, and we can get out of the sun for a bit," Maria suggested.

"Great idea," he agreed.

The riders headed to a group of trees in the distance. As they approached, Carrie noticed a large nest in the top branches of the tallest tree in the clump. She nodded her head toward the tree and asked, "Hawk's nest?"

"Yep," Joel answered. "It's been there since we were little. I still remember the first time I saw it."

"The first time *I* came here," Maria chimed in, "I heard the hawk before I saw it or the nest. I remember how its cry ripped through my heart and froze the blood in my veins. That cry is so haunting and eerie."

Just at that moment, they noticed a hawk flying overhead. They heard it cry as it neared the nest.

"It's very territorial. She just wants us to know this is her place and we're intruding," Joel informed Carrie.

"Should we leave?" she asked.

"No. *She* needs to understand this is our ranch. She's actually here with our permission."

"You're having a territory war with a wild hawk?" Carrie asked incredulously.

"No, not really. I'm just kidding." He winked at her. "She'll squawk and cry for a while, and when she realizes we're not a threat, she'll quiet down."

They walked the horses over to the trees. Maria gracefully dismounted from her horse. Carrie thought, *she made that look easy. Why do I think it won't be quite that easy?* She clutched the saddle horn and began swinging her leg over Misty's back. Just as her leg cleared the horse, she felt two strong hands grab her around the waist and gently lift her down from the horse. As her feet touched the ground, her knees buckled. The man behind her quietly said, "I've got you." Carrie's heart jumped into her throat. Was that really Joel behind her? He continued, "Getting back on your feet after being in the saddle for a couple of hours is hard for anyone who doesn't ride daily. Are you okay?"

Carrie had lost the ability to speak. She could feel the warmth of his hands through her clothes. She nodded her head and held her breath while she waited for him to remove his hands. After what felt like hours, he slowly released her. She was surprised to realize that she had gotten strength back in her legs as she was standing on her own two feet. She went to take a step, and her right leg buckled. *So much for having her legs back.*

"Whoa," Joel said as he once again wrapped his hands around her waist. "Take a couple steps while I hold most of your weight. Your legs need to remember how to work on the ground. Happens to everyone."

Carrie took a few steps and walked over to the trees where Maria was unpacking lunch. As they approached the food, Joel once again slowly let go, only this time, Carrie's legs didn't buckle under her weight. She sat down in the grass and reached for a sandwich and an apple. She listened to the conversation swirl around her, but she still couldn't have spoken a word if she tried. She had no idea what had happened to her when Joel had lifted her down from the horse, but there was a part of her that felt she still had not touched the ground.

Joel, Maria, and Dusty began telling stories. The stories were humorous tales of things that had happened on the ranch. Carrie found herself laughing at the antics of the young Roulston children. She couldn't even imagine living the kind of life they had. So much of her own life had been focused around her sister, Cassie. She couldn't imagine taking a knapsack and running away on the back of a horse and being gone overnight, as Maria had when she was twelve. Nor could she imagine helping a cow give birth to her calf when she was only ten, as Joel had done. She could, however, picture a young Joel sleeping with that same calf because he had been afraid to leave it alone, even in the barn. As they talked, Carrie watched the landscape around her. It was so different from what she saw every day at home. It was open and vast, and she was struck with amazement at the different shades of brown and green dotting the landscape. It was incredible. Suddenly, she caught movement out of the corner of her eye. She moved her head and gasped.

"What is that?" she asked.

Joel jerked. "What? Where?"

She pointed to where she had seen the animal.

He turned his head and looked. Then he turned to her and smiled, "That's a coyote. Stay out here long enough and you're bound to find at least one or two."

"Oh my gosh, Cassie would love to see a real coyote in the wild." The words slipped out of her mouth before she thought of what she had just said.

"Who's Cassie?" Maria asked.

"Ahh, she's, ahh . . . my, my sister."

Maria nodded. "I think that anyone who has only lived in a metropolitan area would love to come out and stay at our ranch. There's so much to see and experience."

Carrie could imagine the joy in Cassie's eyes, seeing all the things she could imagine here at this ranch. It was beautiful and so different from their hometown. Before Carrie could comment, Joel interrupted and firmly stated, "Don't even think about it, Maria."

"Think about what?" She innocently asked.

"Turning this ranch into a dude ranch. We are *not* going to have a bunch of greenhorns getting in the way of ranch operations." Carrie felt her heart painfully squeeze. It actually hurt to hear Joel dismiss the idea of Cassie seeing this beautiful country. As Maria had talked about a city person experiencing this ranch, Carrie pictured Cassie sitting out here with her. Upon hearing Joel's curt words, she shut down that thought. She had to remember that this man had the power to trample on her emotions, and her dreams for Cassie. Additionally, as she reflected on his curt comment, she realized that he was probably talking about her. She was, after all, the only greenhorn on the ranch. While she thought she had insulated her heart from his harsh words, she realized she had not done a very good job of it. How was it that he could make her heart stop one moment and then crush it the next. *Gotta get tougher, girl,* she coached herself.

"Joel, it was just a comment. I wasn't suggesting turning the Double Spur into a dude ranch. Give me a break." Maria turned and slugged him in the arm. With that movement, the tension between the siblings was broken. The tension Carrie felt, however, was not alleviated.

Shortly thereafter, the four of them collected their lunch garbage and returned it to the saddle bags. Carrie walked back over to Misty. Just as she was getting ready to climb back up onto the horse, she heard that deep baritone voice behind her once again, "Need a hand?"

"No, thank you," she managed to squeak out. He watched her swing her leg over the horse. Once she was settled on the mare, he walked over to his stallion and mounted his ride. They set out again, continuing to move in the direction they had been heading. After a little while, Carrie could hear bellowing. As she looked out, she saw a herd of cows grazing. She was astonished. It was so natural and so peaceful. She could watch these cows graze all day. As she was enjoying the natural beauty of the scene, she heard that deep baritone voice again. But this time, it was filled with tension and concern. "Damn."

Carrie turned her head in time to see Joel kick his mount. The horse immediately sprang into action and raced out toward the herd.

"What—"

Before Carrie could get the question out of her mouth, Dusty and Maria were flying in the same direction as Joel. Carrie followed behind them at a much more sedate pace. She was not sure what the problem was, and she didn't want to get in the way. Not to mention the fact that she had never moved that fast while on a horse before. If she tried, she just might fall off. As she neared the herd, she saw Joel quickly dismount and drop to his knees next to a cow that was lying on its side. This cow was pregnant, and even Carrie could tell that she was in distress. *Was she starting to deliver?* Carrie wondered. Joel was running his hands along her extended belly.

Joel yelled to Maria, "Get back to the ranch and call Mac. Tell him 1072 is calving and she's in distress. I think the calf is breach. Tell him we need him ASAP."

"On my way." With that, Maria turned her mare and flew back the way they had come.

Dusty had grabbed his saddle bag and began to empty its contents onto a blanket. Joel got up and walked over to him. They began collecting items that Carrie assumed would help to deliver this calf or at least make the cow more comfortable. Carrie had slid off Misty. She didn't experience the same weak legs as she had the first time. She cautiously approached the cow. She was drawn to help this poor creature. Her heart ached for it. She could tell from the noises she was making that this cow was in great pain. Carrie dropped to her knees near the cow's shoulders. She placed her hand on the animal and began to speak softly to her. "Hey, there, Mama. We're going to help you. It's going to be alright. You're going to be just fine." Carrie gently stroked her hand on the cow's neck and shoulders.

At that moment, Joel turned and noticed Carrie. He was initially concerned with her close proximity to the cow. As he quickly took in the scene, he realized that she had placed herself in a spot where she was least likely to get hurt and yet most able to comfort the cow. She took his breath away. She was trying to ease the animal's distress. He had never met a woman who would have dropped to her knees in the dirt just to help a cow.

"Carrie, can you keep talking to her while Dusty and I check on her?" Joel asked softly.

"Sure," Carrie replied just as softly. "What's her name?"

"Name?"

"Names seem to be so important out here—what's hers?"

Joel chuckled for the first time since he had seen his favorite cow on the ground. "1072."

"What?"

"1072. It's a ranch thing. She's numbered 1072. She doesn't have a name. Often bulls will get names, but it's rare for a cow to get one. They're usually just numbered."

She didn't look up at him, merely staying focused on the cow and continuing to stroke her hand along the cow's neck. "That's sexist, you know."

"I suppose it is. So, are you okay?"

"We're fine, aren't we, Mama?"

"Mama?"

"If you aren't going to give her a name, I am. You can always change it."

Carrie continued to croon to the beast as Dusty and Joel confirmed that there was no way this cow was delivering the calf without help.

"Joel?"

"Yeah, Beauty?"

"How long can she be in this much pain before this becomes dangerous for her?"

"I'm hoping she has some time. She's strong."

"How long will it take Maria to get back and to get help here?"

"Maria should've been able to get cell phone reception back at Hawk's Tree. Hopefully, by the time she reaches the ranch, Mac will be there, and they can come out on the four-wheeler."

"Will she make it?"

Joel could hear the concern in her voice. "This isn't her first calf. She's an old hand at this. In fact, she's never delivered in the barn. It's as if she refuses to have her calves in the safety of the barn. It's one of the reasons why I wanted to come out here and check on her. I'm choosing to believe that Mac will get here and this here cow will be just fine."

"Hear that, Mama? Joel says you're going to be just fine. Joel?"

"Yeah?"

"Who's Mac."

"Mackenzie Adams. He's our vet. He makes house calls."

"How about field calls."

He chuckled. "Yeah, Beauty, he makes field calls too."

"Please, quit calling me that stupid name."

"How about if I shorten it to B?"

Carrie chose to ignore his question. She continued to rub the cow's neck and softly reassure the animal. Joel realized that Carrie was calming the cow with her gentle voice and magical touch. He was glad she was here. He never would've believed this small, spunky woman would be an asset in the field while one of the cows delivered a breach calf.

Carrie didn't know how much time had passed before the roar of a four-wheeler could be heard.

"Do you hear that, Mama? I think that's the cavalry. Ready to meet that baby of yours?"

Carrie continued to talk softly to the cow as the rest of them worked to help her deliver the calf. Things seemed to happen quickly after that. Carrie didn't know what they were doing, but she continued to promise the cow that the people here would help her and her calf would be fine.

"Carrie?" Joel's voice was so soft that she almost hadn't heard it.

"Hmmmm?"

"Look."

For the first time, Carrie looked somewhere other than the head and face of Mama. She turned her eyes and saw the calf. It was covered in afterbirth, and even though it was wet and bloody, it was one of the most beautiful things she had ever seen.

"Are they okay?" She gasped.

"They're both going to be just fine." This comment was from the man who must have arrived with Maria. Carrie had not even looked up when he had come. She looked up at him now and noticed that he was in his mid-thirties, with midnight black hair and a twinkle in his eyes. She immediately liked him.

"Thank you."

"My pleasure, ma'am."

"Oh, please don't call me that." She rolled her eyes. "My name's Carrie."

"It's a pleasure to meet you, Carrie. I'm Mac." The vet turned to Joel and asked. "Where did you manage to find this one?"

"She arrived a couple of days ago."

"Well, well, well—guess I need to make sure to stop and check the ranch stock. How about tomorrow?"

"Forget it, Mac."

"Are you kidding? A woman who can soothe a cow while she gives birth to a breach calf? Even if it was old 1072, this little lady is something special." Mac turned to Carrie. "Do you want a job as a vet's assistant?"

Carrie laughed. "Pretty sure I wouldn't qualify, and I'd only get in your way."

"Darlin', there is no *way* that you would *ever* be in *my* way."

"Enough, Mac. How is Mama?" Joel interrupted.

"Mama?" Mac questioned.

"1072." Joel shook his head as he answered.

"I think she'll be fine. You're going to want to get her back to the barn, though."

"I'll keep an eye on her, Joel, and as soon as she's ready, we'll make our way back to the ranch," Dusty stated.

"She won't be happy if we leave with that calf," Joel asserted.

"Don't I know it. But hopefully, it will give her an incentive to head home," Dusty commented. Joel nodded.

"Thanks, Dusty. Carrie, how about you ride in the four-wheeler with the calf back to the barn?"

"What about Misty?"

"I'll ride her back." Maria offered.

Carrie agreed and climbed into the passenger seat. While they had been talking, Dusty had been wiping down the newborn calf, and drying it off. Dusty lifted the calf into the bed of the four-wheeler. Mac climbed in beside the calf. Carrie turned to look at the calf and placed her hands gently on its head. It was skittish. Mac held onto the calf until it settled down. He then gently shifted the calf so it was resting in the bed. Mac continued to keep his hands on the calf in case it got spooked or jittery. Once Carrie began stroking his head, the calf quieted, just as his mother had at Carrie's soothing voice.

"Hey there, big fella. What are we going to call you? I'd like to call you Dusty, but I think that name's taken."

"How about Early?" Joel called from behind the wheel.

"That's a terrible name for him." Carrie looked back to the calf. "Don't worry, I'll think of something. I won't let him name you Early." Joel shook his head as he turned the vehicle back to the ranch. Mac sat in the back and watched Carrie and the calf.

"So, Carrie, what are you doing at the Double Spur?"

"Filming a reality TV show."

"I heard the Double Spur was going to be the site for a reality show about learning to be a cowboy and bull rider. What's your role in the show?"

"The cowboy-in-training."

"You're kidding, right?"

"Nope."

Things have gotten interesting here at the Double Spur, Mac thought.

CHAPTER 7

They arrived at the ranch to a great hullabaloo. Everyone had heard the story of old 1072 giving birth in the field, and they were eager to know how things had gone. As soon as the four-wheeler neared the compound, every hand raced out to meet it. Carrie noticed the camera crew also moved out. They didn't get too close to the action and instead hung back. They had begun filming as soon as the four-wheeler pulled into the camp. One of the hands stepped up, lifted the calf into his arms, and carried it into the maternity barn. Carrie sat in the four-wheeler and watched all of the action around her deciding to stay in the four-wheeler so she wouldn't be in the way. Joel stepped around the front of the vehicle and reached his hand out to her.

"You comin'?"

"I don't want to get in the way," she voiced her thoughts.

"B, there is no chance you could be in the way. That calf has fallen under your charms, and you should at least come into the barn and make sure he's comfortable in his new temporary lodgings."

"As long as I won't be a hindrance."

"You can help me," Mac piped up.

"With what?"

"I'll come up with something," he responded with a chuckle and a wink. Joel frowned at the vet.

"Everything okay?" Bull asked Joel.

"Yeah. Why?"

"You were frowning just now."

"It's nothing." Joel tried to repeat that to himself as he stepped into the barn and noticed Mac quietly tutoring Carrie about calves and the care necessary for the young creatures. Mac had his head close to Carrie as if he was telling her ranch secrets. *There is nothing between them.* Joel thought to himself. Then Joel wondered why he cared. *Don't ask questions you don't want to have to answer.* Joel merely shook his head. He was pretty sure he already knew the answer to that particular question.

◆ ◆ ◆

After the calf was settled, Carrie walked out of the barn to find Drake. She had to talk to someone. This was one of the most amazing things she had ever experienced, and she couldn't wait to share the story with someone.

"Hey, Carrie."

"Drake. I was just coming to find you!"

"I heard there was some excitement while you were out ridin' fences."

"Understatement of the year! It was so amazing! I can't believe I was there while a calf was born. I was right there!"

"Hold that thought. Let me get Bruce and you can talk about your day on film."

"Oh, okay." Carrie's shoulders sagged, and she realized she was a little disappointed to have to talk about it to the camera. She still didn't feel comfortable around the camera. It was easier if she didn't know the camera was there. They set up on the back side of the equestrian barn. Carrie was sitting on a bench while Drake stood next to the camera.

"Okay, Carrie, let's start with the calf. What happened?"

"We got to the field and the—"

"Carrie," Bruce interrupted. "I need you to look into the camera as you tell the story."

"Oh, sorry."

"No problem. Let's start over."

Carrie looked at the camera and forgot what she was going to say.

"Anytime, darlin'."

"Umm, yeah, so ummm, we ahhh . . . got to the field, and, ah . . . there was, ah . . . this umm . . . cow, and she, umm, was—"

"Carrie?"

Carrie took her eyes off of the camera and looked at Drake. "Yeah?"

"How about we call it a day and we can try this again tomorrow? Is that okay with you?"

"Sure." Carrie looked down at her hands and quietly said, "I'm sorry."

"Don't be."

"Pretty sure I'm messing this up. It's just that, I ah, I—"

"Carrie," Drake interrupted. "Don't worry about it. Doing this tomorrow is just as good as today."

Carrie swallowed and got up from the bench. Drake walked over to her and grabbed her hand.

"Carrie, if I had wanted these scenes to be perfect, we'd have hired an actress. I want this to be real, and that means you. We've gotten some great footage already today of you riding and returning with the new calf. I'll have the crew get some footage of the day's star, and we'll get the story of the calving tomorrow. It's not a problem." Carrie nodded and headed to the bunkhouse.

As soon as she was out of earshot, Bruce turned to Drake and said, "She's way too nervous talking directly to the camera. We need to do something different. This will never work otherwise."

"Ideas?"

"She does great when she's interacting with someone. How about if you interview her?"

"Never work." Drake quickly responded.

"Why not?"

"I'm terrible on camera. I've seen enough of myself on screen when I did the rodeo circuit that even *I* know I'm the last thing this show needs to be a success."

"Well, we need someone she can talk to, someone who could interview her, you know, dialog with her."

Drake's eyes lit up.

"I have an idea. Let me make a phone call."

Drake got up and headed to his trailer. He was hoping he could talk A.Z. into this gig. She'd be perfect onscreen, and she knew ranching, so she could interview Carrie about every aspect of her experience. Drake also had a feeling that the two women would get along like a cowboy and his hat.

CHAPTER 8

The next morning, Carrie woke, feeling her nerves immediately snap into action. She knew that yesterday had not gone well when Drake had wanted her to talk about the calving. She realized if she could convey what she had observed it would do wonders for the ranching industry. Everyone should get to experience what she did yesterday, and if they didn't have the opportunity to do so in person, maybe they could live it vicariously through her telling the story. She just didn't know how to get past her awkwardness talking to the camera. The first day, Drake asked her questions as she was walking around the ranch. She didn't have to just sit and look into the camera and tell the story. Maybe she should try giving herself a rousing motivational talk. *You can do this. Yes, you can—not real inspiring*, she thought. *Got anything else? What if I try to pretend I'm not speaking to the camera? What if I pretend the camera is actually Cassie?* Carrie laughed at herself. She knew she would never succeed at pretending the camera was Cassie. It would be like pretending a bench was the calf born yesterday. Nothing alike. Carrie stepped out of the bunkhouse and headed to the trailer.

Drake stepped out of the trailer when she knocked on the door.

"Good morning, Carrie."

"Morning, Drake."

"How'd you sleep?"

"Okay."

"Why only okay?"

Carrie shrugged her shoulders, "I suppose I'm worried about how much I'm ruining this entire show."

"Carrie, please quit worrying. I have a plan. In fact, I have someone I want you to meet this morning."

"Who's that?"

"Her name's A.Z."

"Is that really her name or some stupid nickname you guys have given her?"

"It's sort of her nickname. When we were young, most of us couldn't pronounce her last name, so we just started calling her by her initials."

Just as he said the words, a red pickup truck drove into the ranch compound. The truck blew in with a cloud of dust and gravel spitting out behind the tires. Carrie was surprised to see a woman step out of the truck. As she got out of the truck, she immediately raised a cowboy hat in her hand and settled it on her long wavy red hair. It wasn't a fashion statement. This hat had been worn for years and was a part of this woman. She wore jeans, boots, and a blue plaid shirt. Just as she circled the front of the vehicle, Drake stepped over to her and hugged her.

"A.Z.! You look great. Thanks for coming."

"You know I would do anything to promote the rodeo circuit, Drake."

"I hoped that would be how you felt." He smiled at her and hugged her again. "Come on—let me introduce you to Carrie."

The two walked over to where Carrie stood.

"Carrie," Drake said, "I'd like you to meet Aubrey Zumronik. A.Z., this is Carrie Nelson."

"Better get that introduction right, Drake. That's Sleeping Beauty," Beans called out.

Carrie rolled her eyes as she held out her hand to the other woman.

"Carrie, please. I can't believe that they're calling me that silly name."

"Welcome to ranch life," A.Z. said with a chuckle.

At that moment, the screen door of the ranch house swung open. Zach walked out the door, bounced down the steps, and strolled over to the women.

"A.Z., it's nice to see you again." Zach smiled at Aubrey and nodded his head.

"Zach," A.Z. said. Her voice was ice cold. Carrie also noticed that all the twinkle that had been in her eyes a moment ago had just evaporated. Carrie frowned. Clearly, A.Z. had an issue with Zach. She didn't understand it. He was the *nice* brother. Carrie would have understood if this reaction had been directed at Joel, but Zach? She wondered if Drake knew what was going on between Aubrey and Zach.

Zach's shoulders sagged a little. "I just wanted to say hi and welcome you back to the Double Spur. Make yourself at home, and just let us know if you need anything."

A.Z. nodded her head once. She turned to Drake and said, "Let's go to your trailer and talk about the show."

"Certainly."

With that, she turned on her heels and headed to the trailers. It was a dismissal of Zach; even Carrie understood the unspoken brush-off. Carrie saw Zach sadly shake his head, drop his head, run his fingers through his hair, and turn and walk away. Clearly, there was history here. Carrie only hoped it wouldn't interfere with Drake's plan for the show.

The three of them sat down in the production trailer, and Drake filled Carrie in on his plan.

"I asked A.Z. to come and act as a host, if you will, for the show. She's going to spend time interviewing you. She'll also add some commentary to the show so the viewers can truly understand what you're experiencing or describe what's happening at the ranch," Drake started.

"How do you feel about me sharing the screen with you, Carrie?"

"I'd be fine if you could have all of the screen time," Carrie replied immediately, which made Aubrey laugh.

"I don't think that's gonna work. Folks are gonna wanna see and hear you."

"So, do you have a lot of experience in front of a camera? Are you an actress?"

"Actress? Me? Hardly." A.Z. rolled her eyes. "I'm just a ranch girl who was active on the rodeo circuit. I got quite a bit of experience being interviewed for both radio and television."

"The camera must have loved you."

"Why would you say that?" Aubrey asked.

"You're so beautiful."

"Not any more than you are," Aubrey responded immediately.

"Oh, I'm not what anyone would call beautiful. In fact, I'm pretty sure it was my plain Jane appearance that influenced Drake into thinking I was the perfect contestant. A regular person with whom the viewers can relate. You know, the girl down the street?"

There was a stark silence at the table. Neither A.Z. nor Drake knew what to say.

The stark silence left Carrie feeling uncomfortable, so she quickly filled the silence. "It's fine, Drake. I know my limitations, and I think I have a pretty good understanding of what you're trying to accomplish here. I'm totally on board. Should we get started?" With that, Carrie stood up.

Aubrey looked to Drake. She had been ready to rip into the man when she noticed his stunned expression. Drake had been just as shocked as Aubrey about Carrie's statement about herself and the reason why she had been chosen for the show. *Maybe I'm here for more than just the show*, Aubrey thought.

Later that morning, Carrie and Aubrey were sitting on the bench behind the horse barn. The camera crew was set up and ready to film.

"So, Carrie, tell me about yesterday. I understand you rode a horse for the first time."

"Yeah."

"How was it?"

"I was so nervous. I felt like I had to do well for Maria, and I didn't want to embarrass myself."

"How'd it go?"

"It was so cool. I couldn't believe how relaxing it was to be sitting on top of a horse. The gentle sway as I rode was even calming."

"Not everyone feels that way on a horse."

"Really?"

"Yeah, some people are so nervous that they make the horse nervous."

"I don't think Misty, that's the horse I rode, could ever be nervous. She's so sweet and gentle. We had a talk before we left. I asked her to take care of me and she agreed."

"You talked to the horse?"

Carrie blushed. She quickly tried to explain herself. "I know that sounds stupid, but I—"

"It doesn't sound stupid at all. I talk to my horses all the time. Not everyone does, but anyone who trusts their life to an animal that size needs to communicate with it. Did Misty give you any kind of response?"

Carrie blushed even more.

"I know she didn't understand me. I don't really think I can talk to horses."

"But . . ." Aubrey prompted.

"But she bobbed her head up and down. I just felt like she was agreeing to keep me safe."

"Knowing old Misty as I do, she probably did understand you and *was* agreeing to keep you safe." Aubrey winked.

"You know Misty?"

"Ridden her a time or two myself," Aubrey answered. "So, the ride went well. Anything else happen?"

Carrie eyes brightened even more. "We rode out to one of the fields, and there was a cow giving birth."

Aubrey began asking questions about the birth, and Carrie responded to each one. Carrie was so animated as she talked about the birth that A.Z. found herself engrossed in the tale. Carrie talked about her anxiety over the cow and calf and about praying that they would be okay. She shared with A.Z. how she had sat on the ground and ran her hands down the cow's neck. She also admitted to talking to the cow. Once the story was told, both women were silent for a moment. Carrie felt euphoric, as if she had relived yesterday all over again. Aubrey remembered her first birthing experience. She had been six and it was a horse, not a cow. But being present for such a miracle touches your soul.

"Ladies, I think we should get some lunch. What do you say?"

Both women looked up at Drake. They had both completely forgotten that they were not alone and that the entire conversation was being recorded. *It's a good thing we didn't swear or say something inappropriate,* Carrie thought.

"Sounds great to me." Aubrey stood up, and Carrie followed suit. They began walking around the barn. As they reached the other end of the barn, Aubrey turned to the ranch house, and Carrie turned to the trailer. Aubrey stopped. "Aren't you going up to the house?"

"Ummm . . . well, ahh—"

Aubrey frowned. "What's the matter?"

"It was made clear to me that I wasn't allowed to eat up at the house." Carrie quietly stated. She couldn't look this other woman in the eye as she explained. She was still mortified thinking about how Joel had treated her that day.

"What?! Are you kidding me?" Aubrey was immediately outraged. "What exactly did Zach say to you?"

"Zach?! Zach didn't say anything."

A look of confusion crossed over A.Z.'s face. "One of the ranch hands told you that you couldn't eat up at the house?"

"No." Carrie was surprised that Aubrey thought of one of the hands—they'd been great so far. "No, of course not. The hands have all been great."

"Well, who the hell told you that you couldn't eat up at the house?"

"Joel."

"J—Joel?" Aubrey stuttered. "As in Joel Roulston, the most laid back, easygoing cowboy in Texas, Joel Roulston?"

"Don't know about the laid back or easygoing part, but if you mean the Joel Roulston who owns this ranch? Then yeah, him."

"Maybe you misunderstood him."

"When he said, 'You are not allowed to go into the house. That's for family and friends only,' I think I completely understood him."

"I don't know what to say. Joel is usually the nice brother."

Carrie laughed. "No he's not—that's Zach."

"Zach? Zach Roulston?! Nice?! Are you kidding?"

"When I first arrived, Zach came out and greeted me. He immediately made me feel at home. He was the one who was so warm and welcoming. Then Joel stepped out of the house. As I walked over to introduce myself, he stated in no uncertain terms that I wasn't allowed up at the house because I was not family or a guest."

"Joel really said that?"

"Yeah," Carrie muttered.

"It's just that Joel really *is* a nice guy. Zach on the other hand . . ."

"So what happened between the two of you?"

"What do you mean?"

"I'm no expert in interpersonal relationships or anything, but clearly, there's some history between the two of you. Wanna talk about it?"

A.Z. looked at Carrie and realized this woman was not asking to be nosy, she was asking because she was concerned. Carrie was probably the most genuine person A.Z. had ever met. It had been a long time since she had let her guard down with anyone other than her sister, Trina. She wasn't ready to share, but she was ready to cultivate this friendship. Drake had been right; the two of them were going to be fast friends.

"I'll tell you the sad tale some other day, for now, let's get lunch. Where *do* you eat if not up at the house?"

"*You* can always go up to the house."

"I'll eat with you. Where do *you* eat, Carrie?"

"At the production trailer."

"Let's head to the trailer."

They grabbed their food and decided to eat outside. It was a beautiful day, and they wanted to enjoy it.

"So, how do you know Drake?"

"Drake and I go way back. Actually, Drake, Maria, Joel, Zach, and I have known each other for years. My family raises bucking broncos. I started going to rodeos when I was little and fell in love with it. I spent every waking moment I could in the stirrups or at rodeos. Eventually, I was invited to be a Belle of the Rodeo."

"What's that?"

"It's a group of women horse riders who promote the rodeo circuit. We perform in horse shows and at rodeos across the country. I have probably been interviewed hundreds of times for both the TV and radio. Drake knows this. He also knows I would do just about anything to promote the rodeo. It's not only my family's business, it's in my blood. I truly love everything about the sport."

"I can understand why."

"How did you get involved in this?"

"My sister Cassie talked me into riding a mechanical bull one night. After I fell off, they handed me a flyer for this show. I, ah, I decided to enter."

"Why?"

"Well, I, umm . . . I thought if I could, ahh . . . win, I could use the money to . . . ummmm . . . buy the, ahhh . . . family hardware store," Carrie stuttered.

A.Z. watched as Carrie talked about her motivation to participate in the show. She watched as Carrie stumbled over her reasons, and she noticed that Carrie was no longer looking her in the eyes. She wasn't being honest.

"Wanna tell me the real reason?" Aubrey gently asked.

Carrie knew that she wasn't going to be able to lie to A.Z.—or at least not do it well. Carrie wasn't good at lying normally, and trying to do so to this incredible woman who was saving her hide was impossible.

"Can we walk?"

"Sure."

After they had walked far enough away so as not to be overheard, Carrie began her story.

"I'm telling you this, and I hope you won't use it against me. Everything I'm doing here is for my sister. Whatever happens, I can't have her hurt or exploited."

A.Z. nodded.

"My sister is disabled. It would take most of the afternoon to explain everything that's wrong and all of the challenges and struggles she's had in her everyday life, not the least of which is being confined to a wheelchair. What's most important is there's some new treatment and therapy here in Texas. It's experimental. She's qualified to be in the program, but it's incredibly expensive. There's no way my family can afford to do it. Doing this show gives her the chance to have the treatment. I know it won't fix everything that's wrong, but it could give her a little more freedom, a little more opportunity to live a normal life. I'm willing to do whatever it takes. I won't, however, have her used to promote the show. What I told you is true. I have always thought I would take over running the hardware store. Like you with the rodeo, I grew up at the store and have always pictured taking it over when my dad retires. For him to leave the store, however, he needs to get his retirement savings out of it. That would mean I'd have to buy him out, and I don't have the money to do that. My best friend, Becky, and I decided that the store provided a good explanation for my doing the show. It also happens to be true. While it might not be my primary reason, it's one of the reasons I'm here."

Carrie held her breath. She had just confided everything to this woman she had just met. She couldn't know for sure that A.Z. wouldn't exploit Cassie for the benefit of the show and the rodeo, but she hoped this woman would do the honorable thing.

"Your secret is safe with me. However, we're going to have to work on the hardware store backstory. It doesn't seem genuine. If I learned anything in all those years doing interviews, being genuine on screen isn't as easy as you might think. The camera tends to see through all of the bull."

CHAPTER 9

The days proceeded with some semblance of a schedule. In the morning, Carrie would work on her equestrian skills. With both A.Z. and Maria helping her, she was starting to feel extremely comfortable riding different horses in the barn. Bull, of course, had insisted she demonstrate some proficiency on a horse before he would allow her to get on the back of a bull. She was wondering how soon the day for bull riding would come.

In the afternoons, Carrie worked in the barns with the livestock. She was starting to help with the different ranching chores, including feeding the bulls. She struggled with the bales of hay, but she lifted or dragged them over to the different stalls on her own. She wanted to prove she could do it. While she would never be able to replace any of the men who did this job, she did feel that they appreciated her attempts. She relished having their respect. What these men did every day was grueling, and she couldn't believe they admired her efforts. She made sure to talk about that hard work during her conversations with Aubrey.

"You sure have been putting a lot of time in at the barns," A.Z. said one evening during their interview.

"Yes. I've learned so much."

"Yeah? Like what?"

"I've learned how heavy a bale of hay is." Both women laughed.

"Seriously, I've learned how much work it is to just keep these animals fed and taken care of. I can't believe how many hours a day you work on a ranch. At my dad's hardware store, we're working before and after the store hours, of course, because there are always shelves to stock and inventory to order. Then there's also the business end of things, which I usually do after hours. We can sometimes put in incredibly long days. However, you can't even compare those days to life on a ranch. They're so completely different. On a ranch, there are chores that need to be done every day, such as feeding the cattle. But then there are chores that you can't anticipate but need to be ready for."

"Such as?"

"The other day, the hands were talking about how worried they were because one of the cows had quit eating. No one knew why. It could've been that the cow was ill or something worse."

"Like what?"

"I heard one of the hands say it could be something in the food or water. They mentioned that a parasite in the water could infect the whole herd and be a huge problem. Even if it wasn't the food or water, if the cow had some kind of virus, that, too, could spread to the rest of the herd. They had to get the vet out right away. It was almost as if everything had to be put on hold until the cow had been tended to, and yet everyone knew the other chores still needed to be done."

"Did they ever figure out what was wrong?"

"The vet figured out the cow had an infection and treated her immediately. She was separated from the rest of the herd, and everyone went back to doing their regular chores. We all worked until well after the sun had set to get everything done."

"Yeah, it happens that way sometimes. The better you take care of your livestock, the fewer the emergencies are, but there's no way to completely avoid them," A.Z. suggested.

"I know how tired I was the next day, and I didn't come close to working nearly as hard as everyone else. I don't know how they do it every single day."

Joel had walked around the corner of the barn just as A.Z. and Carrie had started to talk. He made sure to stay out of the way and out of sight. He was curious to see how the interviews were going. He was surprised at Carrie's observations. When he had agreed to have the show filming at the ranch, he hadn't expected the greenhorn to "see" all of the tasks the others were performing. He imagined the show would shoot some scenes and then the "star" would go back to the trailer and wait for the next scene. He had never expected that the cowboy-in-training would want to be actively engaged in the daily chores of the ranch. He also hadn't expected a greenhorn to appreciate all of the work each person did. Carrie was truly impressed with the daily work the ranch hands did and wasn't afraid to share her impressions with the show's audience. Her comments were genuine and completely heartfelt.

"She's something else, isn't she?" Drake quietly asked him as Joel took in the interview.

"Yeah. I wasn't expecting your show to be so . . ."

"Honest?"

"Yeah. Honest."

"I don't think I can take credit for that. The honesty's all Carrie. She's observant as hell, and she's quick to praise everything she sees. What's so amazing is that none of her comments are frivolous or flowery. She doesn't praise the hands to butter people up or to get something, but instead, it's as if she needs to tell people what's in her heart—and what's in her heart is complete admiration for everyone on this ranch. She really is enamored with this ranch and everyone here, and she can't help but talk about it. It just bubbles out of her every time she talks about being here."

"She's so genuine you can tell she means every word she says."

"Now do you understand why I chose her for the show?"

Joel looked at the other man and smiled. "Yeah, I get it now. She's something special."

"She's certainly one of a kind," Drake agreed.

♦ ♦ ♦

Carrie spent her evenings talking with A.Z. while Drake's film crew recorded those chats. Carrie had begun to feel so comfortable with the other woman that she had a hard time thinking of those exchanges as interviews. They were never that formal, but they were real. One evening, Aubrey let Carrie know that she was going to have to go back to her family's ranch.

"I'll be back, but there are some things I need to take care of at home."

"I understand. I'm so thankful for all you've done for me."

"I really haven't done anything."

"Are you kidding? You and Maria are starting to turn me into a true horsewoman. Additionally, if the show ends up being a success, it'll be because of you. If I had to do all of the talking to the camera without you, this show would've been an absolute disaster. I can acknowledge how much you've added to the show, why can't you? You really should take credit for everything you've accomplished here." Carrie reached out and touched Aubrey's hand. "You've also made a difference in my life. I'm so happy to be able to call you a friend."

"Me, too."

The two women embraced and took a moment just sharing each other's company before A.Z. had to leave. Eventually, Aubrey turned to Carrie and said, "Please make sure to be careful. Listen to Bull and Maria. They'll take care of you."

"I will. I promise."

"I'll be back next week."

"Who knows, maybe I'll be on the back of a bull by then," Carrie joked.

◆ ◆ ◆

The day after A.Z. left, Carrie found herself missing her friend. A.Z. had filled the void Carrie had felt without Becky around. She knew that she was going to have to continue on without either A.Z. or Becky, but it was different not having A.Z. to talk to. She had grown to depend upon Aubrey's insight and knowledge. She shook her head. She couldn't get maudlin over the other woman's absence. She picked up her head and headed into the bull barn. She needed to deliver the hay to each of the stalls. As she walked into the barn, she heard one of the bulls bumping up against the gate. She remembered how unnerving the sound had been on her first couple visits in this barn. She could now walk into the barn and not jump at hearing the gate rattling against the posts.

Carrie managed to lift up the bale enough to get it over the threshold. She then dragged it farther into the barn. She let the bale drop and caught her breath. As she was getting her breath, she heard one of the bulls getting more restless. The metal gate rattled even louder. She wasn't sure which bull was making all the noise, but she reassured herself that no matter which bull it was, he was behind a gate and she was safe. Carrie lifted her arm and wiped the sweat from her brow on her sleeve. Then she grabbed a hold of the twine keeping the bale together and started dragging the bale toward the third stall. The bull in the stall was huge and would get this entire bale. She struggled as she moved the heavy bale and felt her muscles burn. Carrie was so focused on getting her muscles to listen to her and getting the bale to the bull that she was not paying attention to how close to the stall she was. She bumped into the gate and lost her balance.

Carrie fell on her backside right at the gate. The air left her lungs, and she felt the hard metal of the gate as it slammed into her spine. She needed to take a minute to get her breath back. As she was regaining her breath, she felt a sharp stab on the back side of her right rib. She dragged herself away from the gate and realized the bull was right up against the gate, with its horn poking out between the rails. Once she was away from the stall, she tried to see how badly she was hurt. She knew the bull had caught her with its horn, and she was pretty sure that it had broken the skin. She twisted around and realized she couldn't see anything, but it was starting to really sting. She reached around and placed her hand on the spot where the bull had caught her. It was very tender and she felt something warm and wet. She was afraid that she was bleeding more than she had initially thought. She looked to the stall and realized the bale was not quite where it needed to be. She slowly stood up and started pushing the bale toward the bull. As she was pushing the bale, Dusty walked into the barn. She quickly wiped her bloody hand off on her jeans.

"Hey, Sleeping Beauty, whatcha doing?"

"Just getting the hay to the stalls."

Dusty shook his head.

"Do you mind if I help?"

"I can do it."

Dusty frowned and took Carrie by the shoulders.

"I know you *can*. That's not the issue. Will you let me help?"

Carrie looked into his eyes. She was trying to gauge whether this offer was based on pity or just a willingness to pitch in and help. Additionally, she was wondering if he had seen the bull catch her with its horn. She saw no pity or deep concern. She only saw the genuine friendship that had been on his face and the other ranch hands' faces for the past couple of weeks.

"Yes. I'm not so foolish as to pass up good help when it shows up."

Dusty nodded and headed out to grab another bale. It took Dusty no time at all to bring the remaining few bales into the barn. Carrie was so grateful for his help. Once all of the hay was delivered, she stepped out of the barn and headed to the bunkhouse. Her injury needed her immediate attention.

Carrie was relieved to realize none of the other hands were in the bunkhouse. She had the place to herself. She quickly headed into the bathroom with a washcloth in hand. She wet the cloth and tried to look in the mirror to see how bad it was. She reached around, touched the wet cloth to the open wound, and gasped. She hadn't expected the sting of pain at the mere touch of the wet washcloth.

"What happened?" came a growl from the doorway.

Carrie was so startled that she jumped and dropped the wet cloth. She immediately turned and looked up to see Bull standing at the door.

"Nothing, I, ah—"

"Horn or hoof?"

"What?"

"Horn or hoof? I know that gouge came from one of the bulls." He nodded his head at her injury. "Was it a horn or did you get caught by a hoof?"

Carrie let the air out of her lungs and admitted what had happened. "Horn."

"Give me that." Bull took the washcloth out of her hand and pressed it to her injury. Once again, she gasped for air. Even knowing it would hurt when Bull touched it, the pain was intense. After a moment, he removed it and took a look at the gash on her back.

"You're gonna need stitches."

"What?! No! I can't get stitches. No one can find out about this. Please, Bull."

"Saying please to me ain't gonna change the fact that you need stitches. You need to see a doctor to get patched up and to get some pain medication."

"Please, Bull. I don't want anyone to find out."

"Why?"

"If Joel finds out I got hurt, he'll put an end to this show. I need to finish this. Don't let it end before I can finish it. Please."

"I don't like this."

"Can you stitch me up?"

"What?" came his shocked reply.

Carrie turned to the old cowhand with a softness in her voice and a vulnerable look in her eyes.

"Have you ever stitched up another cowhand?" she quietly questioned.

"Beauty—"

She cut him off. "Bull, have you?"

Carrie stood there holding his gaze. She didn't flinch. She implored him to help her with every second she kept her eyes on him. She just waited for the old cowhand to make a decision. Once again, she left it in his hands—as she had done on that first day. The air blew out between his lips in a whoosh of breath. He dropped his head and shook it.

"Yeah."

"I'm supposed to be no different than any of the other hands. Please just stitch me up as you would them," she begged.

"I really shouldn't."

"Bull, please," she quietly implored.

He knew at that moment that he would do anything she asked. She was strong and courageous and had more gumption than most women he had ever met. She reminded him a lot of Sarah Roulston, Joel's mother. She was an original, and Bull was beginning to realize that Carrie was cut from the same cloth.

"If I stitch it up, it'll probably leave a scar," he said, trying one last-ditch effort to dissuade her from this course of action.

"Who cares about that? It's not like anyone's ever going to see it back there."

"If I agree to do this, you have to let me check it every day."

"Fine."

"I'm not done. If, when I check it, I think it's getting infected or I notice any other issue, I'm calling in the doctor."

"Okay." Carrie relented. She knew she was going to have to compromise on this or Bull would refuse to stitch her up.

"I mean it. I want your word you won't argue with me if I think a doctor needs to be called."

"Fine. I agree. Now, can you please stitch me up before anyone else comes in here?"

"It's gonna hurt."

"Figured that out myself."

"Let me get my supplies from my trunk."

Mere seconds later, he entered the bathroom carrying a first aid kit. "Face the mirror and lift up your shirt."

Carrie immediately obeyed him.

"I need to get this wound clean." He started to wipe the gash with a sterilized cloth. The air once again wheezed out from between her lips.

"There, I think it's clean. I'm going to apply a minor numbing cream, it won't be nearly as good as if you went to the doctor, but, hopefully, it will take the edge off the pain."

With that, Bull began applying a cream to the area around her cut. As soon as he had applied the medication, he started to stitch Carrie's wound closed. She clenched her teeth against the pain. Bull was amazed with this woman's determination and strength. He had not met many people, male or female, with her grit. It was an honor to be around her. In that moment, he knew he would keep her secret.

"Bull?"

"Yeah, Beauty?"

"How long before you let me ride a bull?"

"Are you kidding me?"

"No."

"I figured after this, you would want a little break from the bulls."

"Isn't there a saying about falling off a horse and needing to get right back on?"

"This wasn't a horse."

"I figure the longer I stay away, the harder it's going to be to actually get on one of those beasts. Can we get to it tomorrow?"

"You're going to have to let this wound heal."

"How soon?"

"We'll give it a week, Beauty. If your gash is healed, you can ride then—if you think you're up for it."

CHAPTER 10

Carrie climbed onto the back of the bull. Her heart was racing as she cinched the rope around her hand. Bull had reassured her that this bull was not raised or trained as a circuit rodeo bull. While it had the genetics to buck, it didn't really have the temperament. This was, in fact, a bull that had been used to train first-time bull riders in the past. It was a bull that would give her the feel for riding on an actual bucking bull. She reached up one last time to make sure her helmet was secure on the top of her head. Bull had told her not to try to look like a professional bull rider by putting her left hand up in the air. She didn't need that piece of advice. Carrie's plan was to hang on with everything she could, including both hands and her legs. She took a final deep breath and nodded.

The gate swung open, and the bull turned out to the left. As she squeezed the flanks of the bull with her legs, she felt the muscles of the large animal move and contract. Bull had warned her that she needed to pay attention to those kinds of movements. Just as that thought was going through her head, the bull kicked its legs out. Carrie's hands gripped tighter while she felt her body jerk. She tried to stay relaxed and move with the bucking of the bull. As its legs landed back in the dirt, she felt the massive animal jump in the air and turn its entire body to the right. As soon as it landed, it jerked to the left. The movement became too much, and Carrie felt herself falling. Bull had said let go and, if possible, jump off. The most important thing was to get out of the way of the animal's horns and hooves. She tried to jump, and she felt the bull's leg catch her knee. She realized that she was not going to be able to protect herself. She no longer knew how she was going to land. The only thing she knew at that moment was that however she was going to land, it was going to hurt.

"Grab that bull!" Carrie wasn't sure who screamed out the order. It was the last thing she heard before she hit the ground.

Bull jumped into the ring and started yelling at the other hands to grab the beast and get it away from Carrie. As he focused on the bull, he saw a flash of color move past him and head toward the woman in the dirt. Bull was relieved that someone was going to check on Carrie.

Joel ran into the ring. He ignored the bull. His ranch hands would make sure the animal was contained. He needed to check on Carrie. He had been watching her as she flew into the air. All the air had left his lungs when he watched her head crash to the ground. He watched in horror as her head bounced and hit again. He knew immediately that the helmet she was wearing had shifted on her head and because of that, had not been enough to protect her skull. He leapt over the fence and rushed to her side. Carrie was not moving. He knew he shouldn't move her if she had injured her spine. He had watched her fall, and he didn't think the issue was her neck or back, but he couldn't take any chances. He knew she had been knocked unconscious. He wasn't sure how long he should let her lay in the dirt waiting for her to regain consciousness. At that moment, he felt a hand on his shoulder as Bull crouched down next to him.

"How's Carrie?"

"Not sure. She hasn't moved," Joel said, his voice hushed and anguished.

Bull turned his head and hollered over his shoulder, "Call Doc Thorton!"

"Already done. He said he's on his way," someone called back.

Joel sighed. He knew he'd feel better as soon as Doc Thorton arrived.

"I don't think we should move her before Doc gets here," Bull stated.

"Agreed. Hopefully, she'll come back to us," Joel quietly answered. He reached out and took her hand in his own. His thumb began to gently caress her hand as he and Bull knelt in the dirt waiting for Carrie to move. Joel felt his chest start to tighten. She had to be alright. He didn't even want to take a breath. Each breath meant one more second, one more minute, that she was hurt and unconscious.

After what seemed like hours but had been only minutes, Joel heard a small groan. He noticed a slight movement as she moaned and turned her head. Then Joel noticed Carrie moving her legs. He immediately picked her up and cradled her to his chest. As he picked her up, he heard a small gasp for breath. He continued to move to the open gate and toward the house.

"I'm taking her into the house."

"I'll get the doors."

The two men walked toward the ranch house. As they neared the house, Joel heard another person's footsteps behind them. He turned his head and saw one of the cameramen following behind. The man wasn't looking through the camera and was certainly not filming at the moment.

"No cameras in the house," Joel curtly told him.

"I'm not going to film this, just please, let us know how she is. We're all worried about her."

Bull turned to the other man and placed his hand on his shoulder.

"We'll let you know as soon as we know anything."

"Thanks."

Joel continued into the house and headed upstairs. He turned at his bedroom door and gently laid her on his king-size bed. She stirred again. Just as he was removing his hands from her body, she looked up and asked, "What happened?"

"You got thrown from that stupid bull. You must be the unluckiest person on the face of this planet. No one gets thrown from that bull," Joel thundered.

"Oh. Guess I should have realized that," Carrie quietly responded.

All of the air left Joel's lungs. He was taking out his fear on her, and even he knew that wasn't fair.

"How do you feel?" he asked in a gentler tone of voice.

"Stupid?"

He wasn't sure how she could make him smile when only just a few moments ago he had been scared out of his mind and unable to breathe for worry over her.

"How *else* do you feel?"

"Am I supposed to be feeling anything other than stupid? How about incompetent? Like a failure? Are any of those the . . . the right answer?" Her voice became softer and softer as she spoke, and Joel almost missed the last few words.

"Carrie, how is your head?"

"Okay."

"Are you in any pain?"

"Umm, I'm not sure."

"Why's that?"

"It's hard to think over the buzzing noise in my head. Can you give me a minute before you ask me anything else?"

Joel stood up and looked to the door. He saw Bull and Drake both standing there with looks of worry on their faces, which reflected what was in Joel's heart. Joel turned back around to Carrie.

"I'll wait and let the doctor ask his questions."

After a short while, Joel heard the front door open and a set of heavy footsteps climb the stairs. Bull walked out of the room and quietly called to the doctor.

"Hey, Doc, she's in here."

"What happened?"

"She got thrown by Blue Bayou."

"Blue Bayou? Are you kidding? That old bull doesn't throw anyone."

"Thanks for making me feel worse," came the quiet response from the woman lying on the bed.

"Sorry, ma'am, that was incredibly rude of me. I'm Doc Thorton, by the way."

"Carrie Nelson," she whispered.

"So, little lady, let's have a look." He pulled out a flashlight and began checking her eyes.

"Do you have any—"

Before he could finish his question, she sat up and covered her mouth. Joel grabbed the trash can next to his dresser and positioned it under her chin right before she vomited.

"Guess that answers that question," the doctor said with a line creasing his forehead. "I'm pretty confident you have a concussion, little lady. We need to get you to the hospital."

Carrie started to shake her head and was forced to grab the trash can again, afraid she was going to lose whatever was left of her breakfast.

"No. I really don't want to go to the hospital. If it's only a concussion, I'm sure I'll be fine."

"Joel, talk to this gal, you know as well as I do that concussions are serious."

"With all due respect, doctor, this has nothing to do with him. This is my decision." Carrie asserted with the loudest voice she had used since the doctor had arrived.

Doc Thorton's eyebrows lifted so high up on his forehead that they disappeared under the gray hair on his head.

"Ms. Nelson—"

"Carrie, please."

"Carrie, if you have a concussion, you need someone to watch to make sure you're okay. There are some pretty serious complications that can result if you're not careful."

"I understand. How about this, I'll take it easy the remainder of the day, and if there's still some concern, then I'll consider going to the hospital."

"Carrie—"

"Doc, please. You've got to understand. I'm only here for a short time. This has already been enough of an inconvenience for Mr. Roulston and his family. I won't make this drag on any longer than necessary."

"I'll keep my eye on her, Doc," Bull responded.

Carrie breathed a sigh of relief and looked to the doctor for his agreement. The doctor turned to Joel and waited for his opinion.

Joel just shrugged. He wasn't happy about her not getting the medical attention she probably needed, and he was even less happy about the fact she was doing it because of him, but he was pretty confident that there was nothing he could say or do to change her mind. He would just have to trust that they would be able to get her to the hospital if it became an emergency situation. He turned to leave the room when he suddenly remembered the gasp she had made when he had picked her up to carry her into the house.

"Before you go, Doc, you had also better check her back on the right side."

Doc Thorton went to lift up Carrie's shirt to check her side when she quickly grabbed her shirt and held it down.

"I would like some privacy if you're going to examine me further," she asserted.

What the hell is going on now? Joel thought.

"Carrie, what's going on?" Joel probed.

"Doc, I think it's within my rights to *not* have Mr. Roulston present during my examination and treatment. Am I wrong?"

"She's right, Joel. I'm going to have to ask you to leave," the doctor sighed.

"Fine," he answered tersely.

Joel abruptly turned on his heel. As he left the room, he once again heard Carrie gasp. He assumed Doc had lifted her shirt to see whatever injury she had hidden under it. *What the hell had happened?* He didn't think she had hurt her side during the fall, but now he wasn't sure. She was okay with him being in the room while they talked about her concussion, but she wanted him to leave while the doc looked at her back? It didn't make any sense.

"Come on, Joel," Bull said with a sigh, "I've got some things to tell you."

"While you two are chatting, I'm going to talk with the crew and let them know what's happening." With that, Drake headed down the steps and out the front door.

Joel followed Bull down the hallway and down the steps. Bull headed to the kitchen in the back of the house, grabbed a mug from the cabinet, and filled it up with coffee. He took a seat and waited for Joel to take a seat at the table as well. Joel sat down across from the old cowhand and waited.

"She got hurt last week."

"What?!"

"She was working near the stalls. She bent over to pick up one of the bales of hay, and one of the bulls caught her with his horn in her back. The horn gave her a gash about eight inches long. It was bleeding pretty bad."

"Go on."

"She didn't tell anyone what happened."

"How do *you* know then?"

"I caught her trying to clean up the wound on her own. She'd been alone in the bunk house."

"What happened?"

"I walked in while she was touching her gash with a wet washcloth. After she got over her surprise at being caught, she begged me to stitch her up."

"Why didn't you take her to the hospital?"

"She didn't want anyone to know she'd been hurt."

"Bull, what if that cut gets infected? What if it's more serious than either of you realize?"

Bull rolled his eyes at Joel. "I've been working on ranches my whole life. I've seen my fair share of cuts and scrapes and have stitched many of them up as well. Need I remind you of your own cuts? It took all of my persuasion just to get her to let me look at that gash."

"How many stitches did you give her?" Joel asked with tremendous resignation.

"Seventeen."

"Seventeen?!"

"I didn't say it was pretty."

"Why am I only hearing about this now?"

"I promised to not say a word to anyone. I don't know exactly what's going on with that little lady, but something sure is. I agreed to keep my mouth shut if she would agree to let me keep checking on it. I informed her that if I thought it wasn't healing properly, I would force her to see a doctor."

"So why are you telling me this now."

"I suspect the only reason that little filly in there kicked you out of that bedroom was because she was afraid you would realize her injury wasn't from today. She also knew you would blame someone, and she didn't want that to happen."

"She was protecting someone."

"She was protecting me," Bull answered. "The only question now is who's going to protect her."

"I will," Joel vowed.

◆ ◆ ◆

The doctor lifted up Carrie's shirt and noticed the stitches.

"When did you get this injury?"

"Last week."

"Horn or hoof?"

Carrie chuckled.

"Horn. How did you know?"

"Young lady, I've been doctoring in ranch country for over twenty-five years. I've seen plenty of these types of injuries. So, who stitched you up?"

"Ummm, I would rather just leave that question unanswered." Carrie liked Doc Thorton, but she wasn't going to expose Bull to any trouble when all he'd been doing was trying to help her.

"If I tell you I recognized Bull's work right off, will you answer my question?"

Carrie smiled and said, "Still going to be a no to that."

"Fair enough. I can always get Bull to admit it. Well, let me see how he did. He likes to pretend he can do a better job than me. If I'm honest, he's probably had more experience stitching up ranch injuries than I have. I just have more medical training." He winked.

With that, Doc Thorton began examining the wound.

"How does it feel?"

"It's pretty tender."

"It looks pretty good. A couple of the stitches have reopened, but I'm sure that happened just now. The area around the wound still looks pretty bruised but not infected. However, I'm going to give you an antibiotic because it reopened. It doesn't look like I'll need to redo the stitches that have opened, and instead, I'll just put a clean dressing on it. I am also not going to remove the sutures that are still holding. Bull can take them out in a day or so. But I want to make myself clear, someone needs to check on this every day. An infection could still set in if we aren't careful."

"Thank you." Carrie dropped her shirt back down in place and gently laid back on the pillows.

"But, Carrie, I'm still pretty worried about the concussion. Will you please just spend one night in the hospital?"

"I really can't, Doc. I can't risk anything delaying the show's production."

There was a knock on the door frame.

"About done in here?"

Carrie turned her head and looked to see Joel standing in the doorway. The man really could strike a pose. He could probably get a job as a male model for any ranching magazine in the country. He was all male and all cowboy. He could make a woman stop and take notice. She hoped she wasn't noticeably drooling.

"Almost. I was trying to convince Carrie to come to the hospital for at least one night, but she has a mind of her own."

"Doc if I promise she won't do anything more than rest today and that Bull and I will watch over her, will that appease you?"

"I know you and Bull know what to look for as far as concussions go. I'll leave her in your hands, but she can't be left alone. You hear that young lady?"

"Don't worry, Doc, we'll take care of her," Joel responded. "If we think her concussion is more serious, we'll make sure she's taken care of and get her to the hospital."

Doc Thorton nodded. He noticed a change in Joel's demeanor. He wasn't sure what Bull had told him, but Joel was now taking personal responsibility for Carrie, and Doc couldn't be happier. Joel wouldn't let the lady lying in the bed in front of him avoid medical help if things got any more serious.

Carrie sat up and moaned. Doc Thorton stopped to watch her.

"Carrie?" Joel rushed to her side and put a hand on her back.

"Just a little dizzy. I'm sure it will get better in a second."

"Why don't you just lie back down?"

"I have to get back outside."

"No, you don't," Joel responded. "Today, you rest. I just got done promising the doctor you would rest. You do realize that if you try to get up with him still here, he's going to doubt my ability to take care of you."

"Fine. But I need to get back to the bunkhouse."

"You're staying here tonight."

"I can't stay here!"

Joel had had enough of this woman fighting him at every step. He leaned over her and, with steel in his voice, said, "Your only choice is rest here at the ranch house or at the hospital." Joel continued to stare into her eyes and asked, "So . . . what's your decision?"

"I already told you, I'm not going to the hospital." She scowled.

"Here at the ranch house then."

"We weren't done shooting for the day."

"You are now. I've already spoken to Drake, and he and I both agreed that you need to rest, and only rest, for the remainder of the day."

"But—"

Joel leaned farther over Carrie and got closer to her while he continued to stare down into her eyes. He was so intense that she lost her breath all over again.

"Carrie? Today. You. Rest."

Carrie swallowed hard and whispered, "Okay, fine."

As Joel hovered over her, Carrie wondered if she would ever be able to breathe again.

Finally, Joel stood back up again and turned to Doc Thorton. "Thanks for coming over so quickly." Joel stretched his hand out to the doctor.

"No problem. Just let me know if there's anything else I can do."

"Thank you."

Carrie shifted over on the bed and swung her legs over the side.

"Where do you think you're going, now?" Carrie could hear the exasperation in Joel's voice.

"I figured I would move downstairs to the couch or something."

"No, Carrie, you're not going anywhere."

"I'll rest, I promise. I'm just trying to get out of your way."

Joel bent over and picked her back up into his arms. He gently laid her back down in the middle of his bed, careful to not touch her stitches. He suddenly realized how much he liked picking her up in his arms. Additionally, she looked like she belonged there in his bed.

"You're going to rest—right where you are. Bull and I will keep an eye on you the rest of the day and tonight."

"But I can't have you doing that. I'm sure you have much more important things to do than to watch me all day."

"Nothing is more important than making sure you're okay," Joel countered.

"But that doesn't make sense. Joel, I've seen how important this operation is and how much work needs to get done on a daily basis. You don't have time to watch me. Not to mention that if I'm in the house, I'll be in your way."

"You can argue all you want, Carrie, but I won't budge on this. This ranch takes care of its own."

"But I'm not a part of this ranch."

"You are now."

"No, I'm not," Carrie quietly replied.

"Carrie, I can't possibly apologize enough for that stupid comment I made when you first arrived. I truly am sorry. While you are not family, you are more than just an unwelcome visitor to this ranch. Please just stay where you are and rest."

Carrie stared at Joel. She didn't want to cause any trouble. She had no idea what was going on in his head, but her head hurt too much right now to try and figure him out. She couldn't continue to argue with him; it was only making her head hurt more. Her eyelids began to drop.

Joel brushed a strand of hair off of her forehead and gently said, "Close your eyes and rest. I'll be back to check on you in a little while. Trust me. It's going to be okay." Carrie let her eyes drift close, and almost before they were shut, she was asleep.

Joel gestured for the doctor to follow him out of the room.

"I'll keep an eye on her, Doc."

"Good."

"How's her back?"

"I, ah—"

"Bull already told me what happened and that he stitched her up."

"So I was right."

"What?"

"I asked her who stitched her up, and she refused to answer the question. Even when I guessed, she refused to confirm it."

"She was protecting Bull."

"Yeah, I gathered that much." The old doctor smirked.

Both men turned and looked back at Carrie, asleep on the bed.

"Kind of funny to think of anyone protecting Bull," Joel thought aloud.

"Makes her kinda special, don't you think?"

"Yes, it does." *Definitely one of a kind*, he thought.

CHAPTER 11

Joel walked back into the room. He grabbed the leather armchair near his window and pulled it over to the bed. He sat down and gently took Carrie's hand in his own. He began to softly move his thumb over the back of her hand. Her hand was so soft, although he noticed calluses that he was pretty sure she hadn't had before she arrived at the Double Spur. He had heard from the hands that she didn't back down from any of the ranch chores. If it was a job they normally did, then she believed they should expect her to do it as well. She was trying to make sure she experienced everything. He had also heard from A.Z. about how much she had shared in their interviews. A.Z. had told him that she had never met anyone who was such a strong supporter of people in the ranching industry, especially not someone who wasn't raised on a ranch. No person was insignificant to Carrie. She continually inserted comments into the interview admiring all of the work that was done on the ranch and how impressed she was with all of the people who did such hard work every day. Joel recalled how supportive she had been during the interview he had watched. A.Z. expressed her amazement at how sincere and genuine Carrie was in every moment of every interview. Joel knew everyone who watched the show would be impressed with the people who were involved in the daily operations of a ranch. He also knew those impressions would be due directly to Carrie's comments.

As Joel sat there watching over Carrie, Maria walked into the room.

"How's she doing?"

"She's sleeping. I'll probably need to wake her in a while and check on her, but for now, I think she's okay."

"Are you going to stay with her all night?"

"Yes."

Maria moved and sat down on the armrest of Joel's leather chair. The two siblings continued to watch this incredible woman sleep. They were both worried about her and hoped they were doing the right thing in letting her rest at the house and not at a hospital.

After a while, Joel smiled as he spoke, "She's so still, she really could be Sleeping Beauty lying there on the bed."

"You do know she doesn't like that nickname, right?"

He chuckled, "Yeah, but that doesn't mean it won't stick."

"Do you know why she doesn't like it?" Maria quietly asked.

"No." Joel turned to his sister and asked, "Is there a reason?"

"Yeah."

"So . . . are you going to share?"

"I probably shouldn't."

"Ree, is this something I should know?"

"Probably. But I'm not sure Carrie will appreciate me sharing it with you."

"Please tell me. If there's something hurtful about the name, I'll put a stop to it."

"It isn't quite like that."

"Ree, just spill it. She doesn't need to know you shared it with me."

"She told me once that she doesn't care for the name because it doesn't fit her. She said she wasn't a princess and no one would ever think of her as one. She also said it was absurd for the men to call her Beauty because she wasn't beautiful. She told me the name felt like she was wearing someone else's clothes. It didn't fit and was uncomfortable."

Not beautiful? How could she believe she wasn't a beauty, Joel wondered.

He turned to his sister and asked the question out loud, "Why doesn't she think she's beautiful?"

"I don't know." Maria shrugged. "I didn't feel I could push the issue at the time. If I had to guess, I just don't think she thinks of herself as someone who's beautiful. I don't think it's so much a case of low self-esteem as it's more the case of someone who thinks of herself last. If you were to ask her who's smart, she would give you a list of names and never once include herself. The same would be true if you asked her about someone who is kind, compassionate, or beautiful. I just think she doesn't think of herself as anything other than just plain, ordinary Carrie. She's okay with that. But because of that, she doesn't feel comfortable with the guys calling her something that isn't ordinary. Any name that would suggest that she's special is outside of her reality."

"How could she not realize how extraordinary she is? She's so incredibly beautiful. Her beauty was the first thing I noticed about her as soon as she started walking toward the house on that first day. But as I've watched her, I've seen her compassion, her kindness, her generosity, and her strength. There aren't very many people who possess all of those qualities, at least not to the same level she does. How can she not know how special she is?"

Maria looked at her brother for a while and finally asked the question she was dying to know, "Are you . . . are you in love with her?"

"Yeah," he answered, turning back to look at Carrie. "I think I fell in love with her when I saw her sitting in the dirt with old 1072. She took my breath away and, I think, my heart right along with it," he said sheepishly.

"What are you going to do about it?"

"I have no idea. Right now, all I can think about is making sure that she's safe and healing."

"I'll leave you alone then. Let me know if either of you need anything."

"I will. Thanks, Maria."

Joel continued to stroke Carrie's hand and watch her as Maria quietly left the room. As she reached the door, she turned back to watch her brother. Everything had changed for him, and she couldn't be happier. She only hoped he'd be able to convince Carrie that his feelings were genuine. It was not going to be easy, but Joel could handle hard work. He had never backed down from something that was difficult if the end result was important, and this was definitely important.

♦ ♦ ♦

A couple hours later, Zach poked his head into Joel's room. "How's she doing?"

"She's been resting quietly. I think it's time to wake her up again, though. I want to check to make sure she isn't suffering from any side effects from the concussion."

"Perfect timing. I just saw Glenda downstairs. The soup she prepared for Carrie is ready. She was hoping Carrie would wake up to have some."

"Why don't you go down and let Glenda know to prepare a tray. I'll wake Carrie and she can eat up here."

Joel turned back to Carrie, laid his hand on her upper arm, and started to gently shake her.

"Carrie, honey, you need to wake up. It's time to eat."

She didn't even stir.

"Carrie, come on, darlin', you need to wake up."

Joel waited another moment to see if she was responding to him. He tried again. This time, he stood up and bent down to whisper in her ear.

"Sleeping Beauty, if you don't wake up, I'm going to have to find Prince Charming to wake you. Hmmm . . . what do you think? Who would qualify as Prince Charming for you? Should I get Bull to come in here and kiss you, Sleeping Beauty?"

Joel took his hand and caressed her cheek. He tried again, "B . . . please, you need to wake up."

"Please, don't call me that."

Joel smiled. "I'll quit calling you Sleeping Beauty once I know you're awake. So, are you awake?"

"Please just let me sleep for a while longer." She sounded so tired and wounded. Joel was tempted to let her continue resting, but he knew she needed food, and the soup would do her good.

"Once you eat something, I'll let you go back to sleep," he quietly responded. "Glenda is bringing up a tray with some homemade soup for you. I promise you'll want to have some."

Just at that moment, Glenda walked into the room with a tray loaded down with food and drinks.

"Joel, how's she doing?"

"I'm awake—I can answer for myself," Carrie replied, still without opening her eyes.

"She'll let you answer for yourself if you open your eyes. Come on, B, let's see those sparkling brown eyes."

Carrie slowly opened her eyes. As she did so, a sharp pain streaked across her head.

"Arrrgh." Carrie's hand rose to cover her eyes.

"Is it your head?" Joel quickly reacted. "Let me shut off the lights."

"I'll get the lights, Joel. Just make sure that she eats something. She needs to keep up her strength."

Glenda shut the lights off as she left the room. Joel took Carrie's other hand and said, "The lights are off. How about you try opening your eyes again? There's still some natural light coming in through the window, so let me know if even that's too bright."

"My head feels like it's in a vice."

"Yeah, I'm sure it does. I have the pain medication Doc left for you, but you really need to take it with some food. Can you open your eyes?"

Carrie slowly lifted her eyelids. She was surprised that the light did not seem to bother her as much as it had when she had initially opened her eyes. She continued to open them. She blinked a few times to bring things into focus.

"How's the vision?"

"It was a little blurry but seems to be clearing up."

"That's good. Can you sit up?"

"Sure."

Carrie started to lift up and Joel was immediately reaching for her arm and helping her sit upright. He then grabbed the pillows from the other side of the bed and tucked them behind her, careful to avoid the stitches.

"How's that? Are you comfortable?"

"Yes, thank you."

"Let me grab the tray and bring it over to the bed. Just a minute."

Carrie nodded her head and once again groaned. Joel immediately turned back to ask, "What's wrong?"

"I shouldn't have tried to nod my head."

"Once you take the medication the doctor left, that effect will lessen. Let me get the soup."

Joel grabbed the tray and laid it over Carrie's lap. Carrie looked at all of the items on the tray. There were two bowls of soup, a bowl of crackers, and a plate of fresh bread. There were also a couple of glasses of lemonade and a couple of dishes of peaches.

"How much does Glenda think I'm going to eat?"

"I think some of that's for me."

"Ohh, I'm sorry." Carrie started to blush. He just smiled.

"Come on, B, eat your soup." Joel picked up the second bowl of soup and began to eat.

Carrie sat forward and picked up the spoon to eat her soup.

"Joel—"

"B, just eat your soup. After you finish, I'm going to check to see how you're doing."

Carrie started to eat her soup and the bread.

"This is delicious."

"I'll let Glenda know you enjoyed her meal. Now, keep eating, B."

Carrie set her soup spoon back down in the bowl and frowned at the man sitting in the chair next to the bed.

"Every time you call me B, it sounds as though you're referring to me as an insect. Do I look like an insect?"

"No, you don't look like an insect, but you seem to have a distaste for the nickname Sleeping Beauty. Besides, I like calling you my shortened version of the name."

"Your shortened version? I don't understand."

"Yeah, B as in the letter *B* for Beauty. Not bee as in the insect."

Carrie took a moment to process what he had just said.

"I still don't know what to think of you calling me that."

Joel just smirked.

"Joel—"

"Eat your soup, Carrie. I want to check to see how your concussion is."

"Fine." She picked her spoon back up and continued eating.

After she was done, Joel lifted the tray off of the bed and handed her a couple of pills and a glass of lemonade.

"Are these going to make me tired or groggy?"

"Probably."

Carrie moved to get out of Joel's bed.

"Where are you going?" Joel growled and moved into Carrie's way. She couldn't get out of the bed with him standing over her.

"I was going to head to the bunkhouse. I'm feeling better, and if I'm going to fall asleep, I should do it in my bed."

"You're not going anywhere," he rumbled. "I promised Doc I would keep an eye on you. If I have to move down to the bunkhouse to do that, none of the men are going to be able to get any sleep. If you stay right where you are, then everyone else gets some sleep."

"I can't sleep in your bed."

"You're not going anywhere else, B. Now scoot back and lay down." Carrie looked Joel in the eye. She saw steel and determination. She knew that he was not going to give in on this point. She sighed and slid down the bed.

Joel moved the extra pillows out of the way. As soon as Carrie laid back on the pillows, Joel covered her up with the blanket.

"I thought you were going to check on my concussion."

"Been doing that as we've talked."

"And?"

"And you need to get some sleep. Close your eyes, B, and rest."

Carrie closed her eyes and immediately fell asleep.

CHAPTER 12

When Carrie awoke the next morning, she opened her eyes to find Joel sleeping in the leather armchair next to the bed. She quietly lifted the blanket and moved to get out of the bed. Joel stirred. Carrie immediately quit moving, hoping she could get up without waking him. She realized her efforts were unsuccessful when she noticed Joel's eyes were open and focused on her.

"Good morning, B. How're you feeling?" Joel asked with a scratchy morning voice.

"I'm fine."

"How's the head?"

"It feels like I got kicked in the head."

"Well, at least you're being honest with me. Are you hungry?"

"Maybe something light? I don't think I could eat a lot."

"I'll check with Glenda. How about some scrambled eggs and toast?"

"I can go downstairs and check for myself."

"You're not getting out of this bed unless I'm here. Understand?"

"That's ridiculous."

"Please, just stay put until I get back."

With that, Joel turned and walked out of the room. Carrie thought his directive was silly. She was a grown woman, after all. She could get out of bed and get herself to the bathroom without anyone's help. She sat up and felt a little dizzy. She was about to shake her head to clear the fog when she remembered how awful she felt yesterday after nodding her head. She decided to forgo that step and just take a deep breath. Carrie slowly swung her legs off of the bed. She noticed that she still felt a little dizzy. She sat on the edge of the bed waiting for her head to clear. After a few moments, she slid her legs to the floor and cautiously stood up. She turned her head to look if there was a bathroom connected to the bedroom and noticed a couple of doors on the far side of the bedroom. She hoped one of them was the bathroom. It would be a crying shame to get all the way over to the far side of the room and discover that both doors were nothing more than closets. Carrie took a cautious step, then another, keeping her hand on the bed for balance. The dizzy feeling was not improving. She closed her eyes for a moment, trying to get her bearings.

"What are you doing?!" came a growl from the doorway. Carrie felt two strong hands close around her shoulders. Carrie heard the same voice behind her whispering in her ear, "B, what in heaven's name are you doing?"

"I was just trying to get to the bathroom." She continued to stand near the bed while she suffered through the vertigo.

"Are you suffering a dizzy spell?"

"Yes." The answer was a mere breath of a response that Joel barely heard.

"Okay, I want you to sit down for just a moment. Then I'll help you to the bathroom. Okay?"

"Joel, I'm fine. I can get there myself," she insisted.

"Carrie, sit for a moment. Let the dizziness pass," he softly urged.

Carrie sat on the edge of the bed and tried opening her eyes. While it still felt like the room was moving, the spinning seemed to have stopped.

"Better?" he asked.

"Yes." She fudged the truth. She really needed to get to the bathroom, and she realized that Joel wasn't going to allow her to go anywhere as long as she was dizzy. She *was* better, she argued with herself.

"Okay, let me help you up slowly, and I'll walk with you to the bathroom. If the room starts to spin again, let me know, and we'll stop. Alright?"

"Yeah, okay."

Joel helped Carrie up, and they slowly made it to one of the doors on the other side of the room. He turned the knob and opened the door. The bathroom was bright from the natural light pouring in through the windows. Carrie had to shut her eyes for a moment.

"Too bright?"

"No, it's okay. Just let me get adjusted to the brightness."

Joel didn't say anything; he merely stood there holding Carrie's arm and being a source of support. Carrie slowly opened her eyes again, trying to adjust to the new level of sunlight. Once her eyes had adjusted, she took a step toward the bathroom again. Joel walked with her until she was standing next to the counter.

"You can let go now."

"Are you sure you're steady enough?"

"Yes."

"Alright. I'll be right outside. If you need anything, just call and I'll come in, okay?"

"I think I can manage from here."

Joel nodded and walked out of the bathroom. As soon as he closed the door, Carrie sank onto the toilet lid. She still felt lightheaded, but if she were completely honest with herself, she wasn't sure if it was from the concussion or just from having Joel's arms around her. All of his attention was making her nervous and self-conscious. Carrie wasn't exactly sure what to do with his concern and his attention. She took her time in the bathroom. She didn't want to make any sudden moves that would trigger the vertigo, so she moved slowly and cautiously around in the bathroom. She found some toothpaste and used her finger to brush her teeth.

As soon as she had finished everything she wanted to do in the bathroom, she opened the door. Before she could even step a foot outside of the room, Joel was standing there reaching his arms out to hold onto her.

"Here, let me help you to the bed."

"I really need to get back to the bunkhouse."

"After I get you back sitting on the bed, I'll explain the plans for the day."

Joel snaked his arm around her waist and began to move them both over to the bed. As soon as they neared the bed, he bent over and lifted her up into his arms. He gently set her on the bed with her back near the headboard. He tucked the pillows behind her as he had the day before.

"Okay, so the plans for the day are as follows. First, you're going to eat breakfast. If that goes well, we'll take a walk down the stairs and out to the barns. If you are up for it, A.Z. is going to interview you about what happened yesterday. If you're not up for it, then the interview will wait. I'm pretty certain after all of that, you're going to be ready to rest. We'll come back to the house, and you'll rest here. As I said last night, it's much easier for someone to keep an eye on you here in the house rather than at the bunkhouse. Not to mention it's impossible to check on you if you're in the top bunk."

"No one needs to keep an eye on me. I'm fine."

"We'll see how fine you are after breakfast, the walk, and the interview."

Carrie frowned. She didn't want to take anyone away from their work. She felt guilty knowing her concussion was increasing the workload around the ranch rather than helping to decrease it. She looked at Joel and was ready to argue when he placed a finger over her lips and said, "This is not up for discussion. Drake and I have talked it all out, and whether you like it or not, that *is* the plan for the day."

Carrie sat there and tried to figure out a way to get out of the house.

"Quit trying to come up with a different plan."

"What?"

"I can tell you're trying to figure out a way to change the plans. It won't work. Drake and I have agreed on what is best for you, the ranch, *and* the show. We agree that what's best for everyone is for you not to overextend yourself. Carrie, if you don't take it easy and rest, you really may just end up in the hospital. That won't do anyone any good."

"Did I hear someone was ready for breakfast?" The cheery question came from right outside the doorway. Glenda carried a tray loaded down with a multitude of dishes. Joel immediately took the tray from her hands.

"Glenda, I told you I would bring it up."

"Yes, you did, but I was tired of waiting on you. Besides, I'm not the one in bed with a concussion. I can carry a tray of food up a flight of stairs."

Joel shook his head. "Thank you."

"Yes, thank you, Glenda," Carrie said.

"You're welcome. Let me know if you need anything else."

"We will. Thanks."

Carrie looked at the tray again as Joel set it down over her lap.

"You really don't have to eat here with me. I know your routine is to eat with the ranch hands as you talk about the day. In fact, you probably already ate breakfast."

Joel sat down on the bed and grabbed a fresh biscuit.

"I don't *have* to eat with you, but I *want* to. I don't often get to share a meal with a lovely woman. My mama taught me to never look a gift horse in the mouth. So I'm going to enjoy this."

Carrie had no response to his comments. She decided her best course of action would be to just be quiet and eat her breakfast. She hoped Joel would not notice the blush seeping up her cheeks.

♦ ♦ ♦

As soon as Carrie finished eating, Joel stood up and removed the tray from over her legs.

"Are you okay for a while? I would like to bring this back to Glenda and check on a couple of things in the office."

"I'm fine. You really don't need to babysit me."

"Will you stay in that bed while I'm gone?"

"Joel—"

"Carrie, it's a simple question. I'll be honest, if you give me any response other than the right one, I *will* stay here and not get any of my work done."

"Fine." Carrie harrumphed.

"I want *your word* that you'll stay in that bed until I get back."

"Sure you trust my word?"

For the first time that morning, Joel smiled. The grin spread over his entire face. "Oh, yeah, darlin', I trust you at your word. Now, am I going to get it?"

"Yes, I'll stay in the bed until you return."

Joel nodded and turned toward the door. He stepped out of the room and turned to walk down the hall. Carrie could hear his footsteps as he descended the steps. She laid her head back on the pillow and closed her eyes. She couldn't believe how tired she was. Maybe the plan to rest was a good one. She could trust Drake to make good decisions about what was best for her and the show. *You can trust Joel, too,* she heard the little voice in her head say. Maybe she could trust Joel, too.

Joel arrived a while later. He quietly walked into the room. Carrie looked like she was sleeping. If she was, he wasn't going to wake her. She needed her rest. Just as he stepped into the room, Carrie's lashes lifted, and she looked at him. She smiled.

"How are you feeling?"

"Better."

"You're not just saying that to convince me to let you get up, are you?"

"No. I really am feeling better."

"Good. But, Carrie, we'll still be taking things easy and slow today. I won't let you overdo this. Understand?"

"Yes, I understand. I promise not to overdo things today. The sooner you believe I'm fine, the sooner we can get back on schedule."

"Fair enough. Let me help you get to your feet."

"Please, let me see if I can do it? I really do feel better, and I need to do this."

"Fine." Joel sighed. "But I'm not going anywhere. If you start feeling dizzy, let me know."

"I will. I promise."

"B?"

"Yeah?"

"You sure are making lots of promises to me today. I wonder what else I can get you to promise."

Carrie blushed. She wasn't exactly sure what he was talking about, but just the way he had said it, his comment sounded so personal, almost intimate. She took her eyes off him and looked to the floor. Maybe if she looked away, he wouldn't notice her face was as red as a tomato. She slid off of the bed and slowly stood on her feet. She stood up and looked up at Joel.

"So far, so good."

"Great. And, B?"

"Yeah?"

"I have to tell you, that blush on your cheeks is awful cute." He winked as he held out his arm. *So much for him not noticing.* "Ready?" he asked.

"Yes," she squeaked.

Carrie slipped her arm through his and walked with him out into the hallway. They approached the stairs, and Joel stopped.

"I want you to take hold of the banister while I hold onto you. The last thing we need is for you to fall down these steps."

Carrie nodded and felt a wave of vertigo hit her. She stopped and closed her eyes.

"Carrie?"

"I'm okay."

"Are you dizzy again?"

"Yes," she quietly answered.

"I'm taking you back to the bed."

"No, please, let me see if it will pass. I shouldn't have nodded my head. I knew from what happened yesterday that doing so brings on the vertigo."

"Carrie, it means you're not beyond your concussion. Your head is reminding you—and me for that matter—that you need to rest and heal."

"Joel, the plan for the day isn't strenuous. I can do this. The dizziness has passed. I promise. I won't overdo things today."

"Fine. But I'm not leaving your side today. You may be able to persuade Drake or any of the hands that you're fine and all better, but I won't be as easily buffaloed. You have all of them wrapped around your little finger. I, on the other hand, will not be fooled."

Carrie started to laugh.

"Mind telling me what's so funny?"

"You."

He turned to look into her eyes. He lifted his eyebrow and just continued to stare at her as he waited.

"It's just that your comment about having Drake and the ranch hands wrapped around my finger was pretty funny."

"Yeah, we'll see how funny you think it is when you step foot outside this house and you're swamped with all of their worry over you."

"Whatever. Okay, I'm ready. Let's go downstairs."

"Slowly."

"Okay, slowly. I promise."

With that last promise, Joel walked Carrie down the stairs and over to the front door to walk outside. As he opened the door with her still holding his arm, he felt something settle in his soul.

CHAPTER 13

As soon as Carrie stepped foot onto the front porch, Drake stepped up and asked, "Carrie, how are you feeling?"

"I'm okay, Drake."

"If you aren't up for things today, we can wait another day."

"No really, I'll be fine."

"You'll let us know if you're tired or need a break?"

"Yes, I promise."

Joel chuckled. Carrie turned to him with a frown.

"What's so funny?"

"Nothing, B. Absolutely nothing." Joel really did wonder what else she was going to promise today. He wondered more specifically what he could get her to promise *him* today.

Carrie shook her head and once again felt the vertigo come over her. She gasped.

"Carrie?" Carrie could hear the concern in Drake's voice, but at the moment, she had to focus on handling the dizziness. The buzzing in her ears was muting out almost everything else.

Joel quickly picked her up and gently set her in one of the front porch Adirondack chairs. Carrie closed her eyes and took a few deep breaths.

"Vertigo back?" Joel quietly asked her.

"Yeah."

"Just sit here for a moment—see if it passes."

"Okay, thanks."

It didn't take long for the wave of vertigo to pass. She lifted her head. She knew she would need to reassure Drake. As soon as she lifted her head, she realized a few more people had gathered in front of the porch. She looked toward the small group and said, "I'm fine. It's just a little vertigo."

"Carrie, are you sure?" Drake asked.

Before she had a chance to reassure Drake, another voice cut in. "You're overdoing it." That was Bull's rough voice.

"You need to rest," someone else said. Carrie couldn't place the voice, but she thought it could be one of the cameramen.

"Can't take a concussion lightly, Sleeping Beauty, they're serious." That voice she knew to be Beans. He loved to tease her about that stupid name.

"Guys, I'm fine. I just had a little dizziness. It's passed now."

"Don't like it." That was Bull's voice again. He moved up onto the porch and stood next to Joel. "She needs to rest, Joel."

"Bull, I'm fine."

"No, you're not, Carrie. At the rate you're going, you're going to be in the ICU before the two months have finished."

Carrie glared at Bull. She slowly stood up.

"Listen up, cowboy. I'm going to finish this show. I'm fine. I have come to realize I can't shake or nod my head like I just did. When I do, I get a little dizzy. It isn't a big deal. I repeat. I. Am. Fine. I just have to remember not to move my head like that."

Bull looked her in the eyes. Carrie held his gaze. He saw the fire and steel he had come to associate with this woman. They stood locked in a stare-off for a moment before Bull looked away. He turned to Joel and said, "Keep your eyes on her. She won't admit when she's too tired. I don't like the vertigo. Doc would tell us she needs to go to the hospital. You know that as well as I do."

"I know. I've already told her she needs to take it easy."

"Not sure she even knows what that means," the old cowhand grumbled as he stepped off the porch.

The next person to move into her line of vision was Drake.

"Carrie, we can wait another day. It won't affect the production at all. Promise. The most important thing is that you're really okay."

Carrie sighed. It appeared that she was going to spend the entire day reassuring every man on this ranch that she was fine.

"Drake, I've already promised Joel I wouldn't overdo it. I'll make the same promise to you. I'll let you know if I get too tired and need a break. I really just need to remember I can't nod or shake my head. If I can just remember that, I'll be fine."

"It's hard to stop doing something like that when it's a natural part of who you are." He smiled.

"Yeah, I'm starting to realize that. But I promise, I really am doing okay. Joel told me what we were going to do today. I can handle that. Please, can we just get to it?"

"Yeah, okay. Let's go find A.Z. as soon as you think you're ready to move."

"I'm good now. Let's go."

Carrie realized Joel had reached his hand around her waist the minute she had stood up to confront Bull. He had kept his hand on her hip the entire time. As soon as she moved to head off the porch, he turned with her and walked with her.

She looked up at him. "You know, I'm fine. I can walk."

"Yep."

"You can let go, Joel."

"I can, but that doesn't mean I'm going to. If you keep insisting on moving through this day, I'm sticking close to you, B. Get used to it."

Carrie didn't know what to say in response to his comments. She decided that maybe it would be better to conserve her energy for the filming.

The trio walked around over to the equestrian barn. As soon as they stepped foot in the barn, Carrie saw Maria rush down the center aisle and head toward them.

"Carrie! Are you sure you're up for this?"

"Not you too, Maria."

"Me, too?"

"I just got done reassuring Bull and Drake and some of the other men that I'm fine. I was hoping you would understand and not need the same assurance. Please tell me you trust me to know my own body and whether I can handle things today."

"B—" Joel spoke up.

"Of course, I trust you, Carrie," Maria interjected. "That doesn't mean I'm not concerned. You took a nasty spill. I would hope that as *my friend*, you would be just as concerned about me if I had been thrown off of a bull and gotten a concussion to prove it."

"Sorry," Carrie conceded. "Of course, I'd be just as concerned. I'm just not used to so many people being concerned about me. I guess I don't know what to do with all of it."

"I understand. But just remember everyone here genuinely cares for your well-being. That doesn't mean we don't trust and respect you, it just means we care."

Carrie went to nod and stopped herself. She took a deep breath and answered, "Thanks, I'll remember that."

"Well, I assume you're headed to the back side of the barn. I think they have all of the camera equipment set up for your interview."

"Thanks. I'll see you later."

"Sure thing."

Carrie started walking toward the rear of the barn. She noticed that Joel still had his arm around her as she walked.

"I really am fine. You don't need to hang onto me," she quietly asserted.

"You're not getting rid of me that easily, you know."

Carrie chuckled. "It was worth a try."

They stepped out the back doors and found that everything had been set up just as it had been on previous days. It was all ready for her to sit down and talk with A.Z. about her day. As she was letting her eyes adjust to the bright Texas sun, she saw a figure approach her.

"Carrie, how are you doing?" A.Z. asked with concern in her voice.

"A.Z., I'm fine. What are *you* doing here? Joel and Drake mentioned you would be interviewing me, but I just remembered you weren't going to be back yet. Why are you back so soon?"

"Drake called and told me what happened. I wanted to come and check on you myself. I was worried. I know how it feels to be thrown from one of those bucking beasts. While my experience involves horses, not bulls, the landing is the same no matter what animal throws you."

"What about the work you needed to do?"

"I took care of . . . well, enough of my work, for now."

"Are you sure you should be here?"

"Are you sure you should be out of bed?"

Both women stood and looked at each other. Suddenly they both burst into giggles. Carrie turned to Drake and said, "So where do you want us?"

With that, the filming started. Carrie and A.Z. sat on the bench, and A.Z. began to ask her questions.

"I was so nervous, I probably spooked the bull. I'm told no one gets thrown from that bull."

"Just because it doesn't happen often doesn't mean it was an easy ride. A bull's a bull. These animals are bred to buck and turn and spin. Getting thrown by one can happen to anyone at any time. You need to remember that for your next ride."

"Thanks. I will."

"So when are you going to try again?"

"Not sure."

"Worried?"

"Actually, I haven't even thought about it. I've spent so much time trying to convince everyone I'm okay, I haven't even worried about next time."

"My advice? Don't think about it too much. Keep your mind focused on the present. One fall off a bull doesn't mean the next ride will result in a fall. From what I heard, you actually had pretty good form and were doing a great job until you got thrown off. In fact, to hear Joel tell it, you would've been fine, but your leg got caught on the bull's leg, and that's what spun you around in the air. That was really why you landed on your head rather than on your backside."

"Joel said that?"

A.Z. smiled. "Yeah, he did."

Carrie wasn't sure what to think of Joel's comment. He kept surprising her. She had thought she had him pegged, and now it seemed every time she turned around, he said or did something unexpected. That would have to be a puzzle for a later date.

"So, Carrie, what do you think about going for a ride tomorrow?"

"On top of a bull?"

"I was actually thinking of a horse. I think it would be good for you to just get back on top of one of these beasts, but I don't think your head is ready for the jarring of a bull ride. I thought we could take Misty and Sadie out for a ride. What do you think?"

"I think that's a great idea!"

"It will all depend upon how you feel, of course."

"Of course," Carrie quickly answered.

Joel just shook his head. *How could these women even contemplate putting B on the back of one of these animals?* They were going to be the death of him. He was going to be put in an early grave with worry over this woman. However, he had to admit that he wished it had been him putting that smile on her face. The excitement was radiating out of her. She was shining just like the first day she had arrived on the ranch. Joel once again found himself breathless. She was as beautiful as a Texas sunset over this ranch when she smiled like that.

"That's a wrap. Thanks, everyone," Drake called out. He turned to Carrie and said, "That's enough for you today. I want you to rest for the remainder of the day. If you're going to ride, you need to make sure you let that head heal a little more."

"Oh, fine." Carrie turned to head toward the bunkhouse. Joel wrapped his hand around her elbow and gently turned her around.

"Where do you think you're going?" Joel looked into her eyes. His own were intense. Carrie lost her entire train of thought in that moment.

"I, ah, I . . ." she stuttered.

"Let me put it this way, B, if you want to ride Misty tomorrow, you'll rest up at the house tonight."

"Joel, I can't continue to stay at the house."

"Maybe not indefinitely, but you will until I'm convinced you've completely recovered from your concussion. That means tonight you sleep where I can check on you."

"I'm *not* sleeping in your bed again." She had raised her voice, and suddenly, she noticed that everyone else had stopped moving and was watching her. She quickly realized her words were incredibly incriminating. She immediately blushed yet again.

Joel stepped in just as quickly to cover for her gaffe. His voice carried over the still air.

"It doesn't make a difference to me whether you sleep in my bed or in the guest room, but you need to have someone checking on you. I can sleep in the guest room, as I did last night, or you can, but you *will* stay up at the house. We've already talked about this—staying in the bunkhouse is not a viable option for someone checking on you throughout the night. I would have to keep turning on the lights which would only wake the men and make Bull grumpy."

With his comments, the men chuckled and began to move again. They continued to collect the equipment they had used during the interview with A.Z.

Carrie turned to Joel. "Thank you," she whispered.

"You're welcome, B. I would never want anyone to have one negative thought about you staying up at the house when you're there for your health. That's one rumor I won't allow to even germinate."

Joel's words surprised her again. It was getting harder and harder to reconcile this man, the one who was so concerned about her health and reputation, with the man she had met on the first day she came to the Double Spur.

CHAPTER 14

Carrie woke up in the guest room the following morning. She noticed Joel once again sleeping in a chair next to her bed. As soon as she started sitting up, he heard the movement and came instantly awake.

"Carrie, are you okay?"

"Did you sleep in that chair all night?"

"Not *all* night."

There was something about his voice that drove her to question him.

"What does that mean?" she asked.

"For a part of the night, I just watched you sleep."

A blush quickly spread over her cheeks. She had no response except to cover her face.

"Still find that blush adorable. Covering it up with your hands doesn't hide it and doesn't change how cute you are when you blush."

"Joel, just stop."

"Why?" he asked.

"What do you mean why?" She frowned.

"Why would I want to stop?"

"Because it's embarrassing."

"What's embarrassing? The fact that I think that you're cute when you blush or the fact that I enjoyed watching you sleep last night." He stood up and ran his finger down her cheek. Joel knew he had to go easy on the teasing. This was clearly all new territory for Carrie, and he had to be careful not to spook her.

"I'll go see if Glenda has something for you for breakfast."

"Thank you." The words barely made it past her lips.

It wasn't until he stepped out of the room that she was able to take a regular breath. The man was lethal. She was going to have to convince him she was fine and could stay at the bunkhouse tonight. She wasn't sure how many more mornings she was going to be able to wake up to him sleeping in a chair next to her bed.

Before she could get out of bed, Joel was back. He walked into the guest room with a tray laden with breakfast. It looked like Glenda had prepared the tray with breakfast for both her and Joel again. He set the tray down on the bed over her legs.

"How're you feeling this morning, B?"

"Actually, I feel pretty good."

"Truth?"

"Honestly. I'm feeling much better. I'm looking forward to riding Misty today."

"Are you sure that you're up for that?"

"Only one way to find out." Carrie shrugged her shoulders.

"Carrie—"

"Kidding. I'm just kidding." She raised her hands up as if she were surrendering to him. "I really do feel up to riding. Besides, I'll be riding Misty. She'll take care of me."

"Before I let you go riding, I want you to take a shower and get down the steps. If you can do that without *any* vertigo, you can go riding. If you have even a moment of dizziness, you will not ride."

"Joel—"

"I'm not kidding, Carrie. You can't ride a horse, not even one as gentle as Misty, if you might experience a dizzy spell."

"I realize that."

"Good. I just need to make sure we're on the same page here. I won't risk your life."

"Believe it or not, neither will I. I'll see how I'm doing after my shower, and I'll let you know."

"Okay. Fair enough. Now eat your breakfast."

◆ ◆ ◆

After her shower, Carrie walked downstairs and found Joel sitting on the couch in the living room. He turned and stood up.

"How's the vertigo?"

"Fine."

"Is that the truth?"

She rolled her eyes. "Yes, it's the truth. I'll see you later."

"Later?"

"Yeah, when I get back from my ride?"

Joel walked right up to her and reached for her elbow. He cradled it in his hand.

"I'm coming with on this ride of yours."

"Joel, I know how busy you are and how much work you need to do. You don't need to come with me. I'll be with A.Z."

Joel leaned forward even more until their eyes were on the same level and mere inches apart.

"If you think I'm letting you go riding without me, you must have hit your head harder than you're willing to admit."

Carrie looked into his eyes. She was hoping she would be able to convince him to let her go riding without him. As she stared into his eyes, she realized he would not be persuaded. She wasn't sure why she knew it, but she knew he was not going to let her ride without him.

"Joel—"

"B, this has nothing to do with not trusting you—or A.Z. It has nothing to do with your riding skills. This is about my concern that we still have not taken proper care of you and your concussion. I'm still very worried that you should be at the hospital. I won't let you risk your life and health just to go riding today. Okay?"

"Okay, Joel," she quietly responded.

They walked out of the house and over toward the barns. They found A.Z. waiting. Someone had already saddled Misty, Sadie, and Joel's horse, Midnight.

Carrie turned to Joel, lifted her eyebrow, and said, "Obviously, someone else knew you planned on going riding with us."

Joel merely smiled and shrugged his shoulders.

"Do you want a hand up?" he asked Carrie.

"No, I think I can do this."

"Are you sure? I don't want you to overdo this ride. I can help you mount the horse so you don't jostle your head."

"Joel, I'm fine. I'll let you know if I need help."

"Fine," he grumbled.

Carrie turned to Misty and rubbed her hand down the horse's nose. "Are you ready, girl?"

Once again, the horse bobbed her head up and down.

"You're gonna take care of me today, aren't 'cha girl?"

At this, the horse nickered. Carrie smiled, grabbed the reins, and carefully mounted the horse. She knew she was not one hundred percent. She had not lied when she told Joel she hadn't experienced any vertigo yet this morning; however, she wasn't going to take any chances. If she bounced around too much getting on Misty, she could believe the vertigo would return and that would be the end of the ride. As soon as she had carefully lifted herself up and into the saddle, she looked up to see that Joel and A.Z. had already mounted their horses and were ready to go.

The small group rode out.

"Where to?"

"If you'll let me, I'll take you to one of my favorite places on the ranch," Joel prompted.

"Sounds good to me. What do you think, Carrie?" A.Z. asked.

"Sure."

So A.Z. and Carrie let Joel take the lead, and they headed east. This was the opposite direction from where Carrie had ridden before. She had no idea what to expect but was willing to trust Joel to make sure she didn't ride too far.

They had only been riding for about twenty minutes when they came over a rise and Carrie saw the most beautiful freshwater pond. It was clear and blue and serene.

"What is this place?"

"My favorite waterhole. It's where Zach, Maria, and I would come to cool off. We would go swimming as soon as our chores were done."

"I hope you're not expecting me to go swimming. I didn't bring a suit," Carrie said, smiling.

"We could always go skinny dipping," Joel countered as his eyebrows bounced up and down.

"Forget it, Roulston. I'm *not* going skinny dipping with you around," A.Z. answered.

Joel laughed. "Fair enough. I was just kidding anyway. B isn't up for a swim today."

"Who says?"

"You're awfully spirited knowing A.Z. has already quashed any potential for a swim. But seriously, I thought this would be a good spot to just get off the horses. It was a good ride out but not too far for Carrie's first ride."

Joel dismounted. He walked over to Carrie and looked up at her.

"Ready to dismount and stretch your legs?"

"Yes."

"Let me help you."

"Okay."

Carrie swung her leg over Misty, and just as he had the first time, he reached up and wrapped his hands around her waist. He lifted her off of the horse and gently set her on her feet. Joel grabbed Misty's reins. He took both horses and tied their reins up to a stake near one of the trees surrounding the swimming hole. Carrie noticed that A.Z. had already tied Sadie up and had found a rock to sit on. Carrie joined her on the rock. Joel sat down on another boulder near the two women.

"So, A.Z., did you have something like this when you were growing up?" Carrie asked.

"Yeah, we have a similar spot on our ranch. My sister and I used to go swimming as often as we could. How about you?"

"No way. I grew up in the city. The only swimming spot was the local pool."

"Did you go there?"

"Not often. My family was too busy with the hardware store to be able to take me to the pool. I would occasionally go with a friend, but there just weren't that many opportunities."

"So what *did* you do for fun?" Joel asked.

Carrie looked at the man and wasn't sure how to answer him. She knew what she had done for most of her childhood would not be considered "fun" to anyone, let alone this man. Outside of the hospital visits and spending time with Cassie, Carrie had spent most of her time at the store. She didn't feel as if she had missed out on anything because she had loved going to the store and helping her Dad with everything he would let her do. Even more than working in the store, however, she loved spending time with her sister. She cherished the days spent playing games with Cassie in the hospital. She wasn't sure Joel would understand these moments were her version of fun. It was just too different from his life, too mundane. Moreover, she needed to keep Cassie's identity a secret. It was her job to protect Cassie, and she would do it without fail.

"Carrie?" Joel inquired.

She knew she had to have to give him an answer. She went with the only one she could.

"I spent a lot of my time at the store. I used to help my dad with whatever he needed."

"Like what?" A.Z. asked with genuine curiosity.

"I remember sorting nuts and bolts and screws. I would take inventory and refill the containers. As soon as I had mastered taking inventory, my dad started letting me fill out his order forms for re-ordering. Once he was comfortable with my ability to understand the inventory needs, he let me start ordering the nuts and bolts, and then he let me move onto other items we carried in the store."

Carrie looked at Joel and A.Z. They had not said anything, and she figured that what she was describing sounded lame to these two who had such adventurous childhoods on their families' ranches.

"I know it's not anything like your childhood," Carrie quickly interjected. "It must sound pretty lame to someone who grew up riding horses and swimming in their own personal watering hole."

"You loved being in the store, didn't you?" Joel asked, ignoring her interjection.

Carrie turned away and blushed.

"Yeah. I know it probably sounds dull and silly, but yeah, I enjoyed it."

"It doesn't sound silly. Not at all. It's your family's business. Sounds like you fell in love with that business from an early age." A.Z. answered.

"Yeah, I guess I did."

The three of them sat for a while and just enjoyed the tranquility of the water. Joel thought about what Carrie had revealed. He learned that she had not had any of the childhood experiences he had. She had, however, found joy in something as basic as sharing in the work of the family business. She was a woman who was devoted to her family. She was not looking for drama and enjoyed the simplicity that life offered. She had once again shown him that she was a woman of substance.

♦ ♦ ♦

Once Carrie, Joel, and A.Z. arrived back at the ranch, Maria came out to meet them.

"How was the ride?"

"Nice," Carrie answered.

"Where did you go?"

"The swimming hole," Joel answered.

"Really? You took them to that puddle of water? Why?"

"Carrie needed a short ride. I thought it was a perfect amount of time for her to be in the saddle, with a good spot to rest after the ride out."

Maria smiled. Joel was right. That would have been a short first ride for Carrie, but still giving her a chance to be in the saddle.

"How do you feel, Carrie?" Maria asked her.

"Tired, but pretty good."

Joel immediately turned back around to face her.

"B, you should have said something sooner," Joel scolded.

"Joel, I'm fine. I just got a little tired there at the end. We were almost back, and there was no reason to say anything."

"Fine, but you're going back up to the house to rest."

"Okay."

"What, no argument?"

"No. No argument."

Carrie felt Joel's hands wrap around her upper arms. He bent and looked directly into her eyes. She couldn't hide anything from him when he was that close and staring at her so intently. Not to mention that she really was tired—too tired to try to hide her emotions. A frown began to form around his lips and eyes. A breath of air escaped from him. He shook his head and bent and picked Carrie up into his arms.

Carrie shrieked and grabbed his shoulders. "What are you doing?"

"Carrying you up to the house."

"What? Why?"

"I can tell how tired you are. Carrie, you needed to say something sooner. I'm not going to let you exert yourself any further today."

CHAPTER 15

"We need to talk," Joel said as he approached Drake, who was sitting outside of the production trailer.

"About Carrie?"

"Yes. She's pushing herself too much."

"I know." Drake sighed.

"We need to do something about it," Joel pressed.

"I do have an idea."

"What's that?"

"We're going to Canfield, her hometown, to get some background for the show."

"You're taking her away from the ranch?"

"I—"

"I don't think that's a good plan."

"What—"

"Who's going to keep an eye on her? She won't stop, and she certainly won't tell anyone she's too tired to keep going."

"Joel!"

"What!"

"Are you going to let me tell you what my idea is, or are you just going to stand there and tell me it's a terrible idea before you even hear it?"

Joel expelled a deep breath and ran his hand through his hair.

"Sorry, man. I'm just really worried about her."

"Yeah, I heard she was wiped out after the ride this morning."

"She finally admitted it *after* the ride was over. She was exhausted. She didn't even object to me carrying her up to the house."

Drake chuckled. "*That* speaks volumes about how tired she truly was."

Joel smiled for the first time since he had approached Drake.

"Yeah. I laid her on the guest bed and told her to rest. Before I could get her boots off, she was already asleep. She can't continue to push herself. She won't listen to us that she needs to recover from her concussion. We need to take the show out of the equation."

"I know. So my idea is to get her backstory—" Drake lifted his hand to stop Joel from interrupting him and finished, "without her."

"What?"

"I plan to go to Canfield—without her. I figure I can interview her family and friends and learn who Carrie is from their perspective. I really think the hometown perspective will give us more depth for the show."

"Are you going to tell her?"

"Yeah. I figured I would talk to her about the change this afternoon."

"Would you be opposed to having some back-up when you have this conversation?"

"You?"

Joel nodded.

"Nope, I've got no objection. Hopefully, between the two of us, we'll be able to convince her this change is the best thing for the show and for her."

"I'm going to work in the office while she sleeps. I'll keep an eye on her, and when she wakes up, I'll let you know."

"Great. In the meantime, I'm going to take the opportunity to review what we have so far. I need to get an idea of how the shooting is going."

The two men looked at each other. Joel nodded at Drake right before he turned to head back up to the house. He planned to check on Carrie before he went into the office to work.

♦ ♦ ♦

Carrie woke that afternoon, once again in the guest bedroom of the ranch house. She remembered Joel carrying her up to the ranch house and to the guest room, but she didn't remember much after that. This was the first time since she had been thrown off of the bull that she awoke to an empty room. She looked around again just to make sure. Joel was not in the room this afternoon. Carrie breathed a sigh of relief.

"That was an awfully big sigh," came a voice from the hallway.

Carrie turned and noticed that Joel was standing outside of the door. She couldn't say anything.

He walked into the room carrying a tray of food. Clearly, Glenda had sent up more food for her. Carrie wasn't sure what time it was, so she didn't know if this was lunch or dinner.

"Hungry?" Joel asked. Carrie's stomach growled in response. Joel chuckled. "I'll take that as a yes." He walked forward and set the tray over Carrie's lap.

The tray contained waffles, fresh fruit, and juice. The food gave no indication of what meal this was. However, the tray appeared to only have food for one person. It didn't look as though Glenda had sent food up for both of them. Carrie was relieved.

Joel sat down on the bed as he had on the previous occasions.

"How did you sleep?"

"Ahh . . . fine."

Carrie didn't make a move to start eating. She sat on the bed and just watched Joel waiting for him to leave her to her food.

"I know you're hungry, B. Why aren't you eating?"

"Why are you staying?"

"What do you mean?"

"The other times you've brought me food in bed, Glenda included enough food for two people. There's only enough food for one person. Why, ummm, why…"

"Why, what?"

Carrie frowned. This man just pushed and pushed.

"Come on, spit it out, Carrie."

"Are you going to sit there and watch me eat?"

"Maybe." Joel smiled. "Would it make you feel better if I ate some of your dinner?" With that, he grabbed a red grape from her fruit bowl and popped it into his mouth.

"No. Now stop eating my food."

"I'll stop eating your food—if you start to eat it."

"I can't eat if you're going to sit there and watch me."

Joel picked up another grape and asked, "Would you eat if I fed you?"

"No. Now stop it."

Joel shrugged his shoulders and popped the second grape in his mouth.

Carrie's stomach took that moment to growl once again.

"Okay, B, I'll quit teasing you as long as you start eating. While you eat, we're going to talk about the plans for the day."

"Shouldn't I be having that conversation with Drake?"

"He'll be here in a minute. Drake and I spoke after I left you here to rest. We agreed you needed to sleep, so we talked about the schedule and what Drake had planned for the show. The first thing you should know is that Drake reviewed the footage they've gotten so far for the show. We both know you're overly concerned with the production of the show. But what you need to know is that Drake has actually gotten a lot of incredible footage."

Joel looked down at Carrie's plate. She had not started to eat yet. He slowly slid the plate a little closer to Carrie.

"Drake's actually getting nervous that he's going to have an incredibly difficult task cutting material for the final show," Joel continued.

"I find that hard to believe," Carrie replied. Joel noticed she picked up her fork and started to eat.

"It's true. Additionally, he and I are very concerned about you."

"Me?"

"Yes, you."

"But why?"

"Because you're *really* good at taking care of everyone *but yourself*. You make sure everyone eats, including the camera crew, but forget to eat yourself. You pestered Beans about that cut on his hand, and yet you refused to get help when you had a rodeo bull rip a piece out of your back. You nagged Glenda to get some ointment the day she got a bee sting, but let me ask you if you even bothered to do anything about the blisters you have on your own hands?"

Carrie looked down at her hands. She frowned. It was almost as if she was seeing the blisters for the first time.

"You haven't stopped trying to prove yourself since you stepped foot on this ranch. You keep pushing yourself."

Carrie went to respond, and Joel held his hand up to stop her.

"Yeah, I know you're going to tell me you're *fine*. Just so you know, *I* know that isn't the case. I can tell you haven't fully recovered from being thrown during that bull ride."

"What do you mean?"

For the first time, Joel noticed actual fear in her eyes. He needed to back off a little. The purpose of this conversation wasn't to scare her or make her uncomfortable; it was supposed to make her take better care of herself. He reached out and lifted her chin with his finger. Carrie gulped.

"Carrie, I watched you ride back to the ranch after we were at the waterhole. You weren't sitting up in the saddle as you usually do and as you were taught. I could tell that you were doing everything you could to try to limit the amount of jostling that your head felt. I should have realized how tired you were right off. Drake and I are *really* worried. You suffered a *very* serious injury. I'm actually disappointed in myself."

"What? Why?" Now she was confused.

"If I was a better ranch owner, maybe just a better man, I would have insisted you go to the hospital that first day. You would have actually gotten a chance to really rest and heal. Instead, you have only briefly paused. You *need* to rest.

"Furthermore, I understand you're pushing yourself because you're concerned about the amount of time the show is filming on this ranch. You've taken it upon yourself to try to finish the show in record time just so you can get everyone off this ranch. I know *that* is completely my fault. I've left you with the impression I don't want you here. That's not true, by the way. I've actually enjoyed seeing this ranch through the eyes of someone else. I'd forgotten how unique it is to live on a ranch where you can spot a coyote or listen to a hawk cry. You've reminded me why I love this place." He smiled down at her.

"Finally, Drake is blaming himself that your personal drive to get this show done is because you believe he could pull the plug on the show."

Joel watched Carrie swallow at the mention of canceling the show. He once again saw fear in her eyes.

"Sweetheart, no one is going to cancel the show."

"You don't know that. I have to—"

"I do know that. I've seen some of the footage of the show. No one's going to stop this show."

"I just can't risk—"

Another voice spoke from the doorway. "There is no risk of the show being canceled."

"Drake!"

The show's producer walked into the guest bedroom and walked over to the other side of the bed. Drake reached out and clasped Carrie's hand that was resting on the top of the covers.

"Carrie, honestly, there's no risk of this show being canceled. I've been working to put together some teaser footage for additional potential sponsors."

Carrie frowned. She had no idea what he was talking about.

"A show's success is dependent upon one's ability to get sponsors. Before we started, we had a half-dozen guaranteed sponsors. We never would have gone through all the work to even start the process looking for candidates without those guaranteed sponsors. In addition to those we already had, there were a number of other interested businesses. I have sold this show as a reality show that gives an inside view of life on a ranch and one involved in the rodeo industry. There are quite a few companies that can really profit from some national exposure. So, I put together some clips of things we've already recorded—just some teaser moments. I've sent these teasers out to a few of the businesses that showed serious secondary-sponsor interest. In addition to those sponsors, I took the risk of sending these clips to a couple of other sponsors who didn't even know we were producing a show like this. I've already heard from two of them that they are extremely interested in becoming secondary sponsors. One even asked for a contract. They're *that* interested. They only saw a teaser, a small glimpse of the things the show will actually cover. With these sponsors on board, we're not going to have any problem getting this show to air. None at all."

Both men watched Carrie intently. They waited. They needed her to relax and rest. They could both see the toll the show and the injury had taken on this woman. Both men were concerned for her, and they were in complete agreement that they needed to convince her to rest.

Carrie looked from Drake to Joel and then back to Drake. Neither man flinched. They were both intense, but neither man seemed to be hiding anything. Carrie knew they were being completely honest with her.

"Carrie? You do believe me, right?"

"Yes, Drake, I believe you."

She noticed that the tension that both men had held in their shoulders was suddenly released. Both of them seemed to relax and loosen up just a little.

"Good. So, for today, you rest," Joel said.

"Rest, how?"

"How?" he asked, frowning.

"Yeah, what do I do while I rest?"

"Nothing."

"Nothing? But there has to be something I can do while I sit here."

"No, Carrie, that's the point. You're not to do anything."

"But I can't just sit here."

"You could sleep."

"There's no way I'm going to be able to sleep the rest of the day away. Maybe there's some paperwork I could help with?" Carrie turned to Joel with a look of hope in her eyes.

Joel smiled and lifted her hand to his lips. The moment his lips touched her skin, her stomach lurched. She had never felt a man's lips on her hand and was surprised at how intimate it felt.

"B, while I appreciate the offer, and trust me, I will take you up on that offer some day, it won't be today."

"But—"

Joel covered her lips with his two fingers on his other hand. Carrie's ability to breathe left her. She didn't think she would ever be able to take another breath again. Her heart, on the other hand, had decided to do a jig. It was fluttering all around her chest.

"You're smart, and I'm sure you'd be a true asset in my office; however, that defeats the whole purpose of you resting for the remainder of the day. No work. Period. And before you even ask, you're not allowed to offer to help Glenda, either. You're not allowed to get out of this bed."

"What am I going to do all day?"

Both men laughed. They couldn't help it.

"What's so funny?" She didn't understand what they found so funny.

"You have to be the only woman on the face of the planet who doesn't understand the concept of doing nothing but resting. Carrie, have you ever had a friend or a family member who was really, really sick?"

Carrie immediately thought of Cassie. She nodded.

"Was there ever a time they had to stay in bed and not *do* anything?"

She remembered when Cassie had gotten pneumonia. She had had to remain in the hospital for a couple of weeks. She hadn't even been allowed out of her bed for most of that time. She nodded again.

Joel watched the emotions dance across Carrie's face. He saw concern and compassion along with deep-seated fear. Whoever had been in the hospital was someone she loved and had worried about.

"Carrie, who was sick?" Joel quietly asked.

"My sister. She…" Carrie had been scared when Cassie had gone into the hospital. She knew that there had been a strong possibility that Cassie wouldn't be coming out of the ICU. It had been such a horrible time for her and her family. Just thinking about those days made her feelings of worry rise to the surface again. The fear at the time had been so real and even just remembering that time brought the fear back in such a tangible way that Carrie couldn't even get the words out of her mouth.

Drake and Joel waited for Carrie to process the emotions running through her brain. They had never seen this intense fear in Carrie's eyes. Not even when she had ridden the bull.

"I didn't know you had a sister," Drake said softly.

Both men saw Carrie come back from her terrifying memories to the present. As Drake's comment seemed to register with her, they saw a different kind of fear cross her expressive face. Then they saw the wheels turn in her mind.

"Oh, yeah, ummm…" She didn't know what to say to get off of the topic of Cassie. "Okay, so can I read a book or something while I rest?" Carrie quickly filled the uncomfortable gap in the conversation with her question.

"Sure. I'll bring up a couple of choices, and if none of them interest you, we'll find you something else," Joel answered.

Carrie let out a soft breath of air and relaxed. Hopefully, she had been able to avoid the topic of Cassie.

"Okay, I believe you that the show is going to be fine, and I can take the day and rest. I promise not to do anything today. Satisfied?" She tried to smile to prove she was okay with the plan.

Both men watched her smile and waited to see if it would reach her eyes. It never did. She wasn't completely accepting what they had told her, but she was going to go along with it. They each supposed that it was a win if it kept her in bed for the day. However, both of them were worried about what it was that Carrie was not sharing. She was too honest to keep a secret. Drake wasn't worried about whatever Carrie hadn't disclosed. He knew there couldn't possibly be anything in Carrie's life that could damage the show. He worried more about her trying to keep something all bottled up. Hopefully, he would be able to talk to her and she could confide in him, whatever it was.

Joel watched Carrie. He knew that she was hiding something. He wondered what and why. She was so sweet and open and honest. He was pretty sure that whatever it was she was hiding was because she didn't feel she could trust them. He understood her not trusting himself, but he wondered why she wasn't trusting Drake. Joel recognized the fact that he had not earned Carrie's trust, but he thought Drake had. Joel knew he needed to earn this woman's trust, and he vowed to start taking the necessary steps to do just that.

CHAPTER 16

Thirty minutes later, Joel walked into Carrie's room carrying an armload of books.

"I had to not only raid the library downstairs but also Zach's and Maria's bookshelves to make sure you had a wide enough variety to choose from. I didn't know what you preferred to read, so I wanted to make sure I brought you plenty of options. If you would rather watch some television, I can also bring the TV from my room into this room so you can watch that while you rest."

"I would like to make some smart-mouth comment about the sheer number of books you brought in here, but after that explanation, I can't seem to come up with any kind of response. Well, other than thank you."

Joel smiled and bowed his head. "You're welcome."

"So, what did you manage to find?"

Joel walked over to the bed and laid his armload down next to Carrie. She started picking up the books. There were science fiction and suspense novels written by well-known *New York Times* best-selling authors. Additionally, there were romance novels and heartwarming stories.

"*The History of Ranching in Texas*? Do I look like I would be interested in the history of ranching?"

Joel shrugged his shoulders. "I wasn't sure. You've been very involved in every aspect of ranching around here, and I wasn't sure if the topic would interest you. I also brought up *My Life as a Bull Rider* and *Bull Riding: 101.*"

"Are you sure I won't be overdoing it by just reading about bull riding?" she asked with a twinkle in her eyes.

He frowned. "You're probably right. That might be too much. But you're in luck. I also found *The Moon and My Bunny.*"

"The children's story?"

"Too advanced a reading level for you?"

"What?" Her eyes widened.

"Kidding, Kidding." He raised both hands in surrender. "I really brought it to make you laugh. Did it work?"

She tried her best to hide her smile and scowl at him. "No, it didn't."

Joel smiled. "Are you sure? Maybe it's been so long since you laughed or smiled you don't know what it feels like. I think the dimple trying to peak out would suggest I accomplished my goal." He pointed at her cheek.

She couldn't contain her laughter any longer. "Fine. You win. It was funny."

"Thought so."

Carrie continued to sift through the different reading options.

"Find anything you like, or do I need to keep searching for other options?"

"I, ahhh . . . yeah. I think I can find something here."

"So, what interests you?"

"Ummm . . . what?"

"Which one?"

"Why, umm, do you want to know that?"

"Well, I should probably know in case you finish it before supper. I'll need to know what you like, so I'll know what to look for in your second book to read." Joel suddenly felt it was very important for him to learn this information. This was a window into this woman's soul, and he wanted that look. He wanted it very much.

Joel watched Carrie look at the books sitting on her bed. He noticed a blush slowly covering her cheeks. *Oh, this was definitely an answer he would just stand there and wait to get.* He lifted his eyebrow and just continued to watch Carrie.

"Joel . . . "

"Yes, Carrie?"

"I . . . well, you brought me so many. I don't know what I'll read first."

"Hmmm. Maybe I should select one for you." He hid his smile from Carrie, and he pretended to take his time looking through the books. After prolonging her distress a few minutes longer, he reached for one of the romance novels.

"Maybe this one."

Carrie's blush deepened.

"Enjoy it." Joel handed the book to Carrie and winked. He got up off the bed and walked out of the room.

♦ ♦ ♦

A couple of hours later, Joel walked into the guest room carrying another tray. As soon as she noticed him at the doorway, Carrie quickly hid the book she had been reading under the covers.

"I can't believe that you're not sick of bringing me food."

"Oh, B, I'll never tire of bringing you something to eat." Joel's eyes twinkled, and Carrie felt as if he was once again imparting some wisdom about himself. He was so serious at the moment that she felt her lungs constrict. After a moment, her lungs screamed for air, and she was able to take a shallow breath. That first gasp of air was quickly followed by another until she managed to start breathing normally again.

Carrie scooted up on the bed. When she was leaning against the headboard, Joel set the tray over her lap. As soon as he had set the tray down, he leaned over and reached under the covers. Before Carrie knew what he was doing, he snatched the book out from under the covers. He wanted to see which book she had decided to read. It was one of the romance novels that his sister loved reading. He smiled at Carrie and returned the book back under the covers. Once the book was safely hidden under the covers, he patted the covers over it and smiled at her.

Carrie noticed that Glenda had once again put enough food on the tray for two people.

"Glenda must think I'm starving. She couldn't possibly have put enough food on the tray for you to join me. We both know you're way too busy to join me while I eat supper."

"Don't count on it, B. I'm planning on having supper with you, and I asked Glenda to make sure she sent up enough food for both of us."

"But—"

"Trying to get rid of me?"

"No, of course not. Joel, I understand how much work you have to do. I know you really can't spend all of your time keeping an eye on me."

"Not all of my time, but I can certainly spare you some. Let's eat."

Carrie decided to just let that comment go. She picked up her sandwich and started eating.

"How is it this is probably the best turkey sandwich I've ever eaten?"

"Glenda's special kitchen secret."

"Does she share her secret?"

"Nope. She says if she shares her secret, she'll become obsolete."

"Not a chance."

Joel laughed. "Yeah, that's what I tell her, but she still won't share."

Carrie and Joel continued to eat. As Carrie was eating her last bite, Drake walked into the bedroom.

"How's our patient?"

"I'm fine, Drake."

"Joel? Is she really fine?"

"Not sure, but I *can* say she's been resting."

"Good." Drake walked farther into the room. "Well, I have some news."

"What kind of news?" Carrie asked.

"The good news is that you're going to have more time to rest and recuperate."

"Why?"

"There's been a change of plans."

Carrie started to get worried. "What kind of change?" she asked anxiously.

"I've spent the day going through most of the footage we have."

"And?"

"And it's great, but it needs a little something." Joel knew what Drake was going to tell her. In fact, this was the real reason he had insisted Glenda put food for two on her tray. He didn't know why, but for some reason, his gut was telling him that he needed to be around when Drake told her he was going to her hometown to interview her family and friends.

"Like what?"

"It needs your backstory."

"My what?" she choked out.

"Your backstory. We need to add some of your life before you came here for the show."

"Wha—what, why?" Carrie stuttered.

Joel noticed all of the color drain from Carrie's face. "Carrie, are you okay?"

She looked at Joel. She couldn't think—she couldn't even answer him.

Joel reached out and took hold of Carrie's hand. "Carrie, honey, look at me."

Carrie looked up into his eyes.

"B, talk to us. What's wrong?"

"Wrong?"

"What put the fear of God into those beautiful eyes of yours?"

"It's just that there isn't anything in my life that would add to the show."

"I don't believe it. What about your sister? I was thinking that maybe we could interview her." Drake replied.

"NO!" Carrie screeched.

"Carrie, what's the matter?" Joel quietly asked. His response was all the more intense given the fact that it was so calm and quiet compared to Carrie's outburst.

"It's my sister, you can't . . . she can't . . . I . . ."

"Carrie. Take a breath, honey. It's okay," Joel soothed.

"Carrie, I don't have to talk to your sister."

The relief in her eyes was evident. "What if you talked to my best friend, Becky? She probably knows me better than anyone else on the face of the planet. She could give you all the backstory you could possibly want."

"Will she agree to be interviewed?"

"She will if I ask her to."

"Well, that would be great."

"Not to mention that Becky is so beautiful that she'll look great on camera. In fact, you may decide you need less footage of the ordinary greenhorn and more film of the beautiful best friend." Carrie smiled.

Joel frowned. Once again, Carrie was talking about not being beautiful. He wasn't sure how, but he was going to make it his mission to get her to realize what a beauty she was.

Drake ignored her comment about how beautiful her friend was and asked, "So, if you could call your friend Becky, we could make arrangements for me to go and interview her."

"I'll call her tonight. But, Drake?"

"Yeah?"

"What about finishing the show in two months. Will this delay that?"

"That was the other thing I wanted to discuss with you. Would you be okay extending your visit here for another month? While we have lots of great footage, I think extending your time here would really add to the whole show. Extending your visit would mean that we have more time for you to recover and not push yourself to get back in the ring. What do you think?"

"I'm fine extending my time, but, Joel, what about the ranch? What about you and your family? Are you sure it's okay for us to be here another month?"

Joel reached out his hand and gently cupped her chin. "Yes, B, you and the show are welcome to continue filming the show for another month. There has not been the interruption I thought there would be. I think we have all been getting along great, and I have no qualms about

C. Kelly ⬧ 148

you staying here longer." *Much longer than just another month, in fact,* he thought.

"Well, I guess I'll be here for another month, and I'll call Becky tonight."

"Great. I'm going to let you rest, and I'll continue to sort through footage. If you're up for it, we can talk tomorrow, and you can tell me all about Becky."

"Okay. Thanks, Drake."

Drake smiled at her. "No problem, Carrie. I'll see you later."

Drake left the room with more questions than he had had before he had entered. He hoped that he could get to the bottom of this mystery so he could reassure Carrie. She still seemed to be worrying about something, and, in fact, his visit this evening seemed to increase that worry rather than alleviate it.

Joel watched Carrie as her eyes followed Drake out of the room. He noticed the breath leave her lips.

"Carrie, do you want to talk about whatever it is that has you so concerned?"

"What?" She was startled again.

"You were a lot more relaxed before Drake came into this room. Now you seem to be sitting on pins and needles. What's wrong? What has you so rattled? Maybe I can help."

"It's nothing."

"Are you sure?"

"Yeah." She dropped her head and looked at her food. Carrie knew that she couldn't continue to look this man in the face and lie to him. She almost wished she *could* talk to him about Cassie and her fear about Cassie being exploited by the show. She still believed that revealing her secret was not an option. He was devoted to this ranch 100 percent, and if using Cassie helped the ranch, she couldn't believe he wouldn't take advantage of the situation. After all, he didn't know Cassie, and it wasn't like he was going to put Carrie and Cassie ahead of his own family and this ranch. While she believed that he could genuinely care about her as a person, she wasn't fooling herself into thinking that his compassion for her would go so far as to put her needs and desires ahead of his family.

Joel watched her eyes as they dropped down to look at the tray of food she was supposed to be eating. He could see the sadness pouring out of her through them and wished there was something he could do to bring the happiness and joy back into her eyes.

"Do I need to eat your sandwich?"

"What?"

"Your sandwich. Do I get to eat it?"

She smiled a small, sad smile. "No, you don't get to eat my sandwich. If you touch it, I'll tell Glenda."

Joel visibly shuddered. "No. No. Please not Glenda!" he dramatically responded. "Torture me all you want, but please promise me that you won't tell Glenda."

Carrie chuckled just as Joel had hoped she would. However, when he looked into her eyes, he still saw the sadness and fear hiding at the edges.

◆ ◆ ◆

After supper that evening, Joel brought up his laptop so Carrie could video conference her friend, Becky.

"Would you mind if I talked to Becky alone?"

"No, of course not."

"It's just that I haven't gotten a chance to talk to her much since I've been here—and not at all since I fell off of that bull."

"Got thrown from that bull, you mean."

"Yeah, that. I need some girl time. I hope you understand."

"Sure, no problem. I do hope that someday, you'll introduce me to your best friend."

"Ummm, sure. But why?" She frowned.

"Why, indeed." Joel smiled at her and unlocked his computer. "Here you go. Holler if you have any issues with the connection."

"Thank you. I will."

He closed the bedroom door as he left.

Carrie waited to call Becky until she had heard him walk down the stairs. She immediately brought up Becky's profile to call her. She had sent her a text this afternoon after speaking with Joel and Drake. Becky had agreed to be available for the video call.

"Hey, Becky."

"Hi, Carrie. What's wrong?"

"What do you mean?"

"I've been your best friend in the whole world for way too many years not to recognize when you are totally stressed out. What's going on?"

"Becky, I need your help."

"With what?"

"Protecting Cassie."

"Why, what's going on?" Carrie heard the change in Becky's voice from happy to instantly concerned.

"Drake, the show's producer, wants to go to Canfield to interview my family and friends for the show."

"Why?"

"He says that having my backstory will add to the show."

"He's probably right about that."

"Not helping, Becky."

"Yeah, I know. So, what do you want me to do?"

"I need you to run interference."

"How?"

"Well, for starters, I need you to make sure that he and the rest of the show's crew don't meet Cassie."

"Wait a minute. Do they even know about her?"

"Yeah." Becky watched Carrie's shoulders sag with that admission.

"How did they find out?" Carrie could see the concern etched on Becky's face.

"When they were trying to convince me that I needed to rest, Drake asked if I had ever had a friend or family member who needed to stay in bed."

"Oh, wow. What did you say?"

"I accidentally let Cassie's name slip."

"How could you accidentally let it slip? That's not like you. You've *always* protected Cassie."

"I wasn't thinking very clearly at the time."

"Wait a minute . . . why exactly did *you* need to rest?"

"Figured *you* would get to that part sooner rather than later."

"Yeah, so start talking."

"I got to ride a bull," Carrie stated cheerfully.

"What happened? Are you okay? Oh, man, you got hurt, didn't you? What happened? Carrie, answer me! What is going on?"

"Becky, calm down. I'm fine."

"So spill it. What happened?"

"I fell off the bull."

"You mean you were thrown off."

"Yeah, I guess that's a more accurate description."

"Are you okay? Did you break anything? Do I need to come and get you?"

"Becky, I'm fine. I didn't break anything. I bumped my head."

"What exactly does that mean—you 'bumped your head'?"

"I got a minor concussion."

"I knew it! You got seriously hurt."

"No, really, it wasn't that bad. In fact, the doctor wanted me to go to the hospital, but he agreed to let me stay here at the ranch."

"So, what you're really saying is you got a severe enough concussion that they had to call for a doctor, and when the doctor examined you, he recommended you be taken to the hospital. But instead of following the wise medical advice you were given, you somehow manipulated the doctor into agreeing to let you stay on the ranch. Have I got it about right?"

"Yeah. That about sums it up." Carrie chuckled.

"So how are you now?"

"I'm supposed to be resting."

"Carrie, when exactly did you get that concussion?"

"A couple days ago."

"And you're still supposed to be resting?"

"I'm fine. Really, I am. It's been a couple of days since I fell off the bull—"

"You mean it's been a couple of days after you were thrown off the bull," Becky interrupted.

"Today, I went out horseback riding," Carrie said, ignoring Becky's interjection.

"Are you crazy? Why would you get on a horse only a couple of days after you received a severe concussion? Wait, was someone pressuring you to get on a horse? Was it that producer? Is he—"

"Becky, stop. It wasn't Drake. It was me. I thought I could go out riding. We went for a short ride."

"Who's 'we'?"

"It was A.Z., Joel, and myself."

"Joel, the owner of the ranch, joined you? Why?"

"I'm not really sure. He made some excuse about wanting to make sure I was okay."

"Hmmm."

"What is that supposed to mean?"

"Nothing, just hmmmm."

Carrie looked at her friend's image on the screen and just shook her head.

"Anyway. We rode out to the swimming hole on the ranch property."

"They have their own swimming hole?"

"Yeah, Joel mentioned he and his siblings used to go out to it to cool off during the summers."

"Sounds amazing."

"Yeah. It was beautiful. It wasn't that long of a ride. Probably twenty minutes or so."

"Okay, so far."

"So, after we rode out there, we sat on one of the rocks surrounding the pool. We talked and just enjoyed the peaceful tranquility of the setting. Then we rode back to the ranch."

"And?"

"And when we got back to the ranch, I was completely exhausted. Joel noticed and brought me back to the ranch house."

"Wait a minute. He brought you to the ranch house? This is the same man who said that his ranch house was a building you weren't allowed to go into?"

"Yeah, one and the same."

"Why would he bring you to his house?"

"He said someone needed to keep an eye on me and that he couldn't do that if I was sleeping in the bunkhouse."

"Hmmm. So he was the one who was going to keep an eye on you?"

"Yeah."

Becky found the one hundred and eighty degree change in Joel Roulston's attitude toward her friend extremely interesting.

"So where are you right now?"

"The guest bedroom in the ranch house."

"Hmmm."

"What is that supposed to mean?" Carrie frowned.

"Nothing." Becky smiled. "So, is Joel watching you?"

"Yes, he's been checking on me."

"Have you been staying at the ranch house since you were thrown?"

"Yeah. Now can we quit talking about where I'm sleeping and get back to the reason I'm calling?"

"Sure. So you were up at the ranch house in the guest bedroom and you talked about Cassie?"

"No. Drake and Joel were trying to convince me I needed to rest. And by *rest*, I mean they didn't allow me to do anything. I mean, who just lies around in bed all day? I don't even get this. I don't know why I can't at least help Glenda in the kitchen or help with the ranch books. They've got to have some data entry I could do to help."

Becky started laughing. "Now I understand why they were insisting you stay and rest up at the ranch house."

"Anyway . . . when I was just inquiring about helping in the office or doing something, Drake asked if I had ever had a friend or family member who was so sick they had to stay in bed. I immediately thought of Cassie. I couldn't help it."

"Of course not. Who else would you think of?"

"So, anyway, I'm not sure what my face looked like, but Joel asked about who had been sick. Before I could think about my response, I mentioned Cassie's name and that she was my sister. Drake commented that he didn't even know I had a sister. Of course, he didn't. I'd been working so hard to make sure no one even knew that she existed." Carrie took a deep breath and let it out in a puff of air.

"So did you tell them anything else?"

"No, at that point, I finally had my head back together and realized I had screwed up. I changed the subject and asked if I was allowed to read."

"Okay, that's good. So, all they know is that you have a sister. Okay, so how do I play a role in this drama?"

"Well, it's just that Drake and Joel came into the room to let me know they were going to force me to rest by having the camera crew go to Canfield without me. Drake said he had come up with the idea of interviewing my family and friends to get my backstory. Becky, he specifically mentioned interviewing Cassie. We can't let that happen!"

"We? What I think you mean is that *I* can't let that happen."

"Becky, I'm so sorry. I know I'm putting a lot on your shoulders. This is my problem, and I won't be there to fix it."

"I'm only teasing you, Carrie. Of course, I'll help."

"I have to tell you something else."

"There's more?"

"Yeah, to distract Drake from the idea of interviewing Cassie, I kind of suggested he interview my best friend instead. I sort of suggested he would learn more from my best friend than anyone else."

"Are you telling me they are going to interview me?"

"Yeah. I'm sorry."

Becky laughed. "Wow. I guess this is the fates getting me back. It was me, after all, that convinced you to do this show. It's probably no more than I deserve."

"Really, Becky? You'll do it?"

"Of course. You know I would protect Cassie from anyone or anything if I could. I think of her as my little sister, too."

"Yeah, I know. I can't possibly thank you enough for this."

"So, when are they coming?"

"Drake said something about leaving tomorrow and being there for a week."

"Well, I guess it's a good thing we're on summer break at school."

"Becky, you're going to have to help my folks with their interview."

"Already figured that out. I'm going to have to make sure they focus on their first daughter and forget about their second."

"Yeah, that about covers it."

"Any suggestions on how in the world I accomplish that?"

"None. It's a good thing my best friend's a genius."

"Very funny, but don't worry. I can handle this Drake guy."

"Okay. I'll give him your contact information so he only contacts you and not anyone in my family."

"Sounds like a plan."

"Talk to you soon. I love you!"

"Love you, too."

◆ ◆ ◆

"Hey there, Carrie. How're you doing?" Drake asked as he walked into her room later that evening.

"I'm fine."

"How's your friend? Becky, is it?"

"She's good. I told her I would give you her contact information so you can get a hold of her to interview her."

"Okay, that'd be great."

"You should be able to get all the backstory you need from her. She knows everything about my life."

"Okay."

Drake moved forward and sat in the armchair next to the bed. It was the chair Carrie had found Joel sleeping in when she had woken up in the morning. Drake leaned forward and picked up Carrie's hand. He held it for a moment.

"Carrie, is there something you're not telling me?"

"Wh—What?"

"Carrie, you know you can trust me, right?"

"Yes, of course."

"If there's something about your family that's worrying you, please tell me. I want to reassure you that everything will be fine. I can't reassure you if I don't know what's troubling you. Please, will you just let me know what's wrong?"

Carrie opened her mouth to respond and couldn't get any words out of her mouth. She had never lied this much in her life. She knew she wasn't very good at it, and she never saw the need to practice to become good at it. She realized that whatever she said to Drake was going to be a lie, and she knew that she wasn't going to be able to carry it off with any amount of success. She once again opened her mouth and stopped when Drake lifted his hand to stop her from answering.

"Don't worry. I won't ask again. Clearly, you have a great deal of concern about something—or someone." He looked her directly in her eyes, "I just hope at some point you realize that you can trust me."

"Thank you, Drake," she whispered.

With that, he got up and left the room, leaving Carrie to wonder how her best friend was going to pull off this miracle.

CHAPTER 17

Joel walked into the guest bedroom the next morning. "Good morning, Carrie. How are you this morning?"

"I'm good. In fact, I'm ready to get out there and get some chores done."

"Carrie—"

"Yes, Mr. Roulston?"

"*Mister*?" Joel stopped and looked at her. He saw her eyes twinkling. He couldn't help but smile himself.

"You *must* be starting to feel better."

"I really am. Can I get up and *do* something?" She waited for him to approve.

"How about we compromise."

"How?"

"You can get up and help with some of the paperwork in the ranch office. I would be more than willing to have your help. But this way, you aren't physically exerting yourself, and I can keep an eye on you to make sure you're still doing okay."

Spend the day . . . with him? The whole day? Carrie wasn't sure she would be able to be exposed to his level of testosterone for an entire day. But how would she get out of his compromise? He wasn't going to let her do anything physical and that probably included helping Glenda in the kitchen. She really wanted to get out of bed, but could she be around him the whole day?

Joel waited. This was the first test of her trust in him. He knew that the only reason she was hesitating was because it meant she would be around him the whole day. He held his breath, hoping against all odds that her desire to get out of bed was greater than her desire to avoid him.

"Joel, I doubt there's anything for me to do in your office. You'd spend the entire time showing me what to do when it would probably be more efficient for you to just do it yourself."

"Nope, I'm pretty sure you're selling yourself short. If you can order inventory for your dad's store, you can start by ordering some things we need here on the ranch. So, what's your answer? Are you going to help me and get out of that bed, or are you going to keep being a bum?"

"A bum? The only—" Carrie's response was drowned out by Joel's laughter.

"I'm kidding! I'm kidding! But seriously, I would love the extra help. The work has been piling up, and I really could use your help."

He knew he was intentionally playing the guilt card, but at this point, he would do almost anything to spend the day with her.

"Okay, fine, but don't blame me if your office ends up a complete disaster after you let me in there."

"I'm willing to take the risk."

Carrie swallowed. Suddenly, she didn't know if he was still talking about her helping in his office. She was afraid to ask.

♦ ♦ ♦

After breakfast, Carrie and Joel walked into his office. Carrie had never actually stepped foot in this room before. This was Joel's domain, and she had been avoiding it like the plague while she was resting up at the ranch house. The room was lined with bookshelves and had generational pictures on every wall. A large, solid-looking wooden desk sat off to the left. On it was a picture of Joel, Zach, Maria, and two other people who could only have been their parents smiling while standing on the front porch steps. There were also a small loveseat and a couple of armchairs with a small coffee table between the three pieces of furniture. The far wall of the room had windows lining it. If you stood at the windows and looked out, you would be able to see the horse barn and all of the land that surrounded it. Carrie was once again struck with the thought of how beautiful this ranch was and how lucky she was to get to experience it, if only for a short while. She could understand Joel's possessiveness toward this land and the people who worked and lived here.

"Why don't you go ahead and take a seat in the chair behind the desk. Then I can show you what you can do to help," Joel said as they walked into the room.

Carrie merely nodded her head and walked around to the other side of the desk. She would have to look out the windows another time.

Joel followed her to the other side of the desk, and as soon as she took a seat, he reached for the mouse and began unlocking his computer.

"I thought the first thing I could show you was how we go about ordering things for the ranch. With such a large operation, we need supplies regularly. I have the ranch hands give me lists as they notice things they need. Once a month, I place my online order with the local ranching supply company. I figure this process can't be much different from what you said you had done for your family's hardware store."

With that, Joel leaned over and started showing Carrie how to go about ordering supplies. As soon as he leaned in closer to Carrie, he could smell a soft scent of some kind of flower. He supposed she must have used some shower gel like his sister used. Whatever it was, it had Joel's nose taking notice. It was light and fresh, just like the woman herself. It was open and honest, which was also just like Carrie. Joel once again found his mind wandering to Carrie's secret. He was convinced that she needed to reveal it sooner rather than later. She couldn't go on with her pretense. It wasn't good for her to keep secrets locked up inside her. He could tell that keeping it was like a weight around her neck and that she needed to let it go. He needed to get her to trust him, at least enough that she could open up about whatever it was she was hiding.

As soon as he leaned over her, Carrie found herself smelling his aftershave. It was subtle and earthy. She took another breath just to get a whiff of him. She had never wanted to smell a man before. She knew women had talked about liking different colognes, but she had never had the experience of actually being driven to smell a guy before. Just as she was about to take her third deep breath, she stopped herself. She needed to stop trying to smell Joel. She was here to work, not give her olfactory senses a workout. She took her next breath through her mouth just to lessen the impact of his aftershave.

Once she had stopped smelling Joel, she noticed how closely he had leaned over her. It felt as if he was completely surrounding her. One arm was draped over the back of the office chair she was sitting in and the other was on the mouse right next to her hand. She felt petite and—feminine. She had never felt feminine around a man before. She was always just Carrie—just plain, ordinary Carrie. Cassie's big sister and her dad's righthand person in the store. She had been around plenty of men in the store, but not once did she feel this way. She didn't know what it was about this man, but she was going to have to be careful not to let her other senses overwhelm her good common sense.

"—leave the order slips—"

Carrie turned and looked at Joel. He was so close to her that she couldn't think.

"Carrie? Are you okay?"

Carrie shook her head and blinked her eyes. He had been talking and she hadn't heard a thing he had said. *Focus, girl, you need to pay attention to the man's directions, not his nearness.*

"Are you having more vertigo?"

"No . . . I, . . . ummm—"

"Carrie, are you sure you're up for this today?"

Carrie took a deep breath and tried to get her head back on straight. While she could still smell Joel's unique scent and still feel him surrounding her, she knew she needed to come back to the real world.

"No really, I'm fine. I . . . ah . . . what were you just saying? I think I missed it."

Joel looked at Carrie once more. He thought she had seemed better today. He had watched her during breakfast and had concluded she was starting to recover. She seemed the best she had been since she had been thrown by the bull. He didn't want her overdoing things today if she wasn't up for it. He waited and watched for a moment longer. Seeing focus come back into her eyes, he decided to continue to show her how she could help. He made a mental note to keep checking on her and ensure she didn't overdo it.

"So the hands fill out this form and leave the order slips in this inbox."

Carrie nodded. *I can do this.* She continued to repeat the mantra until she could focus on the computer and not the man standing next to her.

Carrie started working through the order forms and the ranch-supply website. Joel had been right when he had said she would be able to pick up this task quite quickly. It was very similar to what she did at the hardware store. Once she seemed comfortable with the process, Joel walked over to the loveseat. He grabbed a laptop computer and began working on it.

"Are you going to stay in here?" Carrie's voice squeaked.

Without looking at her, Joel answered, "Yeah. I have some other things I need to take care of. I can work on those things on my laptop. If you have any questions, I'll be here to answer them. This way, we can both get something done."

In theory, it was a reasonable plan. Now if Carrie could just concentrate with the man in the room, things would be fine. *I can do this. I can do this*, her mantra continued.

◆ ◆ ◆

Carrie had been working for an hour or so when Joel stood up. She heard him moving and looked up from the computer.

"I'm going to get some coffee. Do you need anything?"

"A glass of water?"

"You got it. I'll be back in a moment."

Once he left the room, Carrie took a deep breath. She reminded herself that she needed to keep her mind on the task at hand and not on the man who could be such a distraction.

Joel walked into the room a few minutes later. He walked over to the desk and handed Carrie the glass of water.

"How's it going?"

"Fine. I've been reviewing the orders as well as the supply company's products. I noticed you use the Brighton Branch work gloves. Have you ever thought about using the Trustletime brand?"

"The what?"

"Trustletime. They're a glove we have in the hardware store. They have a product warranty of three years. They're a little more expensive, but they've proven to work well and last longer than any other gloves we've ever carried."

"Hmmm. Does the ranching supply company sell them?"

"No, I don't think so."

"How would we order them?"

"We could piggyback on one of my father's orders. We would have to order a full case, and if we did, we could have them shipped to a separate address—namely, here. You would get the gloves at cost."

"Hmmm. Sounds interesting."

"I know ordering a full case is more than what you currently order; but if the gloves last longer than the current brand you're using, I think you would save money in the long run."

"What if the hands don't like the feel of them?"

"Well, I know my father could always sell them out of the store. If they don't work for you, I could ship them to the store. The hardware store would reimburse you for the cost of the gloves."

"The ranch would still be on the hook for the cost to ship to the store, right?"

"Well, yes, I suppose so. Never mind, it was just an idea."

Joel leaned forward and scooped up Carrie's hand. He cradled her hand in his two big hands.

"I think that sounds like a risk I'm willing to take." He continued to hold her hand.

"You sure are taking a lot of risks today with me in your office."

Joel's lips twitched. Slowly a smile crept up his cheeks. "You have no idea of the risks I'm taking today, Carrie. No idea at all."

With that cryptic line, Joel returned to the loveseat and his laptop with that smile still on his lips.

◆ ◆ ◆

It was late afternoon when Carrie finished working on the ranch ordering. She was shocked at how many different items the ranch used on a regular basis. Other than the gloves, there were a few other items she had ordered through her dad's hardware store. If she were honest with herself, she would admit that she really enjoyed the task. It was similar to what she did at the store, and she had always appreciated that part of the job.

"How are you coming on the ordering, Carrie?" Joel asked.

"I just finished."

"Great, just in time for dinner. Let's head into the dining room." Joel stood up and stretched.

"The dining room?" Carrie squeaked. She hadn't given any thought to where she would eat meals after Drake and the camera crew had left her at the ranch. Up to this point, she had been eating in the bedroom.

Carrie turned and looked at Joel. She suddenly heard his voice ringing in her ears. *The ranch house is for family and guests.* Carrie tried to swallow. *You are neither family nor a guest.* She just couldn't eat with the rest of them. Not without Drake around to act as a buffer. She had made it through the entire day working in Joel's office, and she would take that as a win for the day. She would just need to make up some excuse not to eat in the dining room.

"I, ah—I'm feeling kinda tired. If it's okay with you, I'm going to go upstairs and rest for a while."

Joel immediately frowned.

"Did you overdo it today?"

"Maybe just a little. I only noticed the tiredness just now. Really. I'm sure I'm fine. I'll grab something to eat a little later." Carrie bit her lip and waited to see if Joel would accept her excuse.

"Do you need someone to walk you upstairs?"

"No, I can get up the stairs."

"If you're sure . . ."

"Yes, I'm sure."

"Alright. I'll check on you a little later."

"Sure. Fine." The breath Carrie had been holding quietly escaped her lips as Joel turned and headed to the dining room.

CHAPTER 18

The next morning, Carrie once again woke to Joel sitting on the chair next to her bed.

"Good morning, B. How are you feeling this morning?" he asked.

"I'm feeling much better. Thank you."

"Are you sure?"

"Yes."

"I'm going to have Glenda make up a tray with your breakfast."

"I can go downstairs and get myself something to eat. You don't need to trouble Glenda."

"It's no trouble at all."

"Has everyone else already eaten?"

"Um . . . yeah," he hesitantly answered.

"In that case, let me just get ready and go downstairs. I know you and Glenda have too much work to have me adding to that load." Joel blew out a breath of air. Carrie could hear the frustration in that sound. "Really, Joel, it's fine. I can manage making myself something for breakfast."

"Fine. I'll let Glenda know you're coming down in a few minutes."

♦ ♦ ♦

Carrie entered the kitchen twenty minutes later.

"Good morning, Carrie. How do you feel?"

"Much better this morning. How are you, Glenda?"

"A little out of sorts, if I'm completely honest."

"Why is that?"

"I just found out you don't want me cooking for you."

"I never said that!" Carrie cried. "Did Joel say I said I didn't want you to cook for me?"

"No, I figured it out on my own."

"I only told him that I knew you were busy and I could fend for myself so I don't burden you further."

"Hmmmmph," Glenda responded.

"I mean it. I love your cooking, but I know cooking separate meals for me as well as the ranch hands is an inconvenience for you." Carrie looked at the other woman. She regretted suggesting she could feed herself, doing so had made the other woman feel displaced in her own kitchen.

"Well, if you're truly not too busy, I would love breakfast. Would scrambled eggs be too much to ask?" Carrie asked.

Glenda watched her for a moment longer. Carrie sat down in the closet chair at the table.

"Too much trouble. Ridiculous. Cooking eggs for one person being too much for me to handle," Glenda mumbled.

Glenda turned toward the refrigerator and took out a carton of eggs, milk, and cheese.

"Would you like me to make the toast?" Carrie asked.

"Sure."

With that, the women worked in companionable silence.

After her breakfast, Carrie went looking for Joel. She assumed he would be in his office. As she walked into the room, she noticed Joel concentrating on some information on his computer. When he heard her entering the room, he looked up and smiled.

"Did you have a good breakfast?"

"Yes, thank you. I think Glenda and I reached a compromise on cooking for me."

"Really? I don't think anyone has ever been able to get her to compromise on anything that involves her kitchen."

Carrie just shrugged and asked, "So is there something I can do for you today?"

"Yes. I started to put together some farm records. I'm hoping you would be able to record the information regarding the breeding that we've done in the past three months. If you come over here, I can show you what needs to be done."

Carrie nodded and walked around the desk. She took a deep breath right before she rounded the corner—one last breath before this man once again wreaked havoc with her senses. Carrie sat down to the smell of Joel and his presence completely surrounding her. She took a deep breath and tried to focus on what he was showing her.

Carrie worked for the rest of the day in the office with Joel. As the afternoon progressed, she started to worry about the dinner meal. She knew Joel would once again propose she join everyone for dinner. However, she could still hear his voice from the very first day telling her that she wasn't allowed in the house. It was silly that she could still hear his rejection when she had been sleeping in the house for the last how many days, but she couldn't help it. She guessed her mind had created a distinction between eating at the house with everyone else and sleeping in a guest room. Maybe the difference was due to the sleeping arrangements being directly related to her physical recovery. If she thought about it too much, she was afraid she would talk herself into a headache. She wasn't exactly sure how, but she just knew they were different. Whatever the difference, she started trying to come up with some kind of excuse to avoid being in the house during the meal. She decided that she could use Drake's absence as her out.

"I'm going to head over to the production trailer," she casually stated as she began to rise from the chair behind the desk.

"It's almost dinner time. What are you going to do there?"

"I need to check on a few things for Drake. Not to mention that I want to check in with my parents."

"We'll hold dinner until you're done."

"Oh, don't do that. I don't know how long I'll be."

"What are you going to do about supper?"

"I'm sure there's food in the trailer. I'll just grab a bite as I speak with my folks."

"But—"

"I'll see you later."

Joel watched her walk out of his office and wondered how she had once again managed to excuse herself from the evening meal. He was beginning to suspect that her avoidance of his dinner table was intentional.

♦ ♦ ♦

The next day, Carrie claimed early hunger and went to eat supper at three thirty in the afternoon, way before anyone else on the ranch would be ready to eat. Joel's suspicion that Carrie was intentionally avoiding the family dinner increased. She should be eating with everyone else. She had been living on and working at the ranch for weeks now, and she had not once broken bread at the family dining room table. For Joel, the meal was becoming less and less comfortable. He wanted Carrie at the table with everyone else. She belonged there. He decided that today was the last day she would be eating dinner alone.

♦ ♦ ♦

The next day, Joel knew he needed to get Carrie out of the house and back into the physical work of the ranch. He also knew that he needed to monitor what she did. Someone needed to make sure that she didn't overdo the work, and he had appointed himself as her keeper.

He had spent hours the previous night trying to come up with a plan to get her out of the house but limit what she did. He had finally decided that he would have her work with him. They could go out and check the herd on the far west pasture. It would be too far for her to ride a horse, but they could take the truck out to the shed and switch to the four-wheelers they kept out in the storage building for just this purpose.

He told her the plan when he entered her room the next morning.

"What?"

"I said I thought you were probably healed enough to do some light ranch work. I could use your help checking on the herd in the far west pasture."

"Don't you want someone more experienced working with you?"

"Actually, I don't expect there to be a lot of work, and it would probably be a better use of my ranch hands' time and efforts to work on the other tasks that need doing."

"If you don't anticipate any need for me, why would you want me to go?"

"Our rule here on this ranch is no one works alone. We don't have anyone go out alone, ever. B, I need you to understand there are dangers that can happen with this kind of work. I don't let any of my hands do anything alone unless it's here at the ranch compound. There would be nothing more tragic than having something happen that could have been avoided if more than one person had been doing the task. The policy is not negotiable, and every man on this ranch knows it."

Carrie sighed and resigned herself to spending another day with Joel. She hoped she could stay focused and not get distracted. Even more, she hoped that if she did get distracted, nothing serious would happen as a result of her inattentiveness.

When Carrie and Joel headed out of the house, they ran into Bull.

"What's up, boss?"

"I'm headed out to the far west pasture to check on the herd."

"Do you want me to send Dusty with you?"

"No, I—"

"Boss, your rule is no one goes out alone. I know you would never let any of the men go out by themselves, so why would you try it?" Bull frowned.

"I wasn't planning on going alone."

"Who—" Bull stopped and looked at Carrie and then back to Joel. His eyebrow rose slightly. He asked, "Who's going to go with you?"

"Carrie."

Bull, frowning, turned to Carrie and asked, "Are you up for some physical labor today?"

She took a deep breath. This was her first test. She needed to convince the old cowhand that she was healed. The sooner she could convince these men, the sooner she could get back on a bull, finish this show, and get back to her life and her family.

"Yes, Bull, I'm ready."

He continued to stand there and watch her. While it was incredibly unsettling having the old cowhand stare at her, she didn't move. She saw him nod once. He turned on his heels and headed back into the maternity barn.

Carrie and Joel took one of the pickup trucks and headed out to the west pasture.

After they had been driving for a while, Joel decided to try and get Carrie to open up.

"So, you have a sister?"

"Ummm, yes."

"What's her name?"

"Cassie."

"Is she older or younger than you?"

"She's younger."

"Can you tell me what happened when she was sick?"

Carrie realized that she was going to have to tell him something. Maybe, she could give him enough of the story that he would feel satisfied that he had heard it all.

"She came down with pneumonia, and she had to go into the hospital."

"It must have been pretty serious."

"It was."

"How long was she there?"

"A couple of weeks."

"A couple of weeks? That seems like a long time for someone to be in the hospital with pneumonia. Did she develop complications?"

"Y—yes." Carrie didn't know how else to answer his question. Cassie had developed complications, but more from her other issues than from the pneumonia.

"I'm sorry. That must have been really hard on your family."

"Yeah, it was. We were all so relieved when she was able to come home."

"I'm sure you were."

Joel knew that there was still more that Carrie had not told him, but he felt they had made a start. He would get her to trust him, eventually. He had to believe that.

Once they reached the shed and the four-wheelers, they had no more opportunities to chat.

◆ ◆ ◆

It was a couple of hours later when Joel turned to Carrie and said, "Let's stop for lunch." She nodded and turned to grab the packs that carried the lunch Glenda had made for them. Joel spread out a blanket that had been in one of the four-wheelers. Carrie sat down and started setting the food out.

"So, can I ask you a question?"

"Sure," Joel replied, "you can ask me anything."

"Do you have a nickname?"

Joel smiled at her. It was the first time that she had asked him something personal.

"Yep, B, I've got a nickname."

"I haven't ever heard anyone call you anything but Joel or boss. But yet, it seems that just about everyone else has a nickname. Even Maria's name gets shortened to Ree most of the time."

"I'll share my nickname, but it comes with a story. You have to promise that you won't share what you learn from me with anyone else." Joel paused and let that information sink in before he asked, "Are you ready to hear the tale?"

"Is it bad?" she asked.

He laughed. "No. It's not bad."

"Okay. I guess I'm ready."

"Are you also willing to promise to keep my secret?"

"Sure, I promise to keep your secret."

"When I was probably about eight, my mom and I sat down to watch a telethon. The telethon was raising money for the Free Wheelin' Association. Have you ever heard of it?"

Carrie swallowed. She was definitely familiar with Free Wheelin'. Her family had benefited from many of the services they offered. Even after she had swallowed, she couldn't get any words past the lump in her throat. She nodded her head.

"I don't know if you're aware, but the association does great things for people with disabilities. So anyway, Mom and I were watching the telethon, and we were both so moved by the stories we saw that we decided to raise money and awareness for people with disabilities. I came up with the idea of doing a raffle and silent auction. My mom and I brainstormed what we could raffle off and what items we should get for a silent auction. We worked for days strategizing and planning out what we could do. Then my dad happened to be hosting a meeting for the Professional Bull Riding Association. One of the other ranch owners had heard that Mom and I were planning the fundraiser. He thought it was a great idea, and he asked my dad to have me come into the meeting and speak to all of the people who were there. I had no idea what I was doing at the meeting. I had never been allowed to be at a meeting, let alone participate in one. The other ranch owner, Scott Duncan, asked me to share with everyone what my mom and I had been planning for the fundraiser. After I finished, he issued a challenge; he challenged everyone in the room to match whatever I raised. There was a lot of laughter and guffawing, but before I left the room, he had gotten eighteen other folks at the meeting to agree to match whatever I raised, dollar for dollar. Knowing I was going to get matched eighteen times over, I worked even harder to make the event something special. In the end, my mom and I raised over $10,000 for Free Wheelin'. That meant that with the match, we were able to present to Free Wheelin' a total of $180,000."

"That's incredible!"

"Yeah, it was pretty cool to hand Free Wheelin' a big ole fat fake check for that much money and to know I was helping to make someone else's life easier."

"So, I still don't know what your nickname is."

"After I raised the money, Scott Duncan said I was some kind of King Midas for raising that much money. I had never heard of King Midas before, so I asked him what he meant. He told me the story of King Midas and said I had a golden touch. Zach overheard his comment and started to call me 'Golden Boy.' Sometimes, when they really want to get under my skin, Zach and Maria will call me 'Goldie,' but I hate it. Golden Boy is just a weird thing to call someone who operates a ranch, and therefore, none of the ranch hands ever use it, but as I said, Zach and Maria will use it when they're really hoping to annoy me."

"It's not so bad." She smiled at him.

"I know, but if they were to get wind of the fact that I don't mind the nickname, they'd try to come up with something else. I'm convinced anything else they would think of would be awful, so I let them continue to think I hate the name."

"That's kind of—"

"Genius?" he interrupted.

"I was going to say conniving."

"Yeah, well, so far, it's worked."

"What happens when I tell Zach and Maria that you don't mind the nickname?" She smiled mischievously.

"Awwww, but you promised not to tell my secret."

This time, Carrie laughed. "I think I was tricked."

"Oh yeah, but I did get you to promise." He winked at her. She smiled and shook her head.

♦ ♦ ♦

Carrie and Joel arrived back at the ranch right around dinner time. Joel had made sure of it. Once they had parked the truck and gotten out, Joel turned to the woman beside him.

"Carrie, it's time to eat. Let's go back to the ranch house."

"You go ahead."

"What are you going to do?"

"I just thought I would check in with Drake about the show."

"Fine, I'll come with you, and then we can head up to the house for dinner."

"You don't need to come. Just go ahead without me."

Joel took a deep breath and reached out for Carrie's hand. She was so startled, she jumped a little. He didn't let go. He waited until she looked up at him.

"I know I've already apologized, but please tell me what I need to do to get you to forgive me for that asinine comment I made when you arrived," he implored.

"It's fine."

"It's *not* fine if you still won't come up to the house without me carrying you there."

"I . . . it's..." Carrie couldn't look him in the eye. She let her eyes drop to where he held her hand. She couldn't come up with an explanation while he held her hand. She tried to pull her hand free. Joel gently squeezed her hand and stepped closer to her. He placed his other hand under her chin and cradled it. He didn't force her to look up at him; he just needed to touch her beautiful face. If he was being honest, he needed to hold a lot more than just her chin. He longed to take her completely in his arms. Unfortunately, *that* wasn't going to happen until they hashed this out.

"Tell me," he softly begged.

Carrie took a deep breath and looked up at Joel as she tried to explain what she had realized.

"I finally understand what you meant that day. Why only family and guests are invited into the house. It's a way of making sure your home is always a safe place for your family and your friends. It's your safe haven. If strangers are allowed to traipse in whenever they want, *that* sanctuary is destroyed."

"You're not a stranger."

"I know that. But I'm also not family."

"Neither are the ranch hands."

"Yes, they are. I've watched the interactions between you and every man on this ranch. There's a bond between each and every one of you. This ranch functions like it does because you're all so interconnected.

You would do anything for any one of those men, and they feel the same about you."

"They would do anything for you, too," Joel quietly informed her.

"It's not the same. I'm the transient. They'd do something for me because they're good and decent men. They do for others because it's the honorable thing to do. But I'm not family."

"What would it take for you to *be* family?" Joel softly asked.

"That's just it. I won't ever be family."

"What about a ring? Would that make you family?" he cautiously pushed.

"How in the world would a ring make me family?"

Was she serious? he thought. *Didn't she believe that marriage was a bond that tied people together? Made them a family?* Just as he was starting to get incensed, Joel noticed that she was looking at him with complete and utter confusion shining out of her eyes. Was it possible that she misunderstood what he was asking her?

"I meant a wedding ring," he clarified.

"Why would someone give me their wedding ring?"

Joel stopped and just studied her eyes. She was so honest and genuine that he knew she wasn't being coy or playing any kind of game. How was it possible that she really didn't realize what he was implying?

Joel had been around so many women who had tried to get him to propose. Some would move onto Zach when Joel hadn't moved fast enough. Sometimes they attached themselves to Zach first and then moved on to the other Roulston brother. He was convinced that for some of those women, they didn't even care which brother proposed, they just wanted to be married to a Roulston. But this woman hadn't even given a proposal a thought. She was so naïve that she hadn't even considered the possibility. Not that he was proposing—well, not exactly.

"They wouldn't be giving you their ring."

"Whose ring would it be?" Carrie was starting to lose track of the conversation. *How did they even get on the subject of rings?*

Joel let go of her hand and wrapped both of his hands around her face. He looked down into her eyes and said, "They would be giving you an engagement ring."

"Joel, I don't have any idea what you're talking about. Why would someone give me an engagement ring?" Joel had been watching her expressions so closely that he knew the moment she finally understood what he was saying. "But, I—"

Joel had had enough. He leaned the rest of the way into her and slowly let his lips touch hers. She didn't move. He pulled back and looked into her eyes again.

"Carrie?"

Her eyebrows lifted, and he once again saw that confusion cross her face.

"Carrie?" he asked again.

She swallowed and whispered, "Hmmm?"

"I'm going to kiss you again. Is that alright?"

"I don't..." She swallowed again, "I don't . . . don't know..."

"Sweetheart, what don't you know?" he whispered.

A blush spread over her cheeks.

"I don't know what you expect me to do?"

"What I expect?" It was his turn to be confused. "I don't have any expectations."

"It's just that I, ahh . . . I haven't . . . I..." Joel caught her hand gesturing out of the corner of his eye, "I don't know what to do. I've never..."

His gaze grew very intense. "Sweetheart, are you telling me that you've never been kissed?"

Her blush deepened. She shook her head and answered honestly, "Never."

Joel smiled a slow, secret smile. He couldn't believe that he was her first kiss.

"In that case, how about we try this. You don't have to do anything. You just stand real still and concentrate on what you're feeling. You can let me know what you like and what you don't, okay?"

"Ummm, okay."

Joel slowly bent his head again. He gently touched his lips to the corner of her mouth. Carrie wasn't expecting that.

"Close your eyes," he whispered.

She did as he instructed. She was suddenly more aware of his breath on her cheek right before she felt his lips touch her there and then again a little higher up on her cheekbone. The breath caught in her lungs. He touched her right eyelid, and then he kissed her left cheek. She felt him turn her head, and his lips tugged on her left ear lobe. No matter how much she tried to anticipate where his lips would land next, she couldn't keep up with him.

"I hope your heart is starting to beat as hard as mine," he whispered in her ear. Suddenly, she felt his left hand leave her cheek. The next thing she felt was his hand as it dropped to her shoulder and continued to caress her arm down to her wrist. Then he took her right hand in his left and placed her palm on his chest over his beating heart.

"Can you feel how hard my heart is pounding?" he whispered.

Carrie opened her eyes and saw her hand resting on his chest. She could feel his heart beating through his shirt. It was pounding as if he had just sprinted across the ranch compound. She could only nod.

"Good, you just leave your hand there and feel how hard my heart is pounding . . . for *you*."

His hand moved away from hers, and again, reached up to cup her cheek. He pressed his lips to her jaw as his hands gently lifted her face. As he lifted her head, her eyes fell closed again. She felt his lips move along her jaw.

Joel lifted his head and studied this amazing woman. She was so innocent. She was sweet and kind and the most compassionate person he had ever met. She was open and honest. How was it even possible that no other man had ever recognized her for the unique and quality woman she was? Was it really possible that she was experiencing her first kiss with him? He would make sure to say an extra prayer of gratitude tonight before his head hit the pillow. This was a gift, and he was going to open it slowly, little by little.

In no hurry, he let his lips land on hers again. This time, he pressed his lips to hers and let her adjust to the feeling of his lips touching hers. He didn't dare do anything more than the lightest of touches. He would not rush Carrie. As a first kiss, this needed to be sweet and gentle. Although his body roared for him to go further, he reigned in his passion.

A new pace would be set with this relationship. They would go slowly, and he would love every moment and every new experience with her. He lifted his lips from hers and moved to kiss her on the forehead. He then tenderly asked, "Did you enjoy any of that?"

Carrie opened her eyes, and Joel savored the dreamy expression that had captured them.

"Please tell me you enjoyed that as much as I did."

Carrie could only nod her head. She was pretty sure that Joel's kiss had somehow made her mute.

He leaned down and placed one last kiss on her lips.

"Good."

He stepped back from her just a little to let both of them catch their breath.

"Will you do me the honor of joining me for dinner up at the house?"

Carrie nodded her head again. Joel took the hand he had placed over his heart into his own hand. He bowed, deposited one last kiss on the back of her hand, and then intertwined their fingers. As he stood back up, a broad smile covered his entire face.

"Let's go eat." He turned and headed to the house with Carrie in tow. She was finding resisting this man impossible at the moment. They silently walked up to the ranch house and straight through the front door. Joel continued to walk toward the back of the house to the noisy dining room. Once they entered the room, everyone abruptly fell silent. Joel knew that every person at the table understood the significance of Carrie walking into the room holding his hand. They were all in shock. Joel was concerned, however, that Carrie would interpret the sudden hush as a negative reflection on her presence. He needed to immediately curb that thought before it even had a chance to develop.

"Carrie is going to honor us with her presence tonight."

With that, every man stood and respectfully bowed his head.

"That's wonderful," Maria said.

"About time," growled Bull.

"So glad you're here, Carrie," Zach responded.

"You can sit by me, Sleeping Beauty." Beans winked.

Joel ignored Beans and walked Carrie to the chair to the left of his. He pulled out the chair at the corner and waited for her to take her seat. He then moved around the corner and took the seat at the head of the table. Once Carrie sat down, so too did all of the men around the table.

"Let's say grace." And with that, every head bowed.

Once they had said grace, the dinner conversation picked right back up again as the dishes began to be passed around the table. Joel reached over and squeezed Carrie's hand. She looked at him and softly smiled. For the first time in a long while, this dinner table felt complete to him.

CHAPTER 19

Carrie sat at the dining room table with the conversation flowing around her. She was in shock and was still trying to process what exactly had transpired out in the yard. Joel had kissed her. She wouldn't believe it if her heart wasn't still racing a mile a minute. He had actually kissed her. He had asked her to forgive him for what he had said that first day and then kissed her. No, that wasn't exactly how it had happened. He had started talking about rings. She still didn't understand what he had been talking about. She didn't understand how rings fit into his apology, but then he had kissed her. He was the first man to have kissed her, and she still hadn't recovered. Carrie had taken food as the dishes were passed around the table, but she didn't remember anything she had eaten. Joel Roulston had kissed her. Why?

Joel had watched the many emotions crossing Carrie's face during dinner. She had not participated in any of the conversations around the table. Joel didn't think she had even heard any of the words bandied about. Beans had even teased her about sleeping during dinner and she hadn't had a comeback. Joel was beginning to get worried about what was going on in her head. He needed to make sure that after dinner, the two of them had a chance to talk about that kiss and to come to an understanding. There was no way that that was the only kiss they were going to share, and Carrie needed to know that starting today, they were a couple. He wasn't sure how in the world *that* conversation was going to go, but he kept telling himself that no matter what was said, it was going to end with another kiss.

"Carrie, are you finished?" he asked her.

Surprised by the words said to her, she looked down and realized she had finished all of the food she had dished onto the plate—not that she remembered any of it. She looked up at Joel and nodded. She still wasn't sure her tongue worked.

Joel rose from his seat and held his hand out to her.

"Come for a walk with me?"

Carrie once again looked down at her plate and noticed it was empty. She looked back up at him and heard him say quietly, "Please?"

She couldn't refuse his plea, not even if her life depended upon it. She merely nodded and stood. Joel quickly moved her chair. Once she was standing, he reached for her hand and tugged.

"Let's go out the back."

"Don't we need to help with the dishes?" she responded as she finally found her tongue.

"Don't worry about the dishes—we've got it," Maria quickly interjected.

"Thank you," Joel mouthed to his sister. He saw her wink right before he turned to lead Carrie outside.

Joel led her to the back door and continued to walk away from the house. He had no destination in mind. He only wanted to talk, and he wanted to make sure they were not overheard. He continued to stroll away from the house. There was no path to follow nor did he feel they needed one. This land was made for boots to stomp on it, and he and Carrie were just making their mark, leaving their footprints.

When they were truly far enough away not to be oveheard, Joel stopped and took Carrie's hand in both of his.

"I want you to know how much I enjoyed that kiss."

"Oh?"

Joel smiled. "Yes. It was probably the best kiss I have ever had."

With that comment, a spark flashed in her eyes right before they rolled into the back of her head.

Carrie shook her head and replied, "I can't believe that."

Joel's right hand quickly reached out to cradle her cheek.

"I know I'm a damn lucky man that it was me who got to enjoy your first kiss. Moreover, you need to understand that I intend to be the last man who enjoys those lips."

"What? I don't understand." Carrie shook her head. She didn't know what she had expected when Joel had asked her to go for a walk, but it certainly wasn't this. "You don't even like me."

Joel sighed. He knew this wasn't going to be easy, but he needed to make sure he explained what had been going through his head on her first day. She needed to understand what was in his thoughts and his heart.

"Will you listen as I try to explain?"

Carrie looked up into his eyes. There was sincerity and something else she couldn't identify. But she saw no hate, no malice, and nothing to leave her feeling unsure. She would listen to the man and then decide what to do. She nodded and continued to watch his face.

"Before my parents died, my father decided he would take a risk and drill for oil. It was a big gamble. While there are other ranches around that have oil, there is no guarantee it's everywhere. In fact, it's not. It's also an expensive risk. My dad wasn't a fool; he had good geological evidence to suggest we would find oil in the east pasture. So he decided to invest money into finding it. That first summer after he started digging was a terrible one. Most of the country experienced a drought. We had very little grass that grew in the pastures that summer. What had started to grow got exposed to the harsh sun and lack of water and quickly died. We also grow our own crops, but they too just withered and died. We had to buy feed for the cattle to make sure we would make it through the summer, fall, and winter months. We were not the only ranch that needed food for their herds, and because of the drought, the prices rose through the roof. Normally, this would not be an issue. We usually had cash reserves to get us through two seasons."

"But your dad had spent all of those reserves on the oil well, hadn't he?" Carrie quietly guessed.

Joel released his breath. "Yes."

"What did your family do?"

"Dad took out another mortgage on the ranch. While this sounds risky, it wasn't that much of a risk. The loan proceeds were to get us through the current season, and when we sold the cattle in the fall, we should have been able to pay off the second mortgage. But…" Joel took a deep breath and exhaled.

"But?" Carrie asked.

"Because of the drought, many ranches couldn't pay their mortgages and went out of business. Banks found themselves owning a bunch of cows they didn't want. They needed to unload the cattle and liquidate them as much as possible. Therefore, there were much more cattle sold at auction, more than could have ever been anticipated. The prices were far below what we generally expected when going to market. Not to mention that our own cattle had been smaller than usual. We were not able to pay off the second mortgage. We managed to have enough cash after the cattle market to make our mortgage interest payments, but most of the principal balance remained."

"What did you do?" she asked.

"With the outlook of any good rancher, we hoped and prayed the next year would be better. However, the next summer was just as bad if not worse than the year before. It was that summer that we lost both Mom and Dad in a car accident. Zach, Maria, and I found ourselves in a more precarious position than the ranch had ever been in before. We needed to buy food for the cattle, and we knew the prices would be just as high if not higher than the year before. With the small amount of cash reserves we had from the cattle sale, we held on—but just barely. We have been able to survive each year, but with very little in cash reserves. We have tightened the belt as much as we can and continued to pray each year would get us to a position where we could pay off the second mortgage and get the ranch back on its feet again. But last year was another drought year. It took the little we had been able to squirrel away in cash reserves and left us with nothing to make the mortgage payments. While we have a lot of equity in the ranch…"

"It's all tied up in the land and the animals. You need cash reserves, and you didn't have any."

"Yes. I had finally come to the conclusion there was almost no way we were going to be able to save the ranch."

"What about selling off some of the land?"

"It's a short-term solution. Once you start to sell off land, you need to buy more feed or you can't raise as many cattle as you usually do. It just starts the ranch down a negative cycle of getting smaller and smaller. Eventually the bank just gets what's left. Looking at our own operation, if we didn't sell, the bank was going to foreclose on the mortgages and there would be nothing we could do about it.

"I told Zach and Maria we were going to lose the ranch. Upon hearing that, Zach told me he had heard about this reality show and thought we would be a great location for them to film the show. As we learned more and more about it, it seemed this was going to get us out from the hole we were in. However, I was incredibly reluctant to have a bunch of people tromping all over the ranch."

Carrie smiled. "People like me."

"No. That's what I'm trying to tell you. I had convinced myself the filming would get in the way of our operations. I was completely convinced the show was going to interfere so much with our daily ranching tasks that we would lose the ranch anyway." Joel again let another breath whoosh through his lips as he shook his head. "Zach kept telling me it would be fine. I should have trusted him. Hell, I should have trusted Drake. I knew Drake from the rodeo circuit but had not had all that much contact with him. Zach and A.Z. had hung out with him a lot more than I ever had. They were actually pretty good friends for a while. Drake assured me it would be fine, and I continued to hold onto my doubts and concerns for the ranch.

"I woke up the morning the camera crew was supposed to arrive with a rock in the pit of my stomach. Then I started to think of the greenhorn who was coming to 'experience' the ranching life. I started to imagine all of the things that could happen, and it just made my fear increase. I knew I had to come out and meet the crew and the greenhorn, but all I could see was the ranch slipping through my fingers. I took a few steps out on the porch and looked out over the compound. All of a sudden, I saw this woman step out away from one of the vehicles and my heart stopped. She was the most beautiful woman I had ever seen. She was so full of joy that the sun radiated out of her. My only thought was that she was going to be a complete and total distraction to every man on the ranch, the greenhorn included. There was no way anyone was going to get anything done with this beauty roaming around the ranch. Even behind a camera, she was going to steal the show and each man's ability to concentrate.

"Then she was standing at the bottom of the steps to my home, beaming up at me with a smile that stole my breath away and introducing herself. All I could think of was trying to get her away from every man who was going to fall under her spell and quit doing his job." Joel's eyes dropped from Carrie's for a moment. He lifted his eyes back up and fastened them onto Carrie's. Then she heard him quietly say, "I also needed to get her away from me—before *I* could no longer concentrate and do *my job.*" Joel stopped talking for another moment and just stared into Carrie's eyes.

"I . . . ummm . . ." Carrie stammered.

"To be blunt, you, my dear Carrie, caught me off guard." Carrie noticed a faint smile at the corner of his lips.

"But I'm not—"

"Not, what?"

"It's just that I'm not—" she tried again.

"Hmmm?"

"Joel, your story is ridiculous," she finally managed to get out.

"Why is that?" Joel knew that they were heading into dangerous territory, but he was going to put this particular monster to bed.

"Joel, I'm not . . . I'm just . . . it's just that I'm—"

"You're what?" he prodded.

"I'm just me." She shrugged her shoulders. "I'm not beautiful. I'm not a distraction. I'm just plain old, ordinary me."

Joel shook his head. "You're wrong. You truly are the most beautiful woman I have ever seen. I knew I would be lost around you the moment I saw you. Although I will admit I was wrong on one assumption."

"What was that?"

"Your beauty only seems to distract me. I don't know how they manage to do it, but every other man on this ranch seems to be able to continue to keep his wits about him, whereas I'm at a loss most of the time I'm around you."

"They can keep their wits about them because what you're saying is just nonsense. I'm just plain old, ordinary Carrie. I'm nothing—"

Joel had had enough. He took the hand that had been holding her cheek and wove his fingers into her hair. He clasped the back of her neck and lowered his head. He wasn't going to listen to her put herself down anymore. He was done with all of that garbage.

Carrie felt herself falling. She immediately reached out and clutched onto Joel. He was the only solid thing she could reach to grab onto to stop herself from falling, although if she thought about it, she would have realized that maybe he was the exact reason why she felt like she was falling.

With his other hand freed from Carrie's hand, he reached around and splayed his fingers across her back. He gently drew her closer. He still seemed to have at least a tiny part of his brain functioning, reminding him that he still needed to be careful with her, that he needed to move slow. He gently kissed her and cautiously licked at her lips. She tasted of sunshine. Joel continued to lick and caress her lips. He had initially started to kiss her because he couldn't hear her put herself down any longer, however, now he kissed her to experience joy. She was so full of joy and goodness that he knew if he continued to press his lips to hers, he could taste that joy and latch onto it. She had joy to give away; he could taste it. He knew he could take just a little of her joy for himself without diminishing hers at all.

Joel continued to bask in her sunshine when he heard someone leave out the back door and let the screen door slam against the frame. Joel slowly moved his lips away from Carrie's and tried to take a breath. His lips, hell, his entire being, was not happy. He wanted to go back to soaking up Carrie's joy, but his brain told him that their conversation was far from done.

Joel opened his eyes and found Carrie staring up at him.

"Hey there, sunshine," he said.

"Hmph."

"What are you thinking now?" he said with a small grin.

"I'm thinking that a man like you who grew up around cattle sure knows how to spread the manure pretty thick."

Joel laughed. He couldn't help it. He was so full of joy and sunshine at the moment that her comment just seemed funny. "While it is true that I can spread manure with the best of them, I'll have you know my current conversation included no bull whatsoever. I don't know what kind of idiots you've been around your whole life, but the fact that not a single one of them helped you see how incredibly beautiful you are makes them fools."

"But I'm not—"

"If you tell me again that you're not beautiful, I'm going to kiss you. Okay, in all honesty, I'm going to kiss you again no matter what you say." Then he winked at her and lowered his head. He ran his lips over hers once again. This time, he tasted joy and a little confusion. He didn't know how he could taste her emotions in her kisses, but he knew that she still had the joy that was always a part of her, and yet, she continued to be confused about him. He wasn't done explaining, and he needed to quit kissing her and get to it. Joel reluctantly let Carrie go and inhaled a large breath of air.

"So, there I was, expecting a fellow born and bred in the city to walk onto my ranch, and instead, I get Miss Sunshine and Joy. You took the wind right out of my sails and every thought out of my head. All of my preconceived ideas of how the next couple of months were going to go went flying out the window. The only thing I could see was you. For the first time in my life, I stood on that porch and couldn't see the ranch. I couldn't hear the cows. All I could see was the sunshine pouring out of you, and I knew my life was never going to be the same. It terrified me. I wasn't ready for that.

"With the thought that I was going to be so distracted by you that I wouldn't be able to run the ranch, I panicked. It was the first time in my life I had ever panicked. I lashed out at you, and it was wrong. I'm sorry."

"Joel, it's—"

"Don't tell me it's fine because we both know it isn't. What I said was wrong, and it was hurtful. I'm sorry I lashed out at you, and I hope by now you realize I normally don't behave like that." Joel paused and took another deep breath. "I am truly sorry, Carrie." Joel reached out and gently stroked her cheek with his thumb. "Can you find it within that big, generous heart of yours to forgive me? And I mean honest to goodness forgiveness, soul-cleansing forgiveness, not some cheap carbon copy."

Joel looked into Carrie's eyes, and it was her turn to lose her breath. Suddenly, there was no oxygen in the air, but she didn't care. She was lost in his deep blue eyes and didn't care about anything else in the world. He was telling her something important, and she knew if she stared long enough, concentrated hard enough, she would understand what he was telling her. She felt him brush her cheek again with his thumb and she realized that he was asking her a question.

Carrie shook her head for a moment. She needed to focus on their conversation.

Joel saw her shake her head, and his heart plummeted to his feet. He couldn't let their conversation end like this, he had to do something or say something to get her to forgive him.

"Carrie—"

This time, she was the one to cover his lips with her fingers. Once she had shaken the cobwebs from her brain, she realized that he had asked her if she could forgive him. She knew that she already had. She would not have been able to kiss him if she hadn't forgiven him, and she would have never been able to sit at his table if she hadn't forgiven him.

"Yes, I can forgive you."

Joel heard her softly whispered reply and knew joy like he had never experienced before. Joel took her hand in his and gently kissed her knuckles. He then turned her hand over and kissed her palm.

"I can't tell you how much relief and happiness I feel right now." He smiled.

"I'm glad. I'm also glad you told me about the ranch. I promise I'll do whatever I can to help you get the ranch back on its feet."

"No."

"No? But why not?"

"There's no need. This show is going to provide enough cash so we can pay off the second mortgage and still have cash reserves. All you need to do is be you. I need you to be the woman who stepped out from behind that truck and brought sunshine and joy to this ranch. You've done that since the first day you stepped foot on this land, and it's what everyone here needs from you. I'm sorry I took your joy and sunshine away for a while, but if you can bring it back, I know this ranch will survive for another hundred years. I'm begging you to just be Carrie."

"Are you sure I won't be a distraction?" she asked with a slight grin.

"Oh, on the contrary, I *know* you'll be a complete and utter distraction for me, but now I'm expecting it. I can handle my inattentiveness as long as you continue to bring sunshine into my life."

Carrie looked down at their hands and started to chew on the inside of her lip.

"What's the matter?" he asked.

"I'm not sunshine and joy all the time, you know."

"Oh, I know. Sometimes you can be stubborn and owlish, but I'm okay with that side of you, too."

"Seriously, Joel, I can get moody, gruff, and out of sorts."

"I've lived and worked with Bull my whole life. There's no way I'll ever believe you can get gruffer than that old cowhand."

Carrie opened her mouth to object and then realized that he was probably right. She started to laugh. "Okay, I guess if you can put up with Bull, you can put up with me, too."

"So now, B, the question is, can *you* put up with me?"

She looked into his eyes and saw them twinkle and sparkle. She felt like she could look into those eyes for a lifetime and still not have enough time to fully enjoy them.

Joel lowered his voice. "Please tell me that you can put up with me?"

"Yes, Joel, I think I can *put up* with you, too," she whispered back.

"Thank you, God." He looked up as he prayed those words and then lowered his eyes and head. He placed his lips on hers once again to just enjoy the simple pleasure of Carrie's kiss.

Carrie figured that she must be getting used to Joel kissing her—at least, this time it hadn't come as a complete and total surprise. Once again, Joel's lips were coaxing hers to move and respond. *Nope*, on second thought, she wasn't getting used to his kisses at all. Each kiss was still new and strange.

Joel's lips moved slightly away from her own, and she heard him take another breath. "Carrie, I have one more question for you."

"Yes?"

"Awesome. That's just the answer I was hoping for." And with that, he kissed her again. It was several minutes before Carrie realized he was interpreting her questioning response as an answer to his question. She had to stop him and make him actually ask his question.

"What is your question, Joel?"

"I knew it wasn't going to be that easy." Joel drew back a little farther so he could see Carrie's reaction.

"Carrie, will you be mine?"

"Your what?" she asked.

"My, ahhh . . . date, ah . . . tomorrow night." Joel wanted to answer "mine, just mine," but he knew that he needed a different response. He recalled thinking this relationship was going to take a different course than any other relationship he had been in, but he remembered thinking that that was okay then and it was still okay now. Baby steps, he reminded himself, baby steps.

"Ummm . . . okay."

CHAPTER 20

The next morning, Carrie found herself once again working in Joel's office, although this time she was working alone. Joel had mentioned that he needed to check on some things with Bull and that he would be gone for a few hours. He had asked her to continue working on some of the paperwork they had started a few days earlier. She wasn't sure she was actually helping, but she had agreed to do as he asked. She really hoped she was somehow contributing to the ranch and that this wasn't just Joel's way of keeping tabs on her.

As she worked, she thought back to their conversation last night. Had she really agreed to go on a date with him? Tonight? She couldn't believe it. She didn't even know what "going on a date with him" meant. Was she supposed to dress up? She didn't have anything to wear other than the clothes she had been wearing every day on the ranch, mostly jeans and long-sleeved t-shirts. Was he taking her somewhere? Was he expecting her to do her hair and makeup?

Carrie felt herself beginning to panic when there was a knock at the door. She looked up to see Maria standing outside the office.

"Hey, there," Maria said, "how're you doing in here?"

"I'm okay. I'm not sure that I'm doing everything right, but I hope I'm at least helping somehow."

"Oh, I'm sure you're doing fine. Don't worry, you can't ruin anything, and if you make a mistake, it can always be corrected."

Carrie let loose a big breath and her shoulders dropped. "Thank goodness, I was beginning to worry that maybe I was put here as a way to keep me from getting hurt—that Joel knew he was going to have a huge mess to clean up after I'd gone."

Maria laughed. "Nope, I can definitely tell you Joel would not have entrusted any of this to you if he didn't trust you. There's just no way he would ever do that. He barely lets me or Zach in this office." Maria took a step into the office and in a more gossipy tone said, "But speaking of my brother, I heard a rumor you two were going on a date tonight. Can you confirm the rumor? Is it true?" Maria's eyebrows bounced up and down.

Carrie dropped her head into her hands, and Maria barely heard the muffled yes from her. She then looked up and asked what was most on her mind.

"What does that even mean?"

"What do you mean, what does *that mean*? You've been on dates before, right?"

"No." And with that one word, Maria understood Carrie's question. Maria stepped into the room and closed that door.

"This is the first date you've *ever* been on?"

"Yes."

"What about prom—or any of the other high school dances?"

"Never went. Was never asked. Never thought I was missing all that much." Carrie looked at Maria and decided that she could maybe get a better idea of what was going to happen tonight.

"So can you tell me what we're going to do?"

"Knowing Joel, and as he only asked you last night, my guess is he's going to take you out for dinner."

"Somewhere other than the ranch?"

"Yeah, probably in town. Why?"

"Is he expecting me to get dressed up? Am I supposed to do my hair? What about makeup?"

"Joel's a guy. Trust me when I tell you, he has not put much thought into this date," Maria responded.

"It's just that I don't have any other clothes to wear other than what I wear around here. I don't ever wear makeup, so I wouldn't even know what to do."

Maria looked at Carrie for a moment and asked, "What do you *want* to do?"

"What do you mean?"

"Do you want to get dressed up?"

Carrie had been so worried about what Joel's expectations were that she hadn't even given a thought to what she wanted to do. As she thought about it, she decided that she didn't want to get dressed up.

"Come to think about it, I don't."

"Then you have your answer."

"I just want to be me. I don't want to try to be someone else—and if that's not what Joel wants, then maybe we shouldn't even go on this date."

"I think that's a great reason to just wear what you have on now."

Carrie looked down at the desk. Maria waited. She knew the other woman had something else on her mind, but she needed some time to get her thoughts together.

"Maria?"

"Yeah?"

"Do you think your brother will be disappointed if I just show up in my jeans?"

"Nope."

"Are you sure?"

"Positive. As I said, he's a guy. If I had to guess, he hasn't even given a thought to the logistics of the evening except to know that he would like to spend some time with you—alone. Carrie, I'm going to tell you something else you may not be aware of. My brother is very sweet on you."

"Are you sure?" Carrie still couldn't believe that the handsome rancher had real feelings for her.

"Oh, yeah, I'm sure. Joel has never been one to play relationship games. In the past, when he found a girl who interested him, he would ask her out. If they had something between them, he would continue to date her. But he would never pretend to have feelings for a woman. He's just too practical. He once made a comment about not understanding why a man would lie about having feelings for a woman if he didn't. Joel's comment was that that tactic seemed to be more work than it was worth.

"I also know my brother. He admitted to me he really likes you. I just thought you should know before you go out tonight that his feelings for you are genuine."

"I'm nervous," Carrie whispered.

"You won't be the only one." Maria smirked. She had decided that Carrie needed this inside information. It would make Carrie feel a little less nervous, and it wouldn't hurt Joel's ultimate objectives if Carrie knew he was also nervous. After all, she was only being honest. "Carrie, my brother is very smitten with you, and I'm sure that by this evening he is going to be a nervous wreck about whether he might screw something up."

"Really?"

"Really."

"Thanks, Maria." Carrie smiled.

"No problem. If you have any other questions, don't hesitate to come find me. I promise, if you can just relax a little, you'll enjoy yourself tonight."

Carrie was relieved. Talking to Maria always seemed to calm her nerves. She would take Maria's advice and just be herself, try to relax, and enjoy the evening.

♦ ♦ ♦

It was late in the afternoon by the time Joel had finished in the barns. He and Bull had managed to make some decisions regarding the stock they were going to supply for next season's rodeo circuit. He actually watched a couple of the hands attempt to ride one of the bulls. He wasn't sure Go Easy would be a solid entry and wanted to watch him in action. Watching the rides took much more time than he had originally planned to be gone. He worried about Carrie being left alone, but he and

Bull needed to make their final selections and submit their bulls for the rosters. The only question he had was whether Go Easy would provide a high-scoring ride. He was actually surprised that Bull had recommended it. The bull seemed so mild-mannered in the stall. It was actually how it had gotten the name Go Easy. But the minute one of the men had gotten on its back, it became agitated. It was a challenge just getting the riders enough time to actually get set before they opened the gate. But once the gate was opened, the bull was off. Joel watched, fascinated as what seemed like a mild-mannered bull turn into one of the most challenging rides his men had ever had. Bull had been pushing to add this one to the roster, but Joel had been unsure. After watching three different men try to ride him, Joel agreed that he was a great final submission.

Now, however, it was after five o'clock, and he needed a shower and shave before he picked up Carrie for their date. He rushed into the house and immediately headed to his office. He found Carrie sitting at his desk just as he had left her that morning.

"Please tell me you at least got up and had lunch."

"What?" Joel's voice had startled Carrie. She had been so focused on working on the records that she hadn't even heard him come in the front door.

"I'm hoping you haven't been sitting in that chair for the past eight hours. At least tell me you got some lunch."

Carrie smiled. "Yes, I had lunch. Thank you."

Joel's breath caught in his chest as her face lit up with a smile. She really was the most beautiful woman he had ever met. He took a deep breath and nodded.

"I just need thirty minutes or so to take a shower and we can go."

"Okay. I'll keep working if you don't mind."

"Carrie, you don't have to work yourself to the bone."

"Actually, I just wanted to finish what I was working on and then I thought I would bring my glass to the kitchen."

"Sounds good. See you in thirty."

Carrie nodded and turned her head back to the computer and the log sheets.

Joel ran upstairs. He couldn't think of another time he had been this excited to take a woman on a date.

◆ ◆ ◆

Joel finished getting ready with a few minutes to spare. He didn't want to make Carrie wait for him any longer than necessary. He practically ran downstairs and headed into the office. The office was dark, and there was no one around. He turned to head to the kitchen and once again walked into an empty room. He turned to head upstairs to look for her, but then he heard voices coming from the front porch.

He walked to the front door and saw Carrie sitting on the front porch swing with Glenda. Just as he was about to walk through the door, he heard the two women discussing the flower beds along the house.

"I usually plant the same flowers, but sometimes I change things up," Glenda said. "The problem is, most of the time when I try something new, it just doesn't work. The soil isn't right or the plant doesn't seem to get the right amount of sun or shade. It always seems like such a waste to spend money on flowers that may or may not make it when I can just buy the same ones year after year and know they work."

"I'm never that adventurous. When I find a flower that seems to work in a particular bed, I don't change it. I'm too much of a coward to try something new."

Glenda laughed.

"What's so funny?" Carrie asked.

"Having *you* call yourself a coward. I don't care if it is just about flower beds, there is nothing cowardly about you."

"Shows how little you know me. I'm usually too afraid to try anything new because I'm such a 'fraidy cat."

"And yet, you flew to another state to work on a ranch you had never stepped foot on with a bunch of men whom you'd never met, doing work you have never done. What exactly do you call that?"

"Desperation," Carrie spoke quietly.

"About what?"

Joel saw Carrie look down at her watch.

"I'll have to share that story another time. Joel will probably be looking for me sometime soon."

That's my cue. Joel walked out the front door, turned to his date, and said, "Are you ready to go?"

Carrie stood up and turned to Joel. She had not changed, and his reaction to her look would be the first indication on how the rest of the evening was going to go.

"Yep, I'm ready."

"You look great by the way," he said.

Carrie frowned. His comment was the last thing that she had expected him to say. Maybe he had been coached by his sister.

"Did you talk to Maria?"

"What? Maria? No. Why? Was I supposed to?" He looked generally confused by her question.

"I'll speak plain to you, cowboy. Did your sister tell you what to say when you saw me tonight?"

"Ahh, no. Did I say something wrong?" Joel suddenly looked nervous. Then Carrie noticed that he wiped his palms down on the side of his jeans. *Maybe Maria's right, maybe he's just as nervous about this date as I am.* Carrie decided to let him off the hook.

"No. You didn't. Maria and I had talked a little bit about what I should wear tonight." She smiled at him.

"Well, I say you picked right, because you look great."

"Not too casual?"

"Nope." His smile caused her heart to skip a beat. "Should we go?"

Joel gestured for Carrie to walk down the steps. As she got within his reach, he clasped her hand, and together they walked down the steps. He headed toward one of the ranch trucks. He opened her door and helped her climb up into the cab. He jogged around the front of the truck and climbed up into the driver's seat.

Once he closed the door, he turned to Carrie and said, "I'm so happy you agreed to go out with me tonight." She merely smiled and turned to put on her seatbelt. *Maybe tonight would be okay.*

♦ ♦ ♦

They both managed to relax a little and enjoy dinner. Joel had selected a local ribs and steak place. He made some comment about taking her to a true Texas joint on their first date—something about setting a precedent.

The only uncomfortable part of the whole night was during the conversation on the ride back to the ranch.

"When we get back, I'll grab my things and head back to the bunkhouse tonight."

"No. You can't move back to the bunkhouse," Joel stammered.

"Why not?"

"Because you should stay up at the house where I can keep an eye on you."

"Joel, that's ridiculous. I'm fine. You know I'm fine. In fact, I spent the entire day working in the office, and not once did you check to see how I was doing. I haven't had any issues with vertigo for the past several days, not even when I have shaken or nodded my head. There's no reason for anyone to be checking on me during the night. My head is fine."

"It's not right," he grumbled. "You belong in the house, not sleeping in the bunkhouse with the men."

"They're *your* men."

"That doesn't make me feel any better about this."

"I don't understand why. You were fine with me sleeping in the bunkhouse before—what's changed?"

"I wasn't fine with it before. Remember, I thought you were going to be a *huge* distraction to the men on the ranch. I thought it was a terrible idea. I was trying to figure out a way to force Drake to make you sleep in the trailer when I heard the men had voted to let you stay in the bunkhouse. I couldn't believe even Bull had agreed. At that point, I knew I had lost all of my arguments to move you to one of the trailers. My only hope was the men would snore so loud you would ask to move somewhere else. Then the next morning, you slept through everyone getting up, and I thought maybe then you would want to move. But still, you stayed."

"It seemed like it would be more realistic for the show if I stayed in the bunkhouse." She shrugged.

"Yes, but what about whether it was right for *you*?"

"It was fine."

"Really? Be honest with me, were you really okay with sleeping in the bunkhouse?"

Carrie didn't answer him right away. She took her time deciding how best to answer his question.

"If I'm being honest, no, I was really scared that first night. I was sleeping in a room with a bunch of men I had only just met and didn't know from Adam. If something had happened, I wasn't sure if there was anyone I could go to for help. But just as I started to really scare myself to death, I thought of Bull. I don't know what it is about that old cowboy, but I knew he would never hurt me and he wouldn't let any of the other men hurt me either. So I closed my eyes and tried to go to sleep. I don't know how long I lay in the bed before I actually fell asleep, but I'm sure it was sometime after three in the morning."

"And now? Are you comfortable sleeping in the bunkhouse now?"

Again, Carrie took time answering his question. Joel appreciated that he was getting her honest answer.

"Yeah, I guess I would say I am. It feels a little like I somehow inherited a bunch of brothers and for whatever reason, we all sleep in the same big room. It's a little surreal, but then again, everything about being here has been a little surreal."

"I understand what you're saying. Please don't get me wrong—this isn't about trusting you or my men. I know you are perfectly safe staying down there, but I still don't like it."

"Why not?"

"My girlfriend should not be sleeping down in the bunkhouse when there is a perfectly good bed up at the house."

"Your what?" Carrie squeaked.

"My girlfriend?" he asked uncertainly.

"Ummmm . . . and when did I all of a sudden get that title?"

"The minute you agreed to go on this date with me?" he sheepishly answered. "I know, I know, this is only our first date. But if I'm being completely honest with you, I have to admit I have really come to care about you, and I would really like to start thinking about you as my girlfriend."

Carrie took another moment to think about her answer. When she finally turned to him, she said, "How about we get through this date and a few more before we start calling this a relationship."

Joel smiled and then gave her a wink.

"I can handle waiting a few more dates before calling you my girlfriend."

She laughed and replied, "Are you sure?"

"Oh yeah, I figure that means I have a couple of guaranteed dates with you, and I think it's fair that I expect a kiss at the end of each one of them."

Carrie just rolled her eyes.

♦ ♦ ♦

When they arrived back at the ranch, Joel turned to Carrie and asked, "Will you let me get your door?"

"Why?" she questioned.

"I'd like to end this date being a gentleman, and that means helping you get out of the truck."

"I think that's silly, but yes, I'll let you get my door."

"Thank you."

He opened his door and quickly strode around the front of the truck and opened her door. He held out his hand for her to take as she climbed down from the truck. As soon as her boots hit the dirt, he turned his hand over and threaded his fingers through hers.

"Are you sure I can't convince you to move into the house?"

"Yes, I'm sure. I need to stay in the bunkhouse for the rest of the show. It would seem strange if I suddenly started sleeping at the house."

"I still don't like it, but I'll walk you down to the bunkhouse."

After she collected her toiletries, they strolled down past the equestrian barn, all the while holding hands. He couldn't believe how natural it felt to have his fingers wrapped around hers. There was something about this woman that just settled his soul and made him feel like she was the other half of his heart.

Carrie, on the other hand, was still having a hard time reconciling this Joel with the one she had first met when she had arrived at the Double Spur. She believed his story about why he had said what he had, and she had forgiven him, but this was all so new to her. She was having a hard time believing that he could really have genuine romantic feelings for her, however, whenever he took her hand in his, her toes curled. As they walked down to the bunkhouse, he not only held her hand, but she could feel his thumb gently caressing her hand, and her toes curled even more.

They arrived at the bunkhouse, and Joel walked her to the door.

"Are you going to let me kiss you goodnight?" he asked.

Carrie blushed, which just made his smile grow a little bit bigger. All conscious thought left her when she looked up and fell into his eyes. As she continued to stare into his eyes, she felt him reach up and lift her chin a little bit more. As his head descended to hers, her eyelids slowly closed. She felt his lips caress her own. His lips left hers and moved to press a kiss onto her forehead. His lips pressed there for a moment more, and then he stood up and waited for Carrie to open her eyes.

Carrie could feel Joel's eyes looking at her, and she once again opened her own.

"I had a really nice time tonight," he softly spoke.

She smiled. "I did too."

"Good night, B. Sweet dreams."

"Good night, Joel."

He leaned down one more time and gently placed a kiss on her lips before turning away and heading back up to the house. He was sure that the smile he could feel on his lips was still going to be there in the morning.

CHAPTER 21

The following morning, Carrie awoke in the bunkhouse. It had been more than a week since she had last woken up in the bunkhouse. She could hear the men moving about in the room but waited for them to finish and leave before she got out of bed. Before she had been thrown by the bull, that had been her routine, and it had seemed to work for all of them.

After she heard the last man leave the room, she climbed down from the bunk and headed into the bathroom. As usual, she found toothpaste and shaving gel on the counter and in the sink. She shook her head and thought, *yep, it's good to be home.*

After she had finished getting ready, Carrie headed out to the barns. She needed to find Bull. She wasn't sure what the old ranch hand was going to let her do, but she needed to get on track. She needed to get back to learning and doing the work of a ranch hand, and she *really* needed to get back on one of those bulls. A.Z. was right—waiting was not helping her nerves. She wasn't sure how she was going to be able to convince Bull that she was ready, but that was going to be her task today. She wasn't sure how soon Drake and the camera crew would be back, but when they arrived, she needed to be ready to ride.

Carrie found Bull in the maternity pen.

"Hey, Bull."

"Carrie. How are you doing this morning?"

"I'm good."

Bull stopped checking on a cow and turned and walked up to her. He took her chin in his weathered hand and asked, "How are you, really?"

"Bull, I'm fine. I haven't had any issues with vertigo for days. I had no trouble going out with Joel the other day."

"Hrrrmph."

Carrie looked the old cowhand in the eyes and quietly responded, "I need to get back on a bull and finish this show."

"Hrrrmph," he said again.

"Please, Bull? I need to try it again," she implored.

"I know." He sighed. "But I don't gotta like it."

"What will you let me do today?"

"Give me a second, and we can go check with Maria."

She nodded and watched as he went back to checking on the cow in the pen.

After he finished, the two walked over to the equestrian barn to find Maria.

"Hey, Bull, Carrie. Whatcha doing?"

"Carrie wants to get back on one of the bulls."

Maria immediately turned to Carrie and asked, "Are you sure?"

"Maria, I need to finish the show."

"Why?"

"What do you mean, why? Drake is going to be coming back, and he'll be expecting to finish filming my experiences. Moreover, I'm never going to be able to get on a bull in Las Vegas if I don't get on one here first."

"Of course, of course." She turned to Bull and asked, "What's your idea?"

"I thought we should get her back on one of the horses. Wanna go for a ride?"

Maria's face lit up. As she turned to Carrie, she said, "How about taking Misty out for some exercise?"

It didn't take long to get the horses and the two women ready for the ride. Glenda even packed a light lunch in case they ended up being out longer than they had planned.

"Need a hand up?" Carrie turned and found Joel standing behind her. She blushed.

"What are *you* doing here?"

"I wanted to make sure you were ready for this ride and see you off."

"Joel, I'm fine."

"So, do you want a hand up?" He smiled at her.

"I think I better get on the back of this horse all by myself if I'm going to persuade Bull I'm really okay to go out riding."

Joel moved closer to her and whispered, "How about a goodbye kiss?"

Carrie replied even more quietly, "No way, cowboy. Not with an audience."

His reply was immediate. "No problem. That just leaves me something to look forward to tonight."

Carrie rolled her eyes at the rancher and mounted the horse.

Joel took a step back and tipped his imaginary hat.

"Ready?" Maria asked.

"Yes."

The two women rode for a while, just enjoying the fresh air and the incredible scenery. Carrie loved riding Misty and could hardly believe that just a few short months ago, she hadn't even been on top of a horse. Now she felt like she was a fairly proficient rider. Carrie looked over at Maria, who seemed unusually quiet.

"Hey, Maria, penny for your thoughts?"

"Don't think they're worth a penny. How about we ride to Hawk's Tree and stop for lunch."

"Sounds great. Race 'ya." With that challenge, Carrie kicked Misty into a run. Carrie gave the mare her head and hung on for dear life. It took no more than the kick and loosening the reins and Misty was running. Carrie had never experienced such exhilaration. She was terrified and excited all at once. She was afraid she would fall off while also wanting this run to last forever. The wind whipped her hair and whistled in her ears.

"Run, Misty, run!" she cheered.

It didn't take long for Maria and Sadie to catch up to them. The two women laughed, cheered, and encouraged their mounts to run faster. Eventually, Maria pulled up slightly on her reins, and Sadie responded and started to slow down. Carrie imitated Maria's movements, and soon, Misty was slowing down as well. They proceeded to Hawk's Nest at a much more sedate pace. Both riders and horses were breathless and energized. Maria reached the trees first and dismounted. She grabbed Misty's reins while Carrie dismounted, then she tied both horses to the post near the trees. Carrie grabbed the lunches Glenda had made for them while Maria grabbed a blanket. They settled down on the blanket and started to enjoy the sandwiches and fruit Glenda had sent.

"Sooooo, how was your date last night?" Maria asked.

"Fine."

"Only fine?"

"Good?"

"Carrie, this isn't a test. There isn't a right or wrong answer. Did you enjoy yourself with my brother or not?"

Carrie couldn't contain her grin any longer. The smile burst forth, and Carrie replied, "Yes. I had a really good time."

"And my advice on your outfit?"

"He said I looked nice. I actually asked him if he had talked to you, wondering if you had prompted his comment."

"I didn't see Joel at all before your date."

"That's what he said." Carrie smiled again.

"Was I right? Was he nervous?"

"Yeah, I think so. Or at least he seemed to get nervous when I asked him if he had talked to you first."

"Where did he take you?"

"I don't remember the name of the place. They served ribs and steaks. Joel said something about having a real Texas meal for our first date."

"He probably took you to Hank's. They have great steaks. They also make a killer chocolate chip cookie sundae. Did you get dessert?"

"No, are you kidding? I was so full after eating dinner that I couldn't even look at the dessert menu."

"That's funny, it's always the first thing I look at. If I find a dessert I want, I always make sure to leave room. I've even been known to order dessert first."

Carrie laughed at the idea of ordering dessert first. She was going to have to share this trick with Becky. She could think of a couple of restaurants they had gone to where they had never been able to eat dessert. Becky would definitely support the concept of dessert first.

"I'll have to remember that for next time."

"Sooooo, is there going to be a next time with my brother?"

"Yeah. He, um—"

"He, um, what?" Maria's eyebrows danced up and down on her forehead.

"He called me his girlfriend."

"He did not!"

"Yep. I asked him how I got that title, and he said I got it by accepting his offer to go on the date."

"What did you say?"

"I told him maybe we should go on a few more dates before we started to call what we have a relationship."

"Let me guess, he took that as a good sign."

"Yeah, he said something about how that meant more dates and more good night kisses."

"Did you kiss?"

"What are we, in junior high?" Carrie asked.

"Yep. I never got to really do this in junior high, so I figure I should get to do it now." Maria winked. "But you still haven't answered my question. Did he kiss you?"

Carrie looked at this woman who had become like a sister to her and nodded.

"I'll take that smile to mean you enjoyed it. I don't think I really want to ask for any details about you kissing my brother. That's a little weird." Maria crinkled up her nose.

They both laughed again. Then they heard the horses nicker. Carrie felt like Misty and Sadie were laughing right along with them. They sat for a while longer, and Carrie remembered how distracted Maria had been earlier.

"So, you want to tell me what's on your mind?"

"We've been approached about selling some of our horses."

"Isn't that a good thing?"

"Well, normally it would be."

"But?"

"But there's just something off about this offer. I don't know what it is, but my woman's intuition is telling me we shouldn't do business with these folks."

"Are you worried?"

"Worried? Not exactly. Although I'm the person who would be doing the negotiations, I know that Joel and Zach have my back and will support me in whatever way I need. Additionally, Bull and the rest of the hands are always around if I need them. Like I said, I can't put my finger on anything specific, but there's just something that doesn't feel right."

"The only thing I can tell you is—follow your gut. My mom always said when you got the willies, your subconscious was telling you something was wrong. She also said that your brain processes a lot of information and that sometimes, the subconscious puts together some of those clues before our conscious brain can combine all of the facts and warn us about the potential danger."

"Thanks, I'll keep that in mind."

♦ ♦ ♦

It was about three o'clock in the afternoon when Joel left his office to find Carrie. He hadn't seen her come back from her ride, and he missed her.

Joel walked into the maternity barn and saw Beans mucking out one of the stalls. Beans looked up and said, "Hey, boss. Do you need something?"

"Hey, Beans, I just came looking for Carrie. Have you seen her?"

"I haven't seen her or Maria since they left for their ride this morning."

Joel frowned and turned to head to the equestrian barn. He walked in the barn and found Dusty.

"Hey, Dusty, have you seen Carrie or Maria?"

"No, Joel. They haven't gotten back from their ride."

"What?"

"I was just going to talk with Bull and let him know the women weren't back yet."

"They left hours ago."

"Yeah, I know."

Both men left the barn and headed out to find Bull. They found him out by Go Easy's pen.

"Bull, have you seen Carrie or Maria?" Joel's voice carried the fear he was starting to develop along with his question.

The old cowhand looked directly at Joel, "No. I was just starting to worry. What are you thinking?"

"I'm thinking that it's been way too long for those two women to have been gone. Which way did they go?"

Bull looked at Dusty. The hand merely shrugged his shoulders and replied. "I didn't watch 'em leave. I'm not sure which way they went."

"Hmmmph." Bull said.

"Bull, this isn't good,"Joel asserted.

"No, but don't start to panic. Maria is an expert rider, and she wouldn't have gone far. They were just going to exercise the horses."

"Bull, it's been over six hours."

"Joel, you wouldn't be worried if Maria and Dusty had been out for more than six hours. Don't invite trouble just because it's Carrie instead."

Joel sighed. "I know, but I can't help it. Six hours is a long time to be in the saddle."

"Do you really think Maria would have kept Carrie in the saddle for this whole time?"

Joel looked at Bull and realized he was right. There was no way the women had been riding this whole time. Maria was an expert horsewoman and knew every inch of this ranch as well, if not better, than Joel.

"You're right. Maria would have stopped and let Carrie get off her horse."

"Not to mention Glenda had sent lunch along for them," Dusty added.

Joel nodded. Now that Dusty had mentioned it, he did remember Glenda handing Maria something for lunch and some snacks. "So, how long do we wait before we start sending out folks to look for them?"

"Joel, I don't think we need to send out search parties until at least after five. Maria would not let them miss dinner."

"You're right. I don't like it, but you're right."

Right at that moment, Zach and one of the hands came riding in from the east pasture.

"Hey, y'all, what's up?" he said as he dismounted his horse. Dusty quickly grabbed the reins.

"Maria and Carrie haven't come back from their ride this morning."

"Okay . . . and?"

"Joel's worried," Dusty answered.

"Why?"

Joel turned to his brother and frowned.

"What do you mean *why*?"

"I mean, Carrie is healed from her injury. She didn't have any issues when she went out with you, and we both know you wouldn't have one ounce of concern for Maria if you learned she was out riding for more than eight hours. So, I'm just wondering why all the concern."

Joel sighed and his shoulders dropped. Zach and Bull were right. The only reason he was concerned was because he didn't know where Carrie was and whether she was okay.

Zach moved next to Joel and whispered, "You need to get your concern tamped down before the women come back. Maria won't appreciate the over-the-top worry and you may just scare Carrie off the ranch."

Zach smiled with the last comment so that Joel knew he was kidding, but he nodded anyway.

"Maybe you should head back into the office instead of being caught out here pacing the barn," Zach suggested.

Yeah, Joel thought. *I can just as easily pace in my office, and in there, no one would notice my pacing or worry. Zach's right, though. I need to get my worry under control. Neither Carrie nor Maria would appreciate the concern if nothing is wrong. They would both assume my worry meant I didn't trust them or think them capable.*

Joel nodded to Zach and said, "I'm heading back to the office—let me know when they return."

"Like you won't know the minute those horses arrive back on the ranch?" Zach said under his breath with a smirk.

With that last comment repeating in his ears, Joel turned to the house and headed into the office.

About forty-five minutes later, Joel saw the horses come into the compound. Maria must have taken them out toward the west pasture. As soon as the horses came into sight, Joel took a step toward the front door. Zach's words still in his ears, he stopped and took a deep breath. Zach was right. He couldn't let them know that he was worrying over them and that it was probably for nothing.

Joel heard the front door open a while later and assumed it was Maria coming into the house to take a shower. It looked like he would have to wait to hear about their adventures until they were all at dinner.

◆ ◆ ◆

While they all sat around the dining room table, Joel tried to figure out a way to ask about Carrie and Maria's ride without sounding overly concerned. He looked up and saw Zach laughing at him. Zach rolled his eyes and said, "So, Maria, how was your ride?"

"It was great."

"Where'd you go?"

"We headed to Hawk's Nest. We had lunch under the tree and just rode out a little further. After a while, we got off and just walked with the horses."

"How are you doing after the ride, Carrie?" Zach asked.

"I'm good. Great, actually. I'm hoping Bull is going to let me get on the back of a bull tomorrow."

All heads turned to the old cowhand. Bull turned to Maria and asked, "How is she really?"

"Bull! I am completely capable of answering for myself," Carrie interjected.

"You'll answer all right, but I'm not sure I'd get a completely truthful response."

"Listen here, cowboy. I don't need anyone to speak for me. I told you I felt great this morning. The day out riding was your test to see if I could handle being on top of one of those beasts. I'm fine. I don't know what more proof you need, but I'm good." Carrie's voice had gotten louder as she responded to the old cowhand. By the time she was finished, her voice was so loud it was as if she were yelling. She looked directly at Bull and in stark contrast, quietly said, "We talked about this. I need to get back on a bull and finish this show."

"Why?" Joel asked.

"Why? What do you mean why? Why does everyone keep asking me *why*? I have a life and a family to get back to."

Joel opened his mouth to reply and couldn't get the words to leave his mouth. He hadn't thought too much about after the show was finished. He had started to envision Carrie on the ranch permanently. He had completely forgotten that she might leave. For the remainder of the evening meal, Joel's thoughts were in a jumble. He was afraid of Carrie getting on top of one of his bulls. However, he was more afraid of her leaving the ranch and not returning. She had come to mean everything to him, and he wasn't sure he would be able to go back to the life he had lived before Carrie had stormed into their lives.

Carrie noticed that Joel had been very quiet during dinner. It wasn't like him. He usually participated in the table conversations as much as everyone else, but tonight, she couldn't remember him uttering a single word other than when he asked *why*. She reached over and touched his hand. He immediately turned to her, and she asked, "Are you okay?"

His lips curved up into a small shadow of a smile as he placed his other hand on top of hers.

"Will you go for a walk with me?"

"Of course."

And with that, they both rose from the table. As soon as they stepped away from the table, Joel reached out and took Carrie's hand. He once again directed them out the back door. They walked for a while in comfortable silence. Once they had gone far enough for the ranch to be more shadow than shape, Joel turned to Carrie and said, "I want you to know you are more than welcome to stay on here at the ranch even after the show is finished."

"Offering me a job, cowboy?" She grinned.

"No, more like a—" *A what?* he thought. *A relationship?*

"Hmmmm?" She just turned to him and waited for him to get his thoughts in order.

"Carrie, I know we haven't known each other long, but I have really grown to care about you. You have become very important to me. I know we've only been on one actual date, but you should know, I've started to think about you being here at the ranch for the long term."

"Joel, you can't be serious. You don't even know me."

"I know I don't know everything about you, but I'm pretty sure I know what's really important about you."

"But that's just it, Joel. You don't. I haven't been completely honest with you or Drake. There are things about me that you don't know."

"Such as?"

Such as? She thought. *Can I trust Joel with the information about Cassie? Will he protect her as much as I would? Can I trust him with the real reason I decided to enter the contest?* The questions just kept pounding around inside her head. Then she looked up at Joel and into his eyes. His entire attention was focused on her. He was patiently waiting for her answer, and she realized that he would give her all the time in the world to answer him. She also found herself hoping that she could trust him with her secrets. *Well, here goes nothing.*

"I . . . well, actually my sister. She . . . ummm . . ."

"Carrie, I hope you know you can tell me anything. I also hope that when you share this secret you've been keeping with me, your burden will be lighter. I would never do anything to hurt you or your family."

Carrie just stared at the rancher. The real question was—did she trust him with her secret? Did she honestly believe that he would keep her secret and protect Cassie, even if that meant putting Cassie ahead of the ranch? As she stared into his eyes, she recalled what he had told her about raising money for Free Wheelin'. She had to believe that the young man who was so driven to help disabled people when he was eight would grow into a man who would protect a person with disabilities. She also thought about what he had said about what the ranch needed from her. He had said he only needed Carrie to be who she was. She decided to tell him who she really was. Carrie took a deep breath and started in on her tale again.

"My younger sister, Cassie, is the actual reason I submitted my name for this contest."

"Cassie? Why?"

"It's kind of a long story."

"I've got all the time in the world for you." With those words, she took a leap of faith.

"My mom developed a serious infection when she was pregnant with Cassie. My folks tried for years after I was born to get pregnant. It took eight years, but it finally happened. They were so excited. Actually, I was as excited as they were. I couldn't wait to have a little sister or brother."

Joel snickered at this comment.

"Why are you laughing?"

"I was thinking about when my parents told Zach and me that we were going to have a younger sister. I asked if they could find a different family to give her to. I told them girls didn't belong on a ranch. My mom disagreed, and I knew I was in trouble, although I wasn't smart enough to stop talking because the next thing I said was that there were a lot of families who wanted a baby and that I was sure we could find a good one to give her to. I was sent to time-out and was not allowed to ride my horse for a week. I was only allowed to go for a ride after I apologized to my mom." He smirked as he looked at Carrie.

Carrie chuckled, "Okay, I guess we had very different reactions."

"That's an understatement. But go on, tell me about Cassie."

"So, my whole family was ecstatic. Then my mom came down with what we thought was a cold. After a week of a runny nose and cough, she started to spike a fever. We thought that maybe it was the flu, but her fever was so high my dad decided she needed to go to the hospital. It took them two days to get her fever under control. They gave her antibiotics and tried to figure out what was going on. They finally figured out that she had developed an infection. They never discovered what caused the infection, but she was able to come home after being in the hospital for five days. I was so relieved to have her home, I told both my parents I would be her nurse and I would take care of her while my dad was at the store."

"You were pretty young."

Now it was Carrie's turn to laugh. "What I didn't realize was that my dad had others checking in on my mom. I didn't realize when the neighbor brought cookies for me, she was actually checking on Mom. I also didn't process the fact that Dad was coming home for lunch every day when he had never done that in the past. Additionally, Mom's sister, my Aunt Joan, called twice a day to talk to her. While Mom and her sister were close, they had never talked on the phone twice a day."

"So, your folks let you think that you were taking care of your mom all by yourself, but they really had a whole network of people who were monitoring her condition."

"Yep, that pretty much sums it up."

"I think I'm gonna like your folks."

Carrie chuckled again and said, "Yeah, you certainly have some things in common."

"After about a week or so on bed rest, she was able to get up, and the remainder of her pregnancy went great with no further complications. It wasn't until after Cassie was born that we discovered the infection had had a severe impact on her. She has developmental disabilities."

Carrie stopped talking and looked Joel in the eyes. This was it. There was no going back if she told him the truth.

Joel knew Carrie was trying to assess whether she was going to trust him. He would wait his whole life standing here with her, just waiting until she decided she could tell him about Cassie. She could have all his time until she could take that step. He watched her take a deep breath, and then she quietly resumed her story.

"My folks started to notice little things. She was not developing as quickly as other babies. She was not moving around like other children do. At six months, she still hadn't rolled over, and she couldn't sit up. She was also not speaking like other babies her age. Mom and Dad knew something was wrong. The doctors started doing tests, and we learned the infection had a tremendous impact on her development. In a nutshell, my sister is confined to a wheelchair. She is also mentally challenged."

Carrie let this revelation sit. She looked Joel in the eye and waited to see what his response was. Joel noticed she was waiting for his reaction. Nothing she said deserved to be kept a secret. He wasn't sure what kind of reaction she was waiting for, but he was only confused.

"Okay, so Cassie has some physical and mental challenges. What else?"

"What do you mean, 'what else'?"

"Carrie, what is your secret?"

"My sister. Her condition."

"I don't understand why you're keeping this a secret? What am I missing?"

"I don't . . . I can't . . . you can't . . . the show, I can't . . ." Joel waited. He still didn't understand why Carrie was so afraid to talk about Cassie. "I can't let this show exploit her to get better ratings. I can't expose her to all of that," she quietly said.

"Well, of course, the show can't exploit Cassie," Joel quickly replied. He continued to look at Carrie, trying to figure out what the problem was. Then things started to make sense. She was afraid *he* would use Cassie—well, him and Drake.

Joel reached out and took her cheek in his hand.

"Carrie, I feel like you and I have been getting to know each other pretty well these last few weeks. While I understand your reservation about sharing this with the jerk you met on the first day, I hope you don't think I would do anything to harm your sister. Tell me you know I would never hurt her or you."

Carrie continued to stand there with her cheek in Joel's hand and realized there was nothing but kindness and compassion spilling from his eyes. This man would never use someone else to get ahead. He would stand up for the abused rather than take advantage of anyone. It was time for her to admit this out loud. The tears started to slide down her cheek.

"I do." She exhaled the breath she didn't realize she had been holding. "About nine months ago," she continued, "my parents learned of an experimental treatment here in Texas. There may be a way for Cassie to get out of her wheelchair. The only problem is that it's experimental. This just means very expensive and not covered by insurance. We researched every grant or anything that might help to fund this treatment for her. I learned of one such grant program that would cover some of the costs. Ultimately, my family needs to come up with three-quarters of a million to one million dollars, and the grant will cover the rest. We don't have that kind of money. My parents talked about selling the store so they could use the money for Cassie. I convinced them that that was not a good plan. Without the store, how were they going to live? How would they retire? How could they continue to take care of Cassie without it? As Becky and I talked about this grant, we found the flyer for this show. Becky convinced me that I should submit a tape and that if I could get on the show, we could use the prize money for Cassie's treatment. We both agreed the show could never learn about Cassie. So, we came up with the story about my desire to buy the store. It seemed a plausible story for a reason why I would be willing to go through all of this. Joel, I lied about why I'm doing the show. I only want the money to get my sister this treatment."

Joel leaned down and kissed her. She had once again surprised him. She was going through all of this, risking a concussion—the toll this show was taking on her physically—all for her sister. The depths of her love took his breath away. He lifted his head, looked into her eyes, and said, "You completely amaze me. I thought I had an idea of your strength, your courage, and your capacity for complete selflessness. I have only seen the tip of the iceberg, haven't I? You teach me every day about giving and selfless love. You are the most incredible woman I have ever met, and I have fallen completely head over boots in love with you. I know I will never meet another human being who is so beautiful inside and out."

Carrie's jaw dropped. She didn't know what to say in response to his declaration. What did you say to a man who had just declared his love for you?

"I will keep your secret safe, and Cassie will not be exploited by this show. However, I don't think Drake would ever exploit Cassie for the show. I think he has way too much integrity for that."

"I...Joel, ummm..."

"Carrie, you don't have to say anything. I know I still have a long way to go before you can say you've fallen in love with me, but I know deep down in my soul that God brought you into my life and He will not let you leave it. Well, as long as I don't screw it up. And just so you know, I don't plan on messing this up. Come on, sweetheart—let's sit on the front porch for a while."

Carrie nodded.

♦ ♦ ♦

Carrie laid in her bunk bed that night thinking about her conversation with Joel. She had told him about Cassie, and he had declared that he would protect Cassie. She knew that she could trust him to keep Cassie safe. Then she thought about what else he had revealed. He had said he loved her. Could that even be possible? His words just rang through her heart. *Joel has fallen in love with me. Holy cow!* With that last thought, she drifted off to sleep.

CHAPTER 22

The next morning, Carrie walked out of the bunkhouse and headed out to look for Bull. She started to walk to the bull pens and heard a vehicle coming down the drive. She just stood near the bull pen and watched to see who got out. She realized that the SUV contained some of the guys from the camera crew.

"Hey, guys. Welcome back to the Double Spur."

"Hey, Carrie. It's great to see you again. How are you doing?"

"I'm good. I'm hoping that I'll get to ride a bull today."

"Really? That's great!"

The camera crew went to the back of the SUV and grabbed their equipment. They quickly started to get their cameras ready.

"You're going to start filming already? You haven't even been on the ranch for five minutes. I'm sure Drake will let you unpack," she said.

The guys didn't respond, and that's when Carrie heard another vehicle approaching. She figured that Drake must be in this other vehicle. She figured she might as well go and welcome him back. She waited for the second SUV to come to a stop. As soon as the tires stopped moving, the passenger door flew open, and a woman jumped out. She started to race toward Carrie. It wasn't until she had cut the distance between them in half that Carrie realized the new person was Becky.

"Becky!" she yelled and started running toward her best friend. The two women embraced.

"I can't believe you're here! Oh my gosh, you're really here. You are really here, right? I'm not dreaming, am I?"

Becky laughed and responded, "You're not dreaming. I'm really here. I've missed you so much!"

"I've missed you, too!"

The two hugged again. Becky leaned back and held Carrie at arm's length.

"How are you doing? Drake told me the concussion you got was pretty severe. Are you sure you're okay?"

"It was serious, but I'm really okay. What are you doing here?"

"Drake thought it would be fun if I came back with him and surprised you."

"Well, you certainly surprised me! I can't believe you're really here!"

Carrie looked over to find Drake. Instead, she noticed the camera guys off to the side. They had filmed the whole reunion.

"You knew my best friend was going to get out of this car, didn't you?" She heard laughing coming from behind the camera.

"Yes, they knew. I sent them ahead of us so they could get this reunion all on tape. Hi, Carrie, how're you doing?"

"I'm good."

"I've been talking with Joel, and he tells me you've been out a couple times on the horses. He also tells me you want to get back on one of those bulls."

"Yeah. I need to try again before I freak myself out."

"How soon before Bull lets you ride?"

"I'm hoping he'll let me ride today. Becky, you came just at the right moment to see me ride a big bad bull."

"What? That bull better not be big or bad. Drake promised me you were only going to ride a gentler bull." Her best friend turned and glared at the producer. "What is she talking about—getting on a 'big bad bull'?"

"Carrie, you're getting me in trouble. Tell her you're kidding and that I am not putting you on one of those circuit beasts."

"Becky, he's not putting me on one of the actual working bulls. I only get to ride the tame ones. At least so far."

"That's *all* you're going to ride if it's up to me," a gruff voice from behind Carrie declared. She spun around.

"Bull, I was just coming to find you to see if I could ride today, but look, Drake had a surprise for me. This is my best friend, Becky. She's come for a visit."

Bull turned to her friend and tipped his hat. "Ma'am. Welcome to the Double Spur."

"Thanks, Bull. It's great to finally put a face to the name. I've heard a lot about you from both Carrie and Drake."

"Hmmmph" was the only response they heard.

◆ ◆ ◆

That afternoon, Carrie found herself outside the pen the ranch used for bull riding. It was the same pen where she had fallen and had gotten her concussion. She shook her head. *Don't think about falling off and getting hurt, think about what this money will do for Cassie.*

"Are you sure you're ready to get on that bull?" a deep voice from just behind her asked. She turned and saw Joel standing there.

"I have to. I have to get back on one of these beasts so I can finish the show," she replied.

"If I had the money for Cassie's treatment, I would gladly hand it over to you right now so you didn't have to go through any more of this." Joel reached up and gently caressed her check.

Carrie laid her hand over his and replied, "The fact you would even suggest such a thing means the world to me."

"Can I kiss you now?" he asked.

"No." She laughed.

"Darn. But seriously, I wanted to make sure you remembered you had been doing really great on your first ride. The only problem was that you got caught by the bull's hoof. Try and jump further out from the bull if you feel yourself falling. Got it?"

"Carrie, are you sure you're ready to ride a bull again?" Drake asked as he approached the two of them.

"Yes, Drake. I need to get back on one of these things, and the sooner, the better. Isn't that what they say about riding a horse—you've got to get back up on it?"

"Never liked that saying. I'm sure the idiot who thought of it never got thrown by a bucking bronco—or a bull, for that matter," Drake asserted.

Carrie laughed. "Fair enough." They were suddenly joined by Becky. Carrie could see the worry all over her face.

"Becky, I'm going to be fine," Carrie said before Becky could ask her if she was really going to do this.

"I hope so. This is all my fault. If I had never suggested you entering into this stupid reality show, you wouldn't have gotten thrown by that bull, and you wouldn't have gotten a concussion."

"Carrie and I would never have met, either. So, for that, I will be eternally grateful that you suggested she enter," Joel said.

"We also wouldn't have met," Drake replied to Becky.

Becky turned to Drake and said, "You have a point." A small smile turned up her lips.

Carrie was momentarily stunned. *Becky and Drake?* She had been so excited to see her friend that she hadn't been paying any attention to Drake at all. Now that she thought about it, Drake had made sure that Becky was sitting next to him at lunch. *Were the two of them dating? Was it serious? When had they connected? How?* There were certainly lots of questions to be asked after she got off the bull.

"Come on, all of you. Get out of Carrie's hair so she can focus on what she needs to do on that bull." This came from the old cowhand.

"Come on, Becky, we can watch from over here," Drake suggested. And with that, Becky, Drake, and Joel moved around to the side of the ring where they would be out of the way but still be able to see.

Carrie looked over to the chute. Beans was sitting on the rails waiting to help her get set for her ride. She and Bull walked the few short feet to the shoot. Blue Bayou, the same bull she had ridden the first time, was in the chute.

"Come on up, Carrie. We're all set. Dusty and Rutter are in the ring and ready if you have any trouble. Once you let us know you're ready, we'll open the gate. You won't know what this old bull will do, but be ready for anything. That means staying loose and moving with this beast. You did great your first ride until you got clipped, so there's no reason to think you won't do great again. If you feel yourself slipping off, just let go and jump away, if you can. Ready?"

Carrie nodded and turned to climb up into the chute. Bull grabbed her by the arm and turned her to face him. He double-checked her helmet and made sure it was secure.

"You're gonna do fine. I wouldn't let you get back up on that dang old beast if I didn't think you could ride him. Got that?"

Carrie smiled. Of all of the comments that had been slung her way in the last ten minutes, Bull's meant the most. It also gave her the courage to get back on the bull's back. She climbed up and cautiously straddled the bull. She slowly and carefully let herself down onto his back, and he didn't so much as stir. Beans helped her get the bull rope wrapped around her fist.

"Ready?" he called to her as he got on the outside of the chute.

"Yes!" Carrie called back.

Carrie took a deep breath and waited for the chute gate to swing open. The gate flew open, and the bull didn't move. Carrie looked down at the bull, who didn't seem the least bit concerned about getting out of the chute. Beans climbed over the railing once again and used his boot to prod the beast out of the gate. The bull moved enough to get away from Beans and then just stopped.

Dusty came over to the bull and called out to Carrie, "You good?"

"Yeah. Not quite as exciting as last time."

"You keep hanging on. I'm gonna see if I can get him to move a little."

Dusty moved around the bull and prodded it, trying to get it to move, but nothing the hand did seemed to bother the bull enough to make it move.

"You still good up there?"

"Still holding on, although I'm not sure why." She laughed. "I feel like I could go no-handed on this ride."

Dusty quickly yelled, "Don't even think about it. All it would take is for this dang bull to feel like it had the upper hand and you'd be eating dirt again."

"I was only kidding. I still remember how much it hurt last time when I hit the ground."

Dusty walked to the back of the bull and twisted its tail. It arched its back and took a few steps away from the bothersome hand. Dusty tried it again. This time, the bull moved—but only enough to turn its body away from him.

"Carrie, it looks like this dang old bull is not going to give you any kind of ride today. Sorry."

"It's not your fault, Dusty. Should I just jump off?"

"Yeah, I'm ready. Make sure to try to push off of the bull so you don't come down near its hooves."

"Got it."

Carrie loosened her hand from the bull rope and jumped off of the beast. She tried to push herself so far away from the bull that she was off-balance when her feet hit the ground. She immediately fell to her backside. She looked up to see where the stupid bull was. He hadn't moved a muscle. She could have just slid off of its back and not even gotten dirty.

Dusty had a grip on the bull and called out to her, "You good?"

"Yep, all good."

Carrie stood up and began dusting off her jeans. She looked up to see Joel, Becky, and Drake on the side rail. She turned toward them.

"Don't know what all of the fuss is about. That ride was tamer than the silly mechanical bull you rode at the bar," Becky said as soon as Carrie was within earshot.

"You gonna try the next ride?" Carrie called back.

The two women looked at each other and started to laugh. Joel looked to Carrie and felt his heart drop to his feet. She really was beautiful when she smiled—but especially when she laughed. He looked over and noticed Drake's attention was completely focused on Becky. Drake was clearly just as enamored with Carrie's best friend as Joel was with

Carrie herself. *Probably not what the producer thought would happen when he went to Carrie's hometown to get more background for the show,* Joel thought.

Joel's attention went back to Carrie, who had started to climb up the rails to get out of the ring. As soon as she cleared the top rail, Joel reached up for her to help her down.

"Well, no concussion this time," she said to him.

"Thank the good Lord for that," he replied.

"Clearly, that bull is not going to give you a ride today," Bull said as he approached Carrie. "We can try again tomorrow. I don't think any amount of prodding will get him to do anything today."

"Tomorrow is soon enough," Drake responded. "This gives us time to get cleaned up and go into town for a nice dinner and some dancing. "Joel, do you want to join us?"

"Anywhere Carrie goes, I'm going too."

"Thought so," Drake responded. "Carrie, why don't you get cleaned up, and when you're ready, the four of us can walk around in town for a while. As soon as folks get hungry, we'll eat and then head to the Duck Blind Saloon. The bar usually has a live band."

"Sounds like fun," Becky said.

Hmmm. Very interesting. I'm definitely going to have to grab Becky at some point during the night and get the scoop on whatever is going on between her and Drake, Carrie thought.

CHAPTER 23

A s soon as Carrie had showered and gotten dressed, she walked out of the bunkhouse to find Joel waiting for her.

"How are you doing, B?" he asked as soon as she stepped out of the bunkhouse.

"I'm good."

"Disappointed?"

She looked to the man standing in front of her and was surprised that he seemed to know what she had been thinking. Was it just a lucky guess, or did the man really know her that well? With a small smile and a shrug of her shoulders, she answered, "Yeah."

"Don't worry. We'll try again tomorrow, and if we can't get you a decent ride on that old bull, we'll find another. We have plenty to choose from."

"How about Go Easy?"

Joel's jaw dropped, and his eyes grew to the size of dinner plates. He immediately responded, "No. You can't possibly be serious about riding that bull. Carrie—"

"Joel, I was only kidding," she interrupted.

"That wasn't funny."

"Yes, it was," she replied as a chuckle escaped her lips.

Before Carrie knew what had happened, Joel had moved in and reached for the back of her head. He tangled his fingers into her hair and brought her lips up to his. He swallowed her laughter and deepened the kiss. As his lips took possession of hers, he brought her body closer to his. He held her there against his chest for a moment before he released both her lips and her body.

"I can't wait to go dancing tonight," he whispered.

"Don't get your hopes up. I can't dance."

"Can't or haven't ever tried," he quickly asked.

"Haven't ever tried."

"That's what I was hoping."

"You were hoping I had never danced before?"

"Yep. That way you can learn with me, and I don't have to worry about you taking the lead."

"Do *you* know how to dance?"

"Oh yeah, B, I know how to dance. I'm gonna take you in my arms and slowly move around the dance floor. I don't really care if anyone else thinks that's dancing, because as long as I have you in my arms, that's good enough for me." With that, he winked at her and took another step away from her. He reached out his hand and grasped hers.

"Let's go before someone comes looking for us."

The two of them walked back toward the house. As they neared the front porch, Becky stood up from one of the front porch chairs.

"Becky, I was so excited to see you, I didn't even ask how long you were staying. How long can you stay?" Carrie asked.

"I can only stay for a week. Hopefully, long enough for me to see you actually ride a bull."

"Yeah, today was kind of pitiful."

"Well, at least you didn't end up in bed with another concussion."

"Wait, that reminds me, where are *you* staying?" Carrie asked her friend.

"Here at the house."

Carrie turned to Joel with an eyebrow raised and asked, "So my best friend gets to stay here at the house?"

"You can move your things into the house anytime you want, darlin'. You know I would much prefer you in my house than down in the bunkhouse with the ranch hands."

"Did you know she was coming?"

"Yep. Drake called me a couple of days ago, and we talked about him bringing Becky back here to surprise you. I thought it was a great idea. I let Glenda know we were going to have a guest so she could get a room ready."

"Glenda knew and she didn't say anything?"

"You maybe haven't been around long enough, but there is no person on this ranch who can keep a secret better than Glenda."

"Guess I'll have to remember that."

Joel turned to Becky and asked, "Are you ready to go?"

"Yes. Drake said we should knock on the trailer door as soon as we were ready to go."

"Great. Let's collect Drake and be on our way."

♦ ♦ ♦

The foursome enjoyed a great meal at Hank's. Both Joel and Drake had said Becky needed to taste real Texas beef before she headed home. After dinner, they strolled around Main Street. Becky and Carrie looked at the different shops and occasionally did some window shopping. After a while, they headed to the Duck Blind Saloon. As soon as they found a table where all four of them could sit, Carrie and Becky excused themselves to head to the restroom.

"What's up with you and Drake?" Carrie asked as soon as the two women had some privacy in the bathroom.

"Crazy, isn't it?"

"Are you together?"

"I don't know what we are, but Drake sure gives me butterflies. When he asked if I wanted to come down here to Texas to see you, I jumped at the chance. You've been gone for so long, and I wanted to make sure you were doing okay. Oh, by the way, I called your mom while you were getting cleaned up after your 'ride' this morning."

"You called my mom? Why?"

"She asked me to let her know if you were really doing okay. She's been pretty worried since you called and told her about the concussion."

"I've talked with her since then and told her I was fine."

"Yeah, but she was worried you were sugar coating things so she didn't worry. I promised a fair and honest assessment, which is what I gave her."

"So, what did you tell her?"

"I said you were doing great. I also told her that everyone here on the ranch seems to be concerned with your well-being and that she needn't worry there wasn't anyone here taking care of you. I did *not* tell her anything about you and Mr. Roulston, however. You're welcome, by the way." Becky chuckled.

"Thanks."

"However, just because we're keeping your mom in the dark doesn't mean you can keep me in the dark. So . . . what exactly *is* going on between you and Joel."

"Those butterflies you mentioned?"

"Yeah?"

"They seem to have taken up residence in my stomach as well."

"Are you falling in love with him?"

"How could I possibly fall in love with a man who lives more than a thousand miles from where I live?"

"Lucky for you, we have planes and cars, and you no longer need to try and make that trip on horseback or in a covered wagon."

"I'm serious, Becky. I can't possibly fall in love with Joel. His life is here, and mine's in Minnesota."

"But, Carrie, your life could be here," Becky countered. "If you truly love him and he loves you, what's stopping you from living here in Texas."

"My family? You?" Carrie rebutted.

"You know your folks want you to be happy. I know they would miss you, but they would come to visit you as often as they could. Your mom would never want you to turn away from true love. You and I both know that."

"I don't know if it's true love or not, so this conversation is probably a moot point."

"Oh, I don't know about that. I've seen the way Joel looks at you. If that man isn't already in love, he is certainly well on his way."

"He's told me he loves me," Carrie quietly replied.

"He what?"

"He told me he loves me the other night before you got here."

"Why am I only hearing about this now?"

"Because while he said the words, I just can't believe what he's feeling is actual true love."

"Why don't we test it out?"

"How?"

"Your mom used to teach us all kinds of things about falling in love with a guy when we watched all of those sappy rom coms with her. Remember?"

Carrie laughed. "I had forgotten all about our Romance 101 classes after those movies. What was the first rule?"

"Is the man in question someone who would take care of you in your worst moments? How did your mom put it? Would he hold your hair back when you were puking your guts out?"

"That is so gross."

"Never mind that. Would he?"

Carrie thought about how attentive Joel had been after her concussion. She remembered how he had insisted on helping her to the bathroom and how he had carried her back to his room after they had been out riding. Could she see Joel holding her hair back while she tossed her cookies? Yeah, she definitely thought Joel would do that.

"Yes, he would hold my hair back while I got sick."

"Thought so. Okay, next question. Can you both sit in a room for hours at a time doing your own thing, or does he need you to entertain him?"

Carrie thought back to working in Joel's office. They had sat there, each working on their own thing for hours. The quiet was natural and easy.

"We can entertain ourselves."

"Interesting. Next question. Can you trust him?"

Carrie thought back to her conversation with Joel about Cassie when she had told him everything.

"I told him about Cassie."

"What did you tell him? I know you called me after you let her name slip, but did you tell him more?"

"I told him everything. I told him about mom's infection and Cassie's challenges. I told him about the experimental treatment and that the only reason I was doing the show was so we could pay for the treatment."

"So that is definitely a yes. There is no way you ever would have shared all of that if you didn't think you could trust him. Question number four, you have already answered. That was the one about getting butterflies. That was a resounding yes."

"Is he truthful?" Becky continued.

"I don't know. I can't say I have ever known him to lie to me, but I just don't know."

"So, we don't have a reason to doubt his honesty, it just hasn't ever come up. We'll leave that one for now."

"Is he kind?"

"Yes." Carrie thought of all of the times that Joel had done things for Glenda. She also thought about how he had reacted when she had told him about Cassie.

"Can he admit when he's wrong? Will he apologize when he's wrong?"

"Yeah. He's done that already."

"We already know he's gorgeous."

"Becky!"

"What? That man is a hunk, and you know it."

"*You're* not supposed to notice."

"Oh, I noticed. I'm not interested, but I noticed. Just so you know, I have my own hunk at the moment in Drake, so it doesn't matter that I noticed. Next question, do you know what his dreams are?"

"Yeah, he wants to get the ranch back to being profitable for him and Zach and Maria."

"Can you see yourself helping him make his dreams a reality?"

"Yeah. In fact, when I found out about the financial problems, I offered to do whatever he needed me to do to help."

"What did he say?"

"He told me the only thing he needed me to do was to be myself. He said all anyone on the ranch needed from me was for me to just be me."

"Carrie, honey, I'm pretty sure making a comment like that means he passes the test. That man is definitely in love with you. Now the only question is, do you love him back?"

"I have no idea."

"Well, it's a good thing that you don't have to answer that question tonight."

"Before we go back and join the guys, wanna take the test about Drake?"

"Nope," Becky answered definitely.

"What? Why not?" Carrie dared.

"Because I'm pretty sure my answers would echo yours."

"You think Drake is in love with you?"

"Not sure, and unlike Joel, he hasn't said anything. But he sure seems to have checked off a number of boxes on your mom's test. Oh, and before we go out there, I wanted to let you know that Drake knows all about Cassie."

"What? How?"

"It started when he and I had a conversation about you keeping secrets."

"Secrets?"

"Yeah. He told me that he knew you were scared to share something with him and Joel. He promised me that whatever you were afraid to share would not make it into the show. I was getting ready to share a little about Cassie to see if I could trust him with more when Cassie and your mom came up to our table at Burger Palace. Cassie came right over and hugged me. She turned to Drake and introduced herself. She told Drake that she had a sister named Carrie and that he couldn't meet her because she was working at a real ranch in Texas. She told him how Carrie had ridden a bull and fallen off. She said her sister had gotten a bump on her head, but she was okay. When she stopped to take a breath, Drake told her he knew you and that he had actually watched you ride the bull. Cassie was so excited she scooted her wheelchair even closer to the table and started to ask him all about your bull ride. Drake was patient and kind and answered all of her questions. He offered more information, which only made Cassie ask more questions. She sat with us while she ate her lunch. After about an hour, your mom said it was time to go home. Cassie was so disappointed. Drake asked if he could visit your parents and Cassie. He promised your mom there would be no cameras and that he was only going to share more about your experiences with them. Your mom agreed. After they walked away, Drake turned to me and said, 'So Cassie is her big secret, isn't she? Carrie is afraid we're going to exploit Cassie for ratings for the show, isn't she?'

"I told him that that was exactly what you were worried about. He assured me that he was not producing that kind of show. The next day, he kept his promise. He showed up to your parents' house without any camera crew and talked with them for three hours about your experiences so far. He also told them that if they ever wanted to visit Texas, he would love to show them around. Your mom and Drake actually started making plans for when Cassie needs to come to Texas for her treatment."

"Are you kidding?" Carrie exclaimed.

"No. I'm completely serious. Carrie, you should have seen him with Cassie. He was so kind and patient. I just couldn't believe someone like that would exploit her. I hope you're not mad. I know you asked me to keep him in the dark, but it happened so fast and so completely unexpectedly. I had no time to try to prevent them from meeting."

"I'm not mad. I know you would do anything to protect Cassie, so how could I be mad when fate stepped in and changed the plan."

The two friends hugged.

"We better get back out there before the guys wonder if we left 'em," Becky said.

As they approached the table, the men stood, and each took his lady's hand and led her to the dance floor.

"Don't you want to sit and have a drink first?" Carrie asked Joel.

"No. You were gone so long in the ladies' room, all I could think of doing when you came back was taking you in my arms and going for a spin on the dance floor."

With that, Joel held her hand in his and wrapped his other hand around her waist. He slowly started to sway and move them around the dance floor. When he wanted her to turn in a certain direction, he would softly whisper his directions while at the same time he would use his hands to teach her how to follow his lead. It didn't take long before he only needed to use his hands. As they moved, Joel started to sing along with the band. His soft voice singing in her ear made the butterflies in her stomach take flight. Maybe she was falling in love.

CHAPTER 24

The next morning, Carrie once again found herself listening to the ranch hands as they got ready for the day. She thought back to her experience of waking up in Joel's bed, and for a moment, she wished that she were staying up at the house with Becky. *Oh well.* She shrugged her shoulders and waited for the guys to finish up so that she could get ready. Bull had told her that she could try to ride Blue Bayou again first thing this morning. She hoped this ride went better than the last two.

After she finished her morning routine, Carrie walked out of the bunkhouse and over to the bull ring. She found everyone there, ready and waiting for her. The camera crews were set up and filming already. It looked like Blue Bayou was in the holding stall. There was a second bull in the adjacent pen. She assumed this one was the next in line if Blue Bayou didn't at least give her some semblance of a ride.

"Hey, Bull. Looks like everyone is all set for me."

"Mornin'. You ready to try this again?"

"Yep."

At that moment, Becky, Joel, and Drake all joined her and Bull near the chute.

"Are you sure you're ready for this?" asked Becky.

"I think so."

"Listen to Bull and the other hands. You'll do just fine if you follow their instructions. And remember, you were really doing great on your first ride—well, up until when you landed on your head," Joel said.

"Carrie, please be careful," Drake inserted. "We'll just be over here. Good luck."

Carrie nodded and headed to the shoot.

"Ready?" Dusty said as she climbed up the rails of the chute.

"Yep, I think so."

"Just remember—you can do this. You did really well your first ride. Stay loose and relaxed and pay attention to this beast's movements."

Carrie listened to the last of the instructions thrown at her as she was getting situated on the back of Blue Bayou.

"Okay, Blue, you and I need to come to an understanding. You need to let me at least get a feel for what it's like to ride a rodeo-circuit bull, but please be nice. I can't get another concussion. If you promise to let me have a good ride, I promise to slip you some extra feed this afternoon. Do we have a deal?"

The bull snorted. Carrie felt the movement as she sat atop the beast. Its back arched, and its head dipped low. She dropped back down as the bull released the breath of air in a great rush.

"I'll take that as a yes," she whispered and patted the great beast on its shoulder.

"Carrie, are you ready?"

"Yes."

With her answer barely out of her mouth, the gate swung open, and Blue Bayou turned out into the ring. The beast swung around to the left and Carrie let her body adjust to the movement. After the turn to the left, it dropped its head and kicked out its back legs. Carrie held on and pushed against the bull to make sure she didn't fly over the head of the animal. As soon as its legs landed on the ground, the bull swung around to the right and kicked out its front hooves. Carrie tried to hang on, but she had shifted too much and was no longer centered. She felt herself falling. She tried to push away from the bull but didn't get too far. She once again landed in the dirt, but this time, she managed to land on her backside and not her head. The bull felt her weight leave its back and immediately stopped moving. It turned its head and looked at Carrie as she tried to take stock of whether she had been injured with the fall. Carrie watched as the bull looked directly at her and snorted again.

She started to chuckle. "I guess I should say 'thank you'."

"Thank you? To whom?" came Joel's voice near her ear.

Carrie had been so focused on the bull that she hadn't even noticed Joel had entered the ring and had rushed to her side. He was crouching down next to her.

"Thank you to that crazy bull. I asked him to give me a good ride— one without a concussion. I think that was his way of letting me know we had struck a bargain and he expected me to keep my promise."

"Just out of curiosity, what did you promise him?" Joel asked with a smile twitching his lips.

"An extra helping of feed this afternoon."

Joel threw his head back and let out a roar of laughter. "Well, I guess that old piece of raw hide is going to get an extra helping."

Carrie smiled and replied, "Yep, I intend to make sure he definitely gets some extra food this afternoon."

Joel stood up and held his hand out to Carrie. She took his hand, and he helped her up off the dirt. They both turned to watch Dusty shoo the bull out of the ring and back to the gates that led to its pen. They turned and headed over to where Becky and Drake were watching. As they approached, Becky called out, "You were awesome! I can't believe you actually rode a bull. An actual bull! Oh my gosh, that was so cool!"

"You were great, Carrie! It was pretty exciting watching you actually ride that thing. I'll also admit I was extremely relieved no one needed to carry you out of the ring this time." Drake said.

"No kidding," replied the man standing next to her.

"Yeah, I'm pretty relieved myself."

At that moment, Bull approached the group.

"Well, Bull, what do you think?"

"You did pretty good. I'm glad you didn't end up landing on your head this time," the old cowhand replied.

"You and me, both."

Joel watched as she smiled at the old cowhand. Not only did her entire face light up, she lit up the area surrounding them. Once more, his breath was stolen from his lungs as he saw the joy radiate out of her. She was so remarkable. He couldn't believe his good fortune that she had come to his ranch.

"So, if you're up for another ride, we could put the next bull in the chute, and you could try to ride that one."

Carrie nodded her head.

"I think I'd like to try again."

Bull called over his shoulder, "Load up the next bull—she's gonna ride again."

The ride on the second bull went just as well as the first. Carrie managed to hang on as the bull kicked out its feet and twisted around. She was starting to pay more attention to the bull's movements to anticipate how the animal was going to move next. She even managed to stay on her feet when she jumped off. After she climbed out of the ring, Bull approached and said, "I think that is more than enough bull riding for today."

Carrie smiled once again at the gruff man and said, "I agree."

She turned to Joel and looked up at him with a look of hope and longing. She said, "But maybe we could go riding on the horses this afternoon after lunch? I would love to take Becky out on a ride."

Joel knew in that moment that he would do almost anything she asked.

"Only if I can go with you," he replied.

Carrie turned to Becky and asked, "What do you think? Want to go for a horseback ride this afternoon?"

"Sounds wonderful."

"I can't wait," Drake said.

"You're going to come along, Drake?" Carrie asked.

"Oh yeah. I wouldn't miss this for the world."

CHAPTER 25

The next few days were filled with a tremendous amount of happiness for Carrie. She spent each morning riding a bull. Sometimes, she was able to actually ride it, and other times, she was thrown off its back as soon as the animal cleared the gate. She was bruised and sore from hitting the ground, but it was still better than getting a concussion. The ranch hands praised her for her ability to catch on so quickly and kept telling her that most new riders didn't ever stay on the back of a bull as long as she did. Carrie figured that they were being overly generous, but she soaked up the compliments, nonetheless.

In the afternoon, she and Becky would go out riding. Drake and Joel joined them on most rides, but if they had work to do, Maria would ride with the friends. Carrie laughed as she thought of the morning after Becky's first ride. Carrie had come up to the house for breakfast and met Becky as she was coming down the stairs. Carrie had immediately noticed that Becky was walking very gingerly down the stairs and had asked, "Becky, what's wrong?"

"Wrong? I don't think anything's wrong so much as I'm just a little sore from our ride yesterday."

"Oh, yeah, sorry about that. Did I forget to mention that being in the saddle can wake up a few muscles you didn't even know you had?"

"Yes, you forgot to mention that. All you talked about was how incredible riding a horse was, how beautiful the view was from the top of a horse and how romantic it was for your man to help you down from a horse."

"Pretty sure I never said anything about a man helping me down from a horse. Maybe that's just your romantic heart making up scenes in your head."

At that moment, Joel had walked out of his office. He had come up behind Carrie and wrapped his arms around her waist before saying in her ear, "Don't you find it romantic when I help you down from Misty?"

The butterflies in Carrie's stomach had taken flight again.

"Yes, it's very romantic," she had squeaked.

"Thought so," he had responded right before he had placed a kiss on her neck under her ear.

The two women had shared a look with each other. Yep, Joel was definitely crossing off all of the items on Carrie's mom's list for determining whether a man was truly in love with a woman. They had both sighed and then started to giggle.

"Come on, let's get to breakfast. Glenda won't want her food getting cold."

♦ ♦ ♦

Carrie and Becky stood next to the SUV Becky had arrived in just seven short days ago.

"I can't believe you're leaving already."

"I know. I can't believe I've already been here for a week."

"It's been so fun having you here. I'm going to miss you so much after you go. It won't be the same without you here."

"I know, but you can call me, and we can catch up. I'll know more of what you're referring to now after having been here."

"Yeah, but talking on the phone won't be the same as you being here."

"You could always stay," came a voice behind Becky. She turned to see the producer standing behind her. "I certainly won't object to you staying longer, and I would bet Joel would tell you that you can stay as long as you like."

"I already told her that, but I can tell her again if it would help change her mind," Joel responded.

"I wish I could, but there are some things I need to do at home before school starts, and besides, I need to fill Carrie's family in on what's happening down here. They're dying for me to catch them up. Carrie's mom made me promise to come over to their house as soon as I landed so they could hear all about my trip."

"You could always stay, and we could call them," Carrie replied with a wink.

Both women chuckled and reached out to hug each other.

"I'm going to miss you."

"I'm going to miss you, too."

As they hugged, they both got teary-eyed. The two men watched as the women said their goodbyes. After a few moments, Drake said, "We should get going if we're going to get you to the airport."

"Okay. Bye, Carrie, I love you and I'll miss you."

"Love you, too!"

Becky turned her eyes to Joel, and with her finger shaking at him, she said, "And I expect you to take good care of my best friend."

"You can count on me. I'll gladly accept that job for as long as she'll let me."

Both women exchanged another knowing look and smiled.

Joel stood with his arms around Carrie as they watched her best friend and the producer climb into the vehicle. They continued to stand there as they watched the car drive out through the gate and turn onto the county road in front of the ranch.

"Are you going to be okay?" Joel asked Carrie.

She sniffed and said, "Yeah, but I'll miss her."

"I know you will. I loved seeing the two of you together this week. Everyone here could tell how close the two of you are, and we all know how hard it is for you to say goodbye."

Joel's hands gently turned her around in his embrace. He reached up, took hold of the back of her head, and slowly lowered his lips to hers. He gently coaxed a response from her. He wanted to keep kissing her all day, but he knew she was still uncomfortable with public displays of affection. After a few minutes of kissing her, he drew back and looked into her eyes. He could look into her eyes for days, he thought. Heck, he hoped he was still looking into those eyes decades from now.

CHAPTER 26

It had been a couple of weeks since Becky had been on the ranch. A.Z. had arrived back on the ranch a couple of days after Becky had left. Carrie was sorry that they couldn't have met each other. She thought the two women would have hit it off and become friends. A.Z. had gone back to help with her family's ranch but was now back at the Double Spur and working on the show. There was some kind of trouble going on at A.Z.'s family's ranch, and Carrie could tell that A.Z. was starting to worry.

"So, do you want to talk about what's going on at your family's operation?" Carrie asked one night after they had finished taping a segment for the day.

A.Z. looked at Carrie and said, "I don't know. That's the problem."

"What do you mean?"

"Something's going on—I can feel it. But I can't figure out what it is."

"What do you mean?" Carrie asked again.

"There have been a lot of *accidents* happening at our ranch. You've been around here long enough to know that accidents happen. It's to be expected. But we've had more than our fair share."

"Like what?"

"Remember when I left before your first bull ride?"

Carrie nodded. "Yeah . . ."

"A gate had been left open on one of the pastures. No one noticed it until we couldn't account for all our head of cattle. That's when my dad and our ranch foreman rode around the fence and noticed the gate open. I left to try and help find our missing cattle."

"Did you find them all?"

"Yes, eventually. They had found most of them before I arrived, and my sister and I found a couple more of the stray cows. When we heard about you getting thrown from that bull, my family insisted I return to the Double Spur and make sure you were all right."

"But they don't even know me," Carrie said.

"They had heard a lot about you when I called home and even more while I was there. They all thought it was more important for me to come back here and check on you than it was for me to help find the last few head of missing cattle. I agreed."

"You said they did find them all, right?"

"Yes, the day after I returned, my sister and a couple of our ranch hands found them on the other side of our property taking shelter in the woods."

"I understand the concern over missing even one cow, but why does it seem like you're concerned about more than one open gate?"

"Because it's been more than just the gate. One day, my dad noticed the hay in the maternity pen was moldy. None of our hands would have spread moldy hay in a stall."

"How did it get there?"

"We have no idea. My dad suffers from asthma, and we don't ever keep any moldy hay. It's not good for the cows, but it would be really bad for my dad."

"Is it possible one of your hands put it there without realizing it was moldy?"

"I suppose that's possible, but I just don't believe it. These men are devoted and professional. I can't see one of them being so careless that he would make that kind of mistake. Then there was the incident with the snake we found in one of the horse's stalls. Horses have a deep fear of snakes. My dad and one of the ranch hands heard a terrible commotion in the horse barn. When they went to check it out, they found a rubber snake in the stall with the mare I usually ride. She was terrified and rearing up on her hind legs to avoid the stupid thing. If Dad and Stick hadn't gotten there so quick, she could have really done some damage to herself."

"If horses are afraid of snakes, why was there even one in the barn?"

"That is a question I would love answered myself. I can say with absolute certainty none of our men would have brought one onto the ranch, let alone left it in one of the horse's stalls."

"Has there been anyone else at the ranch?"

"No. That's why we can't figure out what's going on."

"I'm sorry. It does sound like your family has had more than its share of accidents. I understand why you're worried. I would completely understand if you needed to get back home to try to figure out what's happening."

A.Z. looked at Carrie and thought, *I never expected to meet such a wonderful woman when I came here to the Double Spur. I never expected to meet a friend.*

"No. My family has talked about it, and we agree it's important for me to finish the show. Everyone is on their guard watching and waiting for the next incident."

After a moment, A.Z. and Carrie heard Drake call them over to talk about tomorrow's filming. Both women stood and headed to the producer.

As they were walking over toward Drake, A.Z. asked, "So, Carrie, has anyone told you about what you're doing this Saturday?"

"No. What's happening on Saturday?"

"Everyone, including you, is heading over to Brockton for the Brockton County Fair."

"Really?" Carrie said. "I haven't heard anything about it."

"Everyone was hoping to surprise you with the trip."

"Why are we going to the Fair?"

"You need to experience your first rodeo, and Brockton does a pretty good one."

"Really? I'm going to a rodeo?"

"Yep. Excited?"

"I can't wait."

◆ ◆ ◆

Waiting the three days for the rodeo seemed like an eternity. Carrie couldn't believe how excited she was. She had learned from Beans that he and some of the other hands had been entered into the bull-riding event. Carrie was so excited to see someone ride a bull. Maybe she would learn something by watching them.

When Saturday morning arrived, Carrie woke at 4:30. She was so excited that she couldn't sleep a wink more. She quietly climbed down from the bunk bed and walked into the bathroom. She showered and got dressed, trying to be as quiet as possible. She heard some of the men starting to move about the bedroom and realized that she needed to let them into the bathroom so they could shower and get ready for the big day. Carrie walked out of the ranch hands' quarters and headed over to the house. She walked in the back door, hoping to make a cup of coffee that she planned to enjoy on the front porch. As she took a step into the kitchen, she realized that someone was already filling the coffee maker with grounds. She stood for a moment just watching Joel doing the small task. *I swear I could stand here all day just watching the man.* She shook her head and cleared her throat so as not to startle him.

Joel spun around and said, "Good morning! You're up early."

"I couldn't sleep," she answered.

"Excited for today?"

"Yes, is that childish?" she wondered.

"No. Everyone's excited on rodeo days."

Joel slowly walked over to her, smiled, and bent down to give her a kiss. A short while later, he stood up and said, "That, I think, is now my most favorite way to start the day. A kiss with a beautiful woman definitely trumps anything I've experienced to date."

Carrie chuckled and shook her head.

"What?"

"You and your comments about my appearance. I think you may need glasses."

"Nope, my eyesight is better than 20/20, and I know true beauty when I see it. Given your doubt of my assessment, I may have to start mentioning your beauty at least a good twenty times a day. At this stage in your life, I reckon you should have heard how beautiful you are about a hundred thousand times. I get the distinct impression you are way behind in that count."

She laughed some more and strode past him to the coffee pot. After she filled her mug, she asked him, "Would you like to join me on the front porch?"

This was the first time she had invited him to spend time with her, he realized. He wouldn't have cared if the house was burning down around their ears. He accepted her invitation immediately. As they walked out onto the front porch, she asked, "What can you tell me about the rodeo?"

"Well, this one is a part of the county fair. In addition to the rodeo events, there are 4-H demonstrations and projects as well as open-class competitions in things ranging from sewing to canning to baking to woodworking and such. There are many church-sponsored food booths and, of course, the petting zoo."

"Petting zoo?"

"Yes, a couple of the local farms loan out some animals for the kids to hold and pet."

"What kind of animals?"

"Usually, they have chicks and bunnies. They try to get cute and cuddly animals that don't tend to bite. Of course, there is usually a litter of puppies some ranch is hoping to unload on some unsuspecting family."

Joel looked over at her and noticed her eyes had taken on the special glow she got when she was particularly excited about something.

"You know, there's no age limit to holding the animals."

Her smile got even wider, and she said, "Cool," in almost a whisper.

◆ ◆ ◆

A few hours later, Carrie found herself wandering the grounds of the Brockton County Fair with her hand safely tucked away in Joel's. He had taken her hand as soon as she had climbed down from his truck and had not let go of it yet.

"Oh, you have to try some of Miss Martha's blueberry muffins," he said as he towed her along to one of the food booths lining the walking path. They approached the booth, and Joel called out, "We'll take two of your freshest muffins."

"Joel Roulston, you know all my muffins are fresh!"

"Of course, Miss Martha!" he dutifully responded. "How're you doing?"

"I'm well. And how 'bout you?"

"I'm great. I'd like you to meet a friend of mine. Miss Martha, this is Carrie Nelson. Carrie, this is Miss Martha—the best baker this side of the Mississippi."

The two women nodded to each other.

"How did you meet?"

"Carrie is filming a reality show on the Double Spur."

"A reality show, really? What kind of show is it?"

Carrie answered, "They're teaching me how to be a bull rider and ranch hand."

"Why ever would you want to learn how to ride one of those nasty creatures?"

Carrie stopped with her mouth open and her eyes wide.

"Carrie?" Joel asked. "Is everything okay?" She started to laugh. She laughed until tears were streaming down her cheeks. "Carrie?" Joel asked again.

When she was finally able to respond, she merely said, "No one has ever asked me *why* the show would want to teach anyone how to ride a bull. I don't have the foggiest idea why they would want to create a show specifically about becoming a bull rider."

Miss Martha just shook her head and moved onto the next customer. Joel handed Carrie one of the muffins. It was warm, and she couldn't wait to pop a bite into her mouth. A second after the morsel hit her tongue, Carrie moaned.

"Don't tell Glenda, but I think this is probably one of the best things I have ever put in my mouth."

"My lips are sealed, although if you kissed me, that would ensure that they stayed sealed."

With that promise of silence, Joel started walking them over to the rodeo ring.

Carrie climbed the bleacher seats until she could sit down next to Maria and Zach.

"Where have you two been?" Zach asked.

"I wanted to show Carrie at least some of the county fair before we were engrossed in the competition. Not to mention we had to get one of Miss Martha's muffins."

"Oh, man, did you bring muffins to share with the rest of us?" Maria asked hopefully.

Carrie chuckled. "Unfortunately, no, but those muffins are heavenly."

"Oh, yeah," Maria replied.

Carrie watched as the Belle of the Rodeo women came out on horseback carrying the United States flag, the State of Texas flag, the Brockton County flag, and the Professional Rodeo Cowboys Association flag. They rode with the flags waving as the riders circled the ring and then rode to the center of the ring. The horses were positioned as a cross, with the head of each horse facing out to the crowd. The announcer asked everyone to stand and remove their hats. As everyone sang the national anthem, the horses slowly spun so each flag was visible to everyone in the arena. After singing the national anthem, the flags were ceremoniously displayed again to the entire arena as each rider made her final circuit around the ring before heading out the gate.

Carrie was enthralled. The pageantry of the horses being ridden by the Belle of the Rodeo riders was awe-inspiring. Next came barrel racing. Carrie found herself cheering on each rider as they attempted to get the lowest time. After the barrel racing event came calf roping. It was fascinating watching the contestants race out to lasso the calf and tie its legs. Carrie had never seen anything like it before. She turned to Joel after the first pair had gone and immediately asked, "Do the calves get hurt when they flip them on their sides and tie their hooves together like that?"

"No. They're fine."

Carrie nodded and turned back to the arena to watch the other pairs. Eventually, it came time for the bull riding. They knew the line-up of riders, and Beans was the first to compete. Carrie was excited to see someone ride a bull. She had never actually watched someone get on the back of a bull. She only knew of the experience from sitting on top of the bull. She was so excited to cheer Beans on. She hoped he could last the full eight seconds. Carrie was fascinated as Beans climbed onto the large beast in the chute and tried to secure his rope. This bull refused to stay still in the chute. He started to rise up on his hind legs as if he was going to jump out of the enclosure. Carrie's breath caught in her throat as she worried about Beans falling off and getting trampled by the large, dangerous-looking animal while still in the chute. There were a couple of hands around helping to contain the bull and to help Beans get ready. Carrie noticed the bull start to thrash against the side of the rails. She gasped. *Would Beans get his leg broken before the beast even left the chute?* she wondered. Finally, Beans was ready, and the gate flew open. The hulking black mass spun out of the shoot. It immediately lowered its shoulders and head. Carrie watched as Beans fought to stay on the back of the bull and not get thrown over the beast's head. She saw its powerful hind legs kick out. Next, the bull jumped and spun in the air. Carrie could tell Beans had lost his balance and was leaning too far to the right. She knew he was going to fall. She felt herself leaning her own body, trying to help Beans stay on the bull. At that moment, the bull kicked out its hind legs and Beans went flying over the head of the animal. Beans' body landed a couple of feet in front of the bull. Carrie then watched as the menacing creature lowered its head and pawed the ground. She saw its great horns and was terrified Beans would be trampled or gored by one of the long horns on its great big head. Right before the bull rushed forward toward Beans, she saw a man dressed up as a clown wave a big red handkerchief near the bull's face. He started yelling as he waved the cloth. The bull was distracted and turned to the new annoyance in the ring. The clown started to run toward the rails along the side of the arena as the bull once again lowered its head and pawed at the ground. The clown had not quite reached the top rail before the horn of the massive beast caught the man in the back of the thigh. Carrie remembered how much it had hurt when the bull had caught her and sliced her back open. She could just imagine how much pain the clown was in. Another clown had gotten into the ring and was trying to distract the bull from the first injured clown. Thank goodness, the second clown was not only able to distract the bull but also to wave it to the gate where the bull would leave the arena. Once the bull had left the arena, Carrie looked for Beans to see if he was okay. She noticed that he had gotten up off the dusty arena floor. He held up his hands and waved to the crowd. There was a great big cheer from the crowd, and the relief the crowd experienced at discovering Beans was okay was palpable. The breath that had been caught in Carrie's lungs whooshed out, and all the color drained from her face. Joel looked over at her and grabbed ahold of her arms. She looked like she was going to pass out. His full attention was on her.

"Carrie? . . . Carrie? What's wrong, honey?"

Carrie heard Joel's question as if it had come from another planet, but the sheer stupidity of the question was enough to bring her back to the present.

"What's wrong? 'What's wrong?' he says. Are you insane? Beans almost got mauled by that raging beast! He could have died! Furthermore, who was that crazy fool who tried to get the bull's attention, only to end up with the horn tearing into the back of his leg? What was he thinking?! Someone needs to tell him that he could have died. Doesn't he know how dangerous those things are?"

Joel reached out, caught her hands in his own, looked in her eyes, and said, "Carrie, honey, have you ever watched a bull-riding event before?"

"No! Why?"

With that answer, Joel's breath left his lungs. She had agreed to do this reality show to become a bull rider all for the benefit of her sister. She had no idea of the danger she had put herself in, the risk she had taken for her sister.

"Okay, let's see if I can answer some of your questions. First of all, Beans is fine. You can tell by how he waved to the crowd. He may feel some bruises tomorrow, but that's always to be expected when you get on top of one of the bulls. Do I really need to remind *you* of that? And yes, sometimes the riders do get hurt when they get on one of those things, but *usually,* it isn't too serious. Secondly, the crazy guy in the clown outfit was doing his job."

"What?"

"The rodeo has professional handlers who are ready to jump into the ring to make sure the bull gets distracted before it can do any harm to the rider. These professionals get dressed up as clowns and do some pretty ridiculous things to get the bull's attention and to make the crowd laugh. They are the first in the ring after a ride. They know what they're doing, and their first priority is always the safety of the rider."

"He knew he could get hurt, and he still went into the ring?"

"Yeah, sweetheart, he knew. It's his job." He continued, "You probably didn't realize my own hands took on that role for you when you rode Blue Bayou. Dusty and Beans were there to jump into the ring immediately after you left the back of that animal to make sure it didn't come back and injure you."

"They did that for me?"

"Yeah, sweetheart, they did."

"But why? They could have been hurt or killed."

"They knew the risks, and they voluntarily accepted those risks the minute you climbed onto the back of that animal."

"But why?"

"First, they did it because they're professionals and they know someone needs to be ready to distract the bull if necessary. Second, they did it because they care about you. You're a member of the Double Spur family, and they would jump in front of a dangerous bull without hesitation to make sure you wouldn't be hurt."

Carrie searched his eyes and saw the truth shining out from them. He meant every word. She took a deep breath and released it. As she took another breath, her eyes dropped to her hands in her lap. Her heart started to slow down, and her anxiety started to recede.

"Carrie, honey," he said, "are you going to be able to get back onto a bull, knowing what could happen?"

She looked up into his eyes once again. There was no judgment. He was concerned about her and was asking how she felt about continuing with the show.

"I don't know, Joel. I just don't know," she said as she shrugged her shoulders.

"Let's watch a few more riders. Beans's ride is not the typical ride. Maybe after watching a few more bull riders, you'll feel better about getting back on a bull."

Carrie just nodded her head and turned to watch the next rider.

While it had been scary for the first couple of riders after Beans, Carrie realized that Joel had been right. Most of the riders didn't get thrown like Beans, and the bulls seemed very disinterested in the riders once they were off the animal's back. Many just stopped bucking and then seemed to look for the gate to get out. Sometimes, once they spotted the gate, the hulking animal almost galloped to the exit.

After watching the rest of the bull riders, Carrie had a better perspective about the rodeo and the bull-riding profession. It was a dangerous business. She couldn't believe she had been so naïve about becoming a bull rider. Even after she had gotten her concussion, she hadn't realized how dangerous this really was. She had a greater appreciation for all of the ranch hands at the Double Spur. She looked over at Joel and said, "Now I understand why you were so against a woman being on the show."

"I was just worried you would get hurt."

"I understand that now."

"Good. Let's finish watching the rodeo."

After watching the last event, Carrie turned to Joel and asked, "Can we go to the petting zoo?"

"On one condition."

"What's that?"

"You promise me you won't ask to bring one of those cute, cuddly animals home."

"I promise," she quickly responded. *Home.* It sure was feeling like home to her.

CHAPTER 27

That evening, Joel spoke to Drake and Bull about Carrie's scare while watching Beans. The three men talked about her fear and what they thought would be best for her.

"I think we should give her a couple of days before we let her get back on one of the bulls, even one like Blue Bayou," Joel said.

"If she's truly going to get on a bull in Las Vegas, she needs to ride one here as soon as possible. Waiting won't lessen the fear—in fact, it may cause it to become greater. Let her get back in the ring," Bull argued.

"I just don't know. I can't believe she had no idea of what she was getting herself into when she agreed to do this show. She really didn't know what the clown was there for?"

"Nope. She thought he was some crazy fool out doing a stunt or something."

As the three men stared out at Go Easy in the pasture, they each thought about what would be best for Carrie. Each man knew the others were also only looking out for her best interests. They were all concerned and knew they needed to get this decision right.

"I think you should ask Carrie what she thinks would be best for her," said a calm female voice behind them. All three men turned to find Carrie standing behind them with her arms crossed, tapping her foot in annoyance.

"Carrie—"

"B—"

"Carrie—" all three men responded quickly.

She immediately held up her hand to stop them.

"I know. You're all worried and want to do the best thing for me. But truly, the only person who can make that decision is me. You need to let me decide what that is."

Bull walked over to her, looked her square in the eye, and said, "I'll support whatever decision you make." She gave him a small smile. He nodded his head once and turned around to head toward the bunkhouse.

Drake approached her next and said, "So, do you have any idea what's best for you?"

"Yeah. I've been thinking a lot about it, and I think I want to try riding again tomorrow."

"Are you sure? I don't want you to feel any pressure from me or the show. If it means we have to change the ending because you can't get back on one of those beasts, I completely understand, and I'll figure out how to sell that ending."

"Thanks, Drake. I appreciate the support. I can't tell you how much that means to me, but I think I'll ride. Let's see how things go tomorrow before I make any promises about getting on a bull in Vegas."

"Deal. I'll see you tomorrow."

Carrie stood still and waited for Joel to come to her as the other two men had done. He slowly walked over to her and gently placed his hand on her cheek. He lifted her head and placed a sweet, gentle kiss on her forehead.

"I love you," he said.

"You're not going to try and talk me out of this?"

"Nope. I know you didn't make this decision lightly or easily. I absolutely support your decision. Just to make sure you heard and understood me, I will repeat—I love you."

With that declaration in her ears, Carrie felt Joel's lips once more take possession of her own.

I think I love you, too, she thought.

◆ ◆ ◆

The next afternoon, Carrie found herself climbing back up into the gate to get on top of a bull named Sunday Afternoon. The big black Angus bull was moving around in the chute. She wondered if she was even going to be able to get onto its back. She remembered how the bull at the rodeo yesterday had thrashed around with Beans on its back.

"He's agitated, but you should be able to get on," Dusty reassured her.

"Okay," she replied as she wondered how the animal was going to react to her getting on his back. She stretched her left leg over its broad back and gently sat down. The bull slammed into the right side of the shoot. Carrie found her leg pinched between the chute bars and the bulls heaving side. She screamed.

"Carrie?" Dusty called.

"Owww. It's my . . . my leg," she said through clenched teeth.

Dusty immediately put his boot through the bars and started to push on the great beast. In just a moment, the pressure on Carrie's leg lifted as the bull was moved away from the bars.

"Carrie? You okay?" he asked.

"Yeah, I think so," she replied.

"Think so, or you are? I'm not opening this gate to let you out if you're not okay."

"I . . . I'm not sure."

"Okay. Tell you what—let's get you off this ugly bull and check to see how your leg is. If you're okay, we'll just try again. Sound good?"

Carrie nodded. Dusty reached out and took her arm. He pulled her off of the bull and up into the air. She was shocked at how he had been able to lift her off of the bull with one hand. She knew Dusty had to be strong with how he was able to throw the hay bales around and how he lifted and moved other things around the ranch, but she knew how much she weighed and was surprised that he had managed to get her off of the bull while balancing on the top of the chute bars. She grabbed the top bar and hooked her left foot onto the second rung. As she swung her right leg over the bar to climb down the outside of the chute, she heard Joel call out to her.

"B, let me help you down. Don't put any weight on that right leg. We need to get you down without you putting any weight on that leg. Let me help take your weight. We'll check your leg once you're back down on the ground. Understand?"

"How am I supposed to get down without putting weight on my leg?"

Joel climbed up onto the rails. With Dusty still hanging onto her arm, Joel grabbed her around the waist and steadied her.

"Swing your left leg over the bar. We've got you."

She did as instructed and found that Joel and Dusty held all of her weight in their hands. She felt them start to lower her, and then she felt a third set of hands grab her under her knees and around her back. She looked up to see Bull's face.

"I've got her," Bull called to the other men who released her into Bull's arms. He gently set her down on the ground and immediately started checking out her leg.

"Does it hurt anywhere?" he asked.

"Yeah, on the side of my thigh—although the pain has lessened in the time it took for me to get out of the chute."

Once the men were sure that it was only the side of her thigh, they agreed to let her try to stand up on it and see if she could hold her weight on it.

Before they could issue any more instructions, Carrie held up her hands.

"I think I'm okay—the pain is almost gone. Let me see if I can stand on it."

She held her breath as she gently leaned on her right leg. She didn't feel any pain, so she continued to put more weight on it. She let the air leave her lungs as she realized she could put all of her weight on the leg in question. She looked up at Joel.

"I'm okay."

"You sure? I don't want you to try and get back on that bull if your leg's injured."

"I think it's just bruised."

"Keep in mind that if it feels bruised now, it will be even more so tomorrow," Dusty added.

"Gee, thanks."

"Just telling it like it is."

"Okay, I'm ready to try this again."

Dusty nodded and climbed back up onto the chute. Carrie could feel Joel's eyes on her as she turned to climb back up the gate rails.

She looked over her shoulder and quietly told him, "I'm okay, Joel."

He nodded his acknowledgment and continued to watch her as she got ready for her ride.

She was able to mount Sunday Afternoon and get the rope around her hand. She nodded her head, and the gate swung open. The bull immediately turned and jumped out of the chute. Carrie felt its muscle bunch right before it leapt in the air and kicked out both pairs of legs. As soon as the beast landed, it spun around and kicked out its back legs. Carrie felt its muscles contract again and knew the dang bull was going to jump up in the air again. As she tried to prepare for the bull's next movement, she gripped the rope tighter in her hand. Instead of jumping as she had anticipated, Sunday Afternoon swung around to the right, stopped, and swung around again. The spinning caused Carrie to lose her balance. She knew that she was once again going to fall off of one of these beasts. Suddenly, the bull dropped its head and kicked its back legs out. Carrie went flying over the horns of the stupid beast. She felt the jarring contact with the ground. She looked up to see where the bull was and found herself staring the beast in the eyes. The bull dropped its head and pawed the ground. Before she could even think to get out of the way, she saw Beans get between her and the bull. He waved his arms and yelled at it. The beast quickly lost interest in Carrie. Beans quickly moved so the bull was no longer facing Carrie. The ranch hand continued to wave his arms and yell out at the bull. The bull lowered its head again and this time charged the man. Beans had not been all that far from the rails surrounding the ring. He jumped up onto the rungs and was out of the way of the bull's horns in seconds. Carrie noticed that Dusty had also jumped into the ring and was yelling at the beast. Dusty was near the exit gate, and once the bull noticed the gate, he lowered his head once more, snorted, and then calmly trotted out the exit.

As soon as the bull had left the ring, Carrie started assessing the damage her body had sustained. As she was gingerly moving her arms, she heard Joel quietly say into her right ear, "Are you alright?"

Before she could answer him, she heard another voice call from her left side, "Carrie, you okay?" It was Beans.

"Am *I* okay?" she said. "What about you? You're the one who got thrown off of the crazy bull yesterday and were almost mauled. Are *you* okay?"

"Sure. That bull yesterday didn't get me, and Sunday Afternoon is way too slow to have caught me today." He said with a smile and a wink.

Carrie shook her head, and under her breath, she said, "I can't believe you do this for a living."

Even though she had said the comment under her breath, both men started to laugh.

"We can't believe you're doing this for TV!" Beans managed to get out between the laughter.

"Touché," she replied.

Both men snickered once more and asked her again if she was alright. Once she nodded her head, they both reached down, took ahold of an arm, and lifted her off the ground. She started to brush the dust off of her jeans when she looked at Beans once more.

"I'm so glad you weren't hurt yesterday."

"Me, too, Sleeping Beauty, me too."

CHAPTER 28

Carrie stepped outside after dinner. It was almost impossible to believe she had been staying at the Double Spur for nearly three months. As she looked around the ranch compound, she tried to remember what it was like on that first day she had arrived. Everything felt so familiar now. Each building now held memories of her time here on the ranch. She remembered learning about riding and taking care of horses in the equine barn. She remembered arriving at the maternity barn with the new calf, Early. As much as she had tried to come up with a different name, Early had just seemed to stick. Her eyes took in the bull-riding ring, and she thought about her first ride, which just made her think about Joel.

"Hey, there, B, whatcha doin'?" said the man she was just thinking about.

"Just remembering what it felt like on the first day I arrived," she said.

Joel reached out and cupped her face. "Oh, please, don't think about that day. I've tried everything I can think of to get you to forget my terrible behavior that day."

"It's okay, Joel. I've forgiven you for that comment, although I retain the right to remind you of it if you ever say anything stupid again." She smiled up at the handsome rancher.

"I'll make you a deal—you can remind me of it every time you want to share with our kids how we met."

"Our kids?" she squeaked.

Joel took her hands into his, brought them up to his lips, and gently placed a kiss on the back of each hand.

"I realize we haven't talked about what happens after the show is done, but I've not kept my feelings for you a secret. I love you, and now, whenever I think about my future, it always includes you. I refuse to even think about a future without you in it. What about you, sweetheart? Do you think of me when you think of the future?"

"I'll be honest, I've stopped myself from thinking of the future."

"Why?" He frowned.

"Because that meant thinking of a life where I wasn't here—and one that didn't include you. That just made my heart hurt, so I decided to not think about it at all and just enjoy every day, every minute, I have here on the ranch."

Joel released one of her hands and captured the back of her head.

Softly, he said, "I think you should start thinking of the future—and that future means here on this ranch . . . with me."

His lips captured hers in a gentle kiss. Carrie immediately felt the butterflies take flight. Joel opened his lips and deepened the kiss. Carrie felt his tongue cautiously caress her own. She let her tongue start to dance with his. As she began to move her tongue against his, she felt him open his lips even more. Soon, she was drowning in sensation. She forgot to breathe. The rest of the ranch—the rest of the world—ceased to exist. It seemed like hours and also like mere seconds when Joel released her lips. He looked deep into her eyes and said, "I want you to start thinking of the future. *Our future.*"

Carrie nodded. She could not get her tongue to form any kind of verbal response. She was beginning to realize that Joel's kisses were making her mute.

At that moment, Drake walked over to the couple and called up to Carrie.

"Hey there, Carrie, I just wanted to touch base about the remainder of the week."

"Shoot," she replied.

"*Shoot?* When did you start to talk like the ranch hands?" He said, chuckling.

"I think they've rubbed off on me. Must be all the time I spend around them."

"We only have a few more days. I think we've got just about all of the film we need to put together for the show. We'll film your last few days, but I can't think of anything else that the show is missing."

"Sounds good."

◆ ◆ ◆

Carrie's last few days at the Double Spur seemed to fly by. There just wasn't enough time to spend with Joel. She was realizing how much she was going to miss Maria and Glenda, and as she interacted with each ranch hand, she knew leaving them was going to leave a hole in her heart. Each and every one of these people felt like family to her.

"We're really gonna miss you around here," Dusty said as he wrapped Carrie up in a hug. It was her final day. She was leaving this afternoon to catch her flight back home.

As soon as Dusty let go, Carrie felt another set of hands spin her around, "Sleeping Beauty, what are we gonna do without 'cha? No one to be quiet for in the morning 'cuz she's still sleeping."

"I'm gonna miss you, too, Beans. You make sure to take it easy on those bulls." She winked and he laughed.

"I thought you were gonna talk to those bulls and tell 'em to be nice to me," he responded.

"No way. If the Double Spur's bulls are too nice, you won't be ready to compete in Las Vegas. I expect to see you there and watch you ride for the championship."

"Yes, ma'am," he said and tipped his imaginary hat.

She found herself hugging every last ranch hand.

Bull waited until the other hands had had their chance to say good-bye. Then he walked up to her and said, "Carrie, I want you to know you've made a difference here on this old spread. You need to hurry back because nothing will be right until you're back here for good."

"Is that your way of saying I should do another reality show?" She laughed.

"No, it's my way of making sure you know you're family and will always be welcomed on this ranch."

Carrie's eyes started to fill with tears. She tried to blink them away but couldn't stop one tear that fell over her eyelid and rolled down her cheek.

"Oh, stop it, you old cowhand. She's coming back, and we all know it," Glenda said as she wrapped Carrie up in a big hug. "When you come back, we'll figure out what we're going to plant in those flower boxes around the side of the house."

Glenda hugged her again, and Carrie thought she might have seen tears in the cook's eyes before she turned away.

"I can't believe you've been here for three months," Maria said. "I swear it was only yesterday that Joel was saying idiotic things and you were trying to ignore him."

"Oh, come on, can we stop reminding her how much of an idiot I was?" Joel groused good naturedly.

"Why would we stop? It's fun to watch you squirm," his brother replied.

"We know we'll see you in Las Vegas, but know you're welcome here anytime," Zach said to her as he leaned down and gave her a big hug.

The only person left for her to say goodbye to was Joel. It felt wrong saying goodbye in front of the cameras. This seemed like something they should have done this morning with no one else around. Carrie turned and looked up at the man she had fallen in love with. What could she say? Goodbye seemed inadequate, and yet she had no idea when she would see him again. Joel leaned down and hugged her. While it was longer than any of the other men had held her, it didn't seem to be nearly long enough. He took her chin in his hand as he told her, "I'm going to miss you. You've changed this ranch for the better. You've changed me to be better, too." This last comment was said barely above a whisper.

"Goodbye, Joel. I'll miss you, too." They were the only words she could get past the lump in her throat.

"We'll see you in Vegas," he said. He dropped his hand from her chin and stepped back away from her.

"Okay, Carrie, we need to get going if we're going to get you to the airport on time," Drake said as he directed her to the SUV she had arrived in.

Carrie took a few steps and turned back around to wave goodbye one last time to these people who had come to mean so much to her. They waved back, and with that, she walked to the vehicle and climbed in.

Drake started the car and drove them out through the gates of the Double Spur. Carrie sighed as she thought of Joel's goodbye. She knew he hadn't wanted to kiss her on camera, but she was still sad that they couldn't have expressed how they really felt. Drake drove for about a mile or so and pulled the car over.

"Drake? Is there something wrong?" she asked.

"Nope. Just waiting for the camera crew," he said.

"Oh, okay. I thought they had a lot of stuff to put together and would leave much later than me."

"Hmmm," he said. His response wasn't much of an answer, but Carrie was still so wrapped up in her thoughts about Joel that she didn't even notice the non-answer.

It didn't take more than a few minutes for another vehicle to pull up behind Drake's SUV. Carrie's door opened, and Joel reached in, unbuckled her, and pulled her out of the car. He hugged her for a moment and then set her down on her feet and kissed her. Once again, time seemed to stand still. When the kiss finally ended, Carrie looked up at Joel and asked, "What are you doing here?"

"What do you mean, what am I doing here? The love of my life is leaving my home to go back to hers. I'm here to say a proper goodbye and to take you to the airport."

"But you already said goodbye."

"That was *not* goodbye. That was a 'see y'all later' for the cameras. This is my chance to say a real goodbye. I love you, Carrie, and I'll miss seeing you every day. I know we'll talk, but it won't be the same as getting to hold you or giving you a kiss. I just wanted to make sure you knew how important you've become to me and to get one last kiss before you left. It is also *my* job to take you to the airport and see you off. I asked Drake if we could arrange it so I got to give you a proper goodbye without all of the cameras."

"I happily conspired so you could have a little more time together. After all, I understand about a man in love," the producer said with a twinkle in his eyes.

"Thanks, Drake," she said before Joel took her lips in one more kiss. The kiss lasted a few minutes until the producer spoke up.

"Oh, okay, you two, we really do need to get to the airport. Carrie can't miss her flight. Her family's going to be waiting for her at the airport."

With that, Joel released her lips and took her hand in his.

"I'm going to hold your hand as long as I possibly can," he said as he leaned over and kissed it.

CHAPTER 29

Carrie had no sooner left the secured area of the arrival and departure gates than she heard her name. She looked up to see her folks, Cassie, and Becky all waiting to welcome her home.

Home. Within three months, the definition of that word had shifted for her. She couldn't believe that the Double Spur seemed to be more like *home* than here with her family.

"Hungry, honey?" her mom said as soon as she could hug her.

"Yeah, I'm starving. The plane only offered snacks, and I was so nervous about flying, I couldn't eat anything before the plane departed.

"Worried about flying—or worried about leaving your new friends in Texas?" her mom speculated.

"Probably more worried about leaving my new friends," Carrie responded with a small smile.

"Don't worry—I'm sure you'll be seeing them again soon enough. Not to mention, you can always talk on the phone."

"Carrie, do you have any more luggage than these two bags?" her dad asked.

"Nope, that's it. Let's get out of here."

♦ ♦ ♦

That night during dinner, Carrie started to share some of her experiences with Cassie and her folks. She talked about learning to ride a horse and feeding Misty sugar cubes right from her hand. Everyone at the table let Cassie direct the conversation and ask Carrie questions about her time on the ranch.

"Okay, Cassie," her mom interrupted after a while, "we probably need to let Carrie get back to her own place so she can unpack. She'll come back again and tell us all more stories."

"I promise," Carrie said. "I'll come by tomorrow and tell you more about what I saw and did. Is that okay, Cassie?"

Her sister vigorously nodded her head.

Carrie came by every night that week for dinner and to share more stories about her time at the ranch. The more she shared, the more questions Cassie seemed to have. That didn't bother Carrie at all. She loved getting to share all about the Double Spur and the people she had grown to love like family. They made arrangements for Carrie to come over on Saturday to share her pictures and some of the ones Drake had been sending to her during the course of the week.

Carrie spent Saturday afternoon showing her family pictures and regaling them once more with stories about ranch life. After about an hour, she heard the doorbell ring.

"Carrie, dear, can you get that for me? I need to check on dinner."

"Sure, Mom."

Carrie left the family room to see who was at the door. She opened the door and saw Joel standing on the other side. Her heart jumped up into her throat and her jaw dropped.

"Hi, B," he said with a smile on his lips.

"Joel? What . . . what are you doing here?"

"I came to see you and thought I could also meet your family."

"How did you—"

"Carrie, dear, why don't you let your friend into the house instead of making him stand on the front doorstep."

"Oh my gosh, I'm so sorry! Come on in," Carrie said as she opened the door to let Joel into her parent's home. After he was in the house, Carrie went to close the door and then heard another voice.

"Hey, don't close the door on me, I want to come in, too."

"Becky?"

"Yep, that's me, at least you didn't forget who I was in the last couple of days." Becky laughed as Carrie hugged her.

"What are *you* doing here?"

"She was my ride from the airport," Joel supplied.

"She picked you up at the airport?"

"Yes. How about we go into the other room and join your family. I'll answer all of those questions I see swirling about in your eyes."

Carrie turned to lead the group into the family room when she felt Joel grab her around the arm and spin her back around. As soon as she was facing him, his head dropped, and he kissed her. It was not a quick kiss on the cheek, nor was it a passionate display. It was a kiss that was safe to be seen by her family that was also a reminder of how much Carrie meant to the handsome rancher.

"I've waited an entire week to do that," he said with a smile.

The three of them walked into the family room where Carrie started to make introductions.

"Mom, Dad, I'd like to introduce you to Joel Roulston. He owns the Double Spur where I was working."

"Joel!" her sister cried. "You're finally here!"

Carrie watched as Joel walked over to her sister, leaned down, hugged her, and said, "Hey there, Butterfly, how're you doing?"

"I'm great! Carrie has been telling us all about being at your ranch. She's talked about the cows and the bulls. She was telling us that she got to ride a horse!"

"Yep, that horse's name is Misty."

"Misty?"

"Yep. She's one of my favorites."

"Can I come to your ranch and ride Misty, too?"

"Before you can come down to the Double Spur and ride a horse, you need something very important."

"What?"

Joel turned to Becky who handed him a bag. Carrie had been so surprised to see Joel that she hadn't even noticed the bag in Becky's hands. Joel reached into the bag and pulled out a beautifully wrapped gift. He turned and handed it to Cassie.

"Is that for me?" she asked with eyes the size of dinner plates.

"Sure is, Butterfly."

Cassie started to unwrap the present. She lifted off the lid of the box and shrieked. She pulled out a cowboy hat. This was an actual cowboy hat, just like all of the people on the ranch wore, except its hatband had butterflies all around it.

"Look, Carrie, it has butterflies on it!"

"I see that. Why does it have butterflies on it?"

"That's my nickname. Joel told us everyone on the ranch has a nickname. I asked him if I could have a nickname, too. He said he thought my nickname should be *Butterfly*. Isn't it great?"

Carrie turned to Joel and asked, "Why Butterfly?"

"While we talked on the phone, she seemed to flit from one question to the next, from one subject to the next. It reminded me of how a butterfly moves."

Carrie smiled at her sister. Joel was right. Having a conversation with Cassie usually meant verbal acrobatics.

"Besides, butterflies are beautiful—"

"And Joel said I'm beautiful," Cassie finished.

"Yes, you are certainly beautiful, and I think Butterfly is a perfect nickname for you."

Cassie's smile stretched from ear to ear. Happiness beamed out from her eyes, and Carrie felt her eyes fill up with tears at the sheer joy she saw in her sister's face. She turned to the man she had fallen in love with and had no words. He moved back to her side, leaned down, and kissed her cheek. He then turned to her dad and held out his hand.

Her dad stood up and said, "Nice to finally put a face to the voice."

Carrie spun around to look at her dad. Before she could ask the additional questions that started spinning around in her head, Joel turned her back around to face him.

"I've spoken to your parents a few times now."

"What? When?"

"The first time was the week Becky came down to the ranch. I realized I had not met your family and they had not met me. Given my feelings for you, I thought it was only proper to call them and introduce myself."

Carrie felt the blush start to climb her cheeks when he mentioned his feelings for her.

"How'd you get their number?"

"I gave it to him," Becky answered.

Carrie turned to her best friend and asked, "You did?"

"Yes. When Joel mentioned to me that he wanted to talk to your folks, I asked him why. He told me that *he* would be extremely upset if his daughter had started dating a man he had not met. He explained that he knew he would not be able to get away to fly up here to meet your folks, but he figured he could call them and introduce himself. I thought it was so sweet, I gave him their number."

"She also sent *us* a message that he would be calling and let us know a little about him so we wouldn't be caught off guard," her mom said.

This time Joel turned to Becky and asked, "You did?"

"Yeah. I thought before you called them, they should at least be given a heads up."

"No wonder the call went as easily as it did. You did all the hard work."

"Not really. Warren and Diana have been like a second set of parents to me. I knew they would appreciate some advance notice before some guy they had never met called to tell them he was interested in their daughter."

"You were right. Her text gave us the chance to process the idea of a man in Carrie's life and to get over the surprise before you called," her mom said.

"It also gave me the chance to think about what I really wanted to know about you," her dad, Warren, added.

Carrie turned back to Joel. "You called to introduce yourself to my parents." It was not a question.

"We've spoken several times, actually."

"You have?"

Joel took a deep breath, reached down, and took Carrie's hands into his own. He looked into her eyes.

"Carrie, I love you. It was only fitting for me to introduce myself and let your folks get to know me."

Carrie stood there with her hands clasped in Joel's, completely stunned. He had just professed his love for her in front of her family. Was this really happening?

"I love you, B," he whispered.

Carrie looked into the eyes of this man who had become so important to her. This was the man who had crossed off those items from her mom's list and who had, time and again, shown her in countless ways how much she meant to him.

"I love you, too," she responded. While she didn't shout it from the rooftop, she also didn't whisper. She spoke loud enough for everyone in the room to hear her. It felt so natural to admit how she felt about him in front of her family.

"Well, on that note, how about we all move to the dining room to eat dinner?" Diana said with a smile.

CHAPTER 30

Carrie stepped out of the stretch limo and took in all of the lights of the Las Vegas strip. She had seen movies and TV shows that took place in Las Vegas, but she wasn't expecting everything to be so huge. She also wasn't expecting the lights. Everything glowed a different color. There was so much visual stimulation that she was almost dizzy. She moved out of the way to let Cassie get out of the car and into her wheelchair, which the limo driver was setting up at the door.

"Look at all the lights, Carrie!"

"I see 'em. What do 'ya think?"

"They're so pretty!"

"Should we go inside and see what it looks like in there?"

"Yes!"

Carrie took the handles of Cassie's wheelchair and pushed her into the hotel. The minute they were inside, their senses were even more inundated. There were even more lights. Some were holding a steady glow while others were flashing and blinking. The assault on their ears was no less intense. There seemed to be a different sound coming from every machine in the building, and there had to be thousands of machines. Carrie noticed people all over the place on stools sitting in front of the slot machines and wondered how they could sit there with all of the noise and lights.

"Carrie, Cassie! Let's get you checked in and we can talk about what to expect in the next few days."

"Drake!" Cassie shrieked as she spun her wheelchair around and started to move in the direction of the producer. As soon as she was close enough, she wrapped her arms around his waist and gave him a big hug. Drake's face lit up with a smile, and he hugged her back with as much enthusiasm.

Carrie shook her head. She had been so afraid to let this man know about her sister. Seeing him hugging Cassie brought a smile to her lips. He had made friends with Cassie on his first trip to Canfield and that had clearly not changed in the months since his visit. After releasing Cassie from the hug, Drake turned to Carrie and said, "Where are your folks?"

"Right here," Warren said as he approached his two daughters. "We got left in the dust when the girls saw all the lights."

Everyone chuckled as Drake and Warren shook hands.

As they were moving to the registration desk, they noticed a cowboy walking through the lobby. He wore jeans with chaps. His cowboy hat sat perched on his head, and he had a rope slung over his shoulder. Cassie, not one to leave a question unasked, moved her wheelchair to intercept the man and asked, "Are you a real cowboy?"

The man stopped in front of her, and Carrie noticed the smile that stretched across his face. He looked down at her sister and said, "Yep, sure am, little lady."

"Do you ride horses?"

"Yep." He nodded.

"Do ride bulls?"

"Sure do." He chuckled.

"So does my sister. Do you know Carrie?"

The man turned to introduce himself.

"Tad Blackstone, ma'am."

"Carrie—"

"Wait, I know who you are! You're that gal from the reality TV show, Carrie somethin' or other—"

"Nelson, Carrie Nelson," she finished.

"Wow, I can't believe I'm meeting you! My family has loved watching your show. Are you really going to ride a bull here in Vegas?"

"I sure hope so. That's the plan anyway."

"Man, I can't believe I'm getting to meet 'cha. My mom is going to flip out when I tell her I met you."

"I'm Cassie," her sister said.

Tad immediately bent down, looked her in the eye, and said, "Nice to meet you, Cassie. Are you going to watch your sister try to ride that bull?"

"Yep." She nodded enthusiastically.

"I'll be watching, too. I can't wait." Tad moved a little closer to Cassie and, in a stage whisper, said, "I'll be riding a bull. Will you cheer for me, too?"

Carrie watched as Cassie's head bounced up and down with her eagerness.

"You'll need to cheer real loud so I can hear you. Can you do that?"

"I sure can—should I show you?"

As she was about to take a deep breath, Tad said, "Not yet. I don't want all the other cowboys to know I got the best cheerleader in the stands. You gotta wait until I get into the ring and I'm ridin' that bull."

Cassie nodded her head once more.

Tad stood up and winked at Carrie. She smiled. This was one more person in the industry who had treated her sister with kindness and respect.

Tad stood back up to his full height and turned to Carrie. "It's a real pleasure meetin' you, ma'am. Seeing as you are as pretty in person as you are on the TV, I'm only sorry I didn't meet you before that Joel feller did."

"What—"

"Carrie! Cassie! Let's get checked in," called their mom.

Carrie held out her hand and said, "Nice to meet you, Tad. We'll make sure to cheer really loud for you. Won't we, Cassie?"

"Yep, but not as loud as I'll cheer for you."

"That's fair." The bull rider chuckled as he turned and headed to the interior of the hotel.

Tad reminded Carrie a lot of Dusty, and she realized that none of the hands at the Double Spur had met Cassie yet. She was actually looking forward to introducing her to everyone from the Double Spur. Joel had told her everyone was coming to see her ride. Normally, a few folks stayed back to watch the ranch, but this time, no one wanted to stay behind. Joel had made arrangements with a neighboring ranch to watch over the Double Spur while they were gone.

"Come on, Cassie, we've got to get registered and see what our room is like," Carrie said.

After they had checked in, received their room keys, and had their bags taken care of, Carrie noticed the camera crew hanging out in the lobby. She went over to start chatting with them. It had been months since she had seen any of them. Drake walked up to the small group and said, "You guys ready?"

The crew quickly lifted their cameras as they got ready to film.

"We're recording stuff already?" Carrie asked with surprise.

"I want to get some footage of your initial impression of Las Vegas."

"Shouldn't they have been rolling twenty minutes ago?" She smirked.

"Nope. There was no reason to get Cassie's reaction, and I figure you can give us three minutes of your 'initial' reaction now."

"You know I'm not that great of an actress," she said with a laugh.

"Oh, I expect you'll be able to put on a good show for a few minutes. Let's go."

With that, the group headed back outside. The limo had been waiting, and the driver opened the door as soon as Carrie neared.

"Carrie, climb back into the limo and give us a few minutes to get the cameras into position. Tom, here, is gonna open the door, and you can climb out and look around at all of the lights. We'll film that and get some footage of you entering the casino."

With that, the group did as directed, and within moments, Carrie was once again entering the massive hotel "for the first time."

"Alright, Carrie, that's good. I think we have everything we need."

Carrie smiled at Drake and turned to head up to her room. Before she took three steps, she was engulfed in a hug. Her feet left the floor, and her heart set sail. She knew immediately who had wrapped his arms around her.

"Joel!"

"Hey there, B. I've missed you."

"I've missed you, too."

He held onto her for a few more minutes before he gently set her down.

"Are you done with her, Drake?"

"Yep. Tomorrow we'll go to the arena and get some film footage of Carrie being shown the ring and the rodeo setup. After that, we should have enough footage to piece into the live show."

"Great." Joel looked down at Carrie and said, "Let's go meet up with your family."

Carrie nodded.

Just as her feet hit the floor, he leaned down and placed a kiss on her lips. "Oh boy, have I missed you, sweetheart," he said.

"I've missed you, too." She smiled. She still couldn't believe she had found this man while shooting a reality TV show.

"Come on, let's go before you distract me so much I forget where we need to be." Joel's smile warmed her heart.

I sure do love this man, Carrie thought.

◆ ◆ ◆

The next day, Carrie looked around the staging and holding area. It was massive. She couldn't believe there was so much room. She also couldn't take in how much stuff had been crammed into the space. There were pens everywhere containing the animals for the show. Interspersed with the enclosures were nooks that had been loaded with gear. There were ropes and saddles, brooms and hay bales. It looked like these cowboys had brought their entire ranch here with them to Las Vegas.

"I can't believe all of the stuff that's here."

"Yeah, the riders like to make sure they have their own gear. The ranch owners also like to have their own tack. It makes for a lot of stuff to haul in and out of this place."

Carrie was in awe not only about all of the gear that had been brought in, but also about the people. There were folks everywhere, and they all seemed to have jobs to do. No one seemed to be just milling about. Some were moving the gear in while others were handling the horses and cows that were being brought in for the rodeo. There were calves for roping and, of course, the bulls for riding. The crew seemed to be choreographing a ballet as they made sure that everything was where it needed to go. It was incredible.

"I wanted to let you see what goes on here for a while so you were comfortable. Backstage at the PRCA National Championship is a whole different experience than seeing a county fair rodeo."

"I'll say, but everything seems to be so well organized."

"Yeah, they do a great job here. You can't have this many animals and gear and just as many people without being organized."

"Carrie!"

Carrie turned to see A.Z. heading in her direction.

"A.Z.! It's so good to see you again. I've missed you!"

"I've missed you, too!"

"How've you been?"

"Good, and you? Are you ready for this?"

"I thought I was, but seeing all of this makes me realize I didn't fully appreciate what riding a bull at the national championships meant."

"There's a lot to take in here, isn't there?"

"Sure is. I'm a little overwhelmed."

"Don't worry, everyone is overwhelmed the first time they're here."

Carrie smiled, and the two women stood together watching as even more animals and gear were unloaded and brought into the staging area.

As they watched, their attention was drawn to a massive bull that was being funneled through gates to a special holding pen. This bull was as black as midnight and had the biggest horns Carrie had ever seen on a bull. Granted, she had only ever seen the bulls at the Double Spur and the county fair, but this animal's horns were massive compared to those on the animals at the ranch. The men trying to get the beast into the pen moved along the outside of the gates trying to entice it to keep going. Every so often, the bull would stop and drop its head. It would paw the ground and shake its head. As it shook its massive head, the horns knocked against the gates, and the sound drowned out much of the noise of the other animals. The hands would pull on the rope in the bull's nose ring and try to get it to move again. Carrie and A.Z. continued to watch the process. As it neared the two women, it stopped dead in its tracks. The hulking animal turned its head and looked directly at Carrie. She felt her breath get trapped in her lungs as goosebumps broke out on her arms. The bull dropped its horns slightly, and Carrie could have sworn it narrowed its eyes as it continued to stare at her. As the great beast let out a snort, Carrie felt fear. She had never experienced this type of fear from any of the animals on the Double Spur ranch. This one seemed mean. It finally turned its head and moved along until it was in the enclosure designated for this one animal. The stall actually had a double set of gates around it. No one was going to accidentally come in contact with this monster.

She heard A.Z. quietly say, "That's Muerte Negra. It means 'black death' in Spanish."

Carrie swallowed and nodded her head.

"It's the million-dollar bull."

"The what?"

"The million-dollar bull. It has a reputation of being one of the meanest and most vicious bulls in the rodeo circuit. No one has ever been able to ride it for a full eight seconds. More than one rider has been mauled, and one actually died when it gored him."

"That's terrible!"

"Yeah," A.Z. said, nodding.

"So why is it the million-dollar bull?"

"Because no one has been able to ride it, it has become a legend in the industry. The owner has actually put up a million dollars in prize money for the first man who is able to stay on its back for eight seconds. The riders sign up to get the chance to ride it."

"Are you kidding? Someone actually voluntarily signs up to ride that thing?"

A.Z. grimaced. "Yeah. Some do it because they're young and stupid and think they'll be able to ride it. Some do it because they see it as the ultimate challenge and they want the right to say they finally managed to ride the thing. Then there are those few who are completely desperate for the money and sign up for the opportunity to bring home the big prize money."

"That's just crazy."

"Yeah. There was actually talk a couple years back about banning the beast from the circuit. There are a lot of bull owners who think that evil creature gives the business a bad reputation. Then there's the danger that's connected to any ride on that thing. Finally, there's the danger that surrounds it. Just having it here is a risk. If that thing ever got loose, someone would surely die."

"So what happened?"

"Ultimately, the association decided it would continue to allow the bull to come and would let riders volunteer to ride it, but it wouldn't be used in the competition. Additionally, there's extra caution taken in the setup around its pen."

"I'm glad I'm not riding that one."

A.Z. turned to her friend and smiled, "Me, too."

The women smiled at each other, and A.Z. continued to show Carrie around the holding and staging area.

"You ready for us to do some filming?" Drake asked.

"Yep, but I gotta tell you, I'm looking forward to the day you can just be my friend and not feel the need to record everything I do." She smiled at the producer.

"I'm actually looking forward to that day as well," he replied.

After getting some film of Carrie looking around the staging area, they moved to the arena itself.

Carrie looked around the massive ring. Everything here was a hundred times larger than anything she had experienced at the Brockton County Fair or the Double Spur. She tried to see everything while processing what Drake had been telling her.

"—come out on horseback."

Carrie shook the cobwebs from her brain and asked, "What?"

"Carrie, I know it's a lot to take in. Do you need me to give you a minute?"

"I just can't comprehend the size of this place. I think it's bigger than any building I've ever been in. But I'll try to focus so we can get through all of this and back to enjoying this crazy town."

"As I was saying, we'll have you enter the ring with the Belles of the Rodeo on horseback. Your riding is pretty proficient, and I don't have any qualms about you riding in on horseback. The announcer will make a big deal about you and your upcoming ride. You'll make a couple of passes around the ring. You'll leave the ring with the other women. As soon as you get back in the staging area, you'll need to make your way around to the bull-riding chutes. Your ride will start the rodeo off. After your ride, you can wave to the crowd and then head back to the chutes, where you'll be able to climb out of the ring and head to the reserved box your family will be in. You can watch the rest of the rodeo from there. It should be a great show, and I hope you and your family get a chance to really enjoy it."

"As soon as I get past the part where I have to ride one of the bulls, I'm sure it'll be great."

"You're gonna do fine. I've watched you ride these bulls, and the one you're going to ride isn't any different than what you rode at the Double Spur. Trust me, okay?"

"I do, Drake, I do. I'm just pretty nervous to be doing this in front of a live audience, though. It was one thing to have cameras filming me. I could forget all about the audience, but here with so many people sitting in the stands, it'll be hard to forget them. So, you said the bull I'll be riding is similar to what I rode at the Double Spur. Can I meet him?"

Drake shook his head and chuckled. "You're the only bull rider I know who likes an introduction to the bull before she rides."

CHAPTER 31

Carrie sat atop Misty, waiting to ride into the arena. Even with all the noise backstage, she could hear the crowd in the stands. *What would it be like when she rode out into the ring?*

"Carrie? Are you alright?" A.Z. asked. She had joined Carrie backstage and helped her navigate where she needed to be and when. It had been so reassuring to have her friend with her, especially as A.Z. had done all of this before.

"Yeah, just really nervous."

"You'll do fine. Don't think about the crowd. Focus on your ride with Misty. Remember all of the things Maria and I taught you about riding. As long as you focus on that, you'll be fine."

"Pretty sure everyone is expecting me to wave as I ride by."

"Who cares what the crowd is expecting? You need to do what's necessary for you to stay safe, and that means no waving as you ride on by. Wait until you stop, and you can wave to them then. Besides, Joel would kill me if I encouraged you to wave. I think he'd have a heart attack if you fell off this horse," A.Z. said as she patted Misty on the neck.

Carrie remembered arriving at the holding area earlier this afternoon. She had started to wonder what horse she was going to ride into the ring. She had forgotten to ask Drake, and as she had wandered around the staging area, she had gotten more and more nervous about riding a horse she had never ridden before. She had finally managed to track Drake down.

"Drake, I'm so glad I found you!"

"What's up, Carrie?"

"I forgot to ask about what horse I'd be riding on? Can I see it? Maybe meet it?"

Drake had smirked, but his only response had been, "Sure."

He had walked her around until they came to an area decorated with Double Spur tack.

"Drake?"

At that moment, Joel had stepped out from behind one of the horses.

"Joel?"

He had smiled, reached to cup the back of her head, leaned down, and kissed her. He had ended the kiss way too soon from Carrie's perspective.

"Hey, there, B. How're you doing?"

"I'm really nervous. I just asked Drake about the horse I'd be riding."

"Come on, I'll introduce you," he had said with a smirk. *Something was up with these men*, she had thought.

Joel had led her over to a stall and when Carrie had looked at the horse, she had realized it was Misty. She had turned to Joel. "You brought Misty?"

"Of course, I brought Misty. You didn't think I'd let you ride a different horse here, did you?"

"I hadn't given it any thought until today." She had stretched up, wrapped her arms around him, and hugged him. He had wrapped his arms around her and picked her up off the ground.

"Oh, Joel, thank you."

"You're welcome, sweetheart. I knew you would feel so much more comfortable riding Misty. Besides, I think I would do just about anything to get you to throw yourself into my arms like you just did."

Carrie had leaned back and looked up into the handsome rancher's twinkling eyes.

"So, what would you do to get a kiss?"

"Anything you ask."

With that response, she had moved to kiss him. As her lips had touched his, all the noise and the commotion had faded away. It had just been the two of them locked in their own moment of time and space.

"Ahem." The producer had made the not so subtle noise to her left. "You did say you wanted to meet your horse."

"That I did." She had smiled at the producer and as soon as Joel had set her down, she had gone straight to Misty. She had reached out and run her hand gently down the mare's nose. Misty had whinnied and bounced her head up and down.

"Hey there, girl. Are you ready for this?"

Once again, the horse had nodded. Carrie had turned to look at Joel one more time. As he had smiled at her, her heart had dropped to somewhere near her feet. He had brought Misty so that she would be comfortable. "I love you," she had mouthed.

"I love you, too," he had soundlessly replied.

Carrie had turned back to Misty and said, "How about I get you all pretty for the rodeo? I'll take care of you if you take care of me." Misty had nodded again. Carrie had grabbed a brush and begun to brush Misty's coat. As her arms had moved over the horse's frame, Carrie had felt her nerves leaving her body. This horse had been able to calm her nerves from the moment they had met.

Now, as she sat astride the horse waiting for the gates to open, she wished they were back in the stall and Carrie was brushing her again. Carrie ran her hand down Misty's neck and took a deep breath.

"We can do this, right, girl?" Misty bounced her head up and down once again and jangled the reins in Carrie's hands. Misty seemed almost excited to be there. "You're excited to be here, aren't you?" Misty nodded and lightly bounced on her feet. Carrie could have sworn she was dancing in place as they waited for the gate to open. "Got it. You're telling me to enjoy this. Aren't you?" Misty nodded again and danced a little more.

The gate was opened, and Misty followed the other horses out into the ring. Carrie gave the horse her head. She knew she could trust Misty to take care of her. Carrie sat up in the saddle and took in the scene. The ring had been decorated with banners. The dirt had been recently groomed, and the marks from the rake were perfectly visible. Carrie chanced a look up into the seats. This place was massive. She couldn't believe that there were this many people here to see the national championship who were now watching her.

It was at that moment that she heard the announcer say, "And immediately following our flag bearers is Carrie Nelson. How many of you have been watching Carrie as she learned to become a real cowboy?"

With that, a deafening cheer rose from the crowd. Carrie couldn't believe that there had been that many people who had watched the show. Drake had told her that the ratings for the show had far surpassed what he had hoped for and that the sponsors were elated, but it still hadn't really registered with her. It was humbling to think that these people were excited to see her big finale and cheer her on as she rode a bull.

"Let's stand and honor our country by singing the national anthem."

Carrie joined the crowd in singing the song. As the song finished, she turned her head and noticed the viewing stand that had been given to her family. She saw Cassie sitting right up front and practically hanging out of the box. Becky sat to her left, and Joel sat to her right. With a tear running down her cheek, she smiled, looked toward the heavens, and quietly said, "I don't think I have properly thanked you, God, for bringing me to the Double Spur and introducing me to such wonderful people. I am very grateful." Carrie felt Misty bounce her head up and down once more. Then the horse pranced out of the arena.

"Ms. Nelson," a stagehand said, "I've got your mare. Please keep moving over to the bull-riding chutes. We need to make sure we stay on schedule. Thanks."

Carrie nodded, dismounted from Misty, and hustled over to the bull chutes. It didn't take Bull any time at all to start firing last-minute instructions at her.

"You stay focused on the movements of that bull, never mind the crowd. If you feel yourself slipping off its back, you let go and try to jump out of the way. Watch out for the turns. This one likes to do a double turn. He leaps up and turns one way and then jumps and turns the opposite way. It happens in such quick succession, it catches most riders off guard."

Carrie looked up into the eyes of the old cowhand who was once again coaching her about riding a bull. She reached out, wrapped her arms around him, and hugged him tightly.

"Thank you, Bull. I'll remember everything you taught me, I promise."

The old cowhand cleared his thought and croaked, "That's good, that's good."

"Alright, Sleeping Beauty, time to get this show on the road."

Carrie smiled at Beans. He was straddling the gates just as he had done when she had ridden the bulls at the Double Spur. Also atop the gates sat Dusty.

"What are y'all doin' here?"

"You didn't actually think we were gonna let you ride a bull without us here, did you?"

"Nope. I knew you couldn't resist giving me some last-minute advice," she responded with another tear in her eye.

"Now, no crying, Sleeping Beauty. You need to be able to see where the ground is so you don't land on your head again." Beans chuckled.

"Ain't that the truth." Carrie laughed as she started climbing up the gate rails. As she neared the top rail, she heard a great thrashing in one of the neighboring chutes. It reminded her of the bull that had taken a piece of her back at the Double Spur. This one was also crashing about and slamming its body and horns against the rail. She turned to Beans and asked, "What's with the bull next door?" She nodded to the next chute over.

"That's Muerte Negra. Don't worry about him; he's always angry and usually tries to make a lot of noise to get everyone's attention. You can ignore him—we all do."

"Glad, I'm not riding that one."

"No way would we let you get anywhere near that evil creature, Sleeping Beauty. No way in hell," Beans quietly replied.

◆ ◆ ◆

"That noise you're hearing is the million-dollar bull. What do you say, folks, do you want to see someone ride that beast this rodeo?" The announcer called. The crowd responded, cheering. "Think someone can last eight seconds on a bull named Black Death?" Again the crowd cheered. "Well, before anyone gets a chance to ride on Muerte Negra, we have a lot more excitement to see. What do you say, folks, should we start the rodeo?" The crowd roared their approval for the competition to begin.

"To start us off this evening, we have Carrie Nelson. As most of you know, just a few short months ago, Carrie had never even seen a bull-riding event. She hadn't even ridden a horse. Can you imagine that? Getting on a bull here in Las Vegas after only learning how to ride a horse and then a bull a few months ago? Carrie has shown us how courageous she is, don't you all agree?"

The crowd erupted. Joel looked around the arena and saw all of the people cheering for Carrie. He still couldn't believe so many people had tuned in for every show, just to watch Carrie and her time at the Double Spur.

"Remember when she was thrown off that first bull? Who wants to see her ride this bull for the full eight seconds?" The crowd roared again.

I'd just be happy with no more injuries, Joel thought.

"Joel, is Carrie going to be alright?" Cassie asked him with concern in her voice.

Joel turned to the young woman sitting next to him and smiled. He took her hand in his and said, "Of course! We made sure she knew how to ride a bull when she was staying with us at the ranch."

"But she got hurt while she was at your house," Cassie said. The concern creased her brow. "I heard Mom and Dad talking about it this afternoon. Mom said it was really scary."

"Yes, it was. We were all pretty worried about her when she fell off our bull, but she's okay now, and I know she's going to do just fine. Don't you worry, okay?"

Cassie looked him in the eyes for a moment and nodded her head. She turned back to the ring and joined the crowd cheering for her sister.

"You gonna believe those words yourself, or am *I* going to have to reassure *you*?" Maria whispered from his other side. "You know she'll be fine. Green Pastures should be a fairly easy ride for her. You ought to know, you picked it."

"There was a whole committee who selected that bull," he quickly retorted.

Maria chuckled, "Yeah, right. If they had even suggested a different bull, you would have had their heads. I talked to John Freeborn. There was no way in hell anyone on that committee was going to suggest a different bull knowing your feelings for that woman."

"My feelings? No one outside of our families knows about my feelings for Carrie."

Maria laughed outright. "You're joking, right?"

Joel turned to his sister. "What are you talking about?"

"Joel, you watched every episode of the show."

"Yeah, there weren't any scenes with Carrie and me looking like a couple. Drake and I agreed the show didn't need that stuff."

"Drake didn't put in any clips of you expressing your love for her, but he couldn't hide the fact you had fallen in love with her. Joel, the camera doesn't lie. Everyone watching the show knew you two had fallen in love. The fact that there were no scenes with your declaration of love kept people tuning in week after week just hoping for a happy ending. There were even a couple of romantic compilations on YouTube."

"What are you talking about?"

"Your biggest fans spliced scenes from the show together of the two of you and put them to romantic music. They were so sweet."

"Does Carrie know?"

"I doubt it."

"Should I be worried?"

"No. There was nothing in the videos or the blog posts."

"Blog posts?"

"Yeah, there were those, too. But don't worry; there was nothing negative or hurtful about you or Carrie. Most of the comments were encouraging *you* to get off your butt and tell her how you felt. Little did the audience know that you had already done that by episode three." Maria paused for a moment and said, "Joel, everything I saw just underscored your love for each other. The audience could feel your connection as they sat on their couches thousands of miles away. Everyone knows you two were made for each other, and they were just cheering for love all along."

Joel smiled at that. He couldn't agree more. He and Carrie were definitely made for each other, and before the night was over, he was going to make sure she knew it.

♦ ♦ ♦

Carrie cautiously swung her left leg over the bull she was to ride. She had insisted on "meeting" Green Pastures before she climbed onto his back. She wasn't sure they had made a connection, but she felt better for having tried. She also knew Joel had been involved in the selection committee, and she understood that he had been adamant about this being the safest bull for her to ride. She took one last breath as she let her weight drop down upon the large brown animal. As soon as her weight landed on its back, she felt the bull move and shift its weight. She quickly wrapped the rope around her hand, just as Dusty had taught her. She tugged on her hand and was reassured that she had wrapped the rope tight enough that there was no give in the rope. She looked up at Beans and nodded.

"You ready, Sleeping Beauty?" he asked.

She nodded again, and as she looked him in the eyes, she said, "Yep."

She quickly brought her attention back to the bull she was on and started focusing on his movements. She could feel him twisting and shifting his weight from one leg to another. She wondered if Green Pastures was as nervous as she was.

With that last thought crossing her mind, she heard and saw the gate swing out. The bull immediately turned out to the left and shot out of the corral. After it had gone about ten feet or so, Carrie felt it drop its head and kick out its hind legs. She braced herself on the bull's neck to stop herself from flying over its head. Its rear feet landed back on the ground, and she felt her teeth crash together in her head. She tightened her hold on the bull rope as the large beast leaned back on its hind legs and kicked out its front hooves. Then just as suddenly, it spun a hundred and eighty degrees in the air. She felt the jolt as it landed all through her body. Carrie clutched the rope tighter and squeezed the bull with her legs. She had no idea how long she had been on the bull, but she wanted to try and last the full eight seconds if she could. The bull once again dropped its head toward the ground and kicked its legs out. Carrie squeezed her legs tighter and held on. As the hooves hit the dirt, the bull once again spun around. No sooner had the bull landed than it spun around again, only this time in the opposite direction, just as Bull had warned. Carrie felt herself trying to hang on with everything she had. Her hand and thighs were beginning to burn with the effort of staying on the beast. *You can do this, just a little bit more.* She felt the animal's body contract as it once again kicked out its back legs. Just as she was getting ready for the bull to move again, she heard the buzzer. She had done it. She had lasted the full eight seconds. She couldn't believe it. She almost let go and then realized she still needed to get down off this thing. She also remembered that she could get hurt just as easily getting off as trying to stay on. She loosened her grip on the rope and waited to see and feel what the bull was going to do next. As it made a move to spin again, Carrie let go and pushed herself away from it as far as she could. She felt her feet hit the dirt, but her momentum kept her moving away from the bull. She felt the jarring in her spine as her backside forcefully hit the dirt. She looked up to see the bull turn and look at her. In just a matter of a few seconds, however, she couldn't see the bull through the large bodies of the clowns that had jumped into the ring and now stood between her and the bull. The bull turned and allowed the clowns to direct it to the gate that led it outside of the ring.

One of the clowns bent down quickly and asked, "Are you all right?"

Carrie nodded, "I think so."

She went to get up, and he cautiously put a hand on her shoulder and said, "Let's take a minute and make sure. You were jolted around pretty good on that ride."

"Okay." She smiled at the man. It was a little hard taking him seriously dressed as a clown, but he was making sense, so she nodded her head and took stock of her body. She cautiously moved her arms, legs, head, and torso. Her head hurt from all of the jarring motion, and her arm was going to be sore from hanging on so tight, but other than that, she was fine.

"I'm good," she said. She smiled at the clown. He stood up and held out his hand. She let him lift her out of the dirt.

"Okay, Ms. Nelson, take your bow. You definitely deserve it." With that last comment, he moved away from her.

"Ladies and gentlemen, she did it! How about we give Carrie a great big round of applause? She managed to stay on the back of that bull even though he was doing everything he could to oust her." The crowd cheered. "Wasn't she fantastic!" The crowd erupted again.

Carrie looked around the empty ring. Green Pastures had been let out of the ring and all of the clowns had also left right along with it. She was alone standing in the great big circle with thousands of people cheering for her. She had never had so much attention in her life. She took off her cowboy hat and waved it in the air. The crowd's roar grew louder. She turned in a circle, trying to acknowledge everyone who was cheering for her. As she spun around, her eyes found the viewing box where Joel and Cassie and the rest of their families sat. They were all on their feet, and the smile on Cassie's face lit up the whole box. She was clapping wildly, and Carrie waved to her. Carrie's eyes moved to the man standing next to her sister, and the breath left her lungs. She loved him with all her heart. She brought her hand up to her lips and blew him a kiss. He smiled and blew one back to her. Suddenly, she couldn't wait to get out of this ring and back to him and her family, who were waiting for her in that box. With that thought, Carrie turned to head back to the gate where she would be able to get out of the ring.

As Carrie started to leave the center of the ring, she heard a great metal screeching and a loud crash. She looked to the bull chutes and noticed that the gate that usually swung into the ring had crashed to the dirt. While Carrie's bull ride had started the rodeo, the rest of the bull-riding events would happen at the end of the night, so consequently, the bull chutes were empty except for this one stall. Behind the now-missing gate was the million-dollar bull, Muerte Negra.

There now was nothing between her and this terrifying creature. Carrie froze where she stood and watched in horror as the animal jumped out from the enclosure it had been contained in. She watched as it dropped its head and pawed the ground. It snorted and blew the dust into the air. She couldn't move. She couldn't breathe. She couldn't think. As it lifted its head, it looked directly at her. Her breath got trapped in her lungs. Suddenly, the beast leapt toward her. It charged her, and as it neared her, it lowered its head so its horns were directed at her. She was finally able to move. She turned to get out of the way of the charging bull. Carrie had taken no more than a few steps when she felt one of the horns rip into the back of her leg. As she started to fall to the ground, she felt herself fall onto the other unforgiving horn. She was now caught in this menacing beast's horns, and she realized that she needed to do something to get away from it. Before she could react, the bull threw her into the air. The air left her lungs as her body crashed to the ground. Before she could get her breath back, the black beast started to rise up on its hind legs and kick out its front hooves. Carrie knew that if she didn't move, it was going to crash down on her. She didn't have time to get up, so she tried to roll out of its path. She felt one of its hooves catch her in the back. She kept rolling. She knew she would never be able to get away from the hulking mass, but maybe it would lose interest in her and leave her alone. Just as she looked up to see where the great beast was, she saw a flash of bright colors run past her and toward the bull. She had no sooner seen the first splash of color than another and a third. Suddenly, there were three men between her and Black Death. She knew that they would do whatever it took to keep the bull away from her, but now, she was concerned about them. She didn't want anyone to get hurt.

"Carrie, are you okay? Can you move?"

She turned to the voice and noticed the clown who had been at her side after her ride. "I don't know," she said.

"Let's see if we can't get you out of here." This time, there was no taking stock of her potential injuries. The threat was still present. They both knew that she needed to get away from the bull as soon as possible. The clown bent over and gave her his hand. She went to move her legs under her to stand up but realized that she couldn't move her left leg. She looked down at her leg and realized that her pants had been cut open and there was blood and dirt in the open wound. She knew, however, that her injury was more serious than just a cut. When she gasped, the rodeo clown looked at her leg and realized she wouldn't be able to stand on her injured limb.

"Okay, I'm gonna pick you up and carry you out of the ring. Hold on." He ordered. With the words barely out of his mouth, Carrie felt the man pick her up and gently cradle her to his chest. He had no sooner taken a couple of steps when they both heard someone scream, "Look out!"

The clown turned in time to see the bull charging at the two of them. He tried to jump out of the way, but the bull was too close and too fast. The bull caught her rescuer in the knee and lifted them both into the air. Carrie once again felt her body flying through the air. The jarring to her body was even worse this time. As soon as she landed, she looked to see where the foul beast was. It had run past them by a good twenty feet or so. She looked around to see if there was anything she could use to defend herself. When she didn't see anything useful, she looked for the other men who had jumped into the ring to help. As she looked around, she realized that by now, not only had a couple more rodeo clowns jumped into the ring, but so had a dozen other men. She recognized Dusty and Beans as well as Tad, the bull rider she and Cassie had met the day before. The men were all moving the bull away from her and the injured clown. Additionally, she saw the tractor that was used to prep the ground driving into the ring. As soon as the tractor had cleared the gate, the gate was closed behind it. The tractor continued to move toward Carrie. As soon as it got close, one of the clowns lifted her off the ground and gently carried her to the man behind the wheel. The driver leaned over, quickly reached out for her, and set her down in his lap. She was out of harm's way. There was no way the bull could get to her up on the tractor, but that still left the men who had jumped into the ring to save her at risk. Carrie watched as the bull turned, pawed the ground, and turned again. Then suddenly, it charged the group directly in front of it. The men quickly moved out of the way. The bull jerked in another direction and charged the men that way. They had to leap up onto the rails to avoid getting caught by the massive horns, but they each avoided injury. With each turn, the bull charged and the men dashed away. The bull would paw the ground, then charge again. Sometimes, it leapt into the air and kicked out its hooves. Other times, it leaned over its front legs and struck out with it back legs. The men in the ring continued to watch and move and attempt to corral the beast to the exit gate. Suddenly, Muerte Negra stopped moving. It looked up to where Carrie sat and snorted. It stared at Carrie as its hulking sides moved in and out with the rapid breaths it needed because of the tremendous amount of energy it had just expended. It snorted and pawed the ground once again. Carrie shivered.

"Easy, Carrie, you're safe," said the man who held her.

She nodded while she stared at the bull. After what seemed like hours, the beast looked around and casually moved to the exit gate. Once it had cleared the gate, everyone in the ring took a deep breath. They were safe. They were all safe.

♦ ♦ ♦

"Carrie!" The scream was wrenched from Joel's chest. He had heard and seen the gate crash to the dirt and knew that there was nothing between Carrie and that deadly bull. He immediately feared for Carrie's life. He stood motionless. He was too afraid to move, too afraid to make any motion that would draw any attention to Carrie. He prayed Carrie wouldn't move, that maybe—just maybe—if she was still, the bull would leave her alone. The bull pawed the ground. Still, Joel didn't move, didn't breathe, and neither did Carrie. Suddenly, the bull charged forward. Before Carrie could get out of the way, the beast caught Carrie in its horns and threw her into the air.

"Carrie!" he yelled again. He had to get to her. He had to protect her.

He moved to jump into the ring from the viewing box where he had been sitting when he felt an arm grab him.

"You'll break your neck jumping into the ring from up here. That won't help Carrie at all," his brother said. "The guys down there will take care of her. Let them do their job."

As Zach had said, the rodeo clowns had raced into the ring as soon as they had realized what was going on. Joel watched as four of the rodeo clowns hurried over to intercept the bull from getting to Carrie again. He watched as one of them lifted her up into his arms. Joel was sure that she was too injured to even stand on her one leg. But just when he thought she was safe, he watched in horror as the bull charged the clown holding her and threw both of them into the air.

"Carrie!"

This time, the scream didn't come from him. He looked over and saw Cassie's face. She was ashen and terrified for her sister. He had to get her attention away from Carrie. He bent down, took Cassie's shoulders into his hands, and said, "Cassie?"

She immediately turned her attention to him. "Carrie—"

"She's going to be okay. She's going to be just fine, Cassie. I promise."

"Are you sure?"

"I promised, didn't I?" He tried to smile but figured his grin looked more like a grimace. "She's going to be okay, Cassie. I promise," he repeated slowly. As he stared into her eyes, he saw the moment when she decided to believe him. She turned to see what was going on, and Joel spoke again to keep her attention directed at him and not on whatever was going on down in the ring.

"So, did Carrie tell you about the rodeo clowns?"

Cassie looked at him and nodded.

"Did she tell you that it was their job to help the bull riders?"

"Yeah. She said they would go into the ring and make sure the bull left the rodeo ring."

"Yep, that's right. Do you know the best rodeo clowns are here? The very best ones in the whole world are here."

"The best?"

"Of course. This is the championship, so only the best clowns get to be here. They're going to make sure that Carrie's okay."

Joel felt Zach at his shoulder right before his brother whispered into his ear, "They've got her."

Joel turned and noticed there was now a tractor in the ring and Carrie was sitting up with the driver. Joel turned back to Cassie and said with as much lightness in his voice as he could, "Look, Cassie, now Carrie gets to ride in a tractor!"

"She does?"

Joel let her turn her head so she could once again see down into the ring. The bull was no longer in the ring and the tractor was making its way toward the gate. He noticed that there were more men in the ring than just the original clowns who had jumped in to help Carrie. He spied Beans and Dusty. He also recognized a number of other riders and rodeo hands. He looked up to heaven and simply said, "Thank you."

"Cassie, honey, why don't we let Joel go find Carrie. I'm sure we'll see her as soon as she's able to find us." Cassie and Carrie's mom, Diana, had stepped in to watch over Cassie. She turned to Joel and said, "Go on, go see how Carrie is. We'll be here waiting."

Joel nodded and left the viewing box. He headed straight to the staging area. He was glad for his pass allowing him to get back into the staging area. Nothing was going to keep him from seeing Carrie and making sure she was alright.

Joel cleared the gate without any questions. As he got closer to the bull chutes, he realized a large crowd had gathered. He knew these folks were all probably worried about Carrie, but no one needed to know that Carrie was okay more than he did.

"Excuse me. Excuse me. Comin' through."

A few people moved out of his way, but there were still a lot of people crowding in to see Carrie. Finally, one person next to him said, "Hey, you're Joel Roulston."

"Yeah, I am," he replied.

"Hey everyone, let Joel through. Let the man through to Carrie." The voice seemed to carry over the din of the crowd. Soon, people were turning in his direction and moving out of the way. It was as if the Red Sea was parting right before his eyes. He managed to walk right through the crowd. As he got near Carrie, he noticed that Bull, Beans, and Dusty were standing next to her and that one of the rodeo doctors was looking at her leg.

"Carrie!"

She turned her head to see Joel coming through the crowd that had gathered around her.

"Well, I didn't get a concussion," she said as she smiled and shrugged her shoulders. Joel knew she was trying to make light of what had just happened.

"That we know of," the doctor said. "You definitely have a broken leg, and I want you checked for a concussion, too. You're going to the hospital where we can do a proper medical examination."

"I'll be joining her," Joel asserted.

"And you are?" the doctor asked.

"Joel Rouston, I'm—"

"He's with me, doctor," Carrie interjected. "I'd feel better if he could come with me."

At that moment, the stretcher arrived, accompanied by two EMTs. Before they transferred Carrie, the doctor insisted that they immobilize her leg. One of the EMTs turned to Joel and said with a smirk, "I assume you're coming with us?"

Joel chuckled and replied, "You must have watched the show."

"Oh yeah."

"Wait, how do you know he watched the show?" Carrie asked.

"I'll fill you in as soon as I know that you're okay."

"I'm fine. You can tell me now."

Before Joel could respond, Carrie was being pushed through the crowd. It didn't take long before she was loaded into the ambulance and taken to the hospital.

As soon as they were both in the ambulance, Joel typed a quick text to Maria and Zach that read: *I'm in the ambulance with Carrie. Let her family know she's okay and I'll call as soon as I can.*

Will do, came the quick response from his sister.

CHAPTER 32

Joel called Carrie's dad as soon as she was taken down for x-rays.

"We're at University Medical Center. She's getting her leg x-rayed right now."

"How's she doing?"

"She's okay. We're all pretty sure her leg is broken, and the doctor suspects she has another concussion. She has a deep cut on her leg from where that beast caught her, but they cleaned and dressed it, and it should heal just fine. I'm sure she's going to be bruised and sore tomorrow. Between her ride and getting thrown around by that monster, her body went through quite a bit."

"Will they let us in to see her?"

"I think you'll be able to come as soon as she gets a room. I'll keep you posted as to how soon that is."

"You think that they're keeping her overnight?"

"Oh yeah. I was going to insist she spend the night, but I didn't even need to say a word. The ER doctor made it crystal clear the hospital would be imposing strict concussion protocols and that means she will spend at least one night for observation. Tell Cassie she's fine and that Carrie wants her to enjoy the rodeo."

"Thanks, Joel. We'll be in touch."

"Sounds good. See you soon."

It didn't take long for Carrie to be wheeled back into her room in the ER.

Joel stood up and immediately reached for her hand.

"How are you doing?"

"Joel, I'm fine."

"I know when they do those x-rays, they sometimes have to move you into positions that are painful when you have an injury. So, I'll ask again, how are you doing?"

Carrie took a deep breath, looked into the eyes of the man she loved, and replied, "I'm okay. Yes, there were some painful movements, but the medical personnel were so kind and careful, I hardly noticed."

"How's the head?"

"It feels like I had a wrestling match with a semi-truck and lost."

"Yeah, I bet it does. You were thrown around on Green Pastures and then—" Joel swallowed.

Carrie reached over, placed her hand on top of his, and quietly said, "I'm okay. Truly I am."

"It's just that when I saw him charge you in that ring, I saw *your* entire life flash before my eyes. I almost lost you. I would never have let you into that damn ring if I thought you were going to end up in the hospital again."

"It makes for an exciting end to the show, though, doesn't it?"

Joel just shook his head and leaned over to place a gentle kiss on her lips as they waited to hear back from the doctors.

◆ ◆ ◆

Carrie sat in her room at the University Medical Center. Joel had only let her leave his sight when they took her to get x-rays. Her folks, Cassie, and Becky had arrived in her room about twenty minutes after she had been wheeled in. She didn't want to spend the night in the hospital, but no one was going to let her out. The doctor had been adamant, and she knew that Joel was also going to insist that she stay. Although it appeared that he planned to stay as well.

"So . . . is everyone excited to go back and see night two of the rodeo?" Carrie asked.

"You want to go back?"

"Of course. We have to cheer on the other riders, don't we, Cassie?"

Her sister looked at her and asked, "Will anyone else get hurt?"

Carrie immediately knew that Cassie had been deeply impacted by what had happened in the ring.

"Cassie, honey. I'm okay. You know that, right?"

"But you got hurt again."

"Again?"

Cassie nodded her head. "I heard Mom and Dad talking, and they said you got hurt when you were at Joel's house."

"You heard that?" her mom asked.

Cassie merely nodded and turned back to Carrie.

"Yes, Cassie, I did get hurt when I was at Joel's ranch. I hurt my head and had a really bad headache. But once my headache went away, I was fine. Joel and everyone else at the ranch took really good care of me so that I got better really fast."

Cassie continued to watch Carrie.

"Cassie, honey, I know that you're pretty worried about me, but I'm okay. I really am."

No one spoke a word as Cassie stared at her sister for a while.

"You're really okay?"

"Yes. My leg got hurt, but that will be just fine in a couple of weeks. Remember when Sally Jo hurt her leg when she went skiing?"

Cassie nodded.

"Remember she had to wear that hard pink cast on her leg?"

"Uh huh," Cassie replied.

"Well, I'll get to have a cast like that, too."

"Will you get to have a pink one?"

"I don't know. If they let me pick a color, what color do you think I should get?"

"Orange. It's my favorite color."

"Orange it is." Carrie smiled.

Cassie watched her sister for a moment and asked again, "You're really okay?"

"Yes."

"Joel promised that you would be okay."

"He did?"

Carrie turned to Joel and raised her eyebrows. He shrugged and responded, "She needed to know you were going to be okay. I knew in my heart you were going to be just fine, and I didn't have any problem making that promise."

Carrie smiled, "Thank you."

"You're welcome. Now about going back to watch the rodeo—"

"Joel—"

Before Carrie could get her thought out of her mouth, Maria and Zach walked into her hospital room.

"Carrie, how're you doing?" Maria asked.

"I'm good. I was just reassuring Cassie that I'm fine."

"We're so glad," said Zach. He turned to Joel and said, "Everything's all set for tomorrow night."

"Thanks," Joel replied. Then he turned to Carrie and said, "Before we go back and watch night two of the championship, I thought we could all go out to dinner. You good with that?"

"All of us?"

"Yep."

"I think that sounds wonderful." Carrie smiled up at Joel. He leaned down and kissed her forehead.

"Good. I can't wait."

◆ ◆ ◆

The next evening, Carrie hobbled into a conference room in the hotel on her crutches and realized the room had been set up with a buffet and tables and chairs. There had to be seating for at least thirty people.

"This is where we're eating?"

"Yeah, Zach and Maria arranged for us to have this space so we could all eat together without any of the crowds."

"That's great, but why so many tables?"

He shrugged and replied, "They must have just set a standard number of tables."

"Carrie! How are you?" Maria asked as she and Zach came into the room.

"I'm okay. Pretty sore from yesterday, and I have a pounding headache, but I'm not complaining," she said.

"No, because you never complain," said Joel.

"How's the leg?" Zach asked.

"Good actually, it hardly hurts at all."

"That's good."

"Carrie!" a new voice from the doorway yelled. Carrie turned to see A.Z. walking toward her.

"A.Z.! What are you doing here?"

"Joel invited me to join you for dinner." She smiled.

Carrie reached out and hugged her friend. "I'm so glad."

As she let go of A.Z., Carrie realized that Drake had approached them as well.

"Drake! You got invited, too?"

"Of course, I got invited! I'm family, aren't I?"

Carrie laughed and agreed, "Sure are."

Right behind Drake was the film crew. It seemed that everyone who worked on the show was here joining them for dinner. Carrie turned to Joel and said, "Now I understand why there are so many tables. Is there anyone you didn't invite to dinner?"

"Blue Bayou, but we just didn't know how we were going to get the bull in here."

Carrie started to laugh.

"Come on, let's eat."

After everyone had a chance to enjoy the meal, Joel stood up. He reached for his water goblet and began clinking it with his fork to get everyone's attention.

"Thanks for joining us tonight. I know how much it means to Carrie that you're all here."

The room cheered.

Joel turned to Carrie and said, "Having the show filmed at the Double Spur changed my entire life. I never imagined that filming a reality TV show at the ranch would bring the woman God made just for me into my life. You are the woman I—" He had to clear his throat from the frog that had just lodged itself there. "Carrie . . ." He swallowed. "I love you. I knew from the minute you walked up to me that first day that my life was never going to be the same. You have brought more sunshine and joy into my life than I ever thought possible. But more than that, you have filled my heart. I once asked you to start thinking about our future. I hope you did because I have thought about it a lot."

Joel reached into his pocket and pulled out a small black box.

"My future is you." He opened the box and showed Carrie the beautiful ring nestled in the black velvet. "I love you so much. Will you let me enjoy your sunshine and joy forever? Will you let me cherish you and honor you? Will you—" He swallowed again. "Will you marry me?"

Carrie looked up into the eyes of the man who had changed her whole world. She knew she had found a love that would last. He was kind and willing to admit when he made a mistake. He was willing to put in the hard work of keeping a relationship together.

"Yes, Joel, I'll marry you. I love you," she responded as a tear slid down her cheek.

"That had better be a happy tear," he quietly said as he bent over and brushed the tear from her face.

"It is."

Joel removed the ring from its box and slid it onto Carrie's finger.

"I love you," he said as he moved to take her lips into a kiss to seal their promise.

For Carrie, everyone and everything slipped away. In that moment, it was only her and Joel. She basked in his love for a long moment before she heard the cheers from their friends and family gathered in the room.

Zach had stood and said, "A toast to Carrie and Joel. May their life be as peaceful as a Texas sunrise, as exciting as a bull ride, and as full as a belly after Glenda's Thanksgiving dinner."

"Hear, Hear!" called all of the ranch hands of the Double Spur.

CHAPTER 33

Carrie sat on the front porch at the Double Spur. It had been two years since that crazy first summer she had spent here. She had never imagined when she had stepped foot onto this ranch that her whole life would change. Not only hers but her family's lives as well.

Joel and Carrie were married six months after the PRA Championship in Vegas. Carrie had asked Becky to be her maid of honor and Maria and A.Z. to be her bridesmaids. Joel, in turn, had asked Zach to be his best man, and he also asked Drake to be a groomsman. When Drake had questioned whether or not he should be in the wedding party, Joel had firmly stated that had it not been for the producer, he never would have met Carrie, and for that, he deserved a front-row seat to the marriage vows. Joel had also asked Bull to be a groomsman. Bull had also questioned Joel about being in the wedding. Joel had looked at the old cowhand and told him that he had been around for every one of Joel's major life events. Joel had said it seemed wrong for Bull not to be there for his wedding vows. The two men had hugged and patted each other on the back before any tears would be noticed by anyone else. The wedding party had been made complete when Cassie had agreed to be the butterfly girl. Carrie had found a website that allowed you to buy butterflies to release at a wedding. The spring wedding was a perfect time to release a hundred butterflies. Butterfly, as Joel loved to call her, was in charge of the beautiful winged creatures. She released the butterflies right when everyone had gotten outside. Their colorful wings dotted the skies for a mere moment and then they were gone.

The day of the wedding was perfect. The guests were excited to be a part of the couple's happy day, and their families were happy to finally get to see Carrie and Joel permanently joined together. But for Carrie and Joel, everyone else faded into the background. When Warren placed Carrie's hand in Joel's, he felt his heart expand. As he looked into her eyes, he realized that love was the greatest gift he had received and vowed to grow their love every day they had together. Carrie felt Joel's fingers wrap around her own, and she was sure she had not only given him her hand but her heart as well. She knew she could trust him with her heart and that he would protect it forever.

A year after Carrie had ridden in the rodeo in Las Vegas, her sister had had the surgery that allowed her to walk. Cassie still needed a walker, but it meant that she wasn't always confined to the wheelchair. Cassie loved her newfound mobility. As soon as she wasn't limited by the wheelchair, she began to want to do more things, and she wanted to try it all.

As soon as he and Carrie had been married, Joel had brought up the idea of her family moving down to the Double Spur. As the time for the surgery drew near, Joel had encouraged her folks to move down to Texas. He had argued that it would be better if they were closer to the doctors who would be treating Cassie. Her folks had resisted. They didn't want to be in the way. He had insisted that the ranch had been built for multiple generations to live there and that there was no chance they would be in the way. Carrie had known that for her dad, the resistance had come from him wanting to be useful. As soon as Joel had realized Warren's hesitancy was based in part on his feeling useful, Joel had asked how Warren had felt about doing maintenance work. Warren had agreed to try, and from that moment on, her dad had been the ranch handyman. If anything needed repair, it was given to him.

Diana and Glenda also became fast friends. The two shared the kitchen as a team, with Glenda doing the baking and standard ranch fare, while Diana experimented. Sometimes, Diana found a recipe everyone loved, and it was added to the menu. Other times, however, the new creation was met with grimaces and good-natured ribbing. Those disasters were thrown away but often remembered in the teasing and laughter that accompanied every meal at the Double Spur. Diana loved the teasing, and it just encouraged her to find a new recipe to try.

Once her parents knew it would be best for everyone if they moved to the ranch, they sold the hardware store. With the proceeds from the sale of the store, they began to travel. Sometimes Warren and Diana traveled alone, but most of the time, they took Cassie with them. With her newfound freedom, she could do more things, and they worried less about her.

When they learned that Cassie had been accepted into the program for the surgery, everyone rejoiced. Joel had encouraged Carrie to join her family that week. He had told her that she needed to be there for her sister and to support her parents. She agreed. He was right. She had needed to be there and was grateful he had urged her to go. What she didn't realize was he had had his own reason for having her away from the ranch.

She arrived home a week later to find a horse mounting ramp near the equestrian barn. She stood next to the ramp as tears flowed down her cheeks. Joel took her into his arms and gently held her while she cried.

"You did this for Cassie."

"Of course. No matter how the surgery goes, I want to make sure she gets to ride a horse."

Carrie looked up into his eyes and said, "I love you."

"I love you, too." He smiled.

"I can't believe I worried about you finding out about Cassie. Your acceptance of her and your love for her are so obvious. You treat her with such love and patience, sometimes it just amazes me."

"She *is* my sister, after all." Carrie couldn't speak. She nodded her head and hugged him even tighter.

Just that afternoon, Joel and Maria had taken Cassie out for a ride. When Carrie explained that she wasn't up for the ride, Maria had quickly jumped in to replace her. The three of them had been gone for about an hour, and Carrie knew they would be back soon. An hour was Cassie's limit right now. She was always disappointed that they had to return, but Joel always let her know that now that she was living on the ranch, she would be able to ride again.

Just then, she heard Cassie's laugh. She saw the trio come around the barn and head over to the mount. In no time at all, Cassie was heading to the porch to tell Carrie all about their ride.

"Carrie!"

"Hey, there, Cassie. How was the ride?"

"Oh my gosh, it was great! We saw some cows eating grass. We also saw a tree with a rope swing. Joel said he used to swing on the rope and let go and land in the water!"

"He did, did he?"

"Yep! I asked if I could swing, and he told me the branch that the swing was tied to was kind of broken so no one could use the swing anymore."

Carrie turned to Joel and whispered, "Good answer."

He quietly responded, "I'm not stupid. Your mother would kill me if I even suggested taking Cassie out on the rope swing."

"She's not the only one."

Joel just laughed.

"Okay, Cassie, you should get in the house and get cleaned up. It'll be time for dinner soon."

"Okay," she replied as she moved toward the front door. Right before she opened the door, she turned to her sister and said, "Joel also said he would build me a new swing. I'm so excited!"

"Joel!"

"Before you say anything, let me explain. I've been looking at plans for a swing we could build along the same lines as the horse mount. I figure your dad and I could build something that would allow her to swing out and drop into the water."

"She's only just learning how to swim."

"I know, but it might take us a while, and I want to have something ready as soon as she is."

Carrie just shook her head at the man. He reached out and took her into his arms. He leaned down and took her lips in his. They shared a quiet moment with just the two of them. When Joel released her lips, he asked, "How are you feeling?"

"I'm fine."

"Really? Because you usually don't turn down an opportunity to ride Misty."

Carrie looked up at the handsome man and smiled.

"I hope you get better at saying no before our daughter starts to ask about doing something dangerous."

Joel pulled back a little more to look into Carrie's eyes.

"Our daughter?" he squeaked.

"Or son." She smiled.

"You're pregnant?"

"I like to think *we're* pregnant."

"We're pregnant," he corrected. Carrie gave him a minute to wrap his mind around the concept that he was going to be a father. "We're going to have a baby."

She smiled up at him. "Yes."

"Have I told you how much I love you?"

"Yes, right before you went out on that horse ride."

"I am truly a very lucky man." He had to take a moment to get his emotions under control. "Every night, I go to bed and thank God for all of the blessings he has brought into my life. I started saying that prayer the night we first kissed."

"You did?"

"Yes, and I haven't stopped being grateful."

"We are very blessed indeed."

He leaned down and kissed her again. After a while, he lifted his head and asked with eagerness in his voice, "Can we tell people?"

"Yeah, I think my mom and Glenda already suspect."

"Really?"

"Yeah, but we can tell everyone else tonight."

"We're adding a little one to our table. How is it possible that just that thought alone makes me feel like our table is even more complete?"

"I think it has something to do with that table being built for love and family."

He nodded.

As they turned to go into the house, Carrie looked out over the ranch again. She had found such joy at this ranch and with the man standing next to her. She knew this ranch would nurture their love for a lifetime.

EPILOGUE

"There's trouble at Z Stables," Drake said quietly. He was sitting on a barstool at a bar in the Vegas hotel next to Zach.

The final show of *Bull's Life* had aired the night before. The TV station was clamoring for a follow-up. Apparently, word had gotten out that Joel had proposed to Carrie the night after the finale had aired, and now the station was hoping to get an interview with the couple. He had to smile to himself. He was pretty sure no amount of money could persuade Joel to go on national television and talk about his relationship with Carrie. Drake didn't mind. He didn't really need the follow-up show, and he appreciated the fact that Joel wanted to protect his and Carrie's relationship.

During the three days of the championship, Drake had learned that A.Z.'s family's ranch was having problems. A.Z. would never ask for help, but from what he had learned, they really needed some. He had decided to approach Zach. After working on the Roulston ranch for three months, he had a sneaking suspicion that Zach would not only be willing to help but adamant about doing something for A.Z.'s family.

"What do you know?" Zach asked with his brows drawn together in a frown.

"I spoke with Trina, A.Z.'s sister, last night. She said that there have been a rash of problems plaguing the ranch. Open gates causing the cattle to get out and moldy hay in one of the maternity pens. Things like that. Mostly annoyances, but things have started to get worse. Just a couple of days ago, Roger Zumronik, A.Z.'s dad, tripped on a piece of broken gate that was hiding under some hay."

"Is he okay? I noticed he wasn't here for the championship and thought that was strange."

"He broke his arm and sprained his ankle. He figured he would be useless here and sent another one of the hands to help with managing their horses."

"Anything else?"

"Yeah, I think the most troubling thing was the rubber snake they found in one of the horse's stalls."

Zach immediately shifted to look the other man in the eye. "What do you mean they found a rubber snake in one of the horse's stalls? Who the hell would put a snake in with a horse?"

"That's what Trina said. They can't figure out who did it."

As Zach thought about what Drake had said, a thought struck him. "Which horse?"

"Sunset."

"A.Z.'s horse?"

"Yeah."

"Could this be personal?"

"That's what Trina is wondering. She said that she's tried to talk to A.Z., but that A.Z. refuses to believe it's personal."

"If this *is* personal, she needs to watch her back."

"Agreed. But Trina says A.Z. won't listen to her."

"With her father laid up, who's watching out for A.Z.?"

"That's why Trina came to me. She's really worried. She's afraid things are going to get worse and there won't be anyone around to help."

"Let me talk with Dusty. He's pretty good friends with Stick, one of their ranch hands, and he'll get the low down on what's going on."

"Great. Let me know if you need anything."

Zach finished his shot of bourbon and took out his phone as he left the bar. He wanted to find Dusty as soon as possible.

Early the next morning, Zach was on the phone with Z Stables.

"Hello."

"Hello, Mr. Zumronik. This is Zach Roulston. I don't know if you remember me, but—"

"Of course, I remember you, son. I've spent the last couple of months watching my daughter hanging out at your family's ranch."

"Yeah. She was very important in making the show such a success. We were really lucky she was able to come and help out. In fact, that's why I'm calling."

"Oh?"

"I understand that you've been having some unexplained trouble at Z Stables."

"Sure have."

"I also understand that one of those problems just landed you on the injured-reserve list."

Zach heard a chuckle on the other end of the line.

"Injured-reserve list, hunh? That's one way of putting it."

"The Double Spur is deeply indebted to your family for letting us borrow A.Z. for the reality show. I'd like to repay that debt."

"How's that?"

"I'd like to come down to help you. I can also bring one of our ranch hands, Dusty. I think you might remember him?"

"Oh, yeah. Dusty and Stick are pretty good friends. Second cousins, I think."

"Really? I didn't know that."

"Yeah. So let me get this straight. You're offering to come to Z Stables with one of your hands and help us out?"

"Yes, sir. I thought with you being laid up, Mr. Zumronik, it would be helpful if you had a couple of extra hands to watch over your ranch and your family."

"What about the Double Spur? Can your ranch survive without you?"

"I think I can make some arrangements that would get our ranch through for a spell."

"You want to watch over my ranch and *my family*?"

"Yes, sir. I think it would be a good idea to have someone watching your backs."

There was a pause on the other end of the line. Zach held his breath. He knew that if he didn't convince this man to let him help, he would not be able to do anything about it.

"Zach?"

"Yes, sir?"

"If you're going to come down and work at Z Stables, you should probably start calling me Roger."

Zach let out the breath he had been holding in.

"Roger, then. If you've got a minute, I thought we could talk about the logistics of me coming down."

"Let me guess, you want me to keep my mouth shut about your visit? Especially to A.Z.?"

"Yes, sir, ah Roger, I do. I don't—"

"Relax, Zach. I agree. I don't really think A.Z. needs to know before you arrive, so long as we have an understanding."

"What would that be?"

"While I'm laid up, you watch out for my girls until we can figure out who's threatening my family."

"We are in complete agreement." Zach paused and then vowed, "I promise, Roger, we'll figure it out, and in the meantime, we'll keep them safe."

Zack and A.Z.'s story coming soon.

ABOUT THE AUTHOR

 C. Kelly remembers coming home from a sidewalk sale at her local library with an armful of romance novels in junior high. She fell in love with happily ever afters and is thrilled to be bringing her own happily ever after stories to life. When she's not writing, she loves laughing and spending time with her family in Minnesota. She camps every chance she gets, cheers on the Vikings during their season, plays bunco, loves to travel, and finds inspiration for her stories and characters everywhere she goes.